**Praise for**
**of Penny**

***How to Host***

"Penny Warner blends humor and mayhem to create a unique mystery full of fun."

—Denise Swanson, national bestselling author of *Murder of a Royal Pain*

"Penny Warner dishes up a rare treat, sparkling with wicked and witty San Francisco characters, plus some real tips on hosting a killer party."

—Rhys Bowen, award-winning author of the Royal Spyness and Molly Murphy mysteries

"Penny Warner's scintillating *How to Host a Killer Party* introduces an appealing heroine whose event skills include utilizing party favors in self-defense in a fun, fast-paced new series guaranteed to please."

—Carolyn Hart, Agatha, Anthony, and Macavity Award–winning author of *Dare to Die*

"There's a cozy little party going on between this cover. Don't miss Penny Warner's new series."

—Elaine Viets, author of *Killer Cuts*

"The winning and witty Presley Parker can plan a perfect party—but after her A-list event becomes an invitation to murder, her next plan must be to save her own life."

—Hank Phillippi Ryan, Agatha Award–winning author of *Prime Time*

***Dead Body Language***

"The novel is enlivened by some nice twists, an unexpected villain, a harrowing mortuary scene, its Gold Country locale, and fascinating perspective on a little-known subculture."

—*San Francisco Chronicle*

"What a great addition to the ranks of amateur sleuths."

—Diane Mott Davidson, *New York Times* bestselling author of *Fatally Flaky*

# How to Host a *Killer Party*

*A Party-Planning Mystery*

Penny Warner

AN OBSIDIAN MYSTERY

OBSIDIAN
Published by New American Library, a division of
Penguin Group (USA) Inc., 375 Hudson Street,
New York, New York 10014, USA
Penguin Group (Canada), 90 Eglinton Avenue East, Suite 700, Toronto,
Ontario M4P 2Y3, Canada (a division of Pearson Penguin Canada Inc.)
Penguin Books Ltd., 80 Strand, London WC2R 0RL, England
Penguin Ireland, 25 St. Stephen's Green, Dublin 2,
Ireland (a division of Penguin Books Ltd.)
Penguin Group (Australia), 250 Camberwell Road, Camberwell, Victoria 3124,
Australia (a division of Pearson Australia Group Pty. Ltd.)
Penguin Books India Pvt. Ltd., 11 Community Centre, Panchsheel Park,
New Delhi - 110 017, India
Penguin Group (NZ), 67 Apollo Drive, Rosedale, North Shore 0632,
New Zealand (a division of Pearson New Zealand Ltd.)
Penguin Books (South Africa) (Pty.) Ltd., 24 Sturdee Avenue,
Rosebank, Johannesburg 2196, South Africa

Penguin Books Ltd., Registered Offices:
80 Strand, London WC2R 0RL, England

First published by Obsidian, an imprint of New American Library,
a division of Penguin Group (USA) Inc.

First Printing, February 2010
10 9 8 7 6 5 4 3 2 1



Printed in the United States of America

*To Connie, my inspiration,*
*to Matthew, Sue, Rebecca, and Mike, my biggest fans,*
*and to Tom, the mystery man in my life*

"The dying process begins the minute we are born, but it accelerates during parties."

—Carol Matthau

# Chapter 1

*PARTY PLANNING TIP #1:*

*No matter how crazy the gig, the client is always right.*

*And no matter how crazy the client, the event planner is liable.*

Through the thick morning veil of San Francisco fog, all I could make out from the ferryboat deck was the eerie silhouette of an island. It loomed like a giant corpse floating in the bay, its form eaten away by the relentless waves.

I shivered in the penetrating cold as the wind off the Pacific whipped through my purple and gold San Francisco State University hoodie and my black jeans. Even the venti latte, my antidote for my ADHD—attention deficit/hyperactivity disorder—couldn't keep this California native warm.

Slowly, like a desert mirage, the apparition began to take shape.

*Alcatraz.*

I felt goose bumps break out as I thought about the former home of organized crime boss Al "Scarface" Capone, "Creepy" Karpis, "Machine Gun" Kelly, and Robert "Birdman" Stroud. The island exuded a mystique that thrilled tourists and frightened schoolchildren. No wonder this notorious maximum-security prison was the most popular attraction in Northern California. Although no longer home to the most incorrigible criminals, it still housed plenty of legendary ghosts.

Tonight the inhospitable island would play host to the party of the century: San Francisco mayor Davin Green's "surprise" wedding to his socialite fiancée, Ikea Takeda. I held up the wedding invitation I'd created for the event and scanned it.

WANTED!

A WARRANT has been issued REQUIRING<br>your APPEARANCE

At the Capture and "SURPRISE" Wedlock of

MAYOR DAVIN GREEN

to

MS. IKEA TAKEDA

WITNESSES Will Be Remanded into<br>Custody on: OCTOBER 1

CONFINED at: Alcatraz Island

DETAINED from: 8 p.m. until Midnight

ADDITIONAL REMARKS: Come As Your<br>Favorite Criminal or Crime Solver

$200 Tax Deductible Donation will go to<br>the Alzheimer's Association

~ REWARD ~

Seafood Buffet catered by Rocco<br>Ghirenghelli, KBAY-TV's "Bay City Chef"

~ CAUTION! ~

Anyone caught warning the alleged Bride-to-Be will receive a mandatory 20-years-to-life of public service.

For information concerning this docket, contact:

PRESLEY PARKER—"KILLER PARTIES"—415-BALLOON

It would be the biggest event since Caruso sang at the Met.

Or the biggest disaster since the 1906 earthquake.

And I, Presley Parker, was the lucky event coordinator.

*This wedding is going to be the death of me*, I thought, balancing my latte on the boat's guardrail. I shredded the biodegradable invitation into confetti and ceremoniously sprinkled it like cremated ashes into the San Francisco Bay. I only hoped it wasn't a symbolic gesture.

The sudden blast of a warning alarm startled me, sending another chill over my already goose-pimpled flesh. I grabbed the ferry railing, nearly spilling my precariously balanced drink, and pulled my hood up over my bobbed auburn hair.

Prison breakout?

Nothing so exciting. Just the familiar but disquieting sound of the ubiquitous foghorn. As a seagull swooped down, I lost my grip on my latte and watched my life's blood tumble overboard. I cursed into the deafening sound.

Great. Now I'd probably be arrested for polluting the bay.

Even worse, there was no Starbucks on Alcatraz.

At least, not yet.

"Land-ho, Presley!" Delicia Jackson, my thirtysomething part-time assistant, called too cheerily between foghorn blasts. She appeared behind me in her quilted green parka, which made her look as if she'd been entombed in a giant bunch of grapes. Cupping her hand over her forehead like a pirate at sea, she squinted into the fog, then pointed to our destination.

"Good thing too," Delicia said, shivering in spite of the puffy jacket that nearly reached to her matching green Crocs. Her toes had to be icicles; mine were cold even in my black Uggs. "I'm getting seasick."

"How are the others doing?" I asked, referring to my minimal staff.

"They're inside. Too cold out here for those lightweights."

When she wasn't helping me host fund-raising events and kids' birthday parties for extra cash, Delicia was a part-time actress and full-time drama queen. A mixture of many cultures, she was stunningly beautiful, with smooth mocha skin, long black hair, and disconcertingly blue eyes. Girls loved her as characters Belle and Ariel when she performed at my young clients' birthday events.

"Only three hours till showtime!" Delicia said, tapping her princess watch with a sparkly nail. Being an actress, she spoke mostly in exclamation marks.

"What was I thinking?" I shouted through the rumble of the boat engine, the squawk of the seagulls, and the relentless fog blasts. "This is going to be a disaster."

"It's going to be off the hook!" she shouted back. "Perfect for your extreme career makeover!"

Extreme indeed. How did a university instructor like me end up as an event planner? I shook my head, recalling the day six months before—my thirtieth birthday, to be exact—when I'd received the notice in my campus mailbox at San Francisco State University:

*"Due to budget cuts . . ."*

I hadn't bothered to read the rest. I knew what it said. All of us part-timers had seen it coming. My department, psychology, had been hit especially hard. And my specialty, ab-psych—abnormal psychology—was one of the first to go.

That week had gone from bad to worse. Not only had I lost my job, but my mother had been diagnosed with early-stage Alzheimer's, and my so-called boyfriend, a professor of criminology at SFSU, had dumped me for a grad student. I hated being a cliché.

But event planning? That was a stretch. Then again, maybe not. Back in the days of San Francisco café society, my mother had been famous for her Pacific Heights parties, entertaining everyone from the mayor to the governor. I'd grown up helping her fold napkins into swans and drape fur coats in the guest room (when I was done trying them on).

She'd even written a how-to book on the subject called *How to Host a Killer Party,* a best seller in its day. When I started doing event planning, I found her party-hosting hints handy, like "How to Hire a Killer Caterer" and "How to Handle a Party Pooper." But instead of following in her high-heeled footsteps, I had originally gone the more academic route, like my father. Now it looked as if I had inherited her legacy after all.

"I didn't necessarily want a new career, Delicia," I said, tightening the strings on my hood. "But after being downsized thanks to the governor's slash-and-burn method of fixing the education budget, I didn't have much choice, did I? It was this or coffee barista. I should have taken the java job."

"Hey, you're a great party planner! That *Harry Potter* party you gave last night? It was awesome! Seriously. And that Teen *Twilight* party? Getting Duncan Grant to play the vampire was a stroke of genius. You managed to make a nerd look hot—at least temporarily."

"*Event coordinator!*" I reminded her. "And if I have to do one more birthday party for eight-year-old boys or twelve-year-old girls, I'm going to kill someone. Thank goodness this job came up. I still don't know exactly how I managed to get it."

Maybe I was finally receiving the recognition I'd needed. I hoped tonight's gig would get me more charitable events for important causes like Alzheimer's research, and fewer food fights between Harry Potter wannabes. I was still finding blue icing highlights in my hair from last night's frosting free-for-all.

Raising money for deserving organizations was the real reason I'd gotten into event planning. Thanks to Mom, I knew the basics of the business. When I'd been at the university, I'd help coordinate a couple of fund-raisers for the library that had gone well. The mayor's surprise wedding, although under the guise of a fund-raiser, would bring in a bundle for a cause dear to my heart. Since my mother had developed Alzheimer's, I'd done a lot of research on this debilitating disease, which I'd quickly learned was the sixth leading cause of death in the US. Tears sprang to my eyes as I pushed thoughts of my mother's grim future from my mind.

"Are you all right, Pres?" Delicia asked, looking up at me.

I wiped my eyes. "Of course. It's just this fog. . . ."

"Listen, Pres," Delicia said, patting my arm. "You've hit the big time. You've snagged a superimportant shindig at a celebrated city landmark. Imagine! Presley Parker hosting Mayor Green's wedding on the Rock!"

"More like a carnival, don't you think?" I mumbled. The guests had been asked to come in costume, dressed as their favorite criminals or crime fighters. Not my idea—the mayor's. "And a decaying prison isn't exactly the most elegant setting for a wedding. It's Andi Sax who gets all the glam gigs at places like the de Young Museum and the Palace of Fine Arts."

Until the mayor's wedding, Andrea Sax, San Francisco's premiere party planner, was the go-to girl for all the best events—grand openings of prestigious restaurants, inaugurations of political figures, gala fund-raisers for significant foundations. No wonder. She'd long been established in the city and owned her own party supply store. That's why I'd been so surprised when the mayor's administrative assistant called and offered me this job. The event would be impressive enough to garner a lot of publicity, thereby bringing in more gigs—and more money. But I couldn't help wondering why they hadn't used Andi again, and I was certain I'd somehow gotten the job by default.

"Well, bottom line—you need the money," Delicia said, as if reading my thoughts. "Especially now that your mom has to have full-time care."

"You're right about that." I'd had to give up my overpriced Victorian flat in the Marina District and move to cheap former naval housing on Treasure Island so I could afford her care facility in the city. Luckily TI, situated halfway between San Francisco and Oakland, was only a bridge-length away.

Delicia reached up and picked something off my bangs. "Just a little blue frosting on your hair . . . although it does bring out your green eyes."

"Great. Exactly the professional look I was going for." I pushed the hood back and gave my sticky hair a shake to fluff it up before the frosting set like concrete. I'd been too busy finishing up final touches for the wedding to wash my hair since the *Potter* party. Luckily a hat was part of my costume for the mayor's event.

I checked my watch: five fifteen p.m. Since Alcatraz was a national park, my crew and I couldn't set up until the place closed. Before I knew it, it would be eight p.m. and the first guests would be arriving. As the ferry docked, I hustled my coworkers down the gangplank, all arms loaded with boxes of party crap. Most of the big stuff had already been delivered and was waiting for us in the cellblock. Glancing up at the ominous cement building at the top of the hill, I shuddered, hoping the ghosts of Alcatraz would be in a partying mood tonight. Remembering a docent's spiel I'd heard on a school trip to Alcatraz, I recalled some stats about the island's fascinating and fearsome history. For nearly thirty years, the grim maximum-security federal penitentiary had housed around fifteen hundred prisoners. Thirty-six had tried to escape from the Rock. Seven were shot and killed, two drowned, five were unaccounted for, and the rest were captured. Two prisoners made it to shore but were later captured and returned, and three more escaped the island, but not the water surrounding it—presumed drowned. That was it, unless you counted the twenty-eight who escaped by dying—fifteen of natural causes, eight murdered, and five suicides.

If I didn't pull this thing off, I'd be the first to commit career suicide.

My iPhone—a luxury I refused to give up—chirped, jolting me out of my thoughts of danger, detention, and death. *Missed call*, the screen read.

"Service is really spotty here," Delicia said, checking her pink rhinestone-enhanced cell phone.

I nodded, then thumbed to the voice mail screen and found three messages waiting for me. The first was from my mother: "Pres, please call me! It's urgent!" Even though she was safely in a care facility, to my mother, every call these days was "urgent."

The second was from Chloe Webster, the mayor's admin. "Presley? We have a serious situation. Call me ASAP." And with Chloe, there was always a "serious situation." I felt for her. She was seriously overworked and no doubt underpaid, but she seemed to thrive in her status as assistant to the mayor. She'd been instrumental in getting me hired for this gig.

I saved the messages, mentally promising to return the calls—if I could find a pocket of service—as soon as I finished the more pressing matter of decorating the cellblock.

I went on to the third message.

"Presley Parker? This is Detective Luke Melvin from the San Francisco Police Department, Homicide. Would you please return my call at your earliest convenience?"

A homicide detective?

Holy shit.

# Chapter 2

*PARTY PLANNING TIP #2:*

***Like MacGyver, a good event planner can fix just about any party mishap with a toothpick, duct tape, or some crepe paper.***

My first thought was: What would a San Francisco homicide detective want with me? This wasn't about all those unpaid parking tickets, was it?

My second thought was: What had Mother done now? The last time the cops had called, she'd escaped from her care home and was found posing as a statue at the Museum of Modern Art. A nude statue. Things like that had happened more than once recently.

Shaking off other possibilities, my staff and I loaded into a small tram driven by a park ranger and headed up the zigzagging path toward Cellblock B, remaining party gear in hand. We were actually a ragtag bunch of entrepreneurs, all renting office space in an old military building not far from my condo on Treasure Island. The rumor that I'd be hosting a party for the mayor quickly spread through the building like a virus, and within the hour I'd hired TV chef Rocco Ghirenghelli as my caterer, filmmaker Berkeley Wong as videographer, and security guard Raj Reddy for added safety, in addition to Delicia, who pretty much did whatever

I asked. Luckily they came cheap. Like me, they needed the money.

The ride up the steep hill was mostly quiet, all of us awestruck by the eerie surroundings. Delicia gazed wide-eyed at the cellblock as it came into view. Rocco sat stiffly, balancing on his lap several pink boxes of puff pastries and chocolates that he'd whipped up last night. Berkeley fiddled with the video camera perched on his shoulder. And Raj kept rubbing his shiny badge with a handkerchief as if it had magical powers.

The tram pulled up to the front of the cellblock with a jerk, and we unloaded our gear. I took a moment to scan the fog-enshrouded city skyline, but could barely make out Coit Tower through the thick covering. I headed inside to the main hallway, oddly named Broadway, that was flanked on either side by aging jail cells. The hall, wide enough to fit all the expected guests comfortably, would be the main party room. Delicia began unloading jail-themed decorations she'd helped me put finishing touches on last night—prisoner-style tin cups, brass jailhouse keys, striped uniforms and caps, and "Wanted" posters, each personalized for the invited guests.

Berkeley Wong, video camera still perched on his shoulder like a big black bird, began taping—and narrating—our setup efforts. "The Killer Party task force arrives at the infamous prison . . . ," came his overly dramatic voice. "The highly trained team is about to give the penal institution an extreme makeover and turn the ghostly cellblock into a gala celebration. 'Toto, we're not in Kansas anymore.' "

Berkeley looked stylishly gay with his hedgehog hair, how-low-waist-can-you-go jeans, a long-sleeved "Hellboy—Visual Effects Crew" T-shirt, and red Chuck Taylor All Stars. I hoped to use his behind-the-scenes look at the mayor's nuptials on YouTube as a marketing tool for my business. Berk apparently had a different vision; he saw it as his ticket into commercial work at CeeGee film studio, also located on Treasure Island. Berk was always "on"; I'd have diagnosed him as a mild manic. Since I was a former ab-psych instructor, diagnosing everyone I knew was an occupational hazard.

"The wedding," he continued, using his Don Pardo voice from *Saturday Night Live*, "hosted by perky party planner Presley Parker—"

"*Event coordinator!*" I yelled at the camera. "And don't call me perky."

"*Whatever*," Berk hissed, then continued, gangster style, just to irritate me. "Da nuptials'll take place widdin da walls of notorious Cellblock B, and feachah a festive ball 'n' chain theme."

I glared at him as I set the shanklike knives on the buffet table. Berk gave me a sassy smile, then panned the inside of the monolithic cement structure, which was slowly deteriorating thanks to the corrosive effects of time, neglect, and salt air.

"'What. A. Dump!'" he said, summing up the place with a line by Bette Davis. He was always tossing out famous movie quotes, hoping to beat me at Name That Film.

Not in the mood to play games, I ignored him as I surveyed the main hallway for places to hang the "Wanted" signs. The cement walls, covered in peeling pink paint, seemed to close in on me, and my first thought was to look for an escape route, much like the prisoners must have done the first time they shuffled down this infamous hall. I had a feeling I might need one if the party was a total disaster. The dull, thick bars, scarred by decades of angry or bored inmates, gave me a chill that ran down my spine to my cold toes. Or was it cold feet?

"Oh shit!" Rocco Ghirenghelli called from the cellblock dining area, distracting me from my claustrophobia. I headed down to the large mess hall where Rocco was preparing the food. Tall and pale, with a shaved head that disguised his receding hairline, he stood Birkenstock-sandal-footed in his once-white chef's coat and pants, staring into a large pastry box as if it were Al Capone's open crypt.

"What's up, Rocco?" I asked, eyeing the perfect handcuffs and Maltese Falcons he'd formed out of chocolate. Tempted, I wondered whether he'd miss just one. . . .

"My balls are getting soft!"

He looked tired, judging by the suitcases under his eyes. No wonder. He'd pulled an all-nighter sculpting the impressive wedding cake, a giant ball and chain masterpiece covered in silver icing. Rocco dreamed of turning his culinary skills into national Food Network television, but so far he'd managed only to snag a weekly gig on a local cable show, *KBAY Café*. A master at "chocolate art," he'd designed and created dozens of chocolate treats for tonight's party. If I hadn't known better, I would have recommended Prozac for his chronic depression.

I glanced down at the crab-filled pastry puffs he'd prepared the previous night. They looked more like pancakes, deflated thanks to the salt air. I picked up a party toothpick that sported a tiny skull-and-crossbones flag and stuck it into one of the mouth-sized morsels. "There. No one will ever notice your flat balls."

Berkeley giggled. "I'll have what he's having," he said, misquoting *When Harry Met Sally*. I threw a needle-sharp toothpick at him. Missed.

"I'm loving this!" Raj Reddy said, suddenly appearing behind me. He stood grinning at the interior of the cellblock. Glancing at me, he snapped to attention and saluted. "Where are you wanting me, boss?"

A wannabe cop, the Treasure Island security guard looked official in his perfectly pressed khaki uniform and shiny black military-style shoes. Definitely had a touch of OCD—obsessive-compulsive disorder. Raj had been an attorney in India a decade ago, but when he'd emigrated to the United

States, his degree was not honored. In his mid-fifties, he felt he was too old to start over at the university, and went into security work. He seemed to love his job as head security guard on Treasure Island, where most of the crimes tended to be minor break-ins, petty vandalism, or public drunkenness. He especially relished the task of detouring tourists and paparazzi away from the CeeGee film studio, which was disguised in an old Pan Am hangar on the island.

At the moment, he looked prepared to take any and all prisoners, if Alcatraz happened to be missing some. I'd hired Raj for extra crowd control, and to make sure the latest special-interest demonstrators didn't seize the prison and interrupt the ceremony for their own political agendas. Back in the late sixties, American Indian tribes had held Alcatraz hostage for more than a year and a half. With tonight's well-publicized event hosted by our popular but controversial mayor, a demonstration was almost a given.

That would be the icing on the cake.

"How about blowing up some of those black and silver balloons with the helium tank?" I said to him, then turned to the others.

Delicia raised her hand as if she were in school. "Can I help greet the guests when they arrive? I think they'll love my costume!" Dee definitely had a touch of narcissism.

"Sure," I said to her, "but meanwhile would you set out the ball-and-chain centerpieces? And Berk, when you're done shooting the 'making of' video for MTV, would you hang those mug shots of the guests?"

Raj saluted, Delicia clapped, and Berk stuck out his tongue at me.

In spite of the pressure, I was starting to feel good about my first big event. Having ADHD helped—it gave me plenty of energy and helped me multitask—as long as I kept it under control with gallons of caffeine. I'd discovered in high school that coffee, instead of stimulating me like it did other kids, calmed me down and helped me focus. No more Ritalin for me.

It was seven forty-five p.m. by the time we turned on the sweeping searchlights, stationed the uniformed "guard" cutouts, and switched on Johnny Cash's "Folsom Prison Blues." Everything that could go wrong had—popped balloons, burned-out lightbulbs, missing chocolates—but Broadway looked like a scene from *Escape from Alcatraz* when we finished, with stuffed "prisoners" lying in their cots, fake guns poking out from the upstairs guard walk, and jail cell keys dangling from the bars. The chill from the unheated room only added to the authenticity. The setting would have impressed even a hardened ex-con like Martha Stewart.

I inhaled a deep relaxation breath, filling my lungs with the aroma of fresh crab balls mixed with salt air. As I exhaled, I mentally went over the party logistics one more time. This wedding *had* to be perfect. Not an easy task considering the gloomy location, the ridiculous theme, and the fact that it was a "surprise" for the bride.

Its only redeeming value was the mayor's pledge to donate most of the proceeds to the Alzheimer's Association. This was probably the only wedding in history where the guests paid to attend. But it was all part of the ruse to fool Ikea, the bride-to-be. Not an easy task, considering the woman was every bit as smart and savvy—and ambitious—as her political beau. Perhaps more so.

According to local gossip, Ikea seemed to have the mayor wrapped around her little acrylic fingernail. She'd managed to get him involved in all her pet causes: Save the Painted Ladies, Clean Up the Haight-Ashbury, Beautify the City Trash Cans, and even Renovate Treasure Island. Quite the dedicated citizen. Of course, if she got her way with TI, I'd soon be out of an office—and a home. Again.

I checked my cell phone clock for the umpteenth time.

The hours had passed much too quickly. If everything went according to plan, the guests would arrive any minute, followed by Mayor Green and his unsuspecting fiancée of six months.

Time to panic.

"All right, everyone," I called out. "Get into your costumes. We're about to get this party started."

As my crew headed for the public restrooms just outside the cellblock, costumes in hand, I checked my phone again to see if there were more messages. There were half a dozen new calls from the mayor's office, three more from my mother, and another from SFPD, along with a *no service* warning across the screen. I stepped outside the cellblock to try to find service, then listened to the message from the police department.

"Presley Parker? This is Detective Luke Melvin from the San Francisco Police Department again. Please return my call as soon as possible."

Shit. I was sure it had something to do with my mother. What else could it be?

I hiked a few feet away from the cellblock, pressed CALL BACK, and waited for an answer. I felt my underarms prickle at the deep sound of a man's voice.

"Detect— Mel—" Static.

I could barely hear him and spun around, trying to catch sound waves—or whatever they were. "Uh . . . yes, this is Presley Parker. I believe you called me? Is this about my mother?"

"No, ma'am. I'm calling— another ma— You know— woman named— Drea?"

"What?" I pressed my hand over my other ear. "I'm sorry . . . you're breaking up. I can hardly hear you. What did you say?"

"I said— know— An—"

"Sorry—and what?"

"—drea Sax," he said loudly through the crackle.

"No, I . . . wait. You mean Andi Sax. Yes . . . I mean no, that is, not really. Why?"

I wondered what the infamous Party Queen was up to now. Was she jealous I'd gotten the mayor's wedding? Was she trying to sabotage my first big event?

"I— come down— station— a couple of ques— you."

Squinting as if that would help me hear better and twirling around like a whirling dervish trying to capture phone rays, I shouted, "What? I can't hear you."

He repeated most of the words and I filled in the blanks: "Come down to the station. I have a couple of questions to ask you."

"Uh . . . I can't right now. I'm in the middle of something. What's this all about?"

Silence.

I thought for a moment I'd lost the connection. Then his voice came back on the line, and for once—and unfortunately—I heard him loud and clear.

"Andrea Sax was found dead early this morning."

# Chapter 3

*PARTY PLANNING TIP #3:*

*Don't drink alcohol while hosting an event.*
*Especially when the police want to question you about a murder.*

Whoa. I didn't even know the woman, and I felt like I'd been kicked in the stomach. The blood in my head rushed to my feet and I had to squat to keep from falling over.

"Ms. Parker?" I heard a tinny voice from my phone. I brought the phone back to my ear.

"Ms. Parker? Are you there? Ms. Parker?"

"Dead?" I whispered. Then I got my voice back. "You're kidding, right?"

"I'm afraid not. I need you to come down—"

"What happened?" I said, interrupting him. I stood up slowly, using the side of the building for support.

"We're not—" Static. Then, "According to her BlackBerry calendar— your— last scheduled—"

"What?" I rasped, struggling to find my voice again.

"Ms. Parker, I need you to come by the station— answer a few questions," Detective Melvin said, ignoring my question.

I shook my head, even though he couldn't see me. "I

told you, I can't right now. I'm . . . hosting a wedding . . . a fund-raiser. . . ."

"I'm going to have to send an—" More static.

Before he could say more, I added, "For Mayor Green . . . It's his surprise wed— er, big fund-raiser. I'm sure you've heard about it—for Alzheimer's."

Another moment of silence. I thought I had lost him for good, but his voice came on the line, less insistent. "Tomorrow morn— nine sharp—"

The line went dead.

Dead.

Just like Andi Sax. Dead. How was that possible?

Unable to wrap my mind around this stunning blow, I tried to pull my thoughts together and focus—not easy for someone with ADHD. A homicide detective wanted to question me. What had he said . . . that my name was in her calendar? Why? I could easily imagine Andi Sax sticking pins in a voodoo doll with my image, what with my getting the mayor's job. But why would I be her last scheduled appointment? I'd had no plans to meet with Andi Sax. Ever.

Zombielike, I stood holding the dead phone, trying to absorb the news.

"Pres? Presley? You okay?"

I looked at my phone, thinking the detective had come back on the line, then realized it was Delicia, standing beside me. I whirled around and saw her frowning. Blinking myself back to the task at hand, I headed for the cellblock, with Delicia trailing behind me, pelting me with questions.

"Did you get the phone to work? Who were you talking to? Are you all right?"

Ignoring her and forcing thoughts of the detective's call aside, I began my own series of questions. "Where's the champagne? Are the appetizers ready? Why can't I hear the music?"

*Focus, Pres, focus*, I said to myself, repeating my mantra. *You have a wedding to host, not a funeral. Let's get this party started.*

Delicia pointed to a three-foot metal sculpture, supposed to be a mini–guard tower, sitting on a table covered with a black-and-white striped cloth. It looked more like an oil rig, with champagne bubbling up through the middle and spilling over the sides into a crystal bowl. "There's more champagne hidden under the tablecloth," Dee explained. "The appetizers are all arranged on metal prison trays and ready to be set out with the arrival of the first guests. The deejay is taking a smoking break but he'll be back. And the place looks amazing!" She caught my glassy stare and raised a well-plucked eyebrow. "Pres, are you sure you're—"

I blinked, then darted over to the champagne table, ducked under the table skirt, and pulled out a bottle. Aside from the occasional glass of white wine, I wasn't much of a drinker. My mom's fourth husband had died as a result of alcoholism. But seconds later I held a full glass—and gulped half of it down.

"Presley!" Delicia said. I turned around. She had attracted the attention of Rocco, Berkeley, and Raj, who stood in various areas of the room gaping at me as if I'd swallowed poison.

"It's only wine," I said, then waved them off, finishing the last drop with a lick of my lips. "I'm . . . fine. Really. Just a little pre-party pick-me-up."

*Hold it together, Pres*, I told myself. *It's almost party time. No one needs to know anything about Andi Sax—at least, not until* after *the wedding.* Still feeling a little unsteady, I poured myself another glass.

Delicia tore her gaze from me to check her watch; then she clapped her hands like a cheerleader. "Okay, people, the guests will be arriving any second! Make sure you're in your costumes and ready to greet them!"

Dee's up-with-people voice brought me out of my near coma. I nodded to let her know I was back. Slightly tipsy, but back. And I had a new tip to add to my mother's *How to Host a Killer Party* book regarding "Hosting While Under the Influence: Probably Not a Good Idea."

"Rocco, set out the crab balls and chocolate Maltese Falcons," I directed. "Berk, videotape a sweep of the party room before it fills up with wannabe criminals and crime solvers. Raj, take a last look around and make sure Alcatraz hasn't been invaded by party crashers."

I ducked outside, into one of the public restrooms, and changed into a white blouse with a Peter Pan collar, a navy blazer sporting a cameo brooch, a plaid midcalf skirt, bobby socks, and penny loafers. Pulling out a large magnifying glass I'd brought as a prop, I leaned into the mirror to check my makeup. Still pale from the news, I added more blush, then stuffed the magnifier into my jacket pocket. I covered my flat, iced hair with a tan cloche hat and headed out as my new persona: Nancy Drew, Girl Detective.

As soon as I stepped out of the restroom, I collided with Inspector Clouseau. His mustache went flying.

"Whoops! Sorry, Raj." The security guard nodded and shook his head simultaneously as he felt his chest for the wayward 'stache. "Great costume," I added, plucking the strip of fake fur from its landing spot on his trench coat lapel.

"This effing mustache keeps falling off. You got any stickum?"

I dug in my purse and pulled out a roll of double-sided tape. As an event planner, I'm always packing: duct tape, glue, scissors, string, stapler, whatnot. All tools of my new trade. Nancy Drew would be proud.

Raj scanned my costume as he replaced his mustache. "And who are you being?"

I held up my magnifying glass and peered at him, no doubt with an alcohol-induced bloodshot eye.

"Oh, yes, yes. Miss Marple." He grinned and his mustache fell off again.

"No, not Miss Marple. Nancy Drew!"

He frowned. An eyebrow fell off. The "inspector" was coming apart at the seams.

Delicia twirled in, dressed in a trench coat, pillbox hat, and chunky black heels. "How do I look?" she said, waving a slim reporter's notebook for effect.

"Lois Lane! That's so cool," I said. Standing next to each other, me at five ten and Delicia at five feet, we must have been a sight: Amazon Girl Detective and Intrepid Mini-Reporter. We all headed inside.

And froze.

Rocco, wearing a leather butcher apron over his chef whites, held a raised hatchet in his hand. One of his fingers was missing, leaving a bloody stump. A mask and a chain saw lay on the table beside him.

Everything was covered in blood.

Before I could scream "Call 911!" Delicia squealed, "*Texas Chainsaw Massacre*! I loved that movie!" She picked up the chain saw. It was real. What I now realized was red food coloring dripped from the blade. "Do you actually use this thing for slicing and dicing?"

Rocco grinned.

A familiar narrative voice began spouting behind me. "Here she is now, party planner Presley Parker, appearing as her alter ego, Nancy Drew, Valley Girl Detective. Are you ready to solve the Mystery of the Mysterious Marriage, Ms. Drew? Or are you just looking over the crime scene? 'Tis a mystery."

I turned to Berk, not in the mood to play the movie game, and gasped again. My videographer now sported a red-stained bridal gown, torn and tattered, with a ragged veil, and white satin stilettos splattered with more red food coloring. At least, I hoped it was food coloring.

I grimaced. "Oh my God, Berk! This isn't a horror movie theme—it's crime. Don't you know your genres? Who are you supposed to be, anyway?"

"'Wanna play?'" he said, grinning like a crazed doll.

"Not *The Bride of Chucky*?" I said, aghast at his choice. Before I could challenge his questionable taste, Raj rushed into the room, his mustache dangling from one side of his upper lip.

"They're coming. They're coming!"

"'They're heeerrre . . . ,'" Berk added, quoting from *Poltergeist*.

I scanned the cellblock one last time. Incredibly, we'd managed to turn a depressing, decaying prison into a killer party scene, complete with Pose with the Prisoner photo ops. I took another gulp of champagne. "Okay, guys, let's put on a show!"

Delicia, Raj, Berk, and I rode the tram down the dimly lit concrete path to the boat dock. The first guests were just stepping off the ferry. My fingers tingled, either from excitement or terror—or both. My mother was right—putting on a party was a lot more work than it looked. And this one had to be perfect.

As instructed, partygoers were costumed as popular criminals or crime fighters. Delicia couldn't keep from nudging me in the ribs and pointing out the characters she recognized. "Look! Hercule Poirot! Al Capone! Oh, there's Lizzie Borden! . . . *Is she naked under that coat?* OMG—a cross-dressing Hoover from the FBI! And Miss Marple—I love her!"

I nudged Delicia back, sharply, and hissed, "Chill!" But I had to admit, the guests had really gotten into the spirit. Even I got excited when I spotted Jack Jason, a San Francisco resident and the star of CeeGee Studio's current top-secret movie, in production on Treasure Island. He'd come as Inspector Gadget in a trench coat and fedora topped with toy helicopter blades—one of his "gadgets." With him was Lucas "Spaz" Cruz, the producer of the film, dressed as Sherlock Holmes, complete with deerstalker hat, cape-coat, and meerschaum pipe.

After giving a brief welcome to Alcatraz and orientation speech, I gestured toward the waiting trams that would take the guests to Cellblock B on the Rock. Delicia remained behind for the next boatload of convicts and crusaders, while I accompanied the first group up the path to the prison party site. I eavesdropped Nancy Drew–style on their animated conversations as they tried to guess who their alter egos were.

"Right this way, everyone," I shouted over the din as we unloaded and entered Broadway. I indicated the champagne tower, while the deejay played "Jailhouse Rock." As the guests headed for the drinks and appetizers, I checked my iPhone to see if Chloe had called again. She was supposed to alert me when the mayor and his fiancée had left the dock in San Francisco.

Damn. I'd missed her latest call. Stepping outside, I pressed her number.

"Hi, Chloe," I said.

"Presley! Thank God you finally called back. Didn't you get my messages? I've got a major situation here."

Not surprising. The mayor's administrative assistant had called me so many times in the past few days with "major situations," I'd thought about putting her on my "Do Not Call" list, but I couldn't afford to lose this job. Besides, the woman had enough on her plate without me avoiding her calls.

I took another swig from my half-empty champagne glass, vaguely wondering if this was the beginning of a drinking problem. At this point, I didn't give a damn.

"Sorry, Chloe. Reception here is iffy. What's up?"

"Ikea is throwing a hissy fit, and the mayor is about to *lose* it. He's threatened to cancel the whole thing!"

Perfect. The party was dead in the water before it had begun.

I took another swallow. "What did she do this time?"

"She doesn't want to wear the Bonnie Parker costume I got her. She says it makes her look fat. The woman is anorexic, for God's sake. And the mayor can't get her to pick something else."

"Just tell her she can wear whatever she wants—she'll look beautiful. And tell Mayor Green the guests are having a great time, thanks to the champagne. This event is going to top the governor's 'Term-inated!' Ball that Andi hosted last summer."

Shit. I'd managed to put Andi out of my mind for the last half hour. Now she was back. Haunting me.

"Okay, but you know how she is, Presley. I just hope she doesn't ruin everything. The mayor would love to get out from under the governor's shadow and this party could really do it."

He'd love to take the governor's place someday too, I thought.

"Thanks, Presley," Chloe continued. "I'll see you soon—I hope."

I ended the call, took a deep breath, and reminded myself this was all for a good cause. The money for Alzheimer's was guaranteed by the mayor, whether or not there was a wedding.

I returned to the cellblock and circulated, making sure the costumed crowd was noshing, drinking, mingling, and generally having a good time. Nick and Nora were chatting with Eliot Ness, Dick Tracy seemed to be entertaining a small group of attractive women—one in a Wonder Woman outfit—and Jessica Fletcher stood admiring her "Wanted" poster with a giant magnifying glass. The only ones out of place were a thirtysomething man dressed in a plain white jumpsuit and a twentysomething woman wearing the ever-popular trench coat. Who were they supposed to be?

The party had warmed up considerably by the time Raj appeared at the door, waving his arms like a panicked air traffic controller. "The mayor's boat is docking! They're coming!" He shouted into his walkie, alerting the other guards he'd hired to help out.

I checked my watch. Chloe still hadn't called to tell me the mayor and Ikea were on their way. I checked my phone. Another message. Shit! Apparently she had. I tried calling her back, but the call went to voice mail.

I took another swallow of my bottomless drink. "I swear," I said aloud, "if anything else goes wrong, I'm going to slap the mayor, kill the bride-to-be, and take a flying leap off the pier."

Out of the corner of my eye, I noticed the man in the white jumpsuit had sidled up beside me. How long had he been standing there? I caught a glimpse of him as he scanned the crowd, a little grin on his face. He was tall—taller than my five ten. Maybe six two or three. Well built, obviously, even covered in a jumpsuit. Thick, wavy, shoulder-length dark hair, brown eyes. A triangular soul patch that matched his dark hair. A label stitched onto the left side of the outfit read "Crime Scene Cleaners—Our Day Begins When Yours Ends."

Clever.

I wondered if he'd overheard me talking to myself. Or maybe he just had a thing for Nancy Drew?

He caught me staring at him and smiled. I glanced away, feeling my face tingle with heat. He turned to me and lifted his glass. I acknowledged him by raising mine, then drank what was left. As soon as I was done, I bolted for the door. It had been a while since I'd flirted with a good-looking guy, and now wasn't a good time to start again.

On the way out the door, I grabbed a bottle of champagne and two glasses for the guests of honor, cued Delicia to position the minister, then headed down to the dock via tram to greet Mayor Green and Ikea Takeda. I prayed the bubbly would soften the bride-to-be's imminent "surprise."

If not, I'd empty the bottle myself.

With a fake smile plastered on my face, I watched as the couple stepped from the ferry into the pool of light illuminating the dock. Thrusting the glasses into their hands, I said, "Welcome to the Mayor's Ball and Chain Fund-raiser for the Alzheimer's Association!" I could hear the false gaiety in my voice and only hoped I wasn't slurring my words. My tongue felt like a fat dead slug.

Mayor Green and Ikea had indeed dressed as Bonnie and Clyde, only they'd glammed up the notorious bank robbers, Hollywood style. The popular, thirty-five-year-old mayor looked even more dashing in a zoot suit, black roadster cap, and black-and-white saddle oxfords. He was beaming, most likely in anticipation of the upcoming surprise.

Ikea appeared truly anorexic in a slinky sequined black dress, dangerously high strappy heels, and a gray beret with a diamond stickpin placed perfectly in her black shoulder-length pageboy. The outfit hung on her as if she were just a hanger. Aside from a pair of square gold earrings that dangled from her ears and a ginormous diamond on her left hand, she wore no other jewelry. No animal rights activist, she dragged a black stole over one shoulder, and clung to the mayor's arm like a barnacle. Her public smile showed no trace of the tantrum she'd thrown earlier. When she realized there was no one to greet her but "the help," she dropped the smile.

"Where is everyone?" she said to the mayor.

I stepped up. "They're all up at the cellblock, Ms. Takeda. Waiting for you and the mayor. We've got a tram to take you there."

Ikea Takeda looked at me as if I were a prisoner rather than a party planner. She turned to the mayor again, rolled her eyes, and pulled the stole tighter around her shoulders. "God, let's get this over with. It's freezing here! I know, I know. It's for a good cause—what was it again?"

The mayor led her toward the tram.

"Alzheimer's," Chloe said, following them. The mayor's admin wore a long black dress and matching hat from the forties, and carried a black Beanie Baby bird. Even her fingernails were painted black. As Mayor Green and Ikea entered the front row of the tram, I joined Chloe in the seat behind them. She gave me a small hug and mouthed *Thank you*, then nodded at Ikea. If I'd had more time, I'd have guessed some form of anxiety disorder—but then, who wouldn't have anxieties in her job?

"I love your costume!" I whispered to Chloe.

"Do you know who I'm supposed to be?" she whispered back, fiddling nervously with a small silver triangle that hung from around her neck.

"Of course. It's my favorite movie of all time," I said. "You're Brigid O'Shaughnessy from *The Maltese Falcon*. Very San Francisco."

As the tram wended its way up the hill, I overheard Ikea say to the mayor, "How's my hair?" Naturally it was perfect, just like the mayor's.

"Fine," he said, straining his neck to see up the hill.

She shook her head. "You didn't even look!"

Mayor Green turned to Ikea, put an arm around her, and gave her a peck on the cheek. "I've never seen you look more beautiful."

"Well, it won't last if this fog keeps up. That cellblock better be heated."

I thought I saw a flash of irritation cross the mayor's brow before he turned away. Moments later the tram pulled up in front of the cellblock. I hopped out, while Mayor Green helped Ikea from her seat. I made a sweeping gesture toward the large double-door entrance. The mayor took the cue, stepped forward, and pulled open one of the heavy doors, ushering Ikea inside. Chloe winked at me, I crossed my fingers, and we both followed them in.

As Ikea entered, she smiled at the large but suddenly

quiet group gathered in a semicircle in the cellblock hallway.

"Well," Ikea said, seemingly pleased at the turnout, "on behalf of the mayor and myself, we want to thank you all for coming tonight and helping with a great cause, uh . . ."

She paused and looked at the mayor for a moment, who quickly spoke up.

"The Alzheimer's Association."

Ikea nodded and flashed her artificially whitened smile at the group. Several people in the crowd whispered to each other and giggled.

Ikea turned to Mayor Green, looking puzzled. Looping her arm through his, I heard her whisper, "Darling? What's . . ."

She left the question unfinished as the mayor grinned at her in gleeful anticipation. He raised his champagne glass and the smiling crowd followed suit.

"Surprise!" they all shouted.

Ikea frowned deep enough to require Botox. She scanned the room, nearly teetering on her spiky heels, then turned back to Mayor Green. "I don't understand. Davin, what's this all about?"

I cued the deejay to begin the "Wedding March." The cheering crowd shuffled back against the cell bars, clearing a path down the middle of Broadway, as the minister stepped up to the portable altar set up at the end of the hall.

Ikea blinked several times. Under her breath, her smile frozen on her pale face, she hissed, "Davin, what the hell is going on?" As she spoke, she slowly withdrew her arm from the mayor's and nervously ran the finger of her right hand up and down the stem of the champagne flute.

Mayor Green, still grinning like a teenager, took her diamond-studded left hand. "It's our wedding, baby! I wanted it to be a surprise!"

Ikea stared at the mayor, openmouthed.

He raised his champagne glass. "So, are you surprised?"

Her smile unwavering, she slowly lifted her champagne

glass and faced the crowd. I held my breath, waiting for a shriek of joy or a prenuptial kiss. The music quieted, the attendees grew hushed. All eyes were on Ikea.

For one quick moment she gave me a look I couldn't read. Then she turned to the mayor and, with a twist of her wrist, flung the bubbly liquid into the mayor's beaming face.

"How could you!" she said, her eyes as sharp as prison-house shanks.

The crowd gasped at the dramatic display as Ikea spun in her retro heels and stomped out of the cellblock, into the dark night. In the deadly silence that followed, I thought I heard a pin drop. The kind used to stick a voodoo doll.

The deafening crash that followed was the sound of my career hitting the cellblock floor.

# Chapter 4

*PARTY PLANNING TIP #4:*

*You can spin even the most disastrous affair into a successful soiree by turning up the tunes, serving the snacks, and most of all, decanting the drinks.*

I picked up a black-and-white-striped paper napkin embossed with the words "Davin and Ikea—Locked Together Forever" and offered it to the mayor. He snatched it out of my hands, wiped the champagne off his face, and darted after his bolting would-be bride. Chloe shot me a frantic look, then dashed after him.

I signaled to Raj to follow them. He saluted and tore out as if chasing an escaping convict. He was followed by a handful of other guests curious to see the drama unfold outside the cellblock.

"Want ads, here I come," I mumbled, and took another swallow of champagne.

Delicia looked up at me, frowning. "Presley Parker! If you can manage a room full of screaming, hyperactive boys at a birthday party, you can certainly handle a little glitch like this!"

A "little glitch" being a stunned bride-to-be jilting her even more stunned future groom—the mayor of San Francisco, for God's sake—then going AWOL from her own surprise wedding and reception. But Delicia was right, bringing to mind another one of my mother's rules in her *How to Host a Killer Party* handbook on "How to Deal with a Disaster." She'd had a few close calls herself on occasion and had shared her quick fixes in the book. Channeling my ADHD, I moved into fix-it mode.

"Berkeley!" I shouted across the room, then mimed *Start the music!*, cupping my ear and swaying back and forth. I waved to Rocco and gestured *Bring on the food!*, pointing to my open mouth, then waving in my arm. Finally I turned to Delicia and pretended to pour champagne down my throat.

I only pretended because I didn't have an open bottle handy.

My spirited crew went to work—perhaps not quite as "spirited" as I. Berkeley cranked up the marriage-themed tunes, beginning with "Ball and Chain" by Social Distortion. Rocco brought out his mini–crab quiches and tuna tartar bites. And Delicia poured bubbly with both hands.

I headed for the outdoor platform and placed a call to Raj. When he didn't answer, I left the first of half a dozen messages, then headed down a shortcut to the dock to search for Ikea myself. After fifteen minutes of scanning the landing area, questioning the ferry captains, and checking the public restrooms, I hiked back up to the cellblock, shivering from the fog-shrouded night, to check on the guests.

Puffing like a blowfish, I found the party people happy as bay clams, eating, drinking, dancing, and excitedly buzzing about the two guests of honor—the hot topic of the moment, perhaps of the year. I needn't have worried about the entertainment. Who needed a bride and groom when you had juicy gossip like this?

A voice startled me from behind.

"Trouble in paradise?"

I whirled around to see the Crime Scene Cleaner guy grinning at me. I would have spilled my champagne all over him if there had been any left in my recently drained glass. Instead, I fumbled the empty glass and watched it tumble to the floor. Miraculously it didn't break, having landed on the red carpet we'd rolled out for the occasion.

We both knelt down to retrieve it, but I beat him to it. While I was down there, I stole a quick glance at his shoes. New Balance Zips. Great for running, yet seriously comfortable. Not cheap.

Truth is, I have a sort of psychological shoe fetish. I'd worked my way through college selling everything from Birkenstocks to Blahniks, and learned more about people's personalities from their shoe selections than all the psych classes I could ever take. Following even more in my mother's footsteps, I thought about writing a book on the psychology of shoes called *How to Know People by the Shoes They Choose*, but I still hadn't gotten past the cumbersome title.

We both rose. "Well, this isn't exactly paradise, uh, Mr. . . . ?"

"Matthews. Brad Matthews," he said, extending his hand.

I took it lightly, but his grip was strong. And warm. "Presley Parker," I said, suddenly feeling self-conscious. "As for the bride-to-be, I'm sure she was a little shaken by the 'surprise,' but no doubt the mayor will smooth things over. He's good at that, as you may know. Anyway, I hope you're enjoying the party."

Brad Matthews took a sip of his drink, which looked more like water than champagne. "You're right about that—he's great at charming people."

I frowned, wondering what he meant by that, but I couldn't read his expression as he scanned the room. He had to have been a friend of either the mayor or Ikea to be invited to the event, but his tone was ambiguous. He turned his gaze on me. His dark brown eyes were penetrating.

Disconcerted, I traded my empty glass for a full one from a passing tray and shrugged. "Ikea's probably disappointed she didn't get to plan her own wedding. After all, most girls dream of this day from the age of three. To be surprised at your own wedding—it's got to be a shock."

Brad Matthews nodded. "Unique theme—the ball and chain. Your idea?"

"God, no!" I shook my head. "The mayor's." Speaking of whom, I wondered where he and his ex-bride-to-be had disappeared to. Time to call Raj for an update.

"If you'll excuse me . . ." Before I could escape, Brad held out his hand again. "It was nice to meet you, Presley Parker." This time I tried to match his firm, confident grip as I studied his large hand. No rings, not even a suntan ring where a former wedding ring might have been. "Don't you have an office over on TI?"

I blinked. "How did you—"

Before I could finish, Raj burst through the doors of the cellblock, red-cheeked and puffing, his uniform disheveled for the first time since I'd known him. He bent over, trying to catch his breath. I set my glass down on a nearby table and dashed over to him.

"Raj, are you all right?" I put a comforting hand on his back.

He nodded, still gasping, and slowly straightened up.

"I was about to call you," I said. "Did you find Ikea? Or the mayor?"

He shook his head. "No, no. I'm very sorry, but I am scouring the whole area and she is nowhere to be found. She has actually disappeared!"

I made a mental note to add another party tip to my mother's book: "Try Not to Lose the Guest of Honor."

I signaled for Delicia to get Raj a glass of water, then stepped outside and tried to phone Ikea, Mayor Green, and Chloe on my cell. No answer from any of them.

I was about to call the police when I caught a glimpse of the mayor staggering up the hill. I ran to meet him and took him by the arm, out of the chilly night air and into the cell-block. He looked as pale as the damp white shirt he wore, and was breathing rapidly enough to hyperventilate. His black-and-white saddle shoes were scuffed, his suit jacket was gone, but his stiff, gelled hair was still perfect. He grabbed an abandoned, half-empty glass of champagne and chugged it, then looked for another.

"Mayor Green, did you find Ikea?" I asked, pulling up a nearby folding chair for him to use. He looked as if he was about to collapse.

He shook his head and slumped into the chair. "I searched everywhere. I thought maybe she'd taken one of the ferries back, but no one seems to know." He took another swig from his recently refilled champagne glass, and his breathing slowed. As he lifted his hand to wipe his forehead, I noticed one of his cuffs was wet, not just damp, as was one of his pants pockets. He caught my gaze and brushed at the damp spots.

"I ran down to the dock. . . . I saw something caught on one of the ropes near the ferries. . . . I leaned over to get it. . . ."

He pulled what looked like a drowned rat from his pocket. I recognized it immediately as a piece of Ikea's fur wrap. He glanced at me with bloodshot eyes. Had he been crying? Or was the redness due to something else? "You don't think she . . . fell in, do you? She can't swim. . . ."

My stomach flipped. The champagne I'd drunk surged upward. I swallowed, trying to keep it down. Suddenly the door to the cellblock burst open again. I spun around, along with most of the now quiet guests, hoping, praying I'd see Ikea in the doorway.

Instead, Chloe stood there, tears in her eyes. She spotted the mayor and ran to him. "Mayor, are you all right? I've been looking all over for you! Did you find her?" She too was disheveled, out of breath, and goose-pimpled.

Mayor Green shook his head. "I think she may have . . ." He dropped his head in his hands.

Hovering over him like a prison matron, Chloe patted his

sculpted hair. "No, no, Mayor, I'm sure she's fine. She'll turn up. You know Ikea—she has a flair for the dramatic." She glanced at me, her eyes pleading for help.

"Chloe's right," I said uselessly. "Meanwhile, my security team is searching the area."

Delicia appeared in the doorway, her face flushed with color, either from the night air or from hiking up the hill—or both. Puffing, she said, "I just saw one of the ferries headed back to the city. I think she may have been on board—"

Mayor Green rose from the chair. "Really? When?"

Delicia looked at her watch. "Uh, a few minutes ago. We can call the ferry company and check."

"Did you actually see her?" I asked Delicia.

"No, but—"

Before she could respond, I heard a commotion at the far end of the cellblock, near what would have been the altar we'd set up for the nuptials. A young woman, blond, wearing a trench coat, had climbed up on the wooden structure. One of the guests appeared to be trying to pull her down.

The crowd gave a collective gasp as the twentysomething woman, barefoot, began to untie the belt on her coat. In seconds she had yanked it open and was standing in front of the gathered crowd, flashing the already stunned partygoers.

Her naked body was covered in ugly blisters and sores.

"Mayor Green is a murderer!" she screamed.

# Chapter 5

*PARTY PLANNING TIP #5:*

*If your party doesn't have enough drama, add more.*

*There's nothing duller than a party without surprises.*

*Caveat: Just make sure you, as hostess, are not the one surprised.*

Elbowing my way through the crowd, I got close enough to recognize the woman from her frequent photos in the *San Francisco Chronicle*: Xtreme Siouxie, aka Susan Steinhardt. She'd been featured several times over the years for her off-the-wall protesting tactics. A self-described "Earthist" from the quasi-terrorist school of environmental protection, she'd been cited for incinerating SMOKEY BEAR signs ("Hypocritical!"), vandalizing animal spay clinics ("Oppressive!"), and disrupting political events ("Tyrannical!"), all while wearing extreme costumes—a singed bear outfit, a dog in jailhouse stripes, and a shroud made out of an American flag. Hence the nickname.

At the moment, she was sporting her latest protesting getup, which I realized upon closer look was a nude bodysuit covered with glued-on blisters, sores, scars, and fake blood, and accented with streaks of greenish ooze. She'd accessorized with large rubber cockroaches in her hair and plastic decayed-looking "Bubba" teeth in her mouth. Shoeless, she hadn't seen a pedicure, perhaps ever.

Not a good look for this usually attractive young woman.

The crowd stood gawking at her, drinks in hand, appetizers midbite. A few began to whisper, a few laughed, and a few just shook their heads. I nodded to Raj, his top lip curled back in horror, his fake mustache long gone. He rushed forward, reached up, and with the help of a couple of other party guests—including Brad Matthews, the Crime Scene Cleaner—seized Siouxie by the arm. She twisted violently in Brad's grip as he pulled her down and tried to cover her with the discarded trench coat.

Unfortunately, she didn't go quietly into that good night. As the mini-posse escorted her outside, I heard her scream, "Clean up the toxic waste on Treasure Island, Mayor Greedy! You're murdering innocent wildlife!"

A hefty, mustachioed older man channeling Hercule Poirot marched over and clapped a hand on the mayor's shoulder. "Forget it, Mayor. She's just a nutcase. Treasure Island was and will always be a monument to our military, not some tie-dyed, weed-infested, hippy hangout."

"Admiral Stadelhofer, this isn't really the time—" Chloe tried to interrupt before the pompous man could launch full speed into his personal agenda, but she was cut off by another man dressed as a clichéd American Indian in fringed leather pants, wristbands, and a headdress. Only his shirt was out of place—a T-shirt that read in scrawled letters "Indians Welcome" above a sign saying UNITED STATES PENITENTIARY. It was a carbon copy of the actual sign that greeted tourists as they arrived at Alcatraz.

"No, it isn't, Stad," the Indian said. "Besides, no one wants the island to become a reminder of all the contaminated waste the military left behind there, especially not the mayor. That land belongs to us." He pounded his chest with a fist.

"And by 'us,'" said Sherlock Holmes, aka Lucas "Spaz" Cruz, the Treasure Island film producer, "you mean you, don't you, Dakota? So you can build more casinos and bring more tourists to our island? And just how is that going to preserve the place?"

The Indian named Dakota whirled around. "Better to benefit my people than one greedy moviemaker who continues to stereotype people like us."

"Stereotype you?" Spaz laughed. "Look at your outfit! It's ridiculous—"

The mayor held up his hands before the verbal sparring turned into a physical fight. "Enough! Gentlemen, please! Look, Eugene, Dakota, Spaz, I'll make my decision about the island soon, but right now I've got other things on my mind—like making sure my fiancée is all right. So if you'll excuse me . . ."

Ever the politician, the mayor thanked the guests for coming and "for contributing to . . . uh, a good cause. Please enjoy yourselves, everyone. You paid good money for this." With that, he gave a kingly wave and left the cellblock, Chloe shadowing him out the door. Poor girl. She had her hands full. I wouldn't have wanted to be in her shoes—even if they were Juicy Couture. I had my own problems.

"Shouldn't we call the police?" Delicia whispered, her thin dark eyebrows raised nearly to her hairline.

I shrugged. That was all I needed. A police raid on my big party. "I guess so. But let's at least wait until we hear back from the ferry captain. Unless you want to report the premature death of an event planner's career. Besides, Raj has his staff on it. Let's give him a chance to find out what he can."

I signaled to Rocco to cut the ball-and-chain cake, told Delicia to serve the chocolate birds and handcuffs, and asked Berkeley to pour the gourmet coffees.

Raj appeared moments later, holding his walkie in one hand and cell phone in the other. "The ferry company is not responding to my calls, but one of the captains was saying that a boat was returning to the city. He was also giving me this."

Raj held up what was left of Ikea's fur wrap. "He found it at the dock, after the ferry was leaving. It's appearing she was on the ferry. Case solved, perhaps?" he said, in keeping with his Clouseau character.

I nodded, taking the damp wrap from his hand. "Thanks, Raj. Good work."

As the guests headed for the waiting trams to take them to the ferries, I took a last sip of leftover champagne. Then, together with my crew, I packed up the decorations and supplies, leaving only a few crumbs and some spilled bubbly for the park's janitorial staff to clean up.

Where was a crime scene cleaner when you needed one? I mused, boarding the last ferry. This party had certainly been a mess, but it would take more than a mop to clean up after. As the boat left the dock, I gazed back at Alcatraz, once again bleak, moody, and blanketed in fog, and thought about all that had happened. My first big event had been a colossal disaster. The bride had bolted. The groom had been left at the altar. A few of the party guests had made their own scenes.

And lest I forget, the police wanted to talk with me about the death of my primary competitor.

Before I could list more, the boat hit a swell, and I spent the rest of the trip back to the city heaving champagne over the side.

The next morning, with a massive headache, dry throat, and upset stomach, I rolled out of bed and headed for the tiny kitchenette in my one-bedroom, one-story condo. My rental was one of dozens of remodeled former military housing units on this four-hundred-acre man-made island poised between San Francisco and Oakland.

I'd learned from my mother, somewhat of a San Francisco historian along with her other talents, that the island had been constructed from fill dirt washed down from the Sierras. The name, Treasure Island, came from the hope that some of that mother lode dirt still held flakes of gold. While TI may not hold the lure and promise of gold, it has a rich history for such a small plot of land.

I made myself a recuperative latte, took three Tylenol, and stepped out onto my back porch. Inhaling the salt air, I sipped the soothing drink and gazed at the city skyline from my safe harbor. That view of the orange Golden Gate Bridge, Coit Tower, and Transamerica building was only part of the reason I loved living here, in spite of the fact that the island will no doubt sink into the bay if there's another major earthquake. Liquefaction was one of the risks of using fill dirt.

The island was originally planned as an airport for Pan Am's Pacific Rim service—the first of its kind—and during the thirties was home to the glamorous *China Clipper* seaplane. Pan Am only employed male stewards back then, but my grandmother Constance managed to get hired as a nurse aboard the grand ship, and I used to hear tales of her adventures on the "flying boat." What I would have given to have taken a round-trip back then, but today the ticket would cost twenty-five thousand dollars.

At the end of the thirties, the island served as the site for the Golden Gate International Exposition—the World's Fair—and featured such one-of-a-kind amusements as Billy Rose's Aquacade starring Esther Williams and Johnny Weissmuller, and Sally Rand's Nude Ranch along Gay Way. What an exciting time that must have been.

When the navy took over in preparation for World War II, Treasure Island was closed to the public. By the time it reopened in 1997, a few of the Art Deco buildings remained, but sadly the beautiful gardens, fountains, and statues were gone, leaving behind decaying military buildings and a desolate landscape. And the original Pan Am aircraft hangars now house soundstages for film producers like CeeGee Studio. While the island has been designated a historical landmark, it's still a source of continuing arguments over plans for the future.

Luckily for me nothing would be decided until the Environmental Protection Agency cleared the way, which could take years. When the navy vacated the place, it left behind earth and groundwater contaminated with asbestos, plutonium, radium, and other toxic chemicals. I suppose I risked developing cancer, but at least I could keep my home and office for the time being.

When the chilling fog finally reached my toes, I returned to my warm home and sat down at the small oak table that divided the kitchen from the living area. I'd filled the place with garage sale furniture and decorated the walls with posters publicizing *The Maltese Falcon*, *Birdman of Alcatraz*, *Vertigo*, and other movies set in San Francisco. Although my place was small, it was cozy, and the clutter of party supplies, discarded clothing, half-eaten snacks, latte mugs, and even cat hair just made it even homier.

I took a life-sustaining sip of coffee, then courageously scanned the *San Francisco Chronicle* for an obituary featuring last night's fiasco. With only an hour before my scheduled meeting with Detective Melvin at the San Francisco Hall of Justice, I wanted to get in a skate around the island and a hot shower before I faced his interrogation.

I checked the headlines to make sure the city hadn't been attacked by terrorists, sunk into the ocean, or destroyed by another earthquake. The city was still safe. That was the good news. Oddly, there was no mention of Andrea Sax.

The bad news was the lead story on the society page. I reluctantly began reading the review of my first—and no doubt last—big event.

MAYOR'S SURPRISE WEDDING BACKFIRES—
BRIDE BOLTS!
*By Roberta Alexander*

Last evening, at the surprise wedding Mayor Davin Green had secretly planned for his fiancée, chick-lit writer Ikea Takeda, the bride-to-be apparently bolted when she realized the "Ball and Chain" themed fundraiser for the Alzheimer's Association was a shocking ruse. The unsuspecting socialite immediately threw her glass of bubbly at the would-be groom and stormed off into the . . .

*Oh my God, I'm doomed*, I thought, as I threw the paper down without finishing the overwritten tabloidesque story. Changing out of my baggy cat-decorated pajamas and into my baggy, multipocketed safari shorts and "Killers" T-shirt, I grabbed my Rollerblades and headed for the bike path that skirted the island.

No matter how upset or depressed I was, skating around Treasure Island and taking in the breathtaking vista on a clear day calmed me better than any drug. I loved skating by the exposition halls, the clipper ship hangars, and the old navy buildings, trying to imagine what life was like during those colorful times.

Seagulls and sandpipers hovered and dove overhead as I skated from Mariner Drive along Perimeter Road, past decrepit military barracks, abandoned fair pavilions, colorful Windsurfers, and bobbing yachts, toward the rusted, dangling RESTRICTED ENTRY sign. A glimpse of Alcatraz brought me back to last night's fiasco, and I thought about the special interest groups at the party, fighting over the island's future. They all seemed to be trying to sway the mayor to their sides.

Admiral Stadelhofer's agenda to turn the island into a military monument, Dakota Hunter's plan to make it an Indian gambling site, and Xtreme Siouxie's plan to preserve it as a natural habitat were just the tip of the iceberg. I'd heard talk of turning the place into an amusement park, a high-rise housing development, and an exclusive resort—all of which threatened to alter the beauty and serenity of this unique piece of primo real estate.

So far only the radical environmentalists had managed to keep redevelopment at bay by insisting there were toxic contaminants from the former naval shipyard. Until that mess was cleaned up, nothing else could proceed. And in my opinion, the longer it took, the better—or I'd soon find myself homeless again.

This morning the fog had been swept away early by the bay breeze, which whipped my short hair and tickled my fair skin. I spotted house sparrows and hummingbirds among the windswept cypress and palm trees, as well as harbor seals and pelicans that made their homes in the salt marshes and mudflats. Rounding the point opposite Alcatraz Island, I recognized Duncan Grant, a self-described geocaching gamer. Duncan set up treasure hunts for hidden caches on the island using the Global Positioning System. His GPS hunts had become so popular, he planned to expand to the entire Bay Area.

The twentysomething young man with a headful of red curls and a face covered in freckles appeared to be rummaging through a pile of jagged rocks near the water's edge along Avenue of the Palms. He had on his favorite threadbare T-shirt that sported the words "Cache In/Trash Out," along with mandatory skater shorts and green, high-top Nike Dunks, sans laces.

Duncan had taken up squatting residence in one of the empty offices in my building where he kept much of his equipment. He talked of nothing but geocaching, and we'd been discussing collaborating on a fund-raising party featuring some of the historic sites on the island. He'd explained that players would rent inexpensive GPS devices and receive a sheet of quadrants that would lead them on the hunt. At each location they'd search for a hidden "cache" filled with little treasures, everything from baseball caps and small stuffed animals to rubber snakes and cartoon underwear. Players were allowed to take one of the treasures, but had to leave a treasure in its place for future geocachers. The idea was to find all the quadrants, retrieve treasures, and return to home base to share their finds.

I sat down on a large rock to adjust one of my blades. As I got up, Duncan spotted me and urgently waved me over. No doubt he'd found something interesting in one of his hidden caches he wanted to share with me. Curious about his latest treasure discovery, I headed over.

"Hey, Dunk. Thanks again for playing the part of the vampire at that kids' party. You were a hit—"

I stopped short when I realized Duncan wasn't listening to me. Grimacing, he had knelt down at the water's edge and was pointing in the water. His prized Nikes were soaked. But instead of the expected cache, he seemed to be staring at what looked like a large black-and-white fish bobbing on the water's surface.

"What's up, Dunk?" I asked, following his gaze to the water.

Whoa. A dolphin? In the bay? "Oh, the poor thing . . ."

Duncan stood up, suddenly looking pale instead of his usual red-headed complexion. He shook his head robotically.

"What . . . ?" I stepped closer and leaned in.

Oh. My. God. This was no fish. Not wearing a sequined black gown.

It was a floundering Ikea Takeda.

# Chapter 6

*PARTY PLANNING TIP #6:*

*Never say anything bad about anyone at a party. You can bet it will come back to bite you in the ass.*

Looking down at the bobbing body, the swirling water, and the rocking waves, I felt the blood leave my head. To keep from falling down, I sat down hard on some rocks, no doubt bruising my butt. The world spun around me like a whirlpool. I tucked my head between my legs.

"Oh my God," I whispered to my skates. Then I gagged and drooled a little on them.

When I could lift my head, I glanced over at Duncan and wiped the spittle off my lips and chin. He remained rooted to his spot, gawking at the floating woman, his mouth hanging open like a dead fish. Before I could suggest he look away, he bent over and hurled into the cache he'd been setting up.

To keep myself from joining him, I pulled my cell phone from my pocket and punched in 911 with trembling fingers. When the dispatcher came on the line, I rambled incoherently, "I want to report . . . a body . . . a drowning. . . ."

"May I have your name please?"

"Ikea Takeda . . . I mean, Presley Parker," I stammered.

"Where are you now?"

I glanced around. "Avenue of the Palms, at Ninth . . . on Treasure Island."

I answered the rest of the dispatcher's questions as best I could. She told me to stay put, officers were on their way, to remain on the line, and some other things I didn't really hear.

I said, "Okay . . . okay . . . okay . . ." Then, without thinking, I hung up.

Duncan's normally ruddy complexion was now the color of the bay waters. "You all right?" I asked.

He spat and straightened up, jostling a string of saliva that hung from his scraggly goatee. Glancing back at the body, he said the F word, then added, "Think she was a jumper?"

"Huh?" I said.

Duncan nodded toward the looming Bay Bridge. Although not as popular as the Golden Gate Bridge for suicides, the Bay Bridge also served the purpose. Caltrans had put up barriers to try to stop the jumpers, but it hadn't done much good. I'd read once that about twenty-five people jumped from the Golden Gate every year.

But Ikea—a suicide? I supposed anything was possible, but she really hadn't seemed suicidal last night. Shocked. Angry. Humiliated, maybe. I might have diagnosed her as paranoid. But not despondent. Could she have fallen overboard from the ferry on her way back to the city last night?

I shivered. "We'll know soon enough. The police are on their way." Unable to help myself, I glanced at the body in the water. "Poor Ikea."

"The mayor's chick?"

I nodded. "She was the guest of honor at the event I hosted last night."

"Whoa. Sucks for you. But I heard she's a real b—"

Sirens cut off the rest of his words. I spotted a black-and-white coming from the two-man satellite police department located in a corner of the former Exposition Building One, and another black-and-white headed down the winding exit from the Bay Bridge. A third siren seemed to be coming from my pocket. My cell phone.

I could just make out the "Happy Birthday to You" tune. My mother's personalized ring. I hesitated, then answered it in case it was a real emergency.

"Hi, Mom. What's up?"

"Presley?"

I stuck a finger in my uncovered ear and strained to hear her over the incoming sirens. "Yes, Mom, it's me," I shouted. "Now's not a good time to talk. Can I call you later?"

"Sweetie, you know I'd only call if it was important."

"Okay, what do you need?"

"I need help. . . ."

"With what? Are you sick? Are you hurt?"

"No, I was watching one of those infomercials on Channel 58 and they showed this new miracle stuff, it's like medicine, and it makes all your wrinkles just disappear without surgery, and you only have to make three easy payments, but you can only get it by dialing a special phone number, and I could only remember a couple of the numbers, three and seven, I think, so could you call for me and order some? I think Blue Cross will cover it. You know I'm going to need it for the mayor's wedding— Sweetie, what's that horrible noise? It sounds like—"

"Mom, I'm going to have to call you back, okay?"

"Okay, sweetie. I think there's someone at the door. The bell's ringing, or maybe it's the phone—" The line went dead.

Poor Mom. When I told her I was taking on the mayor's wedding, she assumed she'd be invited. In her day, she had not only held the best parties; she'd also been invited to them. In between, she'd also managed to raise a substantial amount of money for the arts, lead roundtable discussion groups, help build a stray animal shelter, and even host her own local TV show. Not to mention marry five husbands.

Now Alzheimer's was stealing away the person she *is*, the person she would have been, but not who she *was*. Veronica Parker Valdez Uawithya Jefferson Heller still thought of herself as the Princess of Pacific Heights. I'd make it a point to stop by sometime today—if no more bodies turned up.

I slipped my phone back into my pocket as the two police cars pulled up on the street near the water's edge. Duncan vigorously waved the officers over as if signaling a distressed ship at sea. The two local officers—Tony Cerletti and Amberly Finarelli—were well-known and well liked around the island. Amberly, tan, no makeup, her hair pulled back into a no-nonsense ponytail, carried so much bulky equipment around her uniformed waist, she tended to walk like a penguin with her arms sticking out. On her feet she wore regulation black SWAT combat boots, more for the look than the necessity, I imagined.

Tony also wore the regulation uniform and shoes, but carried his gun, flashlight, radio, pepper spray, baton, and cuffs as if they were part of his physical makeup. He looked as comfortable in his duty gear as Amberly looked uncomfortable. Amazingly, they made a good team.

An officer from the other black-and-white stepped out wearing a suit, which fit his muscular form perfectly. *Men in Black*–style sunglasses, black high-gloss oxfords, and slicked-back black hair finished the look. This guy cared about his appearance. When he pulled off the dark glasses, his eyes were surprisingly blue.

The flash of his badge distracted me from his eyes.

"I'm Detective Luke Melvin, and this is Officer Carole Price," he said, gesturing toward the uniformed officer who had exited the shotgun side.

Melvin. I knew that name.

Uh-oh. The detective I was scheduled to meet at the station.

Detective Melvin replaced his badge with a small notebook. "Who found the body?" he said, glancing back and forth between Duncan and me.

"Uh . . . I guess I found her . . . but I thought it was some kind of fish or something. . . ." Duncan shot a look at me and jerked his thumb in my direction. "Presley thought it was a dolphin. Then she recognized the body."

"Presley?" The detective frowned. His black eyebrows accentuated his pale blue eyes. This guy was way too good-looking to be a cop. He should have been a male model. He probably knew it.

"Presley Parker?"

Pulling myself from the eye candy, I nodded.

He cocked his jaw and stared at me as if he'd just identified the Zodiac Killer. Flipping a page in his notebook, he scanned it, then looked up at me again with those nearly transparent blue eyes. "We have an appointment this morning. Regarding the death of Andrea Sax." He pronounced it An-DRA-ya, instead of AN-dree-ya.

I pulled out my cell and glanced at the time. "Yeah. Guess we're both going to be a little late."

Not even cracking a grin, he said, "What are you doing out here?"

"I thought I'd get in a little exercise before our meeting, so I skated around the path, and then I saw Duncan—"

Before I could ramble on like my mother, another police car pulled up, and two crime scene techs jumped out. I could tell because they wore dark blue jumpsuits with the letters SFCSI stitched on the fronts and backs, and carried metal suitcases like on TV.

"Officer Price will take your statement," Detective Melvin said, indicating his partner before stepping over to greet the new arrivals. I nodded, unable to escape the nagging notion that I might be in real trouble now that I was connected—albeit randomly—to two dead bodies in less than two days.

Detective Melvin nodded to his partner, and the younger officer took my statement. As soon as we were finished, she reported back to the detective. He nodded a couple of times, whispered something to her I couldn't make out, then turned to me.

"My office, one hour," he called out. Then he climbed into his car and drove off, Officer Price riding shotgun. My legs wobbly, I managed to skate back to my condo, my brain racing faster than my rubbery legs. I couldn't get that image of a floating Ikea out of my head. Nor the idea that I was connected to both victims.

I showered robotically, grabbed the cleanest clothes I had—black jeans and an "Irritable Bowel Syndrome—The DaVinci Colon" T-shirt I had made up for a murder mystery party/fund-raiser. I slipped on a pair of fuzzy black socks and my favorite black Mary Janes, and topped my outfit with a black leather jacket. Grabbing my knockoff purse, I was headed for the door before I remembered to feed my three cats, Cairo, Fatman, and Thursby.

Ingrates. They didn't even bother to look up from their various spots on my garage sale furnishings as I filled the bowls with dry cat food. No doubt they were holding out for seagull tapas and rodent al dente. All three had been strays I'd found on the island when I moved in. Fatman was fat and white, Cairo was an orange scaredy-cat, and Thursby was my black killer attack cat that mostly attacked my feet. At the moment he was asleep in my half-closed underwear drawer, his nose tucked into a Victoria's Secret bra cup.

I knew if I didn't watch out, I'd turn into one of those cat ladies who falls and can't get up, undiscovered for days, ears chewed off by hungry felines—

The theme song from *The Twilight Zone* rang out from my cell phone, ending my death-by-cats vision. I checked the number. Blocked.

"Hello?" I said, multitasking as I glanced at the kitschy cat clock with the big rolling eyes and wagging tail on the wall. Time to go. Didn't want to be late for my interrogation. I wondered whether I should pack a bag or call an attorney.

"Hello?" I said again when there was no response.

I heard a click, then froze as I listened to the voice repeat the same phrase in the earpiece: "I'm going to kill the bride. . . . I'm going to kill the bride. . . . I'm going to kill the bride. . . ."

The phone clicked off, leaving a dial tone buzzing in my ear.

I stared at my cell phone in disbelief.

The voice on the other end of the line had been my own.

# Chapter 7

*PARTY PLANNING TIP #7:*

*To get your party started, prepare some guaranteed conversation prompts, such as "Susan is expecting!" or "Bruce has come out of the closet!"*

I've been to the San Francisco Hall of Justice—referred to as 850 Bryant—more times than would look good on a résumé. Mostly to retrieve my mother, who's been held briefly for various 5150 (official police code for "crazy person") infractions, such as freeing kennel "detainees" at the animal shelter and picketing to "save the pigeons" in Union Square. A couple of the watch commanders know me by sight.

Located in the Tenderloin, across the street from a number of bail bonds shops and a place called the Stud Bar, the block-long building reminds me of the cellblock on Alcatraz, only with fresher paint. The jail portion is curved with lots of smoky windows, but the rest of the building is typical for city structures—pink beige walls, screened windows, and a couple of armed security checkpoints, a result of September 11th. I scanned the sign—WARNING. SUBJECT TO SEARCH. NO SCISSORS, KEYS, WATCHES—to see if I'd forgotten anything and pulled a pair of scissors out of my purse. Dropping them into the contraband container, I placed my purse on the belt and walked through the metal detector. The WC checked my photo ID, issued me a temporary sticker-badge, and directed me to the fifth floor where homicide officers hung out.

I thought about one of my mom's party rules as I entered the elevator car and practiced a few opening lines to help break the ice with Detective Melvin. Naturally I chose quotes from an appropriate film—and my favorite—*The Maltese Falcon.*

*"I haven't lived a good life. I've been bad, worse than you could know. . . ."*

Nah. I was no Brigid O'Shaughnessy.

*"I have a terrible confession to make. That story I told you yesterday was just a story. . . ."*

Trouble was, I didn't have anything to confess. At least, not that I knew of.

*"Haven't you got anything better to do than to keep asking a lot of fool questions—"*

My lip was still curled, Bogey style, when the doors opened on the fourth floor. Two officers read my IBS T-shirt and took a step back, allowing me a wide berth as I left the elevator. I wanted to tell them that not only do I not have irritable bowel syndrome, but that it's not contagious, but I bit my tongue and just smiled.

After we exchanged places in the elevator, I turned and asked, "Detective Luke Melvin's office?"

The cop with his hands clasped over his crotch said, "Five oh two." The other one stifled a laugh.

Spinning around with all the dignity I could muster, I moved down the hall, found the office marked 502 HOMICIDE, and knocked. No answer. I let myself in. A kid who looked right out of police academy greeted me, asked my business in cop-speak, then had me sit down in an indestructible orange chair against a far wall of the small waiting room. Moments later Detective Melvin appeared from behind a closed door. I stood up.

At five ten, I'm tall, but he was taller—at least six four. Imposing, to say the least, even without the classic uniform. He gestured for me to follow him. In an effort to be his equal, at least in stature, I stretched my neck, straightened my shoulders, and stood up straight before heading into his inner sanctum.

Passing several offices, he led me to one at the back. He closed the door behind me and moved around his desk to take a seat. I took a moment to scan the office. The metal desk held a storm of crisscrossed papers, files, and reports. While his in-box overflowed, his out-box held nothing but an M&M'S candy wrapper. The pink beige walls were covered with indecipherable charts, infamous "Wanted" posters, a whiteboard with what looked like football plays, and some bizarre artwork that may have been painted by the criminally insane.

But what surprised me most was the movie poster hanging on the back of his office door. It looked like an original copy of *The Maltese Falcon*, signed by director John Huston. Humphrey Bogart's Sam Spade gazed out at the city holding a smoking gun, while Mary Astor's Brigid O'Shaughnessy leaned on him sorrowfully. The Fat Man and Cairo peered out from small cameos at the bottom corners. The Black Bird—"the stuff that dreams are made of"—guarded the scene from his perch at the top of the poster.

Shoot. Don't tell me I had something in common with this cop.

Shutting my open mouth, I sat down in a wooden chair and tried to look as innocent as Brigid O'Shaughnessy—because I was. But somehow, sitting in a homicide detective's office, I didn't feel that way. Then I remembered Brigid's harmless demeanor hadn't helped her with Spade—and he'd been in love with her.

I straightened up, leaned forward, and met his blue eyes. "'I haven't got the bird, Detective.'"

Detective Melvin blinked. "Pardon me?"

I sat back and waved my hand. "Nothing . . . I was just . . ." I pointed a thumb at the poster. "I'm a big fan of *The Maltese Falcon*. . . . I saw your poster. . . . Never mind. Why am I here, Detective Melvin?"

The detective glanced at the poster behind me, nodded slightly, then shuffled through the pile on his desk and read over what looked like my statement. After a few dramatic moments, he retrieved a file marked "Sax, Andrea." He opened it, pulled out a photograph, and held it up for me to see. The popular party planner was standing between the governor of California and the mayor of San Francisco, grinning as if she'd just won a jackpot at the local Indian casino.

I nodded, making an effort to meet his intense stare. I felt beads of sweat break out under my bangs. I knew he was watching my body language, something I do when hosting a party to see who's bored, who's having fun, and who's having too much fun. I hoped my body was saying, *I'm innocent!*

His, on the other hand, was formal, confident, and seemed to be saying, *"You're going over for this, schweetheart."*

"Ms. Parker, when's the last time you saw Ms. Sax?"

I shook my head. "Like I said before, I never saw her. I didn't even know her—although I knew of her, of course. I heard she was planning the mayor's wedding and then . . . I guess there was an argument or something . . . and he fired her and hired me. That's all I know." I clutched my purse, ready to bolt at his dismissal.

Detective Melvin frowned as he replaced the photo in the file folder. From a locked drawer he withdrew a plastic bag. Inside was a BlackBerry that looked small in his large hands. He set the bagged object on the desk in front of me. I relaxed the grip on my purse.

"Ever seen this before?"

I shook my head. "I mean . . . I've seen a BlackBerry before—I have an iPhone—not the new one—but it has all the apps—" I was rambling, a sure sign of guilt. "Is that Andi's?"

Apparently the answer was obvious, because instead of answering, he said, "Your business address on Treasure Island is in her contacts list. If you say you don't know her, any idea why she might have that information?"

"You're kidding." I frowned. I had no clue why she would have the address of my office barracks in her BlackBerry.

His look told me he was no kidder.

"No, I don't know why, Detective. Maybe she was planning to stop by for some reason."

"It's the last entry in her calendar on the day she died."

My heart started to beat double-time. "I . . . uh . . . you said she died how?"

He nodded. "In a car wreck. She was found at the bottom of the hill, off Macalla, on her way to the island."

A chill ran up my spine. "Macalla? I . . . I don't understand."

"That's the exit you take off the Bay Bridge to Treasure Island."

"I know that," I snapped. I tried to shake my head at his sarcasm, but my neck seemed to have locked up. What was Andi Sax doing on Macalla Road? Had she really been on her way to my office? Why?

Detective Melvin interrupted my silent self-interrogation with a question of his own. "You not only work on Treasure Island, you live there too, don't you?"

"Yes, I have a condo—the old military housing—but—"

He folded his hands on the desk, his eyes steely blue. "I think it's obvious that Ms. Sax was on her way to meet you."

"I . . . suppose it may look that way, but—"

"But she had an accident and never made it."

I didn't like his tone. "Apparently not, but—"

He leaned in. "So why was she coming to see you, Ms. Parker?"

"I. Don't. Know," I said, enunciating each word. "I'm

telling you the truth—I had no idea she was coming to see me—*if* she was. And you said it was an accident."

He shrugged.

What did that mean?

"Well, if it was an accident, I'd like to know why I'm here. Even if I was supposed to meet her—which I wasn't—her car went off the road—which I had nothing to do with. We'll never really know whether she was coming to see me, right?" I felt as if I were trying to convince myself as much as the detective. From the look on his face, I think he sensed it too. It seemed to say, *Let her hang herself.*

I felt my face flush with anger and tried to take a calming breath, something I'd been taught by one of my many special ed teachers as a way of controlling my hyperactivity. I had no reason to be on the defensive, but somehow this Bogart wannabe made me react that way. I sat back, gripping the arms of the chair, and crossed my legs, trying to look relaxed, even if I didn't feel it.

"Is that all, Detective? Because I have a business to run—that is, if I still have a business. . . ." I trailed off as Detective Melvin pulled out another folder that was hidden underneath Andi's. He flipped the cover over and scanned the report. All I could read upside down was the heading in bold black letters: "SF Medical Examiner."

My heart began pumping wildly. There was something more to Andi's death.

The detective took a moment to look over the report—as if he didn't already know what it said. Finally he lifted his eyes and summarized it for me. "According to the autopsy report, Ms. Sax had three broken ribs, a punctured lung, and a contusion to her forehead."

"No seat belt?"

"Yes, but the air bag in her SUV didn't deploy."

I thought for a moment. "Did she die of the head wound, then?" I asked, puzzled. The injuries didn't seem bad enough to cause her death. But then, I'm not a doctor.

He glanced again at the paper. "She died from a myocardial infarction, just before the crash." He looked up with those steely eyes to gauge my reaction.

It felt like the air had been sucked out of my lungs. "A heart attack?" I wheezed. "But she was only in her early thirties, wasn't she?"

"According to the tox scan, there was a high level of KCN in her bloodstream."

"KCN?"

"Potassium cyanide."

"I thought you just said she had a heart attack—"

"With five milligrams of KCN in her bloodstream, she probably lost consciousness. Her stomach was nearly empty, which no doubt hurried things along. The ME found traces of"—he paused to read from his notes, carefully pronouncing the multisyllabic words—"theobromine, endogenous cannabinoid anandamide, N-oleoylethanolamine, soy lecithin, cacao, and cocoa butter."

Cocoa butter? "So . . . what does all that mean?"

"It looks like Andrea Sax was given a toxic substance, had a myocardial infarction, lost consciousness, and her vehicle subsequently collided with a cement beam."

Cop-speak for: She was poisoned, had a heart attack, passed out, and crashed the car.

"How did she get all those chemicals in her?"

"Chocolate."

# *Chapter 8*

*PARTY PLANNING TIP #8:*

*In the competitive world of event planning, do your best to kill the competition by thinking outside the balloon. Caveat: Not literally.*

I felt the hairs at the back of my neck stand up like tiny needles. Somebody had actually murdered my competitor, Andi Sax.

And it was painfully obvious that Detective Melvin considered me a suspect.

I shook my head, trying to gather my thoughts in one place, not unlike gathering a bouquet of helium balloons in a windstorm. No matter how hard I rattled my brains, the important information eluded me, and I was left with a head full of hot air.

"Chocolate? How did they get poison into the chocolate?" I said finally.

He studied me like a wolf would a rabbit. "You tell me."

"How should I know? Are you actually accusing me of something?"

Detective Melvin raised a hand and patted the air. "Simmer down, Ms. Parker. I'm just trying to get some questions answered. Like I said, you were her last scheduled appointment. And her body was found on TI, most likely on her way to see you."

"Well . . ." I started to object again, realized it was a waste of energy, and just shook my head.

"You and Ms. Sax were competitors, weren't you?"

"No! I mean . . . I guess you could say that we had similar businesses, but I was no threat to her. She's been the party queen in this city for years. I'm just starting out, hoping to raise money for some important causes. . . ."

Detective Melvin looked down at my irritable bowel syndrome shirt. I felt my face flush. He lifted another sheet of paper, buried under the files. I recognized the name at the top left-hand side of the page: "Presley Parker."

"What's that—my rap sheet?" I said, half kidding.

He didn't even give a half smile. "So you raise money for good causes? Says here that after you were fired—"

"Downsized."

"Let go . . . from San Francisco State University, where you were teaching"—he glanced at the paper—"abnormal psychology. . . ." He looked at me pointedly, as if checking to see whether I might be abnormal myself, then continued. "You abruptly moved from your flat in the Marina to the former navy housing on Treasure Island, and out of the blue, with little experience, decided to go into the party planning business—"

"Event planning," I said, maybe a little shrilly.

"Says here you've only done a couple of kids' birthday parties and a *murder* mystery for IBS. . . ." He emphasized the word "murder." "And then—in a stroke of amazing luck—you were hired to replace Ms. Sax as host of Mayor Green's 'surprise wedding.' " He crooked his fingers mockingly around the last two words.

I shrugged. "I guess they were desperate, since Andi had . . . quit."

"Quit? Or been fired?"

"I have no idea."

"According to the mayor's admin—Chloe Webster—you were highly recommended to them by former socialite–slash–party hostess Veronica Parker—"

Oh no. Mother. "Shit," I hissed under my breath.

"Beg your pardon?"

"Veronica Parker is my mother—although I'm sure you know that already. I should have known why the mayor's wedding fell so easily into my lap. Although how she pulled it off, I'll never know. She's been out of the business for years."

Detective Melvin pulled yet another sheet out of his ass and held it up. This one featured a front and side photograph of a smiling woman wearing too much makeup in her effort to look younger, with wild red-blond-brown hair and a flirtatious gaze inappropriate for her age and the circumstances.

A mug shot.

Underneath, a list of personal statistics and misdemeanors filled the page. I skimmed it, already aware of most of the contents.

**CALIFORNIA DEPARTMENT OF LAW ENFORCEMENT**
**CRIMINAL JUSTICE INFORMATION SYSTEMS**
**AUTOMATED CRIMINAL RECORD CHECK SYSTEM**
*** CUSTOMER SUMMARY REPORT ***

- - - - - - - - - - - - - - - - - - - - - - - - - - - - - - - - - - - -

**PARKER, VERONICA**

ADDR1: 5224 PACIFIC HEIGHTS AVE, SF

ADDR2: 1710 VAN NESS AVENUE, #222

| SEX | RACE | DOB | HT | WT | EYES | HAIR | POB |
|---|---|---|---|---|---|---|---|
| F | W | 04/14/50 | 5'08" | 140 | GRN | RD/BL/BR | SF/CA |

- - - - - - - - - - - - - - - - - - - - - - - - - - - - - - - - - - - -

**OCCUPATION:**

PEACE ADVOCATE/ARTIST/REVOLUTIONARY/

PARTY PLANNER/ANIMAL ACTIVIST/CITIZEN/

MODEL/TELEVISION PERSONALITY/HOSTESS

---

AKA:

VERONICA VALDEZ

VERONICA UAWITHYA

VERONICA JEFFERSON

VERONICA HELLER

---

ARREST- 1

AGENCY CASE-412084

CHARGE 001-BATTERY-

STATUTE/ORDINANCE CA784—03

LEVEL—MISDEMEANOR

---

ARREST- 2

I couldn't read any more and let my mother's list of arrests and misdemeanors float back onto Detective Melvin's desk.

Oh, Mom.

"She's got quite a rap sheet."

I rolled my eyes. "She's got Alzheimer's. She doesn't always know what she's doing. But whatever it is, it's for a good cause—at least in her mind."

"Like mother, like daughter, huh?"

I bristled. "Look, Detective, if she really did help me get the job—which I doubt—hosting the mayor's wedding isn't a crime. Having a mother with a debilitating disease isn't a crime. And knowing a dead person isn't a crime."

Melvin the Magician opened his drawer of tricks and conjured up another plastic bag. With a twist of the wrist, he dumped the contents onto his desk.

It was a miniature replica of a black bird.

Made of chocolate.

I looked up at him, puzzled. "Where did you get that?"

"In Ms. Sax's car. Four others, including one half eaten,

are at the ME's lab." He raised his eyebrows, apparently waiting for my confession.

"But why . . . how?"

"That's what I want to know, Ms. Parker." He rolled the bird over with a flick of his pencil nib.

Flabbergasted, I couldn't speak for several seconds. Then I said, "Look, Detective. I. Don't. Know. Rocco, my caterer for the event, made a bunch of chocolate Maltese Falcons and chocolate handcuffs for the mayor's wedding. He thought they'd be appropriate for the ball-and-chain theme—falcons for the crime solvers and handcuffs for the criminals. But you're not implying . . ."

Detective Melvin stuck his hand inside the empty plastic bag, grasped the dark chocolate bird and, turning the bag inside out, pulled the bird back in. He placed it in a concealed desk drawer and locked the drawer securely.

"Look, Detective, I don't serve poisoned chocolates at my events. Tends to decimate the guest list, you know."

"Any idea how these got into Ms. Sax's car?"

I shook my head. "Maybe . . . someone took them from the reception, then somehow injected them with poison . . . I don't know. Could have been anyone. There were a lot of people there. Half of them were wearing masks or disguises of some sort."

"You're forgetting, Ms. Parker. Andrea Sax was killed *before* the wedding."

Oh yeah. What a great detective I'd make.

While I tried to come up with a plausible explanation, Detective Melvin watched me squirm. A smug smile played on his face, causing tiny crinkles at the corners of his impenetrable eyes. I could see his jaw working—probably rehearsing the Miranda warning. I was surprised he wasn't salivating.

"Obviously someone stole them from the barracks kitchen. That's where Rocco made them. We've had some break-ins at the office lately."

"That might explain it . . . except for one thing."

"What?"

"Ikea Takeda."

"What about her?" I snapped. "She drowned! I'm sorry, but it was an accident. She must have fallen off the ferry on her way back to the city."

His silence told me everything I didn't want to know. I shook my head and forced the words out. "Not an accident?"

His eyes narrowed.

"Poisoned, right?"

Stone face.

"I guess it won't do any good to say I have no idea what's going on with these two . . . mishaps?"

"Actually, I think you do. Someone overheard you last night threatening to kill Ms. Takeda." He rapped his pencil eraser on the table lightly, as if accusing someone of murder was routine.

"What? I certainly said no such thing!"

He flipped through a few pages of his notebook. When he found what he was looking for, he read aloud. "'Yes, I overheard Presley say, *I'm gonna kill the bride. . . .*'"

All the blood in my body rushed to my feet. The phone call I'd received—of my own voice—saying those very words. "That's ridiculous!" I said, laughing too loudly. "Where did you hear that?"

"I believe your exact words were"—he read his notes—"'I'm going to slap the mayor, kill the bride-to-be . . .'"

Shit. Of course I'd said it. Under duress. Under the influence. "Well . . . if I said it at all, it was just a manner of speaking. Taken out of context. Stress release, you know? Everyone says it: 'I'm gonna keel you!'" I tried to sound like Peter Lorre, but it came out sounding like Shrek with a bad cold. "Nobody really means that when they say it."

He made a note in his book. Apparently he didn't share my understanding of the nuances of language.

I leaned in, trying to read his scribbling upside down. "Who told you, anyway?"

He flipped the notebook closed.

" 'Everyone has something to conceal,' Ms. Parker."

I recognized the quote instantly. How could a jerk like this be a fan of *The Maltese Falcon*, the best noir film ever made? I answered him in kind. "Well, Detective, 'I won't play the sap for you.' " I stood up and slung my knockoff purse over my shoulder like Brigid O'Shaughnessy.

" 'It happens,' Ms. Parker, 'we're in the detective business. . . . It's bad business to let the killer get away with it.' "

It took all I had to meet the detective's gaze. "Am I under arrest?"

"Not yet," he said, grinning, his top lip slightly curled under. I swear he looked like Bogart at that moment.

I felt a jolt of heat flush through my body.

"But as they say, don't leave town."

Sweetheart.

# Chapter 9

*PARTY PLANNING TIP #9:*

*Perfect parties, like perfect murders, are planned down to the last detail. And still, something invariably goes wrong.*

*That's why we have party planning handbooks and jail cells.*

I slammed the hell out of Detective Melvin's door and stormed down the hall to the elevators. By the time I reached my car, fear had replaced anger—I could almost feel the handcuffs snapping around my wrists. And they weren't made of chocolate.

Two murders. Both linked to me. No alibi. Plenty of motive.

Shit.

I pulled the parking ticket off my car's windshield, got into my MINI Cooper, and fought the thick traffic to the Bay Bridge, replaying the detective's words on my way back to Treasure Island. The fog had abated, but the seagulls were out in force, and I only hoped my car wouldn't be covered in gull guano by the time I arrived at my office.

My MINI, like my office and my condo, was full of random party crap—medieval swords, Styrofoam ball-and-chains, sparkly ribbons, and "Killer Party" balloons. I'd gotten the car to save money—besides, it was so cute—then wished I'd bought a big SUV like everyone else on the road so I could haul all this stuff. A couple of black and silver balloons bounced around in the backseat as I drove over the retrofitted bridge toward the midway island turnoff.

I still couldn't believe it, but as ludicrous as it seemed, I was looking like Suspect Number One. I had to figure out a way to clear my own ass or I'd end up being arrested for a double homicide.

I needed an alibi.

Or an attorney.

Or a ticket to Argentina.

Or maybe I just needed to find out who killed those two women. I sure wasn't going to get any help from that wannabe Sam Spade.

Driving with one hand on the wheel, I reached the other hand behind me, feeling for the Kinko's box in the backseat. Removing the box lid (and nearly sideswiping a PT Cruiser), I grabbed one of the fresh event planning forms I'd had made up for my Killer Parties business. Of course, in view of the latest "events," I would probably have to change the name to something less murderous. Extracting a balloon-decorated promotional pen from my knockoff Dooney and Bourke bag, I held it between my teeth and placed the paper on my lap.

My party checklist was based on a diagnostic tool I'd adapted for my ab-psych students to help them differentiate a patient's symptoms. Since it worked for academic problem solving, I'd made a few alterations and turned it into an event-planning checklist. Amazing how useful it was for both.

Holding the paper in my left hand and the pen in my right, I steered with my knees, my eyes shifting back and forth between the road, the wheel, and the planning form. With a last look in the rearview mirror for traffic cops, I began filling in the who-what-when-where-how blanks listed next to the little red balloon icons. But instead of answering questions like, "Who is the party for?" and "What is the occasion?" I substituted details I'd learned from the detective's interrogation.

## KILLER PARTIES—EVENT PLANNING FORM

Who?
Andi Sax—thirtysomething, party planner—victim
Ikea Takeda—thirtysomething, mayor's fiancée—victim
What?
Andi—poisoned, cardiac arrest, crashed her SUV—murder
Ikea—poisoned, drowned—murder
When?
Andi—killed sometime during the day of the party?
Ikea—killed sometime during the night of the party?
Where?
Andi—on the road to TI—coming to see me?
Ikea—fell into the bay?—heading back to the city?
How?
Andi—via poisoned chocolate—from Rocco's kitchen?
Ikea—also poisoned chocolate?—at the party?
Why?

Good question.

And why was someone trying to make me look guilty of two murders?—because that's sure how it seemed. Someone who had overheard me joking about killing Ikea? Someone who knew my address was in Andi's BlackBerry? Someone who just didn't like me—a former student, aka undiagnosed sociopath?

I needed a new category: WTF?

As I merged into the far left lane of the bridge, slaloming through darting cars, someone honked.

I swerved.

Having ADHD, I was usually good at multitasking, but apparently writing notes under the influence of driving a motor vehicle while listening to Amy Winehouse on my iPhone was beyond me. Even my bright red MINI Cooper didn't seem to help my visibility in the light mist.

I honked back, cursed the driver via my rearview mirror, then switched off the iTunes. Perhaps if I tried to limit my attention to two tasks—driving and deducing what the hell was going on—I'd make it off this bridge.

Alive.

Unlike Andi.

Another question occurred to me and I jotted it down. Why was Andi on her way to Treasure—

Another honk!

I checked my mirror. A white SUV—the same one that had honked at me a few minutes ago?—was riding my tail.

*Go around, you idiot*!

What was his problem? I wasn't about to change lanes with my tricky off-ramp coming up. Someone needed to give him a ticket for stupidity. Where was a cop when you needed one?

That thought reminded me of my interrogation with Detective Melvin, who was no doubt filling out a warrant for my arrest at this very—

Another honk!

What the *hell*?

I strained to see the driver's face in the mirror but the windshield was too high for my short car. I tapped the brakes a couple of times to signal for him to back off, but he clung to my bumper.

"Go around me, you stupid jerk!" I shouted at the mirror. It didn't take a *Diagnostic and Statistical Manual of*

*Mental Disorders* (Fourth Edition) to spot road rage in the lunatic behind me. I slowed down to force him to go around but he stuck to me like frosting on a cake.

I glared at him in my rearview mirror, hoping that in spite of the angle, he might see the signs of "posttraumatic police interrogation disorder" in my face and realize I shouldn't be antagonized.

Switching my focus to the road ahead, I suddenly slammed on my brakes—this time to keep from hitting a Hummer that had cut me off.

I swerved, knocking the plastic sword off the seat. The tip hit one of the balloons and popped it, causing me to jump and nearly hit an orange traffic cone. When I tried to step on the brake again, I found the sword had slid underneath the brake pedal.

Shit! I leaned down and tried to dislodge the sword, while trying to keep an eye on the road and a hand on the wheel. Finally I pulled it loose, dislodging my shoe in the process.

My exit jumped out of the mist. Jerking the wheel, I oversteered as I took the Yerba Buena/Treasure Island off-ramp and skidded with a screech onto the narrow lane.

I stole a glance in my mirror, hoping I wouldn't be hit from behind.

The white SUV was right behind me!

Seconds later it shot past me on the narrow, one-lane road. It disappeared around a sharp curve.

Still skidding, I slammed on the brakes in an attempt to gain control of my car, but the wheels slid into the hairpin turn, tires squealing like angry seals. The MINI Cooper continued its course, slipping onto the shoulder of the precarious road, out of control.

I was headed right toward a sheer cliff that would plummet me straight down and into the bay.

# Chapter 10

*PARTY PLANNING TIP #10:*

***Always carry a bag of balloons to a party. They perk up any event with color and cheer. For added fun, fill one with confetti, then pop it over the guest of honor's head and watch the surprised reaction!***

The MINI choked, spasmed, and died at the edge of the cliff overlooking jagged rocks and swirling water. Adrenaline racing, I jerked the parking brake and rested my head on the steering wheel.

Asshole. Idiot. Lunatic. Shithead!

Not very professional terms for an ab-psych instructor to call an obvious sociopath, but sometimes layman's terms were more satisfying.

Releasing my death grip on the wheel, I took stock. My heart raced under my T-shirt. I wiped the sweat from my forehead with the back of a shaking hand. I was lucky I hadn't peed my pants. They were my only clean pair.

I sat back, took in a lungful of salty air, and peered at the water a hundred feet below the jagged escarpment. Normally the postcard panorama—the whitecapped bay, colorful sailboats, San Francisco skyline, landmark Golden Gate Bridge—calmed me, but at the moment, the view did nothing for my jangled nerves.

I glanced over at Alcatraz Island in the distance. Last night it had been lit up like a birthday cake. Today, standing alone, stark and severe, it looked like dried-up, crumbling leftovers.

A fish out of water.

Sort of how I was beginning to feel.

How had I ended up here . . . with a deadly cliff in front of me, a determined cop at my back, and a deranged driver on my ass?

One thing was clear. That white SUV had nearly run me off the cliff.

Deliberately? Or was the driver just crazy?

As I turned the ignition, my cell phone blasted an electronic version of "Beauty and the Beast"—Delicia's personalized ring. I punched the phone icon.

"Presley? Pres? You there?" Her high-pitched voice sounded frantic.

"Delicia?"

"Where are you?" she hissed, her voice changing to a whisper.

"I'm . . . I'm on my way back to the office. What's up?" I found myself whispering back.

"There's someone . . . here . . . in the building . . . hurry. . . ."

Delicia had a penchant for drama. That's probably why she was such a good actress, albeit mostly unemployed. The trouble was, she tended to create problems when there weren't any. I took her theatrics with a cup of salt.

"I'm on my way, Dee. Did you call Raj?"

The image of the white SUV barreling down the road toward the island flashed through my mind. What if the driver actually *had been* after me? Would he—or she—be waiting at my office on the off chance I survived the trip?

"Delicia?"

Static.

"Delicia? Are you there?"

I thought I heard whispering but it could have been interference.

Checking my rearview mirror for other speeding white vans, I shoved the gearshift into reverse and backed up slowly until I reached the road. Turning the car around, I stepped on the gas and continued down the hill toward the main gate, once manned by the navy. When I reached the bottom of the hill, I redialed Delicia.

The call went to her perky voice mail.

Something was up.

MINI Coopers, although too small to hold all my junk, are built for curves. I put mine to the test by pressing a Mary Jane to the metal. The car hugged the turns like a racer as I sped down the winding road that led to the flatland. In a matter of moments, I'd arrived on the flat, man-made island.

Thanks to Delicia's call, my near-death experience was almost forgotten. I usually enjoy cruising the ghostly remnants of the island's lost eras. In spite of the contaminated waste, a high crime rate, and spirits of the past, TI retains a mystique, popular with tourists, windsurfers, picnickers, brides, and GPS treasure hunters searching for hidden caches—not bodies.

Cursing cell phones, I jammed mine in my bag and tried to focus on reaching the barracks office in record time. I whizzed past the dangling NO ENTRY sign and onetime armed guardhouse turned Snack Shack, the Art Deco administration building and the World's Fair Exposition Hall that now housed various government agencies, and finally the Pan Am Clipper hangar where CeeGee Studio filmed special effects for such movies as *Indiana Jones and the Last Crusade*. I felt a little like Indy, but a tingling at the back of my neck reminded me this wasn't fiction. In spite of her histrionic history, this time Delicia had sounded seriously scared.

I flashed on the recent break-ins we'd been experiencing

on the island. The place had become host to a variety of taggers, vandals, and burglars. Some of the "perps," as Raj called them, were transients currently housed in a section of military barracks at the north end. While the island is regularly patrolled by our two-officer police squad and security guards like Raj, there are still ongoing problems with bored teenagers and the unemployed.

Most of the rental barracks had been broken into, but as far as I knew, Barracks 2, my co-op office building, hadn't been hit yet. The five of us renters were extra cautious about locking up at night, and I'd felt safe there, until recently.

Was someone actually trying to break in—in broad daylight?

And was Delicia alone?

Another chill grabbed the back of my neck.

I jerked the wheel right and sped into the barracks' gravel lot. The bark of the harbor seals basking on the rocks nearby welcomed me—warned me?—as I shut off the engine.

Next to my MINI sat a white SUV.

I glanced at the barracks building. The front door of the blue-trimmed, white clapboard building stood ajar.

We never left the door unlocked, let alone open.

I hopped out of my car, tiptoed up the rickety steps, and peered inside. The reception area stood empty, the lone desk deserted. Delicia was nowhere in sight.

"Delicia?" I called quietly. I wanted to let her know I was here, without alerting the—what? Robber? Killer? Crazy driver?

The hairs on my neck stood on end. Maybe it was going to be a new—and permanent—look for me.

I thought for a moment. If she really was in trouble, I couldn't go in unarmed. I hated when those fictional heroines went down into the dark basement to check out a noise. Without a flashlight. In their skimpy underwear.

I dashed back to my car to get my cell to call Raj, but when I'd thrown the phone down, it had slipped between the seats. It would take too long to retrieve it. Instead I did a quick search for some sort of weapon—a tire iron (didn't have one), my mini-laptop (too expensive), the cigarette lighter (broken). . . .

Glancing at the floor, I grabbed the medieval sword and two inflated balloons, and rushed back to the open barracks door.

Holding my plastic sword in one hand like a crazed pirate and the two balloons in the other like Mary Poppins, I slipped inside the reception room, straining to hear Delicia's high, nasal voice. The only light came from the small windows flanking the building.

The smell hit me like a slap on the face.

I scrunched my nose. What reeked? Decaying fish? Decomposing fungus? Dead feet?

*Something had died in here.*

Or someone?

I fanned the smell away with my sword and tiptoed past the phony receptionist's desk. No one in the co-op could afford a real receptionist, so we took turns manning the spot when we needed to look professional. But the scarred beige walls probably didn't help our image.

I moved through the open reception doors that led to a hallway. Offices lined both sides. Each door featured a glass window, allowing anyone to peek inside. There were windows inside each office as well, offering an instant view of everyone inside, from the waist up. Great if you happened to be nosy or bored, but distracting if you had ADHD. Each room was furnished with a mishmash of garage-sale desks and purloined chairs, and decorated with personalized posters, cartoons, and boredom-busting office toys.

Moving slowly, I tiptoed onto the distressed hardwood floor of the hallway, looking for movement, listening for sound, all the while trying not to inhale the rancid smell that seemed to be coming from the kitchen at the back of the building.

The place looked deserted.

"Delicia?" I whispered.

Cautiously, I started toward the first set of offices—mine on the right and the unoccupied office across from mine on the left. I peered into the windows. Empty.

I moved on to the next set—Delicia's adjacent to mine, and Berkeley's on the opposite side. No sign of her.

And then I spotted her grande soy chai sitting on her desk among the clutter of film scripts, acting manuals, and glam photos of herself. Her computer screensaver, a picture of Edward the Vampire, looked at me lustfully.

I stepped inside and reached for her desk phone to call security, then froze.

A muffled voice.

As in gagged.

Coming from behind the closed door to the kitchen.

# Chapter 11

*PARTY PLANNING TIP #11:*

***When setting the scene for your party, accessorize, accessorize, accessorize! For a Pirates and Wenches party, use plastic swords as creative invitations, costume accessories, dangling decorations, and even for a game of silly sword fighting.***

Delicia.

I started toward the kitchen, then came to my senses. Picking up the phone, I dialed security and punched SPEAKERPHONE. After setting the receiver on the desk, I backed into the hallway, raised my plastic sword as menacingly as I could, and tightened my grip around the nub of a balloon.

"Whoever's in there, you better get out!" I shouted toward the closed kitchen door, hoping Raj would hear me over the speakerphone. "I've got a gun!"

To make my point, I stabbed the balloon with the tip of the toy sword. It gave a loud *pop*!

Another muffled shriek.

I inched forward, my sword raised in my sweaty palm. My heartbeat went into hyperspeed.

The door to the kitchen clicked open. The smell hit me in the face like a rotten cream pie. I reared back, fanning my nose with the sword.

Out stepped a giant marshmallow monster.

Either we were being invaded by an alien, or this was a robber uniquely disguised in a white hazmat jumpsuit.

I threatened the Thing That Came from the Kitchen with my plastic sword while screaming, "The police are on their way!" The Thing raised its hands like a zombie and headed right for me. It held a pair of wicked-looking tongs in one gloved hand. In the grip of the tongs was a large plastic Baggie.

Inside: something pink, gelatinous, and foul.

Body parts?

"Don't come any closer!" I screamed.

Where in the world was Raj? He should have answered my call and been here by now. The island wasn't that big. I swished my sword, but The Thing kept coming. I took a step backward, ready for flight if fight didn't work, but one of my shoes caught on something and I lost my balance.

I fell backward on the hard floor and landed on my ass. My sword skidded across the floor, out of reach. In a clatter, half a dozen glass bottles labeled with little skulls and crossbones rolled in every direction from an overturned box.

The box that had tripped me.

As I scrambled for my weapon, the creature stopped dead in its tracks, grabbed the smoky mask that obscured its face, and pulled it off, revealing a head with wavy brown chin-length hair, chocolate brown eyes, and a soul patch.

I'd seen this robber before.

"You all right?" it—he—said.

"Where's Delicia?" I asked, scooting back like a frightened crab, in spite of the pain in my rear.

"I'm right here, Pres!" came a voice from the kitchen doorway. Dee stepped into the hallway, took in the scene, and scowled. "What happened to you?"

Stunned into silence, all I could do was stare at both of them. The guy in the hazmat suit grinned. I recognized that grin too.

He'd been wearing a similar outfit at the mayor's wedding.

Finally I managed to sputter, "What the hell is going on here?" I stood up, ignoring the offered assist from the hazmat guy, and brushed myself off. For good measure, I kicked the stupid box that had brought about my downfall.

"Careful with that," the hazmat guy said. I glanced at the bottles strewn about, all covered with warning labels. What—were robbers using explosive chemicals these days?

"And just who the hell *are* you? And what are you doing here?"

Delicia stepped over to brush me off and pulled at something in my hair—a dust bunny I'd picked up in my fall. "Presley, this is Brad Matthews." She held out a hand, as if serving him up on a platter.

Brad Matthews. Oh yes. That's how he'd introduced himself at my disastrous party. I peered at him in recognition. I looked at Delicia. Dressed in her latest vintage outfit—a gauzy shin-length dress, thick strappy heels, and pink socks with little bunnies on them—she certainly didn't look like she'd been in recent jeopardy. Must have been the grin on her face that gave her away. "Brad, this is our resident party girl—"

"*Event planner*," I snapped.

"Event planner—Presley Parker. You may have heard—she hosted Mayor Green's wedding last night. It was off the hook!"

"We've met," he said, extending his hand.

I ignored his greeting. "I said, what are you doing here?"

Delicia smiled up at him as if he were a rock star instead of some kind of janitor. "Brad just rented the empty office across from yours. For his business." She tucked a loose curl seductively behind her ear. So transparent.

"Then what was that frantic phone call about?" I said to her. "You scared the shit out of me!"

"Oh, that. I wasn't *frantic*. . . ." She blushed, shook her head, and grinned again at Brad. The tight curls bounced flirtatiously.

"Actually, that was my fault," Brad Matthews said, still holding the disgusting Baggie of what looked like giblets in the pair of tongs. "In this outfit, I'm sure I scared her a little." He flashed her a toothy smile.

"No, no!" Delicia said, giggling. "Well, maybe a little. . . ."

I pointed to the bottles on the floor, then looked at Brad. "What's with all the poison? Are you some kind of Unabomber chemist or just an ordinary serial killer? Because if you are, I'm sure your rent is going to be a lot higher."

Brad Matthews gave his lopsided grin, but before he could respond, Delicia answered for him. "He's a crime scene cleaner! Isn't that cool, Pres?"

"I gathered that," I said, then nodded at the plastic bag he held in his hand. "What *is* that? Did somebody die in here? It stinks to high heaven." I fanned my face.

Delicia giggled again. "Oh, Rocco—I guess he forgot to clean up the crab puffs he made for last night's reception. The kitchen's a disaster. Looks like Emeril meets Lucy Ricardo in there."

Rocco. The chocolates. I darted past Delicia and Brad, into the kitchen, and scanned the counters. The smell kicked up a notch. Delicia was right—it looked like a bomb had gone off in there. Scrunching my nose, I took a quick inventory.

"Where are the leftover chocolates?" I called out.

Delicia stepped into the kitchen and shrugged. "I didn't see any. Rocco must have tossed them."

Rocco was a perfectionist. If any of the chocolate falcons or handcuffs hadn't turned out perfectly, he wouldn't have taken them to the party. But he knew I loved his leftover desserts—especially chocolates.

So where were they now?

I looked back at Brad Matthews, still down the hall, kneeling over his box of cleaning supplies. A siren went off in my head as I recalled my near-death experience on the bridge off-ramp.

Was he the one driving the white SUV that nearly got me killed?

I moved past Delicia and Brad, down the hallway to the reception area, and glanced out the front window to the parking lot.

The white SUV. I'd forgotten all about it.

I stormed back down the hallway and stood over Brad, still hunched over the box of cleaning supplies.

"*You!* You're a lunatic!"

He looked up at me and blinked. "Excuse me?"

"You almost got me *killed*!"

He stood up, brushed his hands on his pants, and shook his head. "No, those chemicals are perfectly safe . . . as long as you don't trip over them—"

"Not that! At the bridge exit. You nearly drove me off the road, tailgating and speeding in that stupid SUV of yours. What was your *problem*?"

Brad ran his fingers through his hair. "Oh, was that you I passed? You were driving kind of funny, like you weren't really paying attention to the road, and I was sort of in a hurry. . . ."

"Yeah, and after you ran me off the road, you didn't even stop to see if I was okay."

He held his hands up. "Look, I'm sorry. I didn't know. I just wanted to get around you. You were all over the road. . . ."

He paused and leaned in. I ridiculously thought for a moment he was going to kiss me. Then I realized—*he was checking my breath*!

I glared at him. "I haven't been *drinking*! It's eleven o'clock in the morning!"

He shrugged. "Well, you were hitting it a little hard last night—"

"That was—God! You're unbelievable! I don't drink . . . in the daytime, anyway. And I don't get drunk . . . usually. Today I was just—"

I stopped. What was I going to say—I had been "writing while operating a motor vehicle"? So maybe I had been driving a little erratically. Doesn't everyone these days?

Before I could argue more, my office phone rang.

Delicia, standing near my office door, stepped in and picked it up.

"Killer Parties!" she said in her Cinderella voice. Covering the speaker, she whispered, "Pres, your phone has been ringing off the hook all morning!" She waved at a small pile of yellow sticky notes on my desk. "The calls have all been about that article that appeared in the *Chronicle*. Did you read it? The reporter went off on how cool the party was—even with the disappearing bride!"

Apparently the writer didn't know about the body in the bay.

She listened for a moment, then asked, "Who shall I say is calling?"

*Take a message*, I mouthed to Delicia. I gave Brad Matthews a last scowl as he carried the refilled box into the empty office across from mine.

"Where's the newspaper?" I asked Delicia as she hung up.

She looked at me, wide-eyed. "OMG."

"What?" I asked, suddenly alarmed by her expression. I hadn't finished the article. Could it have gotten any worse?

"That was the governor!"

"What?"

"On the phone!"

Oh my God. First the police. Now the governor.

What was in the rest of that newspaper article?

# Chapter 12

*PARTY PLANNING TIP #12:*

*Personalize your party setting to the theme.*
*Host an Over-the-Hill milestone at a mortuary, a Redneck bash at a trailer park, or a Murder Mystery at a haunted mansion.*

Although I had my reservations about Brad Matthews, I set them aside when he offered to help clean up and remove all the rotting fish carcasses from last night's wedding prep. "No charge," he'd said, grinning in an attempt to make up for giving us a scare. Meanwhile Delicia and I went to work on the countertops, appliances, and floors, mainly by squirting everything with Lysol and other mysterious chemicals Brad brought in, until the whole office building reeked like a hospital. I had to admit, we did an impressive job. Now that we wouldn't be poisoned by botulism, we'd no doubt be asphyxiated by industrial-strength cleaners.

Poisoned.

I returned to my office and slumped into the seat at my desk, trying to ignore the strong smells coming from the kitchen and the new activity in the office across from mine. Not easy for a person with ADHD. Dropping my purse in the middle of the desk sent yellow sticky memos fluttering around like giant confetti. I leaned over to pick up a handful that had sailed to the floor and caught a glimpse of the new guy across the hall.

Stripping.

I watched as the white jumpsuit fell to the floor like shriveled snakeskin, leaving behind yet another outfit, this time a well-filled-out white T-shirt with the company logo embossed on one pocket and low-rise, well-worn jeans. His shoes: New Balance. Not a blood spatter on them.

He caught me peering and grinned.

I snatched the notes off the floor and spun around, trying to focus on the stack of calls I'd gotten while at the police station. But when Brad left his office to retrieve more boxes from his killer SUV, I stood up in the hall and leaned in to check out his stuff.

Everything was sealed with crime scene tape.

So what did he have in those boxes besides bottles of poison?

Poison. There was that word again.

"Can I help you?" Brad said, startling me from behind.

I jumped. "I . . . was looking for today's newspaper. Delicia!" I called out, trying to cover my snooping. I spun around, took a few steps, and leaned into her office. "I can't . . . um, find the *Chron*. Did you do something with it? I've searched all over. . . ."

"I think I left it in the kitchen," Delicia said, eyeing me oddly. "I'll get it." She popped up from her chair and bounced down the hall. I returned to my desk, ignoring Brad's eyes on me, and riffled through the pile of messages again. Two were from Chloe at the mayor's office, both marked "Urgent!" They probably wanted their money back. Tough.

I took a second look and realized Chloe's messages were dated yesterday. Probably more pre-wedding panic attacks. One was about the reception food. "Did the caterer know that Chilean sea bass was endangered? The mayor didn't feel it was politically correct to serve it. Could it be replaced with Dungeness crab, the 'new lobster'?"

I wadded up that message and its twin—one about a couple of last-minute guest additions—and tossed them into the wastebasket.

The next five were from my mother, also marked "Urgent!" as usual. I set them aside, promising myself I'd see her as soon as I had a moment. I knew she was lonely—and confused—and my visits had a way of grounding her, at least temporarily. Thankfully the return phone number wasn't the San Francisco Police Department.

The rest of the messages were from a variety of businesses, all wanting parties.

Friends of the San Francisco Library: "We'd like to do a Murder Mystery set in the stacks. . . ."

Gay Pride Coalition: "Can you do a kind of Queer Eye Makeover party for the Exotic Erotic Ball? . . ."

Glide Memorial Church: "Looking for an American Idol in Heaven karaoke fund-raiser for a new organ . . ."

The de Young Museum: "When are you free to host a gala for a new wing?"

Overwhelmed by all the prospects, I shuffled through the rest—Morrison Planetarium, Mark Hopkins Hotel, Angel Island State Park, Industrial Light and Magic. A group of Red Hat ladies wanted a Chocolate Decadence theme. The Sally Rand Madams were asking for a Pimps and Hos party. Even my former employer, San Francisco State University, was looking for a Cheerleaders and Jocks alumni party.

Whoa. What was in that article I hadn't finished reading?

I set all the messages down, except for the last one. As usual, Delicia had written it in text messaging code.

"OMG! Gov. wd like to mt w/U to discuss his 60th b'day pty—a MM theme! Pls call ASAP! OMG!"

Oh. My. God. was right. The governor wanted me to host his Big Six-O birthday party? With a murder mystery theme? This was beyond the society page—this was front page headline: MARTHA STEWART DOES THE WHITE HOUSE.

Where was that damn newspaper article?

"Delicia?"

Delicia appeared in the doorway and handed me the paper. "Did you call him?"

"Who?"

"Johnny Depp. Duh! The governor!"

"I will. I want see what this says first." The paper was already folded open to the article.

Delicia pirouetted out and, with a curious glance at Brad's office, headed back to her own office. "BTW," she threw over her shoulder, "if you see Rocco, tell him he owes us for cleaning up his mess. Where the frick is he, anyway?"

Delicia never swore. She used every word but the actual expletive. I figured that was because she'd never really had a reason to. Just wait until she'd been fired from her job, lost her longtime boyfriend, run through five fathers, dealt with a crazy mother, and become a murder suspect.

But that was a good question. Where *was* Rocco?

He'd pestered me relentlessly to cater the mayor's event the moment I'd been hired. As soon as I agreed, he'd been in the kitchen twenty-four/seven. Being the star of his own local access cooking show wasn't enough for this culinary artiste. He was constantly cooking up ways to make the leap into the Food Network fry pan. He saw the mayor's wedding as a way to highlight his gastronomy—and frost his résumé.

Now, with this chocolate fiasco, was he out of the frying pan and into the fire? *Enough with the food metaphors*, I decided.

I held up the newspaper and skimmed the article to the point where I'd left off in a huff.

MAYOR'S SURPRISE WEDDING BACKFIRES—
BRIDE BOLTS!

*By Roberta Alexander*

Last evening, blah-blah-blah, Mayor Davin Green blah-blah-blah, Ikea Takeda . . . threw her glass of bubbly . . . stormed off . . .

When I reached the point where I'd stopped, I read more carefully:

After making the scene—and making a scene—Takeda bolted, leaving her guests, creatively dressed as crime stoppers and criminals, to continue their merry-making without her—which they did, with gusto.

Everyone from Inspector Gadget (actor Jack Jason) to Sherlock Holmes (producer Luke "Spaz" Cruz) to Hercule Poirot (Retired Admiral Eugene Stadelhofer) was there, with a surprise appearance by a garish Lizzie Borden–wannabe (uninvited protester Xtreme Siouxie), all drinking festive "cellblock hooch" and dining on "prison mess hall" food—expertly prepared by local celebrity chef Rocco Ghirenghelli of KBAY-TV's *Bay City Café* fame.

According to several of the guests—and seconded by this reporter—Rocco's Ball & Chain–shaped wedding cake was nothing short of edible art worthy of the SF MOMA, and his Chocolate Maltese Falcons were "to die for."

With or without the guests of honor, the event—planned and presented by Presley Parker from Killer Parties—was a "cellblock riot," delighting guests while garnering over $100,000 for a good cause: the Alzheimer's Association.

Parker replaced premiere party queen Andi Sax at the last minute, when Sax bowed out for "personal reasons," according to Chloe Webster, Mayor Green's administrative assistant. "We were lucky to get Killer Parties on such short notice!" Webster said.

After the breakout success of this clever caper, it would be criminal not to let Killer Parties host all the mayor's future events. While the guest of honor could not be reached for comment, the groom-to-be was overheard saying, "I was hoping for twenty-years-to-life with Ikea."

Now that the runaway bride is on the lam, it looks like our marriage-minded mayor won't have to do the time—this time.

Whoa! Was I at the same party as the purple-penned reporter? Guess she hadn't heard about the deaths—murders. At least, not in time for the morning edition of the *Chronicle.*

And thank God for that.

Now the phone was ringing off the hook and I had more "Please call back!" messages than business cards. I let the next few calls go to my voice mail and listened in while school principals, museum coordinators, and restaurant owners left requests for party info.

I hated to be a party pooper, but I didn't see how it could be helped. Number 1: How was I going to manage all these potential events? And Number 2: How was I going to manage them from jail?

Still . . . the governor? I thought of the amount of money he could raise for a good cause. And hosting a murder mystery for him would be a piece of cake. I already had a plot in mind:

*Detective Luke Melvin lay dead in the foyer of the Governor's Mansion, impaled by an ornate medieval sword dipped in the rare poisonous oil of the Amazon puffer fish, garroted by a string of Chinese lantern party lights (provided by Killer Parties), and bludgeoned by a priceless Golden Falcon encrusted with rare jewels—*

The phone rang, jangling my nerves and bringing me out of my murderous daydream. What was the matter with me? That's all I needed—one more murder on my hands, even if it was the detective's.

Letting the call go to voice mail, I glanced at the newspaper article. Jeez, until today I'd have used any excuse to host a party—just to bring in a little money. I'd even taken to reading the want ads for some part-time temp work to keep me going until the party business kicked in. I glanced over at the section where I'd circled half a dozen dead-end jobs: process server, personal shopper, coffee barista, convalescent hospital assistant, meter maid, dog walker. . . .

I wadded up the section and tossed it into my wastebasket. The trash was filling up nicely. If the phone kept ringing like it was, I might even get my own *Killer Parties* show on HGTV.

After I was paroled, of course. Like Martha.

Before I could start planning my Going Away for Good party, a blast of salt air swept in through the front door and into my open office, whipping my daydreams out to sea.

I looked up to see a gun pointing in my direction.

# Chapter 13

*PARTY PLANNING TIP #13:*

***Choose your event caterer carefully. Nothing ruins a party faster than a bunch of toilet-hugging guests who've been poisoned by bad sushi.***

"Watch out with that thing!" I screamed. "You might put an eye out!"

Raj Reddy, the island's foremost security guard, looked more dazed and confused than armed and dangerous. Of course, just arming Raj was probably dangerous in itself.

"I got your 911! What is going on?" Raj said, glancing around, his eyes wild with anticipation.

"Nothing—*now*. You're a little late. And put that gun away before you shoot someone."

Raj holstered his gun awkwardly, finally jamming it home. He'd only recently completed the weapons requirement for his security guard job, and it showed.

"Actually, they were shooting over at CeeGee Studio."

"Shooting?" I raised an eyebrow.

"A live-action scene. Actually, they were needing an extra for playing a police officer and they chose me." He puffed up visibly.

I glanced at his badge. His TI ID had been replaced by a realistic-looking SFPD logo.

"Well, it's impressive, but you'd better take that off. You could get arrested for impersonating an officer." I grinned.

Raj nodded. "Ha. You are pulling my legs again." He plucked off the badge and replaced it with his real badge, tucking the bogus one into his pocket.

"So why were you calling me? Was there another break-in?" He sniffed the air. "It's smelling funny in here."

"False alarm." I jerked my thumb at Brad Matthews, who had closed his office door while he worked on his box collection. "Delicia thought the new guy was an intruder. Turns out he's our new renter."

Raj looked through the door's window at Brad. "Actually, there was another breakin-in last night. When I was doing my rounds early this morning, the back door to our own barracks was open. I was looking around to see—"

"What?" I bolted up from my chair.

Startled, Raj pulled his head back. "Yes, that is what I am telling you now. Someone was breaking into the kitchen—"

I ran down the hall, where I found Delicia reheating her gourmet tea in the microwave.

"What's up?" she asked, looking up.

I glanced around the kitchen and shook my head. Not only had we apparently had a break-in, but if there had been any evidence, it was now completely wiped away—by crime scene cleaning products. I ran a finger along a countertop.

"Great. Just great."

Delicia frowned. "Hey. If you don't like the way I clean, next time you can do it all yourself!"

"That's not it." I turned to Raj, who had come up behind me. "Raj said we had a break-in last night, probably sometime during the wedding. He found the back door open early this morning."

Raj nodded.

"Oh my God!" Delicia glanced around the kitchen. "Did they take anything?"

I did a spot check for the espresso maker, Cuisinart, and the rest of the appliances that weren't nailed down. Nothing was missing as far as I could tell.

Not that it mattered to me. I never cooked, aside from brewing lattes when I couldn't get to Starbucks or microwaving Rocco's leftovers. The Cuisinart container occasionally came in handy to drink from when there weren't any clean cups.

"Where do you keep your cleaning products?" came a voice from behind me.

Brad Matthews had silently stepped up behind us. He slid in between us and pulled open two cupboard doors.

"Uh . . ." I shrugged. "No clue."

"Up there." Raj pointed to a cupboard over the refrigerator.

Brad found a stool and stood on it to open the cupboard door. Inside was a collection of bottles I'd never seen before. Mainly because I'd had no reason to. We had a janitorial service to clean the building, and aside from some Lysol, we'd used Brad's cleaning stuff to get rid of Rocco's stinky leftovers.

"What's all that?" I said stupidly.

Brad shuffled through the bottles in the cupboard, one by one. "Drain cleaner, glass cleaner, sink cleaner. Bug spray, roach motels, ant traps." He looked at me. "Essentially a bunch of toxic chemicals."

"Poisons?"

He nodded, then glanced back at the cupboard. "Where's the rodenticide?"

"Rodenticide?"

"Rat poison."

"Rat poison?" I was beginning to develop echolalia. "Why would we have rat poison? We don't have . . ." Oh God. Of course we did. We had a kitchen. A kitchen meant rats—especially in an old barracks like this.

I looked at Delicia and Raj. Both shrugged.

"Maybe Rocco would know," Delicia offered.

Rocco. Where the hell was he?

Brad closed the cupboard and stepped down from his perch. "Next time you have a break-in, don't touch anything." With that, he left the room, leaving us standing there feeling like naughty children caught with our hands in the poisoned cookie jar.

How had he known about the break-in?

Back at my desk, I quietly steamed. *Don't touch anything?* Who did he think he was? Detective Melvin in a white jumpsuit?

"Enough!" I said aloud and stood up. I needed to clear my head. Too many thoughts were rattling around inside my brain—Detective Melvin, the deaths, the phone calls, Rocco, the new guy, the break-in, the questionably missing rat poison.

A skate around the island was the best way to jostle those loose ends into some sort of cohesive order. When I skated, I did my best thinking. I twisted my hair up and clamped it with a giant clip, put on my Rollerblades, knee and elbow pads, and headed for the running path that circumnavigated the island.

Rarely used except on weekends by a handful of locals, the path was originally created by the navy to keep their enlisted men in shape for war. The scenic trail was another of the best-kept secrets in the San Francisco Bay Area. But all the talk of redevelopment—Indian casinos, exclusive high-rises, film studios, military monuments—loomed over the island like an insidious fog bank.

As the October breeze whipped my hair and goose-pimpled my skin, I found myself drawn to the rocky spot where Ikea's body had been discovered floating. How had she ended up there? The currents? Maybe one of the windsurfers would know.

Or was it something—or someone—else?

More importantly, how had she ended up dead?

Once again I spotted Duncan Grant just outside the crime scene tape. What was he doing here? When he looked up, I waved and headed over to the rocky edge.

"Hey, Dunk. Find any more bodies?"

He glared at me. "Very funny. I'm just checking one of the caches." He knelt down and withdrew a box hidden between some jagged rocks. Standing again, he opened it and began picking through the whimsical objects left by geocachers—a Mickey Mouse figurine, a dot-com pen, a snow globe, a decoder ring, a magnifying glass, and an earring shaped like a tiny book.

"Wait!" I said as he started to close the cache. I lifted the earring from the box and turned it over in my hand. There was an inscription in miniature print, almost too small to read. "Hand me that," I said, indicating the Cracker Jack–sized magnifying glass. He picked it up and passed it to me; I held it over the engraving and read the fine print: TO I.T. LOVE D.G.

Oh my God. The earring belonged to Ikea. I remembered she'd been wearing it at the party.

So how did it end up inside this cache box?

# Chapter 14

*PARTY PLANNING TIP #14:*

*When arranging your seating chart, be careful not to place a warhawk next to a peacenik, or you may find your party becoming a combat zone.*

I pocketed the earring.

"What are you doing?" Duncan asked. He looked at me as if I'd just robbed a grave.

Perhaps I had.

I didn't want him to think I was stealing evidence from a crime scene, but before I could come up with a good lie, he added, "TSLS."

"What?"

He pointed to the cache. " 'Take something, leave something.' It's the rule. If you take something from a cache, you have to leave something in its place."

"Oh . . . uh . . . sure." Whew. I searched my pockets for something I could leave in exchange for the earring and pulled out a Killer Parties business card. Talk about an advertising opportunity. You never knew who might find it and suddenly want a party. I set the card in the box.

"That's pretty lame," Duncan said, closing the cache box. He set it back in its hiding place between a couple of large jagged rocks.

"Not any lamer than half the things in there," I said.

But Duncan was no longer paying attention to me. Something in the distance held his gaze. I turned to see a familiar man in a white jumpsuit. He was taking down the crime scene tape left behind by the police techs.

Brad Matthews again.

"Hey, what are you doing?" I called to him, then headed over.

"Doing my job," he said, rolling up the tape. "I'm a crime scene cleaner, remember? Question is, what are you doing here?"

*None of your business*, I thought. "Just getting some exercise." I pointed to my skates. "And talking with Duncan."

Brad raised an eyebrow and smiled. "Find anything?"

My hand went to the pocket that held the earring. "Nope. Uh-uh. Nothing. You?"

He eyed me. "Like I said, I'm just here to clean up. SFPD sent me." He nodded toward Duncan. "Who's that?"

"He's the guy who found the body. Duncan Grant. He organizes GPS games."

"Geocaching, huh?" Brad watched Duncan for a few seconds, then returned to whatever it was he was doing. Looked like he was just puttering around. He got paid for that?

"Not much to clean up, is there?" I asked.

"Nah. A few loose ends."

Curious, I asked, "Do you ever find anything the cops missed when you're cleaning up a crime scene?"

He shrugged. "Sometimes, but usually the scene is pretty well picked clean. Cops aren't as stupid in real life as they are on TV."

I thought of the earring in my pocket. The sound of a car engine pulled my attention away. I turned to check out the rubbernecker.

Uh-oh.

Detective Melvin. He had just arrived in a white, unmarked, but obviously police-issue car.

"I gotta go," I said abruptly, and skated down the path before the detective could slap the cuffs on me. When I was just about out of sight, I glanced back to see him engaged in a serious-looking conversation with Brad Matthews.

They were both staring at me.

What was the detective saying to Brad?

And what was Brad telling the detective?

By the time I reached the office, I had a plan. Since it was business hours, the office door was unlocked, but at least it wasn't standing open. I let myself in and skated down the hall, looking through the glass partitions of the other offices for signs of life. I spotted Delicia talking on the phone, Raj hunched over his desk, and Berk staring at his monitor, probably editing the party video.

The only ones missing were Brad Matthews and Rocco.

While the others were occupied, I tried the doorknob to the newly rented office across the hall from mine. Locked. Shit.

Raj. He had a master key.

How unprofessional, even illegal, would it be if I got him to open Brad's door?

How badly did I want to know more about the crime scene cleaner and his sudden appearance on the island?

If Brad caught me, I could always claim he must have left the door unlocked. People forget to lock their doors all the time. But what would I tell Raj to get him to open it?

My office phone rang, giving me an idea. Letting the call go to the answering machine, I skated down to Raj's office, the last one before the kitchen. To my surprise, he wasn't reading a weapons catalog or studying for a cop exam or doing anything that might keep us safe on the island.

He was eating a bagel and reading what looked like a movie script.

"Raj! Hi. Hey, I wondered if you could do me a favor and open the door to the new guy's office? I think I left my cell phone in there."

He looked at me as if I'd just said, "Stick 'em up!"

"Oh no, Ms. Presley. Actually, I cannot."

"But my cell phone—I need it, Raj. I've got some business calls to make and my office phone is . . . broken." Not only was I lying, now I was whining.

"It is going against my ethics, actually. I'm sure Mr. Brad will be back soon. Until then, you can be using my telephone."

Shit. Shit.

"Never mind," I said, and pulled the door closed a little too hard.

I skated back to my office to figure out a new plan. Dropping into my chair, I leaned over to untie my skates and noticed my top drawer was open an inch. It must have caught on my stapler when I'd tried to close it earlier. Stupid stapler.

But I hadn't used my stapler this morning. Or anything else in that drawer today.

Slowly I pulled out the drawer until everything was fully displayed. Instead of being tucked into the back right-hand corner where it belonged, my stapler lay on its side at the front—blocking the drawer from closing.

Not where I kept it. So how did it get there?

I scanned the contents of my drawer. Nothing appeared to be missing.

But on second glance, I noticed my chocolates were not in their usual groups. I always sorted my See's Candies—dark chocolate raspberries, dark chocolate butters, dark chocolate caramels, and dark chocolate–covered nuts.

One of the dark chocolate–covered nuts was in with the dark chocolate caramels.

So I have a little OCD along with ADHD. Right now I was happy to have the additional disorder, since I now knew someone had been snooping in my drawer.

Brad Matthews?

I popped a chocolate in my mouth as I flashed on those strong hands of his in my drawer—then I froze.

*Chocolates.*

I spit the bite-sized candy onto a sheet of paper and wiped the chocolate drool from my mouth with the back of my hand.

What if someone had tampered with my private stash of chocolates too?

I pulled out another chocolate and looked around for something to save it in until I could get it to Detective Melvin. I found a small box among a stack of party gift boxes on a shelf and set the chocolate inside. Returning the stapler to its proper position and place, I slid the drawer closed, then bent over and pulled off my skates, replacing them with pink flip-flops I kept in another drawer. Releasing the clippie that held up my hair, I stuffed it in my pocket—and felt the earring.

I pulled it out.

Ikea's earring.

Where had it come from? And how had it ended up in the cache treasure box?

I set the earring on my desk and got out the sheet of paper with the notes I'd started in the car, hoping I could decode my scribbles. After reviewing them, I drew a line under the who-what-when-where-how-why party questions. Beneath that I wrote a heading, then began making notes on Andi and Ikea's deaths. Murders.

***Possible Suspects:***

People who knew both Andi and Ikea?

For a start—the mayor. Besides me, that is.

Or people who had a grudge against the mayor?

Like Andi Sax—for firing her from hosting the event?

Or could Ikea Takeda have angered the mayor enough to make him kill her? They say it's often a loved one who commits a murder. Maybe that wedding was just a setup for his plan. Maybe he knew Ikea would bolt—giving him the opportunity to get rid of her, under the cover of darkness and fog. And maybe the mayor was completely innocent and I thought I was Nancy Drew.

I crossed his name off and wrote down "Motive?" Underneath that I wrote:

Adultery (Ikea?)—Was the mayor cheating on her? Or was she cheating on him?

Jealousy (Ikea?)—Was Ikea jealous of the mayor's power and status?

Humiliation (Andi?)—Was she devastated by losing the mayor's prime event?

Revenge (Andi?)—And did she do something about it, to get even?

Or was it larceny? (Follow the money.)

I realized I'd just listed five of the seven deadly sins—adultery (lust), jealousy (envy), humiliation (pride), revenge (wrath), and larceny (greed.) The only two missing were gluttony and sloth. Could I make overeating or laziness possible motives too? If so, I could be guilty of both at times.

I didn't have much to work with, but if the detective planned to follow his course in suspecting me, I had better come up with something more viable than what I had.

I couldn't interrogate the two major players—they were

both dead. I needed to talk to the mayor, but that wasn't going to be easy, between all the security he had and his busy schedule. Maybe I could have a little chat with the people who knew him—and weren't dead yet.

Obviously his administrative assistant would know a lot about her boss. But would she share that information with me? Probably not, if she was the loyal secretary type. Still, I would give her a try.

Who else might know something about the mayor and his connection to both women? Without being familiar with his social circle, I didn't have a large selection. Best to start with the scene of the crime—Alcatraz—and those attending the party. Surely someone there would know a few secrets about our popular mayor.

I pulled out the guest list and underlined the names I recognized. I put stars next to a few of them who stood out:

- *Admiral Eugene Stadelhofer. He seemed to know the mayor well, and was one of those involved in that little altercation at the party. Something about wanting a military memorial on Treasure Island.
- *Lucas "Spaz" Cruz. He talked about his interest in turning the island into some kind of Hollywood movie-making Mecca of the North.
- *Dakota Hunter. Wasn't he the one lobbying to build an Indian casino on TI?

Those three stood out among the rest of the costumed criminals and crime solvers as having some kind of stake in the mayor's pending decision. They might just have something interesting to say about him.

Looking over my notes, I realized one name was missing—that tree-hugging young woman who called herself Xtreme Siouxie. She'd made quite a scene at the wedding, accusing the mayor of "murdering" Treasure Island. I had a feeling she'd have plenty to say about the mayor. But how much of it would be true?

There was another name not on the guest list: Brad Matthews.

He'd attended the wedding uninvited. What was he doing there? He'd nearly run me off the road the day after the party. And he'd suddenly arrived at the barracks to rent office space for his "crime scene cleaning" business.

I reviewed my notes. At least I had a list of people I could ask about the mayor and see if they knew of any secrets he might have had. True, my name looked the most promising, at least according to Detective Melvin. The way he saw it, not only did I benefit from Andi's death—taking over the wedding plans—but I also benefited from Ikea's disappearance and death, with all the lurid publicity.

I was sure of only one thing—the mayor was somehow connected to all this. But before I could jot down any more notes, I felt a breeze through my open office door. The salt air wafted in, along with Brad Matthews. Moving to his office, he turned and nodded at me, then unlocked his office door and slipped inside.

It was time to pay a Welcome Wagon visit and get this party started. I pulled open my top drawer again, selected three dark chocolates, and arranged them in a tiny gift box I pulled from the shelf.

Would he eat them? Not if he'd poisoned them.

I headed across the hall.

Just as I was about to knock, Brad saw me and waved me in. He was out of his white jumpsuit and back in his T-shirt and jeans. I opened the door, leaned in, and smiled, ready to kill him with kindness.

"Hi." I thrust out the small box of chocolates. "I wanted to apologize for this morning. I was . . . rude. Uh, welcome to Barracks B."

Brad smiled, stood up, and reached over to accept Pandora's box. As he did, his shirt rose, revealing a glimpse of his tan, tight waist.

That wasn't all. There was a definite bulge in his pants. As flattering as it would have been, Brad Matthews wasn't necessarily happy to see me.

That was a gun in his pocket.

# Chapter 15

*PARTY PLANNING TIP #15:*

***Always keep a video camera handy to catch those spontaneously funny, embarrassing, and blackmail-worthy moments to show on YouTube.***

"My God!" I said, staring at the gun.

"What?" Brad frowned.

I quickly recovered. "Oh, uh . . . my phone! It's been ringing off the hook. I'll, uh, see you later, okay?" I backed out and pulled the door closed behind me before he could ask any more questions.

I slipped into my office and picked up the phone receiver, pretending to answer it. I caught Brad eyeing me suspiciously and turned away, listening to the dial tone buzz in my ear. I nodded, shook my head, laughed, pretended to jot down a note, and hung up. When I looked over, he was still watching me. I waved. He nodded, frowning.

Great. The crime scene cleaner was packing heat, as Sam Spade would say. Why would someone who's essentially a janitor have a gun?

There were just too many coincidences connected to Brad Matthews. I had to get into that office the next time he stepped out. And I had to make sure I could get in without a key.

I headed for Delicia's office and waited for her to hang up her phone. It sounded like she was talking to her agent about a part in a TV pilot being shot in San Francisco. I heard her mention something about playing the sidekick to a deaf private investigator who solves crimes by using his heightened other senses. I wished I had that kind of superpower.

"What's up?" she said, replacing the receiver.

"Got any gum?" I asked.

"I thought you didn't chew gum. Said it was like drinking decaf coffee—pointless." She opened her purse and offered me a stick of Big Red.

"Thanks." I took it and left without explaining my intentions.

Back in my office, I opened the wrapper, rolled the gum into a spiral, and popped it in my mouth. After exactly ten chews, I spit the wad into my left hand and headed back to Brad's office.

"Hi," I said, sticking my head inside. "I . . . uh . . . saw you talking to that detective earlier. Looked like a pretty serious conversation. Anything new on Ikea's murder?"

He shrugged. "Not that I know of. We mostly talked about the weather. Doesn't this fog ever get you down? It's depressing."

"You're not from around here?" I said, eyes searching the room for something out of place, something telltale.

He shook his head. "LA."

"I'd rather have fog than smog. Well, I better get back to work." I started to pull the door closed, my gum hand resting inside the lock.

He held up a hand. "Wait a sec."

I froze. "Yeah?" I tried to sound innocent. Wasn't easy.

"Thanks." He gave a half grin.

I frowned. "For what?"

"The chocolates. That was sweet of you." His grin broadened. He licked his lips.

I felt the color rise in my face and smiled. I wasn't ready

for the compliment. Was he flirting? I hadn't meant the gesture to be a come-on. And if he actually ate those chocolates, then apparently he hadn't poisoned them after all.

Feeling guilty for the ruse—and what I was about to do—I was caught off guard and stammered, "Uh . . . good, glad you liked them." Sticking the gum into the lock slot as magicianlike as possible, I pulled the door closed.

Then I had a thought. What if someone else poisoned the chocolates? Brad could be dying right now. I swung the door open—it slammed against the wall. "Uh . . . did you eat . . . all of them?"

He looked down and shook his head. "Uh, no . . . I'm not much of a chocolate lover. But I appreciate the thought." He met my eyes, and I felt a jolt of electricity. Where had that come from?

Coming to my senses, I realized I had to get those chocolates out of there before someone ate one—just in case. But it would have to wait until Brad left the office or he'd be suspicious, even more than he was now. Returning to my office, I spent the next hour trying to catching up on work—returning phone calls, scheduling dates for events, and playing phone tag with the governor's office. Most of the time I was just distracted, waiting for Brad to leave. When I finally ran out of party related tasks, I called my mother.

"Yes?" came the familiar voice, instead of "Hello." I'd signed her up for caller ID, so she must have known I was calling.

"Hi, Mom. It's me."

"Yes, I know, dear. How are you?"

"Good. I just called to check on you. See how things are going. You all right?"

"Oh yes. I'm planning a fund-raiser for this care center. Seems they don't have enough money for one of those Wii gadgets"—she pronounced it "why"—"so I'm organizing a Halloween party and charging everyone a fee. Guess what my costume's going to be."

Oh boy. “I have no idea, Mom. What?”

“Priscilla Presley! In her big-hair heyday. Won’t that be a hoot!”

I should have known. She was obsessed with Elvis. Hence my name, a constant source of teasing in my youth.

“Sounds fun, Mom. Hey, listen. Did you happen to talk to anyone at the mayor’s office about me or my party business?”

“Which mayor? Joe? Or George?”

While her memory for current events wasn’t so great, she had no trouble recalling names, dates, places, and lurid details from the past. Joe was Mayor Joe Alioto from the early seventies, and George was Mayor George Moscone, late seventies.

“Davin Green, our current mayor.”

“You mean the one who’s gay?”

“No, Mom, he’s not gay. He supports gay rights. . . . Never mind. I was just wondering.”

“Okay, honey. Now don’t forget the Halloween party. I think you should come as Lisa Marie. Don’t you think we’d be cute together?”

“Adorable. I’ll stop by later to see you, Mom.”

“Don’t forget to bring your sweetheart. I want to meet him.”

I shook my head as I said good-bye and hung up the phone. I really needed to work on getting one of those sweethearts. Ever since I’d caught my administration of justice professor “boyfriend” with his hot young assistant at their “crime scene,” I hadn’t been interested in starting up again.

I glanced over at Brad’s office. He was stepping into his crime scene jumpsuit. I pretended to ignore him as he left his office, closing the door behind him, then hid behind a party catalog as I watched him exit the front door of the building. As soon as the coast was clear, I ducked into the reception area and peeked through the front window of the barracks to make sure he left. After he drove off in his white SUV, I tiptoed back to his office. Glancing around to make sure the coast was clear, I tried the doorknob.

Locked.

I pushed on the door.

It didn't budge.

I leaned against it, hard, with a shoulder and hip.

Nothing aside from a sore shoulder and hip.

I jiggled the circa-1940s doorknob.

The lock released. The door opened.

The gum trick had worked—finally. I wondered if Brigid O'Shaughnessy had ever used that one, or if it was strictly Nancy Drew.

I slipped inside, hoping my office mates were too busy with their own mischief to notice mine. If any of them caught me, I could always use the old "door was unlocked, left my cell phone inside" ruse.

First I checked the boxes Brad had brought in. They'd been emptied of their contents and stacked neatly in a corner. The shelves were now filled with what looked like a variety of chemicals—all toxic, I assumed.

Next I invaded his desk drawers. Sparse—nothing but basic office supplies and some official-looking forms with the Crime Scene Cleaners logo at the top. So far, it appeared to be a one-man shop.

Finally, I riffled through the papers on his desk. Rental agreement. Take-out menu from the Pirate Cove Diner. Map of Treasure Island. Sticky pad with a phone number.

I read the number. Local. And familiar. On a hunch, I pulled out my cell and checked "Recently dialed numbers."

A match.

Why was Mayor Green's number written on Brad Matthews' notepad?

The phone rang in my office. I dashed out, closed the door behind me, and picked up the phone.

"Killer Parties," I said absently, still distracted by the phone number I'd found on Brad's desk.

"Yes, this is Governor Brien's office calling. Is this Presley Parker?"

My heart went into overdrive.

"Yes, this is Presley." I sat down.

"This is Arden Wong. The governor asked me to call regarding the possibility of your hosting a party at the San Francisco Library. I understand you produce murder mystery dinner parties? If so, he'd like to employ you to host one as a fund-raiser."

So it wasn't a prank—the governor had really called. I took a deep breath to keep myself under control, something I'd learned to cope with ADHD, and mentally chanted my mantra: *Attend. Discern. Heed. Deliberate.*

"Uh, sure, I do murders all the time. I mean, murder mysteries. What kind of fund-raiser? And when do you want the event?" In spite of my efforts, my speech had gone into hyperdrive.

Delicia came out of her office, eyebrows raised, and peeked in through my door. She could tell I was excited. No doubt she'd been waiting for me to return this call. I gave her a thumbs-up, and she fake-clapped her hands.

"The governor would like the mystery to take place at the San Francisco Main Library, as a benefit for the Friends of the Library. And he'd like to play one of the parts, if that's possible."

"Uh, sure," I said stupidly.

"Good. How about we discuss the details next week?" she said.

"Great." *As long as I'm not in jail*, I nearly added.

Delicia grew giddier by the second. Her antics started to distract me, not to mention her knockoff perfume. I managed to arrange a time and place to meet Arden Wong before I hung up and joined in a modified version of Delicia's happy dance.

"How cool! Tell me all about it!" she said, pulling out the folding chair and plopping herself into it. "Can I help? We made a great team for the mayor's wedding, didn't we? I can play one of the parts. Maybe the victim!"

Remembering the victim at my last party, I was jerked back to earth.

Delicia caught the change in my demeanor and patted my arm. "Listen, that thing about Ikea? That was just a tiny little glitch. A fluke."

"A *glitch*?" I raised an eyebrow. "She was murdered, Dee."

"I know, Pres. But lightning never strikes twice—usually. This is the governor, for goodness sake! I'll help with the décor. Berk can film it for local access TV—that'll put you on the map for sure. And Rocco can make, like, chocolate weapons—a candlestick, a wrench, a gun!"

Before I could say *Been there, done that*, Berk popped his head in, his ubiquitous video camera at his side.

"A Cinderella story, out of nowhere," Berkeley said, adding his own touch of drama. "Former psychology teacher–turned–master party planner gets the gig of a lifetime. . . ."

"More like *Caddyshack*, you mean, with a few editorial changes," I said.

"Hey, it's 'the stuff that dreams are made of,' " Berk said, using a bad Bogart accent. Instead of a trench coat, however, he wore a tight green T-shirt that read "FX Crew—Shrek IV" and Lucky jeans. "And I'll be your videographer! Maybe then Spaz will finally take me seriously."

"What is going on in here?" It was Raj, trying to crowd into my increasingly crowded office. "I'm trying to work back there and am hearing all this commotion."

"Presley's going to do a murder mystery party for the governor!" Delicia said. "And we're all going to help!"

I glared at her. Too late. Raj straightened his shoulders. "Actually, I have been studying the actors over at CeeGee and I think I would make a very good suspect in your murdering play."

I checked my watch, hoping the others would get the hint. In case they didn't, I said, "Well, if you'll excuse me, guys, I'd better get back to work." They reluctantly shuffled back to their offices, leaving me to the ever-growing pile on my desk. But instead of returning any calls, I pulled out a fresh who-what-when-where-how-why sheet and began to fill in the blanks with what I already knew about the governor's event. I was halfway through when an apparition appeared at the door.

Brad Matthews, in his hazmat suit and mask, held tweezers at arm's length, as if the small object being tweezed was highly toxic material.

Where had he come from?

I blinked. "What—?" I stopped.

Between the prongs of the tweezers was a wad of pink gum.

# Chapter 16

*PARTY PLANNING TIP #16:*

*A sign of a successful party is the amount of mess you have to clean up afterward.*
*Unless it's blood.*

"You scared the hell out of me!" I said, slapping my chest. "What are you doing, sneaking up like that?"

"I wasn't sneaking. You looked pretty lost in thought." Brad Matthews pulled off his mask, then raised the tweezers with the small wad higher. "This belong to you?"

I shook my head automatically, but felt my face flush as I said, "No." I'd never survive a lie detector.

"You know what it is?"

I leaned in to peer at it. "Looks like gum," I said.

He leaned in too. "And you smell like cinnamon."

I pulled back. "I . . . It's Delicia's. . . ." *Lineup, here I come.*

He raised an eyebrow.

"What I mean is, Delicia gave me a stick of her gum . . . but I don't know how it ended up in your . . ." My voice trailed off.

Shit! When would I learn to think before I lied? "I mean, wherever it ended up." I turned back to my work, hoping he'd disappear.

He didn't. Instead he stepped into my office and closed the door.

Uh-oh.

"What are you doing?" I scanned the other offices looking for backup. No sign of immediate aid.

"We need to talk." Brad sat in the unfolded chair opposite my desk and placed his face mask on his knee. The last time a guy said, "We need to talk," he was breaking up with me. Too early for that.

Shaking the tweezers, he dropped the gum on my desk. "I could always have the police run the DNA on that."

"Who do you think you *are*?" I demanded, turning from evasive to defensive.

"I told you, Brad Matthews." He crossed his arms over his chest. Even through his uniform I could make out arms of steel. The room seemed dwarfed by his presence.

I thought of the gun in his pocket.

I felt for my purse under my desk. If I could reach my cell, I could call Raj surreptitiously, without arousing Brad's suspicion—in case things got nasty. "No, I mean who *are* you? You're not just a crime scene cleaner, are you? What were you doing at the mayor's wedding? Why do you have the mayor's phone number? And how come, all of a sudden, you start renting space in my office building?"

Moving my hand slowly so he wouldn't notice, I eased out my cell.

He leaned back in the chair and stretched his long legs out in front of him. "I'm a crime scene cleaner. I told you." His eyes narrowed and his signature half smile appeared. "Why are you so suspicious?"

I got the feeling he was toying with me. Or was he flirting? It had been so long, I'd forgotten the signs. Glancing down, I keyed the phone icon, then thumbed down to Raj's number and pressed it. "Look, Brad, I saw you talking to Detective Melvin. I want to know what you two were discussing."

Brad shrugged. "He thinks you might know something about Ikea Takeda's death."

I punched SPEAKERPHONE. "But I *don't*! I told him that. I don't know anything I haven't already—"

Brad raised his hand to calm me. "First of all, hang up the phone."

I blinked, paused a minute, then lifted my iPhone from its hiding place and tapped END. I set the phone on my desk hoping Raj might call me back.

"Secondly, I'm pretty sure you didn't kill Ikea that night."

My mouth dropped open. "You believe me?" I closed it and sat back. "Why?"

"You were way too drunk to kill anybody. Except maybe yourself."

I bit the inside of my lip. He was right. I could barely function by the time that party was over. Of course, maybe I'd had a blackout, killed Ikea, and just didn't remember. That happened on the Lifetime channel a lot.

"Okay, so you know who *I* am—not a killer. Now what about you?"

He relaxed into the chair and sighed, as if he got that question a lot. "I clean up after dead people. Suicides, accidents, murders. And contaminations—distressed properties, biohazards, meth labs. Situations that most people don't want to deal with. The stuff no one else wants to do, that makes them wanna hurl."

I wanted to hurl just hearing about it. But like gawkers at the scene of an accident, even though I thought it was revolting, at the same it was riveting. "You help the police a lot?"

He nodded. "The cops, public service agencies, private sector. Twenty-four/seven, three hundred and sixty-five days a year."

"So you basically clean up blood and stuff?"

"Pretty much," he said, reaching over to a nearby shelf

and pulling out another of my Nancy Drew–style cloche hats. He played with the felt, punching it in, smoothing it out, while he talked. "Blood is the toughest, once it dries. Sort of like Jell-O at first, then it turns hard, like icing."

I made a face. Now I wouldn't be able to eat a frosted cake without thinking of dried blood.

He replaced the hat, trading it for an oversized magnifying glass. He held it up to his face, enlarging his brown eyes, and looked at me as if I were a bug under a microscope. An interesting bug.

"Brains are worse. They dry like cement, solidify like superglue. I have to use putty knives and steel brushes, then steam them with injection machines that melt them, then suck them up into a chemical treatment tank."

I nearly gagged. He was twisting the putty knife—on purpose? I imagined he found it entertaining to gross me out. I snatched the magnifying glass from his hands and set it on my desk like a teacher confiscating a toy from a mischievous student. I tried to distract him from the gruesome topic with another question.

"Is it dangerous—cleaning up crime scenes?"

"The meth labs are. And the hantavirus-infested homes. That's when I have to use really strong solvents. And wear a full-face filter respirator—a mask—and my white jumpsuit. It's nonporous and disposable."

"So they're the worst?" I asked, half curious and half wishing I weren't so curious.

"No, decomps are. Places where there's body decomposition." He glanced around my office as if looking for a body. A decomposing one. "And kitty houses."

"Kitty houses?" I thought of my three cats. Did I have a "kitty house"?

"Slang for places filled with decaying animals, feces, garbage, stuff like that."

I grimaced. "Gross. How did you get into this type of

work? I mean, it's not your everyday kind of business." Oh my God. Was I starting to flirt again?

Reaching for a small box from another shelf, Brad said, "You're right—the death business isn't for everyone. Most guys burn out after a few months." He opened the box and laughed. Must have been the fake teeth inside.

Speaking of which, he had lots of nice white teeth. And a nice laugh. With tiny laugh lines around the mouth and eyes.

Good heavens, what was wrong with me?

"Truthfully," he continued, returning the box to the shelf, "I got interested in this when I saw *Pulp Fiction*. Remember the guy they wasted in the car? They called in the Wolf—Harvey Keitel—to clean up the mess. That's when I decided to become a crime scene cleaner. Thought it would be cool."

I laughed. "I guess that's one way to choose a career. You got lucky though. You seem to love your job. Which, in this case, is kinda creepy."

He scrunched his nose. "I don't love everything about it—especially the maggots. Those little buggers are smart and strong, and they don't die easily. Plus they make these weird chattering sounds. Sometimes I dream about them. God, I really hate 'em." He pulled out the box with the fake teeth again, held them up, and made them chatter.

I snatched the teeth from his hands and set them next to the magnifying glass. "So you can deal with the worst of life, so to speak—death—and yet you can't stand a few tiny little bugs."

He shrugged. "I'm a janitor, not an entomologist."

"A janitor with connections to the police," I said.

"Yeah. And that detective—Melvin? He thinks you're somehow tied to those two dead women—more than you're letting on." He leaned forward and tried to pick up the magnifying glass again.

I slapped his hand. "No shit, Sherlock."

He sat back, rubbed his chin, then said. "I think I can help you—if you're willing to share."

I frowned. "Share what?"

"Information."

I took this in for a moment, studying Brad's eyes as he scanned the shelf for something else to play with. They were dark, deep set, fringed with lashes a little longer than average.

"How do you know I have any information worth sharing?"

He rolled his eyes. "Come on, Parker. I'm a crime scene cleaner. I see things other people miss."

"All right. First question: How do you know the mayor?" I asked.

He shrugged. "He comes to some of the crimes scenes—depending on who died."

"Like who?"

"Anyone who has a name. He likes to show the citizens of San Francisco that he's a hands-on kind of mayor."

"Like who?" I pressed.

He took a Sherlock Holmes–style deerstalker hat, put it on, and shook his head. "I'm not at liberty to say. My services are discreet and confidential."

"You're kidding. You're not like a doctor or lawyer or priest, right? You shouldn't have any kind of confidentiality issues."

"Listen, if someone asks me not to discuss a scene, I respect their wishes." Another trip to the shelf and he was sporting Sherlock's pipe.

"You look ridiculous. And you still haven't told me why the mayor's phone number was on your desk."

He looked at me. "How did you know . . ."

"I figured—"

"I knew it! You were in my office!"

I plucked the pipe from his lips. "Is this how you share information?"

"Okay, okay. I answered your first question. Now it's my turn. What do you know about the deaths of Ikea Takeda and Andi Sax?"

"*Nothing! Nada! Niente!* Jeez!"

"Look, Parker," he said, removing the hat. "Maybe you don't realize it yet, but whoever broke into the building may think you know something—and that could be dangerous for you."

A shiver ran down my back.

"Let's start with the evidence you pocketed at the scene this morning," he said.

Shit. This guy didn't miss a thing. My eyes darted to the gold, book-shaped earring that lay on my desk, nearly obscured by papers.

Brad reached out an open palm.

I sighed, then handed over Ikea's earring.

"You know, it's a felony to remove evidence from a crime scene," he said as he studied the deceased's jewelry.

"It was in the cache!" I said, a little too loudly.

"Don't suppose we can check it for fingerprints now that you've obviously handled it."

*We?* Who did he mean by "we"?

I squirmed in my chair. "I was going to give it to Detective Melvin," I protested. "The next time I saw him. He wouldn't have found it in the cache anyway. Besides, the cops aren't doing anything to help me, so I'm trying to save myself from relocating to the city jail—or San Quentin." Thank goodness Alcatraz was closed to criminals—and innocent victims.

"So who put it there?" Brad dropped the earring into my hand, then met my eyes. I shrugged. Maybe Duncan knew something more about it.

"Well," Brad continued, "you'd better give it to Melvin. It might help take some of the suspicion off you."

Or make things worse. I felt little beads of sweat break out on my forehead. How was I going to prove I'd really found the earring in the cache when the detective would probably assume I removed it from her body—after I killed her—and planted it there? Even Duncan couldn't back me up, since I could have put it in there before I discovered it.

"My turn," I said, shaking the negative thoughts away.

He shrugged. "Shoot."

I reflexively glanced at his hidden gun. "Can you find out the results of Ikea's autopsy?"

Brad slowly rose to his feet. "I'm a crime scene cleaner, Presley," he said, finally using my first name. "And that's a request, not a question. But I'll see what I can do—*if* you keep me informed about anything else you learn. Deal?"

I pressed my lips together, then said, "Deal."

He reached out a hand; I shook it. His was warm, firm, strong—and not very calloused for a janitor, I noted.

I wondered how mine felt to him. Cold, clammy, shaky? Like a murderer's?

My office phone rang. I waited for Brad to leave before I answered it. He grinned as he closed the door behind him.

"Killer Parties," I said. I really needed to rethink the name of my event planning business.

"Presley Parker?" a male voice whispered. I hadn't recognize the caller ID. Crank call? I was about to hang up when the voice came again. "Pres?" This time it sounded urgent—and used my nickname. "It's me. Rocco."

"Rocco!" I glanced over at Brad's office. He was busy at his desk. I spun around so he couldn't see my face and said, "Where are you?"

"Quiet! Don't say my name. Is anyone in your office?"

"No, why? What's going on? Rocco, why haven't you

been to your office? You left the kitchen in a mess and—"

He cut me off. "Pres, listen. The chocolates. Were there any leftover chocolates in the kitchen?"

"No, they were all gone when we—"

"Shit!" he said, just before the line went dead.

# Chapter 17

*PARTY PLANNING TIP #17:*

*When your dessert soufflé falls flat, dump the disaster into the disposal and bring out your backup stash of gourmet chocolates. One bite of a Christopher Norman, MarieBelle, or Lake Champlain chocolate and your guests will be eating out of your hands.*

I could tell by our brief telephone conversation that Rocco knew the chocolates had been poisoned.

Except, how would he—unless he poisoned them?

But he would never do that.

Would he?

I thought about the chocolates in my drawer, and a chill ran down my spine.

*Brad! He still had the chocolates I gave him. . . .*

I ran from my office into his, sweat breaking on my forehead. "Spit that out!"

Brad stopped chewing and stared at me, his mouth frozen open.

"Spit it out!" I repeated and extended my hand. Obediently, Brad spit the saliva-soaked wad into my waiting palm.

I grimaced as I stared at the steaming glob of what looked like upchuck. "What the hell is this?"

"My breakfast," Brad said, wiping his mouth with the back

of his hand. "Cinnamon raisin bagel with walnut cream cheese. At least, it was."

I flung the nauseating clump into his wastebasket as if it were covered in blood. "That's disgusting!" I looked around for something to wipe off my hand and spotted his white jumpsuit.

Brad looked as if I were about to spew maggots. He leaped from his chair and caught my wrist. "Don't even think about it." Pulling open a file cabinet drawer, he grabbed a roll of paper towels and some disinfectant wipes and handed them to me.

I ripped off an arm's length of paper towel and wiped my hand, then scrubbed it with the disinfectant as if it were highly toxic before tossing the refuse into the wastebasket.

"I don't have leprosy." He sat back in his chair and crossed his arms. "So, you want to tell me what the hell that was all about?"

I rubbed my hand on my pants, hoping to destroy any last germs. "I . . . those chocolates I gave you. I thought you were eating one. They may have been tampered with."

Seemingly unfazed, he pulled open another drawer and removed the small box of chocolates I had given him earlier. Only now they were encased in a plastic Baggie. "You mean these?"

"Why are they in a bag?"

"I thought I'd take them down to the station and see if I can get someone to analyze them."

"What! Why?" I said, shaking my head in disbelief.

"Like you said. In case they've been tampered with."

"But why would you suspect something like that?"

Brad folded his hands like some kind of patient counselor. "Look, Presley, I know about the poisoned chocolates. A friend of mine at the station just sent me a copy of the autopsy report. As you probably know, Ikea Takeda didn't drown. She was poisoned. The tox scan found cyanide in the chocolate."

Oh my God. Were Rocco's chocolates really poisoned?

But how did Ikea get them?

And how did she end up in the water?

And what about Andi Sax?

He nodded toward my Welcome Wagon gift of chocolates. "I doubt these are poisoned, but I'm taking precautions. You don't have any more of these stashed away, do you?"

I glanced toward my office. Only a desk full.

I wondered if I should tell him about Rocco's odd phone call. After all, he'd shared the autopsy information with me. I reached out and closed his door to keep the other office mates from overhearing, then opened a folding chair that was propped against the wall and sat down.

I took a deep breath. "Listen. I need to tell you something. It's about Rocco. He called a few minutes ago."

Brad leaned forward conspiratorially. "Where is he?"

"I don't know. He asked if there were any chocolates left in the kitchen, and when I said no, he hung up. That was it."

"He needs to call the police. They'll want to talk to him."

I nodded. "I don't know why he hasn't come into the office yet. Maybe he figures he's a possible suspect. But I'm sure he didn't poison those chocolates. He's just not the poisoning type."

"Well, if they suspect *him*, that might let you off the hook."

I shook my head. "I'm not going to shift the blame to him to save my own ass. He didn't do anything wrong." I hoped.

Brad swiveled to his computer and opened up a search engine I didn't recognize—not Yahoo or Google. He typed the name "Rocco Ghirenghelli" and pressed ENTER.

"How did you know Rocco's last name?" I asked. I didn't recall telling him.

"It's on the mailbox outside."

Duh.

Seconds later the search brought up several links. Instead of clicking on Rocco's Web site, Brad moved the cursor down to an article published in the *San Francisco Chronicle* a couple of months ago.

I skimmed the details over Brad's shoulder—and caught a whiff of Brad's herbal shampoo. I inhaled, deeply. Momentarily distracted, I forced my eyes back onto the screen and read the review.

> Rocco Ghirenghelli, host of *Bay City Café* on KBAY, the San Francisco cable station, has been delighting hungry audiences for the past three years with his signature selections from local markets. Known for his unique Pacific Rim dishes, he often combines fresh catches from the bay with popular California produce. Among his award-winning specialties are his Crab and Avocado Tart in Quince Paste, Shaved Manchego with an Artichoke Chiffonade, Lobster Confit with Crispy Lavash, and Lemon Pepper Brined Mussels with Wilted Pea Sprouts. And what he does with chocolate is to die for.

Ah yes. The article brought back taste memories. I had sampled all of the above. They'd tasted like crab Pop-Tarts, artichoke paste, fish Jell-O, and rubber thingies. But people seemed to like his food. And the chocolates really were to die for. So to speak.

"It's just a review," I said to the screen. "What are you looking for?"

Brad typed "Department of Motor Vehicles" into the search engine. Up popped the Web page. He typed some numbers—an access code? And finally he typed in Rocco's name. The screen filled with more numbers, as indecipherable as my college trig homework.

Brad leaned to the side so I could see the screen.

"What am I looking at?" I asked.

He pointed to a line that read "CPC 192b," along with what appeared to be dates from over ten years ago.

"Yeah?"

"He's a con," he said matter-of-factly.

I stared at him. "What do you mean—like a con artist? Rocco? That's ridiculous."

"No, con, like convict. A 192b is a violation of the California Penal Code."

I reread the line, then turned to Brad. "What's a 192 whatever?"

He narrowed his eyes. "Manslaughter."

Uh-uh. No way.

Not Rocco.

Yes, he was a little eccentric. What semi-celebrity chef isn't? But he wasn't a murderer. Or a manslaughterer.

I crossed my arms. "I don't believe it. If he really did . . . kill someone, I'm sure it was an accident."

Brad glanced back at the screen, as if avoiding my eyes. Odd.

"How did you get that stuff, anyway?" I nodded at the screen, referring to his ability to access the information.

He shrugged. "Like I said. I have friends at 850 Bryant. We work hand in hand."

"Yeah, about that . . ."

"Look, Presley," he said, finally meeting my penetrating stare. "Rocco's obviously in some kind of trouble. He's gone AWOL from his job. His chocolates were probably poisoned. He has a record. And you just got a suspicious phone call from him. If you know anything, you need to—"

I stood up. "I don't! All I know is he called me and hung up before I could find out what was going on." I headed for the door, then turned back. "I thought we were going to help each other."

He threw his hands up in surrender. "Me too. I told you

about the autopsy. Now it's your turn. It's called quid pro quo."

"I did! I have! I—"

I heard the front door of the barracks creak open, interrupting me from my defense. I stole a peek out the door—two men in suits had stepped in and were glancing around the reception area. I recognized the one with the slicked-back hair immediately: Detective Luke Melvin.

Any chance he was here to hire my services for the next Policemen's Ball? Not likely.

"I gotta go," I whispered and slipped out the door, hoping the detective hadn't spotted me yet. I ducked into Delicia's office, startling her, and scrambled under her desk, startling her even more. My thinking was, if they couldn't find me, they couldn't arrest me. Scrunched into a human ball between Dee's legs, I whispered up to her, "Where is he?"

Delicia leaned down and whispered, "Who?"

"Stop talking to your crotch! They'll see you. Pick up the phone and pretend to talk."

Frowning, she did what I told her.

"Now, where's the detective?"

She swiveled in her chair, almost rolling over my fingers. "He's talking to the new guy—Brad."

"Can you hear what they're saying?"

Seconds passed. I couldn't see her face. "I think they're talking about . . . you. They keep looking toward your office."

Great.

I hoped Brad wouldn't give me up. This would be a test of his sincerity about wanting to help me.

"What are they saying now?"

"Shhh! I can't hear them when you keep interrupting. Besides, the detective is a mumbler. There's another cop with him . . . uh-oh. He's . . . going into your office. You left the door open."

What was that dickwad doing in my office? Wasn't that illegal without a warrant? "What now?"

"Uh, he's looking around. . . . Wait, he's sitting at your desk. He's . . ."

"What?"

Delicia didn't answer. I pinched her ankle. She jumped. Her knee hit my chin. We both said, "Ouch!"

Rubbing my chin, I asked, "What's he doing?"

"Quiet—they'll hear you. I don't want to be charged as an accomplice if you're arrested, you know."

I pounded one of her purple Crocs. She had a pair in every color.

"Okay, he's picking up something from your desk. . . . A sheet of paper . . . He's getting up. . . . He's taking it to the other cop."

Sheet of paper? What sheet of paper?

My notes about Ikea's and Andi's deaths!

I sat up and bumped my head underneath the desk. Shit! I rubbed the bump.

"Wait—he's bringing it back to your office. . . . He's putting it on your desk. Uh-oh."

"What?" I pulled on Delicia's long patchwork skirt like a kid wanting her mother's attention.

"He's calling the other cop over . . . showing him something . . . in your drawer."

Oh God. I'd left my drawer open too!

And they'd found my stash of chocolates.

# Chapter 18

*PARTY PLANNING TIP #18:*

*To perk up a placid party, introduce a surprise guest—a magician with something up his sleeve, a fortune-teller who can predict the future, or a cop . . . who doubles as a stripper.*

When the coast was clear, I scooted out from my hiding place. My knees and back cracked as I eased myself to an upright position. I was sure I had a lump on my head and a bruise on my chin. Brushing cobwebs from my clothes, I said to Delicia, "You really should clean under there."

"You really should find a better hiding place!" she snapped back.

"Thanks, by the way," I said in parting, then turned around to find myself face-to-face with Brad Matthews. I froze, feeling like I'd just been caught breaking and entering.

"What were you *doing* under there?" he said, frowning and grinning at the same time.

"Uh . . . looking for something." I felt beads of sweat break out along my forehead.

"The detective wanted to talk to you."

"Really." I arched my back, trying to squeeze the remaining kinks out. "Did he have a warrant?"

"No. Should he have?" He gave that half smile he was so good at.

I rolled my eyes. "He was in my office snooping through all my stuff!"

"Actually, there's a loophole called plain view, which means you don't need a warrant if you can clearly see what you're looking for. Like papers on your desk in an open office and stuff in your open drawers. But I think he just wanted to talk to you about Rocco, who seems to have disappeared from the face of the earth."

"What did you tell him?"

He leaned back against the doorjamb. "Nothing, obviously, since I don't know anything more than what I read on the Internet."

"What did he say about me?" I ran my hand through my hair, hoping to remove any spiders that might have set up residence. I certainly didn't mean for it to come off as sexual. But Brad reached out toward my face. Reflexively, I pulled back. His hand paused; then he plucked a cobweb from the side of my head. I felt a blast of heat rise like an erupting volcano.

Flicking away the cobweb, he said, "Melvin wanted to know where you were so he could ask you some questions. Your car's out front, so he knew you were around. Didn't you hear me calling you?"

"No." Yes. "What else did he say?"

"He did mention something . . . ," Brad added, rubbing his chin.

"What?" I may have screeched.

"Calm down. He found some kind of notes or list on your desk, along with some chocolates in your drawer. He wanted to know why you were writing down a bunch of names. And where the chocolates came from."

Jeez, didn't everyone have chocolates in their drawers?

"So . . . ," Brad said, raising an eyebrow. "What's up with your list?"

I shrugged, spun around dramatically, and went into my office. I found my list almost right where I'd left it. Before I could pick it up, a muscular arm came out of nowhere and snatched it away.

"Give me that!" I said, grabbing at it.

Brad raised his arm, holding my list out of my reach like a school bully. When I stopped reaching for it, he lowered his arm and scanned the names. A few moments later he handed it over, frowning. "Is this a list of suspects?"

I glared at him. "No. Just people I want to talk to, who might know something about Ikea and the mayor."

"Why's my name there?" Was that a smirk on his face?

"You're a person of interest, just like the others," I said. "Even *I'm* on my list—thanks to Detective Melvin. So don't take it personally."

The phone rang. I snatched it up. "What!—I mean, Killer Parties."

"Pres! Thank God." It was Rocco. I turned away from Brad in an attempt to have some privacy, but he didn't get the hint. He stayed planted right where he was—inside my office.

"Hi . . . Mother. How are you?" I said a little too dramatically.

"Are the cops still there?" Rocco whispered.

"Oh no, I'm fine. What's up, Mother?"

"Did they find anything?" He sounded urgent.

"Not that I know of, Mom." I sneaked a glance at Brad. He was busy flipping through my stack of phone messages. At least, he was pretending to.

"What about the chocolates?" Rocco said.

"No, Mom, sorry." I shook my head as if he could see me.

"Shit! Listen, Pres, you've got to help me. In the kitchen cupboard, over the refrigerator where we keep the cleaning supplies, there's a box of rat poison. . . ."

A chill ran down my back. I hesitated, then said, "Uh,

yes, Mom, it's gone." I looked at Brad—he was no longer pretending not to listen. I quickly added, "My rash has finally cleared up."

Brad made a face. Great. What sort of rash was he imagining I had?

"No!" Rocco hissed. "It's got to be there! I use it all the time—"

"You do?"

"For rats, of course. My fingerprints will be all over it—"

I heard him cough. "Are you okay?"

"Where could it . . . who . . ." Rocco coughed again, more violently.

My heart skipped a beat. "Ro— Mom? You don't sound well." More coughing, gasping. "Mom?"

The phone went dead.

I turned to Brad as I hung up. He was staring at me.

"Is your *mom* all right?" He frowned, feigning concern.

I opened my mouth to continue the lie, then sighed. "Okay, okay. It wasn't my mom."

"No shit, Sherlock," Brad said. "So where's Rocco? I'm guessing he's in some sort of trouble."

"I think he's sick. . . ." I trailed off, trying to guess where Rocco might have called from. Wherever it was, he obviously knew the cops had been here. "We've got to find him. He sounded . . . awful."

Brad reached for the phone. "I'll call the police, see if they can—"

I pushed his hand down, replacing the receiver. "No! No cops. Listen, I have a hunch where he may be, but you have to promise not to call the police. If anything, he may need an ambulance."

Brad frowned.

I raced out of the barracks to my MINI with Brad right behind me. I slid into the driver's side, and Brad got into the passenger's side, ducking to avoid hitting his head in the tight quarters. As he turned to fasten his seat belt, I caught another glimpse of his gun.

Momentarily distracted, I switched on the ignition—twice, by accident—causing a horrible noise. I jammed the gearshift into reverse and sped out of the parking lot, shooting pebbles in my wake. Driving back toward the main gate, I turned onto California Avenue, which ran along the marina. Just before the Treasure Island Yacht Club stood the Windsurf Café. It was the only restaurant on Treasure Island, run by the Job Corps Culinary Academy. Housed in what looked like a double-wide trailer on blocks, the place was easily overlooked by tourists.

The café served breakfast and lunch, six days a week, and was a favorite spot for us locals—even Rocco, who needed a break from his own gourmet cooking from time to time. The bacon, crab, and cheese omelet beat a fancy eggs Benedict any day. And nothing cost over ten dollars. No wonder we all loved it.

I pulled in front of the café. Bingo. Rocco's SUV was in the parking lot. I could smell frying fish as I got out of the car. Leaving Brad in my dust, I ran inside and scanned the patrons, mostly young men and women with still-damp hair, wearing wet suits.

"Bosun!" I called to the overweight balding man behind the lunch counter. Behind him were colorful photos of the Chinese Dragon Boat Races, held every August in Clipper Cove off Treasure Island.

He finished pouring a beer from a tap, then looked up. "Hey, Pres. The usual—"

I cut him off. "Where's Rocco?"

He wiped a beer-soaked hand on his apron, glanced around, and shrugged. "Hmm. Was here. Left, I guess. S'up?"

I turned to Brad, who'd finally followed me in. "Check the men's room. I'll check his SUV."

Brad headed into the lavatory as I made a dash for the

front door. Before I stepped out, I heard him yell, "He's in here!"

Ignoring the boundaries of society, I joined him in the men's room. Rocco lay slumped on the floor, his legs sticking out of the last stall. From the blue coloring in his lips and fingertips, he looked cyanotic.

"Call 911!" I screamed.

"How is he?" Delicia said, following me into my office when I returned from the hospital. Rocco was in critical condition. They'd pumped his stomach after I mentioned he might have been poisoned. He was still unconscious when I left.

I slumped back in my desk chair, frowning, my legs stretched out in front of me. "I don't know, Dee. He's in pretty bad shape."

I gave her a brief summary of the past couple of hours.

"You think it's another poisoning?" she said, blinking rapidly.

I shrugged. "They haven't confirmed it, but . . ." I thought about Rocco, lying in that hospital bed, all those wires hooked up to him. At least he was still alive, unlike Andi and Ikea.

"Well, if he was poisoned, wouldn't that prove he didn't kill anybody?" Delicia said, leaning against the doorjamb. "I mean, why would he eat his own poisoned chocolates?"

Raj appeared in the doorway. "Perhaps the police will be thinking he tried to off himself." Apparently he'd overheard us.

Delicia turned toward him. "What do you mean, Raj?"

"Perhaps he was committing suicide, knowing the jig was up."

Off himself? The jig was up? Raj had been watching too many bad cop films. He was starting to sound like a Bollywood Gangsta. But he had a point.

What if the police thought the same thing? And at the moment, Rocco wasn't able to defend himself, lying in that hospital bed unconscious. Now I had two people I needed to clear of murder—Rocco and myself.

What had Rocco said about the missing rat poison in the kitchen? That it had his fingerprints on it? And where was it now?

"Where's the CSC?" Delicia asked, peering into Brad's office across the hall. When I frowned, she explained her text-talk: "Crime scene cleaner."

I shrugged. The last I'd seen him he was at the hospital, but he'd disappeared sometime before I left. At least, he hadn't ridden back to the office with me.

"Ms. Parker?" A familiar voice boomed from the doorway of the reception area. Raj and Delicia parted like the Red Sea, allowing me a full view of the dapper Detective Melvin.

"What?" I snapped, not in the mood to be arrested, let alone interrogated. I had just about lost a friend—and still might, if Rocco didn't make a turn for the better.

The detective glanced at Delicia and Raj, who both got the message and disappeared into Dee's office. Once there, they pretended to work while surreptitiously watching the proceedings behind the glass partition. I was so onto them.

The detective helped himself to the empty folding chair. As he did, I caught a glimpse of Brad slipping into his office and wondered if he'd been at the hospital all this time. Or had he come with the detective? I watched as he started to shut the door, then noticed he left it open a crack. Since his office was directly across from mine—and only five feet away—he'd be able to hear everything the detective said. I was onto him too.

"Ms. Parker, I understand Rocco Ghirenghelli called you," Melvin said, flipping open his notebook.

I couldn't lie. They'd probably checked the call history on his cell.

"Yes, but—"

"What did he say?" The detective lifted his piercing blue eyes from the notebook page and looked at me.

I bit the inside of my mouth, then shook my head and said, "Nothing, really. He started to say something and then coughed and wheezed. I couldn't understand him. Then the phone went dead."

"He must have told you where he was. You showed up at the Windsurf only a few minutes later."

"Nope. I just guessed. He hangs out there a lot, so I took a chance and headed over. We—Brad Matthews and I—found him lying on the floor of the men's room, unconscious. I called 911. End of story."

"Matthews was with you?" he asked.

I nodded. *As if you didn't know.*

The detective squinted. "Why did Ghirenghelli call you?"

"I don't know." *None of your business.*

"What did he say?"

"I told you. Nothing. He just coughed." I glanced over at Brad's office. The door still stood ajar. I wondered if he'd rat on me later.

No doubt.

"By the way, they've done a partial analysis of his stomach contents, thanks to your heads-up." The detective flipped a page of his notebook.

"Rocco was poisoned, right?"

He looked at me and frowned. "How did you know?"

I swept my arm around the office. "It seems to be contagious around here."

Detective Melvin looked back at his notes. "Do you know any reason why Ghirenghelli might have wanted to poison Ikea Takeda? Or Andrea Sax?" He met my eyes again.

"No, of course not! He had no reason at all. And whoever poisoned those two women probably poisoned him too. I'd think that would be pretty obvious, Detective."

Without taking those penetrating blue eyes off me, he reached into his jacket pocket, pulled out several folded sheets of paper, and handed them to me.

I unfolded them and skimmed the contents, like I do nearly everything I read, thanks to ADHD.

SUPERIOR COURT OF CALIFORNIA
*Search Warrant*

> . . . *To authorize a search and seizure of property, articles, materials, or substances* . . .
>
> blah, blah, blah . . . *Whereas* . . . blah, blah, blah . . . *constitutes evidence of a violation* . . . blah, blah, blah . . .
>
> Then the words jumped out:
>
> *Cyanide* . . . *in conjunction with other chemicals to form compounds such as hydrogen cyanide, sodium cyanide, and potassium cyanide* . . . *specifically, Diphacin 110, aka concentrate rodenticide anticoagulant powder* . . . *in the premises described below* . . .

A warrant. To search the barracks. For rat poison.

"You really think you have probable cause?" I asked, thrusting back the papers.

The detective stood up and waved me aside. Jerk. Crossing my arms in hopeless defiance, I stepped away from my desk and watched him open the top drawer. He glanced inside, then looked at me, raising an eyebrow.

"What? You think I'm going to poison my own chocolates? Get real." I didn't take my eyes off him.

He nodded toward the drawer. "What did you do with them?" he said.

"Do with what?"

I dropped my arms and glanced at the open drawer.

My chocolates were gone.

# Chapter 19

*PARTY PLANNING TIP #19:*

*Think of yourself as CEO of your party. Don't try to host the event alone. Hire assistants, bribe friends, or blackmail relatives, then delegate and micro-manage, while taking all the credit.*

"Where are the chocolates, Presley—Ms. Parker?" Detective Melvin, slipping for a second from his usual formality, nodded toward the open drawer.

"I . . . I . . ."

I glanced at Brad, who had appeared behind the detective in the doorway. He gave me a blank look I couldn't read. *Thanks for the support, buddy.*

"Wait a minute!" I said, recovering part of my brain. "Why did you think there were chocolates in my drawer?"

Melvin turned to the young woman a few steps away. "Officer Price?"

The wide-eyed rookie couldn't have been more than twenty-five.

"Anonymous tip?" she said. I thought I saw her steal a glance at Brad.

Brad caught it too and backed away, holding up his hands. "Innocent bystander," he said.

"Go check Ghirenghelli's office," Detective Melvin told the kiddy cop. Meanwhile, Melvin busied himself by searching the rest of my office, opening party gift bags, snooping into prop boxes, looking behind cardboard cutouts of Elvis, Britney Spears, and Captain Kirk. All he found was a bunch of party crap. If he was looking for method, there were a few plastic swords, but no bloody weapons. No pointed clues. No detailed murder plots.

I stood there smugly, my arms crossed again, while he completed his search. When he'd just about finished, he bent down and checked beneath my desk, then reached under and pulled out my Rollerblades. He looked as if he'd discovered Lizzie Borden's ax.

"You keep these hidden under your desk?" he said, rising.

I shook my head, more in exasperation than denial. "Not *hidden*. Just out of the way. Seemed as good a place as any, since the rest of my office is pretty well filled with party paraphernalia."

He peered inside one of the skates, no doubt checking for stashed evidence.

Then he reached in.

To my surprise, he pulled out a small plastic bag that had apparently been stuffed inside. I felt myself blush and leaned in. "What's—"

"Funny place to keep your chocolates, don't you think, Ms. Parker?"

Struck dumb, all I could do was shake my head in disbelief as he held up the bag. Inside were half a dozen tiny black birds from last night's party—all chocolate. He dropped the bag into a large paper evidence bag.

"But . . . those aren't my—"

"You'll be hearing from me, Ms. Parker," Detective Melvin said, glancing around as if searching for an overlooked clue. "Don't leave town." His last glance was directed at me, just before he left my office.

* * *

I felt the rope tighten around my neck and pulled at my T-shirt collar.

A voice came from the doorway. "You okay?"

I looked up at Brad, frowning. "Are they gone?"

He nodded.

"Did they find anything else?"

He shook his head.

I leaned back in my chair, still tugging at my T-shirt collar as if it were strangling me. "So what are they going to do now?"

He shrugged and plopped into the folding chair. "Run a tox on the chocolates. That'll take some time."

I nodded listlessly, playing with the now overstretched neck of my shirt. Up until now I'd been going round and round with possibilities but had come up with nothing substantial. It was time to start seriously investigating some of the mayor's friends and acquaintances—not to mention the mayor himself, if I could get to him. He was the only link to the two dead women. Besides me.

Brad nodded toward my notes, now a mess of scratch-outs, arrows, additions, and question marks. "Want help?"

I pressed my lips together, then said, "You weren't much help a few minutes ago. Besides, why would you help me? What's in it for you?"

"Nothing," he said, leaning forward. "Just seems like you could use a little professional assistance."

"Professional assistance—from a crime scene cleaner?"

"Looks like I'm all you've got." He grinned. I couldn't help but smile back, then bit my lip to cover it.

I thought about my options. I had my coworkers—Delicia, Raj, Berk—and Rocco, who was out of commission at the moment. They meant well, but what could they do to help? Play themselves in my Lifetime movie during "Women Who Kill" week?

I'd lost contact with most of the staff at the university.

Of course, there was always my mother. She was my best friend, supporter, and cheerleader, in spite of her illness. But I couldn't exactly ask her to help me find a murderer. Could I?

I spun the list of the mayor's associates around toward Brad.

He took it in his large hand. "Tell me what you know about them."

As I ticked off the names, I gave Brad their connections to the mayor and what information I had so far, which wasn't much.

"Xtreme Siouxie: She's been pressuring the mayor to clean up the island and make it a natural habitat. Eugene Stadelhofer: He wants TI to become a permanent monument to the navy. Dakota Hunter: He thinks the site should be turned over to his tribe for a casino. And Lucas Cruz: He's trying to make this place Hollywood North. They all know the mayor—and in fact want something from him—so I figured they'd be good to talk to. Maybe they know something about the mayor or Ikea or even Andi. I know it's not much to go on, but it's better than nothing."

In the silence that followed, Brad rubbed his chin. I ran my fingers through my hair. They caught on a snarl. How long had it been since I'd brushed my hair?

"Look," I said, breaking the silence, "I know I don't have shit, but I think the key lies with the mayor. He knew both of the dead women. But how that ties in, I don't know."

"All right," Brad said, setting my notes on the desk. "When the cops work on an unsolved murder, they usually begin with the victim. In this case, there are two. Let's start with Ikea." Brad sat forward. "You said you heard she had a lot of influence over Mayor Green. That's a start. Now, how do you find out more?"

"No clue," I said.

"You were a college instructor, right? Who did you schmooze when you needed classroom materials or whatever?"

A light cut through my fog of thoughts. "The admin."

Brad grinned. "Now you're thinking like an investigator."

I opened my cell, checked my call history, then pressed the number for the mayor's office. A few seconds later, a familiar voice answered.

"Mayor Green's office."

"Chloe? It's Presley Parker."

"Presley! Hi. Sorry I haven't called to thank you for the great job you did, in spite of everything that happened. It's been totally crazy here, as you can imagine."

"Actually, I wondered if you had time for lunch or coffee? I wanted to talk to you about something else." Out of the corner of my eye, I saw Brad give me a thumbs-up.

"Um, sure. I'm a little overloaded with work right now because of all this—the mayor's taking it hard, you know—but if you want to come by, I might have a couple of minutes. Is it about the party? We'll cut you a check soon."

"Actually, it's about Ikea's death."

"Oh God, it's been awful. The mayor is just devastated."

"That's what I wanted to talk to you about. The police seem to think I'm somehow involved. I could use your help."

"You're kidding! Of course. I'll do what I can. Can you come by, say, in half an hour?"

Brad stood up. "Nice work, Holmes. You're a natural. And that's kind of a scary thought."

I shrugged. "Hmm. Planning a party and solving a mystery aren't that different, really. It's all about the dynamics of a group of people brought together for a purpose."

"Maybe. But one's a lot more dangerous than the other," he said, raising an eyebrow. "Want me to come with you?"

"No, thanks, but you could do something for me." Oh my God, was I actually batting my eyelashes now?

"Like what? Destroy incriminating evidence?"

I frowned. "Not funny. I thought you believed me."

"Just kidding. What do you have in mind?"

"Find out how Rocco's doing?"

"Sure." He reached in his pocket and pulled out a business card. "Here's my cell number. Call if you need me." The card, with the words "Crime Scene Cleaners" at the top in red, looked as if it had been printed by computer. "Got any idea what you're going to say to the mayor's admin?"

I looked down at my notes. "I have no clue. But I'll think of something."

As soon as Brad left my office, I pulled out my mom's *How to Host a Killer Party* manual, silently thanking her for writing it. The more I read through it, the more I believed preparing for a party *was* a lot like solving a mystery. It was all about planning—and timing.

The cover featured a picture of my mother in her thirties, wearing a polka-dot party dress, her dyed-blond hair styled in a classic pageboy. She held a martini glass in one hand and some sort of fancy canapé in the other. Colorful balloons filled the background like giant pieces of confetti.

I smiled as I remembered the day the photo was taken. I'd been watching the shoot from a short distance away, admiring my beautiful mother's poised and confident demeanor. She still retained those qualities, in spite of her illness, and I envied that.

Flipping open to the first chapter, already dog-eared and latte-stained, I inserted a few handwritten corollaries next to the Perfect Party Planning to-do list:

Step 1. Start with a Theme

Party Plan—What's the occasion?

Investigation—What's the crime?

Step 2. The Guest of Honor

Party Plan—What are the GOH's interests?

Investigation—What was the victim like?

Step 3. Timing Is Key

Party Plan—Plan the party from start to finish.

Investigation—Note the events before and after the crime.

Step 4. Location, Location

Party Plan—Set the stage.

Investigation—Check out the crime scene.

Step 5. Greet the Guests

Party Plan—Welcome the attendees.

Investigation—Interview the suspects.

Step 6. The Element of Surprise

Party Plan—Expect the unexpected.

Investigation—Expect the unexpected?

It looked so simple on paper. Six easy steps for hosting a party. Or solving a crime. The only difference? My life didn't depend on the success of a party.

# Chapter 20

*PARTY PLANNING TIP #20:*

*When planning your event, consider creating a flowchart to outline the sequence of events. That way there won't be any awkward surprises or embarrassing lulls at your party.*

*At least not on your part . . .*

As I entered the historic Hall of Records, a massive gilt-trimmed concrete building that encompassed the entire block and housed the mayor's office, I felt as if I were stepping back in time. I'd heard it referred to as the Crown Jewel by the docents and tour guides I'd half listened to over the years. Only recently had I come to appreciate the Beaux Arts architecture that is rare in eclectic California construction.

I glanced at the plaque bolted near the door and skimmed the brief description. The original building was destroyed in the 1906 earthquake. The current one was built in 1915, then retrofitted after the 1989 Loma Prieta earthquake. The three-hundred-foot domed structure was now a national landmark, considered "one of the most important buildings in America." Architect Arthur Brown Jr. designed a number of other buildings in the city, including the San Francisco Opera House and Coit Tower, often referred to as a phallic symbol. Each one was considered a masterpiece. But like all construction, safety renovation and historic restoration seemed never-ending, as state-of-the-art technology continued to be introduced and installed, "without compromising the historic character of the building." So said the plaque.

I entered the expansive rotunda and took in the vast grand staircase—the same one used in another Indiana Jones film—that led to the mayor's office on the second floor. I gawked like a tourist at the pinkish Italian marble walls and huge domed skylight overhead. Two indoor courtyards currently offered art exhibits and educational displays. Now playing: "Before and After the Quake of 1906" and "The Universe Within—A Look Inside the Human Body." Passing the pre- and post-quake photos I'd seen dozens of times over the years, I stole a quick peek at the poster for "The Universe Within." My stomach lurched at the graphic photos of real human beings with their innards dipped in some sort of resin and put on display for all to see.

Passing busts of assassinated Mayor George Moscone and Supervisor Harvey Milk reminded me that even Mayor Green was only a bullet—or a bottle of poison—away from having his bust made. Moving on, I walked by courtrooms, public offices, and familiar names on nameplates in reverential awe, as if I were in church. Marble, pillars, and domes did a lot for a business professional's image.

My decrepit military barracks office could use a few pillars and domes, not to mention a little gilt.

At the top of the stairs, a little out of breath, I entered the mayor's office and was greeted by a young man sitting at a large oak desk. "Greeted" as in, he looked up from his phone call and held up a manicured finger, indicating for me to wait a minute. I nodded and took that moment to enjoy the ostentatious surroundings of the reception area.

The mayor's outer office encompassed the past and present nicely, with a mix of heavy antique office furniture and state-of-the-art electronic accessories. Dark hardwood floors were covered with intricate Oriental carpets. Velveteen-covered Victorian chairs sat tastefully arranged around the room beneath oil portraits of previous city mayors. I recognized the infamous—Emperor Norton—as well as the popular—Joseph Alioto, Willie Brown, and Gavin Newsom—all looking regal in their suits and smiles.

"May I help you?" the man at the desk finally said, putting down the phone.

I spun around, took several steps to the desk, and reached out my hand. "I'm Presley Parker, the mayor's event planner. I have an appointment to see Chloe Webster."

The anorexically thin man in the tailored dark suit and closely cropped highlighted hair took my hand with slim fingers and shook it lightly, as if I might have cooties. "Do you have an appointment?" he said without making eye contact.

Hadn't I just said that? "Yes, sir." I tapped an invisible watch on my wrist as if officially verifying it.

"Have a seat. I'll let Ms. Webster know you're here."

He lifted the phone, pressed a button, and said something so softly I couldn't make it out. After a brief couple of "Yes, Ms. Webster"s, he hung up and more or less mouthed to me, "She'll be with you in a few minutes."

I sat down in a stiff chair underneath Davin Green. He looked like a movie star in his portrait with his professionally whitened smile, green-contact-lensed eyes, molded dark hair, and Italian suit. As any event planner knew, a few fancy decorations went a long way to cover up a less-than-perfect venue. The same axiom worked for people too.

A few minutes stretched into a quarter of an hour. While I waited, I thought about what I was going to ask Chloe. As I pulled out my notebook, a small sticky note floated onto my lap. Written in Delicia's curly handwriting, it was the note to call the governor's office. Damn. The timing couldn't be worse. I wanted that job, but I felt overwhelmed by the current circumstances. How could I put on a murder mystery for the governor while trying to solve a real one?

That got me thinking. I'd done a small mystery event for the university to raise money for the campus library, and it had been a great success. The sponsors were able to supply the library with several new computers. Plus, it'd been a lot of fun putting the event together—although working out a not-too-easy, not-too-hard plot on the university's limited budget had been a challenge.

First I'd chosen the victim—in this case a professor who was appearing at the school library to sign her latest book, *Deader Than a Doornail*. Then I jotted down the most likely suspects connected to the victim—the frumpy librarian, the tweedy bookseller, the stuffy publisher, the bitter critic, the bimbo star of the book's miniseries, and the local crooked politician. Stereotypes always got the biggest laughs.

Next, I gave each one a secret and a motive for offing the victim—standards like jealousy, blackmail, larceny, lust. Finally, I wrote alibis for each one—which of course turned out to be questionable when the "detective" interrogated them. While the amateur sleuths attending the mystery tried to sort the red herrings from the real clues, they were distracted by the suspects' psycho personalities and suspicious statements. Only those who looked for physical evidence guessed the real killer. Source: *Murder, She Wrote*.

As the minutes ticked by, I started to brainstorm a plot for the governor's mystery. But after tapping my pen on the pad for several minutes, all I'd come up with were two dead victims and a very suspicious-looking party planner as the killer.

"Presley?" a voice called. I looked up to see Chloe Webster standing in her office doorway. I stuffed the notebook into my purse and rose.

"Hi!" Chloe reached out and took my hand in both of hers. She looked completely different out of her costume and in her fashionably tailored blue suit, with its cropped, closely fitted jacket and short skirt. Even her dark blue, sky-high Manolo Blahniks blended perfectly with her outfit. Around her neck she wore the small triangle necklace she'd had on at the party.

"Hi, Chloe. Thanks for seeing me. I know this is probably a bad time. . . ."

She'd turned and headed for her office, leading the way. With a last glance at the portrait of Mayor Green, I followed her through the door labeled CHLOE WEBSTER, ASSISTANT TO THE MAYOR. I shot a glance at the office next to hers: MAYOR DAVIN GREEN. His door was shut and the room looked dark through the frosty window.

As Chloe moved around to her desk, I took a moment to read her room. It was sparse, simple, and tastefully appointed. A steel desk and file cabinets, functional gray carpet and chairs, gray wainscoting on white walls. A framed picture of the Golden Gate Bridge and one of the Painted Ladies filled two walls. On her desk were tiny figurines popular with tourists—a Victorian house, a cable car, the Transamerica building, a replica of the MOMA. Even a cup from the mayor's party on Alcatraz.

But it was her clothes and shoes that told me she was making the big bucks at this job.

I sat down in the sleek steel chair opposite her.

"As I told you, it's been crazy here. Mayor Green is devastated over Ikea's death, as you can imagine, and it's meant a lot more work for me. But you're not here to listen to me complain. So, what's this all about?" She played with the triangle around her neck.

"Well, as I mentioned, I want to help the police figure out who did this."

"Great." She raised a well-drawn eyebrow. "How can I help?"

"I think the police are on the wrong track. They're even questioning me and my staff."

Her face clouded and she fiddled with her necklace. "The police were here too."

I leaned in, waiting for her to go on. Like me, had they suspected the mayor too? When she didn't continue, I asked the obvious. "So what did they want?"

She cleared her throat, looking uncomfortable. "Uh, well, they asked about you. And your caterer."

I bit the inside of my cheek. I knew it.

"Okay, so now you know why I'm really here. That's why I need your help."

"I don't know what I can do but I'm happy to help any way I can, Presley. I didn't tell them much. Mainly because I really don't know anything."

I remembered Brad's advice—start with the victim—and asked, "Can you tell me something about Ikea? How did she and the mayor get along?"

She grinned. "They were a great couple. Obviously, or the mayor wouldn't have planned that whole wedding party."

"Was there anyone who might have had a reason to do this? Anyone who—"

She cut me off with a laugh. "Oh sure. Plenty of people didn't care for Ikea. She was talented, beautiful, powerful, and engaged to the mayor of San Francisco. Maybe having that kind of life makes you a lot of 'friends' "—she put the word in finger quotes—"but it also makes you some enemies."

"Really?" I pulled out my notebook. "Like who?"

"Oh, don't quote me, but goodness, too many to count. I suppose you could start with the people who saw her as a connection to the mayor. Granted, she had a lot of influence over him, but some people thought she could actually affect his decision making." She rolled her eyes.

"You knew Ikea pretty well?"

"I suppose. She was here all the time." More fiddling with the necklace. Was she bored, nervous, or hyperactive like me?

"What was she like?"

Chloe sighed, as if reluctant to give a big speech. "Well, she was beautiful, you know. Tall, slim, gorgeous almond eyes. I think she was a model at one time. Then she started writing chick-lit novels and became a minor celebrity. Began hitting the city social circuit. That's when she met the mayor. He was just coming off an ugly divorce and fell head over heels immediately."

"You said people thought she had a lot of influence over the mayor. Do you think that was true?"

Chloe shrugged and looked down at her necklace. "I don't really know. Like I said, some people thought so. That's not to say the mayor didn't have his own agenda, but I know she encouraged him on a few city projects."

"Like . . ." I was practically sitting on the edge of my chair.

She tapped her pen. "Mostly special interest groups. As you know, the mayor is in the middle of making some decisions about the future of Treasure Island—and that's causing major issues. Things are . . . intense, to say the least, and there are a few people who are trying—tried, I should say—to sway the mayor through Ikea."

I thought of the three men who'd argued at the wedding—Dakota Hunter, Spaz Cruz, and Admiral Stadelhofer. And then there'd been that scene with Siouxie, the activist. Was there anyone else I could add to my list?

"Did Ikea actually help any of them? I mean, did she support any of those causes?"

"Honestly, I don't know. Ikea and I weren't that close. Like I said, I met her after I got the job here. She didn't confide in me or anything." Chloe put the pencil down and looked at her watch. "Look, I want to help you, Presley, but I've probably said too much already. My job is to protect the mayor, and I could get in trouble—besides, he has a press conference in a few minutes."

Protect the mayor? Odd choice of words, I thought.

"Sorry. Just one last thing. Do you have any idea where she got the earrings she wore that night?"

Her hand went to her necklace again. "Which ones?"

"They looked like miniature books."

"Oh sure. The mayor gave them to her. That night, in fact, as a special pre-wedding gift, I guess. She was having a tantrum about her costume, and when he whipped those earrings out, she forgot all about her little snit."

"By the way, I love your necklace. Does it symbolize something?"

"Just my old sorority. Tri Delta."

I rose to leave and reached out my hand. She came around the desk and gave me a light hug. "Don't worry. I'm sure the police will figure all of this out. And feel free to come to me if you need my help—or the mayor's."

"Thanks, Chloe. You've been a great help already."

She smiled wanly and looked away. "I wish I could do more. It's really been hard on the mayor."

Did I see something more in that smile and those eyes besides concern for the mayor?

I started for the door, then turned back. "Oh yes, I almost forgot. Did the police tell you that Ikea was poisoned?"

Chloe nodded. "Yes, I heard. The mayor is sick about it."

"They think it was the chocolates at the wedding party," I added.

Chloe's eyes narrowed as she had a thought; then she shook her head. "God, that means it could have been anyone. . . ."

I nodded. "Well, if you have any ideas, let me know."

She nodded. "Hang in there, Presley."

Did she have to use the word "hang"?

A bunch of newscasters and reporters were gathered in the rotunda when I came out of the elevator, checking camera angles, checking their hair, testing microphones.

The mayor's press conference. This might be a good time to ask a few pointed questions of our bereaved mayor. I pulled out my little notebook and a pen and tried to blend in with the newspaper reporters, hoping the mayor might not recognize me when I started grilling him. Ha. Then I had a thought and ran out to my car, where I still hadn't unloaded the costume I'd worn at the party. I dug out the blazer, cloche hat, and a pair of Groucho glasses, then slipped on the blazer and hat as I dashed back to the rotunda. Mayor Green had just arrived at the podium and was about to be introduced by Chloe. As subtly as I could, I broke off the mustache and nose from the black-rimmed glasses and put them on, hoping I could at least fool the mayor from a distance.

Seconds later Chloe took the microphone. "Ladies and gentlemen of the press, Mayor Davin Green has been through a very devastating experience. He knows you have questions, but please keep them brief. You have five minutes. And now, Mayor Davin Green." She lifted her hands in applause.

The room followed suit as Mayor Green took over the mic. He waved his hands to calm the crowd, then began reading his professionally (but over-) written speech. "People of San Francisco"—pause, look at notes, blink back tears—"I want to thank you for the tremendous outpouring of support for me at my time of loss. . . . The death of my fiancée has been difficult . . . but I appreciate all your good wishes. . . . I am confident the San Francisco Police Department will fully investigate her death and apprehend the perpetrator in a swift and timely manner. . . ."

I couldn't stand it any longer. Why wasn't anyone asking questions? Chloe had said he'd only be available for five minutes. At this point, I had nothing to lose.

"Mr. Mayor!" I called out, interrupting his prefab talk. "Do you know of any reason why someone might want to murder Ikea Takeda?"

The mayor blinked, put a hand over his brow, and tried to see who had asked such a boldly rude question. In the harsh lights, I doubted he could see me, but I pulled back behind another reporter in an attempt to hide, just in case.

"Uh . . . ," he stammered, not having any notes on the sudden subject change to refer to. "Who's—"

"Is it true," I continued, lowering my booming voice an octave so he wouldn't recognize it, "that you and your fiancée were arguing over something the night of the surprise wedding and that—"

Someone grabbed me by the shoulder and pulled me back from the crowd—a man in a black suit. His twin joined him, and together they "escorted" me from the rotunda and "helped" me through the door and onto the sidewalk.

Rubbing my shoulder where the first guy had grabbed me with "unnecessary force," I headed back to my car. I sat in the front seat a few minutes, shaking my head at my stupidity. What had that accomplished, other than to make me look like a fool, get me thrown out of the building, and no doubt draw sympathy for the mayor? If he were really as devastated as he'd proclaimed to the press, he sure didn't look like it. Maybe he was good at hiding his feelings when he was in front of the public. Maybe he was good at hiding more than his feelings. . . .

As I removed the hat and switched on the ignition, I only hoped that Chloe hadn't recognized me. If she had, I could cross her off as a source of more information. And at the moment, she was my best bet for uncovering any of the mayor's secrets.

# Chapter 21

*PARTY PLANNING TIP #21:*

*To personalize your party for the guest of honor, secretly interview friends and family to find out little-known facts—such as her first job, his first car, their first date. Then use those telling details to make the event memorable.*

"*Cherchez la femme*," I said aloud as I got into my MINI Cooper. *Look for the woman*. This advice had certainly been true in *The Maltese Falcon*. Brigid O'Shaughnessy was the real clue, not the black bird. Hitchcock had called this the McGuffin, and defined it as something that seemed to be the pivotal point of the mystery, when in fact it was simply misdirection—there was so much more going on.

In this case, there were two femmes—both connected to the mayor.

Speaking of femmes, I made a U-turn out of the dead-end street in front of city hall and headed up Van Ness to my mother's care facility. I parked on a side street and walked half a block to her building, inhaling the smell of roast beef and gravy coming from Tommy's Joynt, my mother's favorite lunch spot. Entering the three-story renovated Victorian home, I waved to Holly Dietz, one of the LVNs at the front desk. The tantalizing aroma of Tommy's Joynt evaporated among the heavy odor of cleaning products, mildew, and left-over cafeteria food.

"She's in the community room," Holly called cheerily. It took a special kind of nurse to work in a facility like this, and I was grateful for her.

I spun on my flat Mary Jane heels and headed over to the "Grand Parlor," where half a dozen elderly men and women were sitting in comfy chairs, chatting, playing games, or watching TV. My mother, who never watched TV, didn't like small talk, and only hosted games—never played them—sat alone, hunched over a craft table filled with papers.

"Hi, Mom!" I said almost as cheerily as the nurse. Sitting down opposite her, I gave her a quick once-over in an attempt to evaluate her status. Today she wore a bright orange floral dress and scuffed black heels; she'd twisted her hair into a French roll and tied a green ribbon in it. Her makeup, albeit a little heavy for daytime, was expertly done, and her manicured nails were painted bright red. A throwback to the Donna Reed/June Cleaver days, my mother was not the type to sit in a housecoat and slippers with no makeup or unstyled hair, no matter what the circumstances. She had "an image to preserve," she often told me.

She looked up as if she'd been expecting me—and I was late.

"About time," she said, placing a colorful piece of paper in a large binder.

"Whatcha doing?" I asked, noticing a pile of old photographs taken at some of her favorite parties years ago. I cleared a small shoe box off of a chair, set it on the floor, and sat down opposite her.

"I'm scrapbooking. It's the latest thing. I'm putting all my party pictures together so I can present them to clients and show them what I've done."

"Great idea," I said, sifting through a few of the photos. There were two schools of thought in dealing with Alzheimer's patients—either try to bring them back to reality or go along with their fantasies. I chose the latter. She was happier that way.

I looked down at the floor. Next to her feet were three more shoe boxes filled with more photos. "Wow, you've got a lot."

"That's why I'm making each scrapbook a different theme—just like a party. This one is for my political parties. That one will be for my surprise parties, those over there for weddings and showers, and then I'll make some for my children's parties." She pointed to a stack of binders on a chair next to her. It would take her years to finish all her planned projects.

I noticed her *How to Host a Killer Party* book lying open, facedown, on the table. I lifted it up and found it had been cut to pieces.

She caught my surprised look and said, "Oh, I'm adding pages from my book. . . ." She took the book from me, flipped through what was left of it, and found the page on party themes. She ripped it out. "Like this."

She began cutting out the page with scalloped scissors. While she worked, I watched her artfully arrange photos, party tips from her book, and what she called "embellishments" on the page. I had to admit, she had a knack for this. My mother seemed to be good at whatever she did, even with Alzheimer's.

I lifted a shoe box, set it on my lap, and flicked through the pictures. Some were familiar to me and brought back memories from my childhood and teen years; others were new to me. I was halfway through the box when I discovered a photo of a man I recognized. I pulled it out and held the faded snapshot up for my mother to see.

"Mom, do you know this man?"

Over the top of her decorative reading glasses she glanced at the photo of the man in a military uniform. Returning to work, she said, "Sure. That's Gene. He was such a sweetheart."

Gene? "You mean, you knew Admiral Eugene Stadelhofer?"

"Of course. Handsome, isn't he? I hosted a party for him a few years back, when he retired from the navy. Why? Do you know him too?"

I inserted the photo back into the box. "He's . . . uh, trying to get the mayor to erect some kind of military monument on Treasure Island. Did you know him well?"

She looked at me and smiled wickedly.

Oh. My. God. Don't tell me he'd been another one of her many "paramours," as she called them.

I set the box on the floor and stood up. "Well, I can see you're busy, so I'm going to take off. I'll come again soon, okay?"

She nodded, concentrating on her page layout.

"Do you need anything?"

"No, I—" she started to say, then added, "Oh! More of this." She held up some sort of tape dispenser. "I go through them like chocolate."

Chocolate. Great. "Okay, Mom. Well, take care of yourself. You look wonderful."

"You too," she said, peering over her glasses. "And say hello to Gene for me when you see him."

I headed for the door, then had a thought and turned back to my mother. "Mom? Would you like to go on an outing with me, maybe later today?"

She brightened. "Certainly, dear. I always enjoy our outings. Where are we going this time? Sausalito? Tiburon? Angel Island?"

"How about Yerba Buena Island?" I said. It was about time my mother saw her old "paramour" again.

Driving home, I thought about my mother's connection to the admiral. What had their relationship been? More than I wanted to know, that's for sure. But maybe she could help me get the opportunity to question the admiral about his ties to Treasure Island—and possibly Ikea Takeda. Maybe the admiral had more of a connection to Ikea than anyone suspected. . . .

A chill ran up my back, and I shuddered. Was it possible the admiral had something to do with Ikea's murder? Even more disturbing—could my mother have been romantically involved . . . with a potential murderer?

Whoa. Where had that thought come from?

When I arrived at my desk, the office across from mine was curiously deserted. Where was our crime scene cleaner? Cleaning up after another crime? There was something about that man I didn't trust. And yet he seemed so—

The phone rang.

Not in the mood to talk, I let the machine answer. Turned out to be another request for a party, this time from someone at Pier 39. I wondered what kind of event this tourist area wanted. Didn't matter, as long as it didn't involve another body.

I got out my notes and updated the list of people I wanted to question about the mayor and his connection with Ikea and Andi. Although I was tempted to put a big fat circle around the mayor's name, it seemed unlikely that he'd kill his own fiancée—at a wedding he himself had planned. Still, stranger things had happened, especially in the name of passion. Maybe she'd said or done something that really, really ticked him off. And maybe the wedding party was just a cover.

But how did Rocco tie in to all this? Although he had means and opportunity, he had no motive—that I knew of. Still, the physical evidence didn't bode well for him.

I was convinced Ikea's drowning and Andi's car crash had been misdirections. Poison via Rocco's chocolates was the real MO. But there was no way I was going to add Rocco's name to the suspect list—he was a victim, I was certain of that. The only other possibility was that he'd attempted suicide. But why?

I didn't buy it.

Almost as if I were channeling automatic writing from the dead, I found myself writing down the name of the mystery man who'd shown up right about the time all this was taking place: Brad Matthews.

He'd been at the party: opportunity.

He had access to all kinds of chemicals and poisons: means.

But what would be his motive?

If he knew the mayor, he probably knew Ikea too.

How well?

And Andi?

I grabbed a black marker and obliterated his name. Underneath the heavy black mark, I jotted the initials KTBNL—Killer to Be Named Later. I didn't want him to know I suspected him if he stumbled onto my notes. Meanwhile, I'd have to watch my back around him. If Brad was involved in this, I could be in big trouble.

Back to the femmes fatales. I had to find out more about Ikea in order to know who had the strongest motive. And I had to find a credible link between her and Andi Sax.

There's a saying popular in my former teaching occupation: "Go ask the administrative assistant." As Brad had pointed out, admins, including those at the university, were the ones to befriend if you wanted anything. Mine, Linda Barnes, had managed to get around all sorts of red tape, while keeping me supplied with materials I needed. She was also a great source of information about the subculture of academia. I learned from her that I might lose my job long before I was officially fired.

Chloe had been a good source of info on Ikea, but I had a feeling she knew more. I wondered if Andi Sax had someone like an administrative assistant. Surely she couldn't have been the most successful event planner in the Bay Area all by herself.

I turned to the computer and did an Internet search for her company, Party People, then clicked the link to her site. The dazzling display, full of floating balloons and flashing lights, listed links to many of her biggest parties, along with her lengthy bio, suggested party themes, information on how to hire her, and her Party Talk blog. I scrolled down to the bottom of the home page and found, in fine print, a snail mail address. Andi had an office in Sausalito, just on the other side of the Golden Gate Bridge.

Grabbing my purse and a copy of the address, I was on my way out the front door when I bumped into Brad—literally—who was headed inside. As I hit solid muscle, I caught a whiff of lime. Beer? Or aftershave?

"Whoa! Where's the fire?" he said, backing down the front steps. Brad Matthews always seemed to be running me off the path.

"Uh, I . . . was just about to run some errands. Party stuff, you know."

He nodded a *Yeah, sure* kind of nod.

"What about you? In a rush to get back to work?" I said, massaging my shoulder where he'd slammed into me. If I didn't stop getting hurt in the shoulder, I'd soon be needing rotator cuff surgery.

"Nope. Got some information for you." He rubbed his chin. I was beginning to wonder what this "tell" meant—that he felt a little self-conscious? Or he was about to tell a lie?

"Oh? What did you find out?" I asked suspiciously.

He stuffed a hand in his pocket, pulled out a wrinkled piece of paper, and glanced at it. "Your friend, Rocco? Same poison, same MO—chocolates."

I felt my stomach drop. I'd suspected as much, but the confirmation still hit hard. "How did you find out?"

"I have my sources," he said mysteriously as he stuffed the note back in his pocket.

I looked down at him as he stood on the bottom step. "The police just *happened* to tell you this?"

He shrugged. "Like I said, they know me from my cleaning business."

"So, how's Rocco? Any news?"

He shook his head. "Still unconscious."

Poor Rocco. He didn't deserve this. I'd stop by the hospital later and check in on him. I stepped down the three stairs and started for my car.

Brad caught me by the arm. "Hey, wait a minute. It's your turn."

I looked at the grip he had on me. He released my arm and crossed his own arms, causing his biceps to double in size. The guy worked out, and his white T-shirt didn't hide anything.

"My turn to what?" I said, stroking my arm as if he'd seriously wounded me.

He rolled his eyes. "Your visit with the mayor's chick. What happened?"

"Oh." I sighed. "Not much. She was kind of tight-lipped—you know how it is with them." I decided not to mention the press conference fiasco.

Brad set his jaw and waited.

I sighed again. "Honest. She said there might have been some special interest groups urging Ikea to influence the mayor about the island, but she didn't have anything concrete."

"Hmmm," Brad said, rubbing the stubble on his chin. "Think she's hot for him?"

I laughed. "Who? Chloe? For the mayor? No way. She's not his type."

"Oh, you can tell people's types?"

"I read people like fortune cookies. I have a background

in psychology, remember. Abnormal psychology, as a matter of fact." I eyed him.

"Really?" he said, his voice full of doubt.

I looked down at his shoes. "New Balance athletic shoes. Expensive. Good for both work and play. But awfully clean, even for a crime scene cleaner."

He checked his shoes, then looked up at me and smiled, obviously impressed. "What do your shoes say?"

I glanced at my black, round-toed Mary Janes. "Isn't it obvious? Comfortable, casual, but still feminine." Talking about my own shoes reminded me of my skates—and the chocolates that someone had placed inside. *Better get moving, Pres*, I told myself, *before Detective Melvin shows up with a pair of prison slippers.* Definitely not my style.

He watched me as I moved on to my car.

"MINI Cooper, eh?" he called out. "Does what you drive mean something too?"

"Sure. It means I'm smart with money, but playful, independent, yet flirty. . . ." I stopped before I told him too much. Instead, I nodded toward his SUV parked next to mine. "Your SUV? All business. Dirty—could use a wash. A magnetic sign for easy removal. And paneled—no way to see what you're hiding inside."

He laughed. "That's just for work."

"Really? So what's your other car?"

"A Harley."

It figured.

As I drove over the Golden Gate Bridge toward the boutique town of Sausalito, I wondered if tourists were a little disappointed to find the famous Art Deco bridge painted bright orange instead of gold. What they didn't know was that the bridge had been named after the Golden Gate Strait—the entrance to the San Francisco Bay—not the color.

In addition to walking across the Golden Gate, committing suicide from the bridge has been a popular activity.

Someone once said, "The Golden Gate Bridge is to suicides what Niagara Falls is to honeymooners." Years ago, one of my college friends jumped from the bridge just before finals. It haunts me to this day. I can't think of a worse way to die, but when she talked about it a few days before she jumped, she'd romanticized it, imagining it to be some kind of swan dive. In essence, it was. Still, even though we'd talked about it, I didn't think she would follow through.

Ironically, she'd planned to be a psychiatrist.

There had been lawsuits and demands to erect barriers—one led by my mother—and a recent exposé by a renegade filmmaker who had actually videotaped jumpers in the act. But even after the city put up the barriers, the suicides continued.

As an abnormal psychology instructor, I retained morbid facts like these: A bridge jump is called a 10-21 in police code; every two weeks someone jumps from the bridge; there have been twelve hundred jumps since the bridge opened; only twenty-six people have survived.

And the most common fear among San Franciscans is gephyrophobia—the fear of crossing bridges. I have a touch of it—especially when being run off the road by a white SUV.

Another irony—now I lived in the middle of a bridge. In earthquake country.

In truth, death by jumping isn't romantic at all. People don't hit the water cleanly, like an Olympic high diver. After the four-second fall, they hit the surface at about seventy-five miles per hour, and die of multiple blunt-force injuries—bruised, broken ribs; lacerated spleens, lungs, and hearts; bleeding from the ears; snapped vertebrae, ruptured livers, and heads smashed like day-old Halloween pumpkins. According to those few who have survived, many change their minds—just after they let go. For most, it's too late. And if the bodies aren't found immediately, they sustain "severe marine depredation"—shark attacks, feeding crabs, and other indecencies. That's the kind of stuff kids remember from their field trips. And every time I drive over the bridge, I think about all that crap.

When I reached the end of the span, I spotted the familiar rainbow tunnel that leads to Sausalito. Driving out the other side, I was greeted by houseboats on the right and stilted houses on the left. In this cute little bayside town, neither type of lodging came cheap.

After cruising the cute downtown area three times in search of parking, I finally found a car pulling out from a metered space close to my destination and hovered until I could take over the spot. I got out of the car and looked up at the three-story artsy-craftsy building with boutiques—cookie boutiques, clothing boutiques, jewelry and juice boutiques, scrimshaw and T-shirt boutiques, even dog and cat boutiques. I thought about picking up some new toys for Cairo, Fatman, and Thursby, but a glance at a price tag for a fake mouse sent me running from the place.

I found Party People on the third floor of the high-rent building. The door stood open to a cluttered store with narrow aisles filled with party supplies. A woman wearing a plastic tiara sat behind a cramped counter covered with Halloween party favors. Fake lips. Rubber ears. Bleeding fingers. The kind of crap I love.

She looked up from an Oriental Trading Company catalog when I stepped on the PARTY HERE! mat, which instantly played a version of Eddie Murphy's "Party All the Time!"

That would get annoying fast.

I looked around, envious of all the party props available. A life-sized Brad Pitt posed between Angelina Jolie and Jennifer Aniston, and other giant cutouts of famous stars were propped here and there. Mylar balloons in various shapes and metallic colors hung from the ceiling, above piles of Balloon Time! helium kits. Aisles were packed with themed paper products and props, everything from tropical luaus to over-the-hill birthdays. Apparently Andi's business had been doing well for her to have so much party stuff on hand. I could barely afford to order it over the Internet in time for each event.

"Can I help you find anything?" the woman said, resting her hand on the catalog. Her name tag, pinned to a pink top that read "Princess in Waiting" in rhinestones, said "Staci McLaughlin." She looked familiar. I wondered if I'd met her somewhere.

"Yes, hi. I'm Presley Parker."

The woman sucked in a breath at the sound of my name and sat up. "Oh dear."

Apparently she'd heard of me. "I was sorry to hear about Andi," I said quickly. "Are you her . . . partner?"

She stood, closing the catalog slowly, and came out from behind the counter. The pink top was filled to capacity by her ample bosom and matched a long silky pink skirt, also studded with rhinestones. Pink ballet slippers peeked out from under the hem of her skirt. I felt underdressed in my black jeans, blue SFSU T-shirt, and sockless Mary Janes. "You're the one who took over planning the mayor's wedding, aren't you?"

I nodded, distracted by her costume. "Love your outfit," I said, trying not to giggle.

"Andi likes—er, liked me to dress up for the customers. Helps sell the merchandise. Today I'm Pretty, Pretty Princess." She spun around, then curtseyed.

"Very . . . pretty," I said, mortified for her. I glanced around the crowded store to collect my thoughts, then turned back to her. "I wondered if you could tell me a little about Andi. I'm trying to help the police find out who might have had a reason to harm her."

She shook her head, nearly dislodging her crown, and took a moment to push it back into her puffy hair. "They've been here already—the police. I told them what I could, which wasn't much. It's all so sad."

Funny. She didn't look all that sad in her pink getup. "What did you tell them?"

She took in a deep breath before speaking. "That I don't know anyone who would want to kill her, if that's what you're asking. Not even after that thing with the mayor."

"That thing?"

"You know. That little tiff she had with him a couple of weeks before the wedding. But—"

"What kind of tiff?"

She shrugged. "I overheard her arguing with him on the phone, something about how ridiculous the wedding was becoming. You know, the ball-and-chain theme. Having it on Alcatraz. Andi thought it was all terribly tacky. Andi didn't do tacky. But when he fired her, she was pretty upset. Then hiring you only made it worse."

I forced an apologetic smile. "Sorry about that, but I had nothing to do with any of it. I just got the call one day—"

She waved me silent. "I know, I know. It's not your fault. Andi could be a bit of a diva. Actually, we aren't—weren't—exactly partners. She did all the party planning; I run the boutique. But I helped her out a lot. And, of course, she had a freelance staff that worked for her too."

"Freelance?"

"Oh, no one permanent, other than me." She gave a little princess laugh. "Truth is, no one would work for her for very long. Like I said, a bit of a diva. I only got along with her because we kept our businesses separate. And she knew if she didn't treat me well, I wouldn't give her a big discount on all the party stuff she needed."

"Do you have any names of these freelancers?"

She shook her head. "They came from a temp agency. No one lasted more than once or twice. Except me. Like I said, I helped out when I could."

"Hmmm." I started down one of the aisles, hoping to find a clue to the mysterious Andi Sax. All I saw were festive supplies, party props, and costume rentals. One costume in particular caught my eye. I turned to Staci, who'd returned to her perch behind the counter and was fiddling with a bloody, severed arm.

"This Miss Marple costume. It looks just like one I saw at the mayor's wedding. Did it come from here?"

She shrugged. "Could have," she said, still focused on the rubber hand.

"Do you know who might have rented it?"

She shook her head so abruptly this time, one end of the tiara fell over her forehead. She shoved it back into place with a little more force. "I'd have to look. . . ."

I stared at her. She wouldn't meet my eyes. I leaned over the counter, in her face. "Staci?" She looked up. "Would you mind checking to see who rented this costume?"

She dropped the fake arm and hung her head. "Oh, I suppose it doesn't matter now."

Puzzled about her response, I asked, "What are you talking about?"

"Andi . . . she sort of hired me to wear the costume. . . ."

"So you could attend the party!" I finished her sentence, then stood back, stunned. "You were there to spy on me?"

She shrugged. "Andi wanted to know how it went. She was so jealous, you know?"

I picked up the severed arm and slapped its hand menacingly in mine. "Did she want you to sabotage the party, Staci?" I thought about the poisoned chocolates. Maybe Andi had poisoned them. But then she wouldn't have eaten them herself. Would Staci have done it?

"Oh no. No. I'd never do that. I was just her eyes and ears. She knew she couldn't be caught there, but not that many people know me. And she paid me a nice bonus, you know. I figured it was harmless." She looked at the arm I was batting in my hand. "Oh dear. I shouldn't have said anything. Especially about Andi. I don't like to speak ill of the dead. Poor thing."

I raised the hand up to face her, as if it might strike her if it had a life of its own. "Did Andi say anything about me, specifically?"

She eyed the hand and laughed nervously. "Oh yeah. Like I said, when you got the mayor's job, she was royally pissed. Checked you out on the Net. Wanted to know all about you. She saw you as a major threat to her future business. Said something about going over and having a little chat with you."

I thought about her body being found on TI. Apparently she *had* been on her way to see me. For a "little chat"? Why? Was she going to threaten me? Try to bully me out of doing any more business?

Or had there been another reason?

I set the fake bloodied arm on the counter and stepped back. "Do the police know you were at the party, Staci?"

She shook her head. "I was too embarrassed to tell them. See, the thing is, I left before the mayor arrived. I got seasick coming over on the ferry and took the next one back to the city."

Delicia had said she thought she'd seen a ferryboat return—with a woman on board.

"Can you prove that?"

"Oh sure. When I stepped off the ferry, I saw the mayor and his fiancée boarding—although I kept out of sight so they wouldn't notice me. I looked pretty real as Miss Marple. Anyway, I got a cab back to Sausalito. I suppose you can call the cab company. I'm sure the driver would remember me. I took off my wig and wiped off my makeup in the car."

"What did you do when you got back?"

"Went home. I didn't want Andi to know I'd come back."

"And you can prove that too?"

"Well, my husband was at home, watching *Survivor*. He can vouch for me. Although sometimes he falls asleep watching TV."

Good heavens. This woman was something else. I headed

for the door. "That's quite a story, Staci, but you'd better let Detective Melvin know. He's bound to find out anyway."

"I know, I know. The whole thing's got me a little discombobulated. Until this thing is solved, I told my husband I'm sleeping with the lights on and the doors double-locked."

I nodded.

"And I've given up chocolate."

I blinked. Apparently she knew about the poisoned chocolates. That reminded me. "One more thing. Did Andi ever do parties for any of the mayor's acquaintances, like . . ." I pulled out my list and read the names: "Dakota Hunter, Eugene Stadelhofer, Xtreme Siouxie, or Lucas Cruz?"

"Oh yes. She hosted an Over-the-Hill birthday party for Jack Jason, that TV star, last month. It was given by Spaz Cruz. Really lavish. Held at a funeral home, of all places. Everyone wore black, gave funny eulogies while Jack lay in a casket. He kept sitting up and making jokes."

"Andi didn't consider that tacky?"

"I guess not. Anyway, it was a great party—one of her best."

"What about Dakota Hunter?"

"He's the Indian, I mean, Native American, right? The one who wants to build a casino on Treasure Island? She met with him about hosting a Vegas-style party if the Indians—Native Americans—got the land. But it was still in the planning stages."

"Xtreme Siouxie?"

She stuck out her lower lip. "No, that name doesn't ring a bell. Wait—is she the gal who does all that crazy protesting?"

"That's the one."

"No, Andi never did a party for her. That gal nearly ruined an important event Andi was hosting for a big meat company. She came running in, naked except for a cowhide draped over her. And she'd sprayed red paint on the hide to make it look like the cow was bleeding. It was a fright."

This, coming from a woman who was fondling a bloodied, disembodied arm.

"Luckily the meat people were used to it—they get protesters all the time. The security guards carted her away."

Just like at the wedding reception. So Andi had had to deal with the extremist too. I checked my list for the last name. "How about Admiral Eugene Stadelhofer?" I thought about my mother, who had hosted an affair for him years ago—and possibly had another kind of affair with the admiral.

Staci shook her head. "Don't think so. She did a few military parties at the Presidio and Yerba Buena Island, but I couldn't tell you for who specifically. He might have been involved."

"If you think of anything more, will you give me a call?" I started to give her my card, then decided to write my number on one of her sticky notes. It didn't seem appropriate to leave a card with the words "Killer Party" on it.

Talk about tacky.

# Chapter 22

*PARTY PLANNING TIP #22:*

*With a few creative touches, you can transform the party room into Frankenstein's laboratory, Cinderella's castle, Indiana Jones's archaeological dig, or a CSI crime scene—and transport your guests to another time and place.*

Staci McLaughlin had been helpful.

Too helpful?

I wondered what the detective would think of her story. Did she really leave the party? Or did she just say that? With everyone in costume, it would have been hard to tell who belonged and who didn't. And spouses were known to lie for their loved ones.

I thought of the mayor. Spouses were also known to kill their loved ones.

Apparently there was no love lost between Staci and Andi, but it didn't sound like she disliked her coworker enough to kill her. After all, a good portion of her income came from Andi's purchases of party supplies. And Staci didn't appear to have any plans to take over Andi's business. Or did she?

This whole thing was getting complicated. Every time I talked to one possible suspect, another one popped up. How did the police keep it simple? Oh yeah. They blamed the most obvious suspect. That would be me. I reflexively checked my cell phone clock—time was running out. I felt beads of sweat break out on my forehead and wiped them off with the back of my hand.

Sitting in the cozy comfort and temporary safety of my MINI outside Andi's building, I looked at the list of addresses I'd printed out from the computer for the people I wanted to interview.

Dakota Hunter. He lived up in the Gold Country. Too far to go today, but I'd get to him ASAP.

Lucas Cruz. His film company was located in my own backyard. I'd stop by on my way home.

Eugene Stadelhofer. He still lived on Yerba Buena Island in upscale military housing, where all the high-ranking officers once lived. Before I went there, I'd pick up my mother to help me break the ice.

For now, that left Xtreme Siouxie, aka Susan Steinhardt. Her address was listed as the High Times Commune in the Haight, hippie heaven circa 1969. I revved up the MINI and drove along the scenic Sausalito highway back to the Golden Gate Bridge, stealing a glimpse at the peaceful sailboats in the bay.

In its heyday, the Haight-Ashbury was the place to find anything counterculture—psychedelic clothes, music, and drugs. The area still reeks of incense, weed, and dog droppings, even though an influx of new-age hippies had joined the aging hippies.

As I turned onto Haight Street, I saw balding men with long ponytails and leathery skin, and women with graying hair in tie-dyed skirts and worn Birkenstocks. Most were sipping espressos at non-chain coffeehouses, while reading well-worn copies of books by Kesey and Kerouac. And everyone seemed to own a dog.

Tourists still came to see the show, but exclusive boutiques, high-end vintage clothing stores, and hip—not hippy—restaurants had replaced much of the free-love culture of the sixties. In addition to getting pierced, you can now get tattooed, buy old clothes at higher prices, and obtain marijuana legally. The Haight was now one of the most commercial centers in the city, in spite of the fact that you can also still purchase an LP, give money to a panhandler, or find "paraphernalia."

I drove by a holistic healing center, an anarchist bookstore, a bead store, a Tibetan boutique, a tattoo parlor, a costume shop, a medical marijuana outlet, the Grateful Dead house, and nine cafés—none of them Starbucks—on my way to find a parking spot.

The High Times Commune, an old Victorian painted every color of the rainbow, was located on a side street. Tie-dyed sheets covered the windows, and the door sported a dozen bumper stickers, mostly political clichés. My favorites: "Save the Bay; Drink Hemp Tea," "Compost Happens," and from the Bush days, "Dr. Jack Kevorkian for White House Physician." I felt like I'd gone back in time.

Stepping over a German shepherd/rottweiler mix sleeping on the second of five cement stairs, I knocked and rang the bell. A towering emaciated man with blond-turning-to-gray wispy hair tied back in a long, thin ponytail answered the door. He wore ragged jeans and a torn T-shirt with the words "More Cowbell" on the front. I couldn't begin to guess his age—anywhere from thirty- to fiftysomething. The lines in his face could have come from poor skin care, too much smoke, or simply aging.

"Yeah?" he said. His eyes were bloodshot, his teeth stained, and I had a feeling his frown was permanent.

"Hi, I'm looking for Siouxie."

"What for?" He reeked of pot.

"Shut up, Stone," came a voice from inside the house. Siouxie appeared from behind the half-open door, dressed more normally than her usual getup. She wore an ankle-length retro floral dress, gauzy and too large for her tiny frame. No doubt she'd picked it up in one of the Haight's secondhand stores. The contrast between her youth and the old clothes was arresting. She didn't look any older than a high school girl, although the newspaper had listed her age as twenty.

The man stumbled back, and Siouxie took his place at the door. "I'm Siouxie. Sorry about him. He's a few ounces short of a kilo." She brought her thumb and index finger to her lips and pretended to inhale. "Are you from the welfare department? I haven't been getting my checks. That's why I called."

I shook my head. "I'm Presley Parker. I'm looking into the death of Ikea Takeda."

She jerked the door tight against her side. "You're a cop?"

I laughed. "Oh no, nothing like that. I'm a . . ." I almost said *event planner*, then realized it sounded ridiculous. Why would an event planner be investigating a murder?

"I'm a psychologist. I'm sort of helping the police." Could I be arrested for impersonating an assistant to the cops? Hell, better to be arrested for fraud than murder.

Instead of inviting me in, she stepped out, closing the door behind her. Apparently she didn't trust psychologists either.

She sat on the porch step and began petting the dog, which until this moment I'd thought might be dead. It hadn't moved a muscle.

I sat next to her, carefully eyeing some dog poop not far away. "I'm trying to find out what I can about Ikea Takeda—the woman who was supposed to be the bride at her surprise wedding. Did you know her at all?"

"Why are you asking me?" she said casually, still petting the dog. She looked so innocent rubbing the animal's black and brown fur, it was hard to believe she'd been dressed like a blistered corpse the other night.

"Because you were at her wedding the night she died."

She stopped petting and stared up at me. Her green eyes

flashed in the late afternoon light. "Wait a minute. I was only there to make a statement. That's how I fly. You can't think I had something to do with her death?"

"No, no, of course not." Maybe. "But you might have seen something that night that could help." Like someone poisoning chocolates. "Does anything stand out in your mind?" Say, murder?

She shrugged. "All I saw was a bunch of rich drunk people, oblivious to the fact that wildlife is dying on Treasure Island while they get wasted on Alcatraz. That's the only reason I was there—to get Mayor Greed to save TI."

I nodded. "How's that going?"

"Sucks. Ikea was supposed to talk to the mayor and get him to come around. My group, Endangered Earth, paid her a lot of money for her help. Now everyone's mad at me because the bitch is dead, the money is gone, and we've got squat."

"You *paid* Ikea?" I asked, surprised at this revelation.

"Duh," she said, playing with the beaded necklaces around her neck. "Isn't that the way things really work in this capitalist society? She promised—practically guaranteed—the mayor would agree to our demands—I mean, requests. Said she had a lot of influence over him. Even told me to show up for that little demo I put on."

"She *told* you to come and do that?" Holy crap. I guess she didn't know it would be her wedding reception entertainment.

She laughed. "How else do you think I got into the party?"

"Why did she want you there?"

"She said my demonstration—I call it performance protest—would help sway the mayor to my side. She was supposed to talk to him right after the gig. Said she'd have it locked in and TI would be turned into a natural habitat for the seals and shit, after all the toxic waste was cleaned up."

"And for that you paid her? How much?"

Siouxie patted the dog. "A lot."

"How much is a lot?"

She met my eyes. "A lot lot."

"How does a group like yours get a lot lot?"

She laughed. "Bake sales."

"Drugs?"

"No!" she snapped. Was she overreacting? She stood, brushed off the back of her dress, and stepped up to the front door. "I mean, well, I work at Pot for Patients, the medical marijuana outlet. Part-time. But that's not dealing."

"You get welfare, but you work part-time?" I asked.

She shrugged. "You just have to know how to work the system, you know? Listen, I gotta go. You're a psychologist, right? So everything I just told you is in confidence, right? I don't want anyone to know I paid that bee-otch all that money. Someone might start asking the wrong questions."

I rose and wiped off the back of my black jeans, praying I hadn't sat in something. Just to make sure, I pulled my T-shirt down over my butt. Ignoring her question, I asked, "So after you paid Ikea, you found out she wasn't going to help you after all?"

She spun around. "Anything Ikea did, she did for herself. She couldn't have cared less about doing the right thing for the planet—not even for a bagful of cash. Unfortunately, I figured that out a little too late. Stupid me."

She turned the knob. I took a step toward her. "Susan, where did you go that night, after your 'performance'?"

She looked startled. "How did you know my real name?"

"One of the newspaper articles mentioned it."

Nodding, she pressed her lips tightly together, then said, "I came back here, of course. I wasn't about to hang around for champagne and cake—" She stopped suddenly. "Wait a minute. You really *do* think I had something to do with her death. Now you're asking me if I have an alibi? Fuck off, you psycho headshrinker."

Siouxie stepped through the front door, then turned to the dog and said, "Cujo! Sic 'er!" before slamming the door shut.

I looked at the dog, ready to run, my heart pounding.

The dog lifted his head, looked at me, then laid his head back down.

And farted.

# *Chapter 23*

*PARTY PLANNING TIP #23:*

*Deal with party crashers quickly, quietly, and discreetly.*

*You want to read about your event in the society section of the newspaper, not in the police blotter—or the obituaries.*

While driving back to TI, I added Susan's name to my short but growing list of possible suspects. The young woman had a motive—she hated Ikea. And she had opportunity—she'd been invited to "crash" the party. As for method, she could easily have poisoned the chocolates when no one was looking. No one noticed her until she began her "performance."

And she'd tried to bribe Ikea for control over TI. She'd paid a lot of money—*whose* money was still in question—but hadn't gotten what she wanted. Had Siouxie killed her after she learned Ikea wasn't going to follow through?

As for the money, was Siouxie selling drugs to support her causes? In addition to defrauding the welfare department, she was working part-time at Pot for Patients. Perhaps she also did a little embezzling? Sold some on the side? Her house had certainly reeked of the stuff.

The fog was rolling in over the Bay Bridge, bringing with it an eerie, luminous cast to the evening. I checked my cell phone clock. Good God. It was after seven. Too late to track down anyone else. The rest would have to wait until tomorrow.

I rubbed the back of my neck, stiff from the tension of the day. And I was hungry. I could hear my stomach growling over the Morrissey song on my radio. No doubt I probably had a hundred messages waiting for me back at my office. Passing up the turnoff for Yerba Buena Island, I took Avenue of the Palms to the Snack Shack, bought a crab Louis and a beer to go, and headed for the office barracks.

As I headed into the building, Berkeley was on his way out, camera in tow. "You're baaaccckkkk!" Berk said, misquoting either *The Shining* or *Poltergeist*. He held the door for me. "Thought maybe you'd skipped town, gone to Ar-gen-tin-a." He sang the last word, à la *Evita*.

"Errands," I said, to avoid a long explanation. I glanced at his ubiquitous camera and remembered something. "Berkeley, did the cops take all your footage from the party?"

"Yep," he said, then grinned.

"You made a copy!"

"I soitenly did," he said, nodding like Curly Howard and beaming with pride at his cleverness.

"Can I borrow it?"

"Help yourself. It's in my office. Top drawer of the filing cabinet. Not quite ready for your close-up yet, but you'll get the idea."

"No problem. I just want to see what you've got. Is your door locked?"

"Yeah, but Raj has a key. Tell him I said to let you in." He gave me Spock's "Live long and prosper" hand sign.

Remembering the last time I'd asked Raj to open a door, I said, "Would you mind telling him? He's gotten tight with the keys lately."

Berkeley nodded and headed out the door to his VW camper, calling back, "E.T., phone Raj. Gotta run, Forrest, run. But I'll be back," he said, switching from *E.T.* to *Forrest Gump* to *Terminator*. It was mind-boggling—I didn't know who I was talking to anymore.

I yelled back the titles, plus *The Three Stooges*, *Sunset Boulevard*, and *Star Trek*, before closing the front door, thankful Name That Movie was over. Glancing at the other offices as I headed for my own, I saw that Delicia was out—who knew where—Raj was just locking up, and the office across from mine was dark.

"Ms. Presley," Raj called from down the hall. "I am opening Mr. Berkeley's door for you now. But you must be remembering to lock it. I cannot be responsible for it if it is left unlocked, you see."

"Thanks, Raj," I said, unlocking my own office. "I promise. Where are you off to?"

"Actually, the Jack Jason movie is filming at Pier 39 tonight. Perhaps they are having a part for a security guard again. But my cell phone will be available for your call, if you are needing me."

I nodded as I slung my purse on my desk and set down my salad and beer. "Good luck. Break a leg."

Raj wrinkled his nose at me.

"It's just an expression," I explained.

"Oh, yes, yes. Well, then, you break a leg too. And an arm." He laughed as he made his way out of the building.

The office grew uncomfortably quiet. I'd never felt unsafe working in my office at night alone. Until now.

Something strange was going on and it had to do with Treasure Island itself—at least in part. I pushed the feeling aside and dug into my crab Louis, hardly tasting it. When the phone rang, cracking the silence, I jumped.

After fumbling for the phone, I said, "Hello?" I could feel my heart racing under my T-shirt. Why was I so nervous? I'd been alone in the building before. Raj was just a phone call away. And I had my plastic sword.

"Hello?" I said again. No answer.

I hung up. It rang again before I could lift my hand from the receiver. I hesitated, letting it ring a few more times, then picked it up.

"Hello?" I said slowly.

I heard a voice whisper something I couldn't make out.

"What?" I said stupidly when I should have hung up. But something about the whisper kept me on the line. What if it was Rocco calling from the hospital?

"Rocco? Is that you?"

Silence. Then the whispered voice came again. This time, in spite of the low volume, I heard it loud and clear:

"Got chocolate?"

I slammed down the phone, took a deep breath, then picked it up again, my hand shaking so hard I could barely dial Star-69. Blocked. Of course. What kind of obscene phone caller—or killer—would leave a callback number?

I slammed the phone down again.

What was that about? "Got chocolate?" As in poisoned?

Gathering my purse and food, I was about to get the hell out when I heard a noise at the front door.

Someone was jiggling the door handle.

I froze, listening, waiting for a key to unlock the door, for familiar footsteps to ring out in the reception room—the shuffle of Delicia's bunny slippers, the squeak of Berk's skull-covered Vans, the tap of Raj's steel-toed military boots.

Nothing.

I dropped my food, ducked down behind my desk, hoping whoever was there hadn't seen me through any of the windows. Of course, my office light was on. In fact, it was the only light on besides reception.

I switched it off, eased up, and tiptoed into the hallway,

hoping the old floorboards didn't give me away. Maybe the would-be intruder knew I was there, but at least he couldn't see me now. And maybe, if I was careful, I could catch a glimpse of him in the reception room light.

The reception light went off.

Shit!

The building went pitch black. My eyes searched the darkness. I felt rivulets of sweat slalom down my back. My throat went dry. I could hear my heartbeat, amplified in my chest—and hoped the intruder couldn't hear it too.

Scenes from old movies filled the blackness. I had learned a lot from those old films and had sworn off a few important things:

*Never go into the cellar in your lingerie* (*Prom Night II*).

*Never call out "Who's there?" when you're alone* (*Halloween 4*).

*Never go into a dark room unarmed* (*Urban Legends 3*).

Suddenly, in the blackness, the phone rang. An icicle stabbed my heart.

*And never answer the phone* (*Scream 1*, *2*, and *3*).

I whirled around and ran toward the kitchen. As soon as I stepped inside, I heard a loud thud at the back door.

Shit! Surrounded.

Then came more pounding—the sound of someone trying to break down the door. Shit! Shit! Was this the same person who'd been at the front door? Or were there two of them? If the place was surrounded, my only chance was to hide.

Where?

Under my desk? Been there, done that. Too obvious.

In the kitchen? There were several closets and cupboards that I could probably fit into.

Just as I started for the front office, the thudding returned at the front door, jarring my already jangled nerves. I ran back toward the kitchen, the only place I could think of to hide from the lunatic who was trying so hard to break in.

As I reached the kitchen, in the darkness I saw a light flickering from under the closed door. I froze, unable to move or think, just panting with fear.

Then I smelled the smoke!

# Chapter 24

*PARTY PLANNING TIP #24:*

*Hosting a party can be stressful for even the most experienced party hostess. Take some time to relax with a flute of champagne, a glass of wine, or, if necessary, a keg of beer.*

"Fire!" I screamed to no one. Except maybe the burglar/arsonist/killer.

Foolishly I opened the door. The kitchen was engulfed. The rest of the old wood-slatted building was a tinderbox waiting to fully ignite. I dashed to my office, already coughing, and grabbed my purse and my cell phone, knocking over the crab Louis.

I started for the front door, but smoke filled the reception area. In seconds it lit up with flames.

Trapped!

Frantic, I ran back to my office, racking my brain for another way out. The only escape I could think of was through one of the narrow office windows. I scanned the room for something to knock out the glass and grabbed a balloon tank filled with helium.

I hoisted the tank up, chest level, and stood back five feet. I was ready to toss it at the window when the glass imploded with an ear-shattering screech.

Reflexively I ducked, dropping the tank as I covered my eyes and face. It hit my foot, and I screamed in pain. As soon as I got my wits back, I spotted a crowbar lying next to me.

The killer had thrown it through my office window!

I had to get out of that room.

Brushing glass shards from my shoulders, I hobbled toward the door.

"Parker! This way!"

Turning back, I could just make out a figure through the smoke. Someone was knocking out the jagged pieces of leftover glass with some kind of stick.

Brad.

What was he doing there?

I had no choice. Smoke had completely filled the hallway. Coughing, my lungs beginning to burn, I grabbed the folding chair opposite my desk and dragged it over. Stepping up on my good foot, I climbed out, holding on to Brad's outreached hands. Halfway out I lost my balance and started to fall; he caught me, and we both tumbled to the ground.

In the near distance, while lying on top of Brad, I heard the scream of fire engines.

The flames were put out in less than twenty minutes. Brad said he'd called the fire department as soon as he'd arrived and smelled the smoke. Firefighters were crawling all over the place, squirting hoses, chopping walls, clearing out debris. Brad had quickly joined the effort, spraying what he could with the emergency can of extinguishing foam he kept in his SUV.

At least, that's what he said.

Wrapped in a blanket, I asked him, "How did you happen to show up here when the fire started?" We'd just finished exploring the water-soaked reception area—a total loss, along with the kitchen. The offices were mostly untouched, thanks to fire walls the navy had included when they'd built the structures in the forties. But the place reeked of smoke and the building was no longer secure. We'd have to relocate whatever we could salvage to the similar but unoccupied building next door.

"I had paperwork to do," Brad said, staring at the building. "When I got here and smelled the smoke, I tried to get in through the front door, then the back. Didn't you hear me pounding?"

That had been Brad? "Why didn't you use your key?"

"I tried. The lock was filled with dirt."

What? Someone had jammed the locks?

"Did you see anyone?"

He shook his head. "Too dark. I was focused on the fire and getting you out."

"How did you know I was in there?"

He nodded toward my car.

Duh.

I had run out of questions. Except one: Who had done this? It didn't look like the work of the recent vandals. This was way beyond their MO. What was the fire supposed to accomplish? Obscure evidence? Tie up loose ends?

Loose ends like me?

"I'll deal with moving my stuff in the morning," I said, handing the blanket back to the cute firefighter who'd provided it. "Right now, I'm going home to bed."

"I'm going with you," Brad said.

I looked at him with a raised eyebrow. "I don't think so."

"I mean . . . I don't think you should be alone tonight. This may have been meant for you."

"You think someone tried to . . . kill me?" I felt a wave of dizziness sweep over me at the thought I might have been the next target.

"Makes sense, doesn't it? Someone knew you were alone in there. Whoever it was did his best to trap you—setting fires at both ends—to keep you from getting out."

I took a deep breath and squared my shoulders. "Well, I can take care of myself. Really. And you didn't need to rescue me. I was just about to toss a balloon tank out the window when you threw that crowbar in. You hit my foot, by the way," I lied. I didn't intend to tell him I'd dropped the tank on my own foot. For emphasis, I limped a couple of steps.

"What were you thinking, throwing a tank full of helium? Do you know what could have happened if it had landed in the fire?"

I shivered, trying to remember what was on the warning label. Something like "Rupturing a tank may cause it to explode or to take off like a rocket. . . ."

Whoa.

Brad rubbed his arm. "Well, I'm taking you home. No argument, so let's go. I'll follow you in my SUV."

I looked at him. "You cut yourself. You're bleeding." A line of blood ran down his arm.

He shook his arm. "It's nothing."

"You need to have that looked at. Get a tetanus shot. Some antibiotics."

He shrugged. "I'm not much of a drug taker. Don't like doctors much. Beside, I'm fine. It's just a scratch."

I was too tired to argue. If nothing else, Brad seeing me home might discourage the arsonist/killer from doing anything more tonight.

As I watched him get into his car, I noticed something odd. There was no CRIME SCENE CLEANER sign on the side of his SUV. I called to him, "Where's your sign?"

"Took it off," he called back.

"Why?" I said, frowning. If I didn't stop doing that, I'd need Botox.

"I get too many weirdos asking me about my business. I only put it up there when I'm on duty. Or forget to take it off."

I flashed on the white SUV that had chased me off the road. Had it sported the sign? Or had it been removed for some reason?

I drove the short distance to my condo, past the usual empty buildings and deserted warehouses, until I entered the former military housing area. My end unit was a one-story/one-bedroom, in an eclectic neighborhood of artists, writers, and musicians, as well as recovering addicts, former homeless people, Job Corps graduates, and grassroots leaders of various causes. Duncan Grant, the geocacher, had a unit nearby, even though he stored most of his stuff in a back office at our building. Berk lived with other artists in a communelike setup a few blocks away. Rocco sometimes crashed at his ex-girlfriend's place, when he was too tired to drive to his flat in Noe Valley. Dee lived with her mother in the Mission. I had no idea where Brad slept at night.

I drove into the carport. Brad's white SUV pulled up behind me in the driveway, blocking me in. I got out of the Cooper and locked it with a button on my key.

"Thanks for seeing me home."

Brad hopped out of the SUV and closed the door. "Yeah, well, I want to make sure your place is safe—and smoke free—inside."

I started to shake my head, then nodded instead. Good point. If the killer knew where I worked, he probably knew where I lived. A cold hand gripped my spine at this thought. I wondered if I would be safe anywhere.

With Brad looking over my shoulder, I fumbled with my keys and finally managed to get the front door open. He entered first, his hand resting on what I thought was his belt buckle.

Then I remembered the gun.

"Don't shoot my cats," I whispered, following him in on tiptoe.

He sneezed. "Cats?"

"Yeah. Fatman, Cairo, and Thursby."

He looked at me. "Cute." He sneezed again.

"Don't tell me you're—"

"Aller—" He sneezed again. "—gic."

I shook my head. "Great. I hope the killer isn't armed with cat hair."

He ignored me, moving forward to check my compact living/dining/workroom, my kitchenette, and my tiny bedroom the size of a walk-in closet. I stood back, scanning the place to see if anything of value was missing. My papers were scattered on the little coffee table that served as a workstation and dining table. Party props were strewn over every available space. Dirty clothes covered most of the floor, along with random holiday books, craft magazines, and party catalogs.

"Looks like it's been trashed," Brad said, returning from the bedroom. "Did you leave a window open or something?"

I swept my arm around the room. "Actually . . . it looks just like I left it this morning. . . ."

Brad gawked at me as if he'd seen a dead man. "Tell me you're kidding."

I shrugged, picked up a pair of jeans I'd meant to put in the laundry basket, and tossed them over the back of a wooden chair I'd found at a going-out-of-business sale. I didn't think the place looked so bad. Maybe I didn't have OCD after all.

Brad shoved aside a jean jacket resting on my maroon corduroy futon and sat down. "Got any beer?" he asked, picking up a Halloween party catalog. Apparently he wasn't in a hurry to rush out the door.

I pulled open the refrigerator door, grabbed a bottle of Michelob Light, and handed it to him.

He took it, examining the label. "Light? That all you got?"

I glared at him. He nodded, popped it open, and took a long swallow. As he held his beer to his mouth, I noticed a red ribbon running down his arm.

"How's your arm?" I asked, leaning over and lifting it gently.

He looked at it and shrugged. "No big deal."

I returned to the kitchen and pulled out a box of balloon-decorated Band-Aids I'd bought for kids' party boo-boos and wet a paper towel. Sitting next to him on the couch, I gently wiped the dried blood from his arm, then covered the long, superficial slice with multiple balloons.

"Thanks," he said, admiring my work, and returned to his beer and party catalog. I spent the next few minutes gathering strewn-about items and sorting them into piles. Before long I had the place looking lived in instead of vandalized.

Brad reached under his butt and pulled out something lacy, pink, and embarrassing. I snatched it from his hand. My bra, of course. One of the first things I do at the end of the day is break free from female bondage. Must have slipped between the cracks in the cushions.

To cover my oncoming blush, I leaned over and retrieved half a bag of Cheetos from under the coffee table. I dumped the contents into a bowl that had obviously once held some other snack and offered him access. He took one and popped it in his mouth. I grabbed a handful and jammed them into my mouth to prove they hadn't been poisoned. Then I licked my orange fingers.

The sound of food brought my cats out of their hiding places. Fatman found a spot on the coffee table and went back to sleep. Thursby climbed onto the back of the futon and kept watch over Brad's every move. Cairo hid under the futon.

The sneezing picked up dramatically. Brad finished his beer and stood up. I found myself reluctant to let him go. Was I nervous about being alone after the events at my office building? Or was it something more?

"So, you've got my cell number, right?" he said, then sneezed.

I nodded. It was in my purse somewhere.

He took a couple of steps toward the door, then said, "Be sure to lock up."

"I will," I said, wrapping my arms around myself.

He pulled the door open and stepped out into the salty night air, then turned to face me again. A burst of bay wind swirled my hair.

"Remember. Call me. Now that I know where you live, I can be here in a few minutes if I'm on the island." He started to reach for my face—probably to dislodge the wisp of hair caught on my cheek—but the wisp flew off and he let his hand drop.

I felt a wave of disappointment. "Do you live here too?" I said, stalling, not wanting him to leave.

"No, but I'm sleeping in my SUV tonight, over by the office building."

"Why?" I rubbed the goose bumps on my bare arms.

"Keep an eye on things. I've got some stuff in there that I don't want to fall into the wrong hands. You better get inside. The wind's come up."

He didn't look cold at all. In fact, at that moment, he looked hot.

As he stood there looking at me, I lost the power of speech. He leaned in, and for a second I was sure he was going to kiss me. A jolt of electricity zapped through me as if I'd touched a live wire.

Instead, he plucked a small piece of glass from my hair—a remnant of the broken window. So that's what he had been after. "Good night, Parker," he said, returning to calling me by my last name. He pulled back.

I swallowed and gave a limp wave as he backed away. It was all I could manage to do in my disappointment. As he headed for his SUV, I started to close the door, but stopped when I caught a glimpse of something odd.

Just before he got into his SUV, his eyes seemed caught by something lying on the ground. To me it looked like one of my business cards, but rumpled and dirty. He bent over, picked it up by the corner, and carefully slipped it in his pocket before getting into the driver's seat.

I was left standing in my doorway, puzzled.

If he wanted my card, he could have just asked for a fresh one.

So what was he planning to do with the rumpled one?

# Chapter 25

*PARTY PLANNING TIP #25:*

*If you don't get an RSVP from an invited guest, don't assume it's a no-show. Be prepared to welcome him or her graciously, even if you harbor a tiny bit of resentment.*

After watching Brad's SUV pull away, I closed the door and scanned the room. Shit! I'd meant to clean up earlier, but I hadn't expected company—and I'd been a little distracted with the murders on my mind—so I hadn't gotten around to it. What kind of impression had all this chaos made on Brad Matthews? As a crime scene cleaner, he'd no doubt seen worse. Right?

So why was I overthinking this?

"Boys! Suppertime!" I poured rainbow-colored kitty food into the cat bowls, each labeled with the owner's personality: "Attack Cat," "Fat Cat," and "Scaredy Cat." I'd once read a book on cat personalities, written by an imminent psychologist. She'd studied cats using the California Personality Index (CPI), the Myers-Briggs Personality Profile Analysis, and the Kiersey Temperament Sorter, and had come up with cat personalities similar to people—Sexy Cat, Hyper Cat, Psycho Cat, Diva Cat, Bossy Cat, Attack Cat, Lazy Cat, and Scaredy Cat.

If only people were as easy to analyze and diagnose. How would I classify Brad Matthews? Diva? Bossy? Attack? Psycho?

Sexy?

Enough. Bedtime.

My body might not have been tossing and turning, but my mind was doing flips. Maybe I couldn't sleep because there were three cats lying on my legs. Or maybe it was Killer to Be Named Later. I couldn't escape the fact that someone was trying to make me look like a murderer, if not trying to kill me.

I got up, straightened my flannel cat pajamas that had become twisted, pulled out my notes, and sat on the floor with a box of granola. Scanning the chart I'd made, I filled in some of the blanks, using a basic axiom of psychology: All behavior is motivated.

In other words, whoever killed the two women had motives. Including the mayor. Once again the seven deadly sins reared their ugly heads. The way the detective probably saw things, he suspected me of greed (I wanted the party business all to myself?), envy (I was jealous of Andi?), wrath (I secretly disliked Ikea?), and pride (I was embarrassed about the mayor's silly theme?).

All I was missing were lust, sloth, and gluttony. *I could be guilty of gluttony*, I thought, as I stuffed another handful of granola in my mouth.

I kept circling back to the mayor. He was the one link to everyone, dead or alive. But he couldn't have pulled off those two murders without some help. Was there someone willing to do anything for the mayor—in order to get what he, or she, wanted?

Like Dakota Hunter, who wanted TI for a casino? Or Spaz Cruz, who wanted to keep it for the film industry? Or the admiral, who thought it should be a monument to the navy? Or Siouxie, who thought the mayor was "murdering" the island?

Or someone else entirely?

I threw my pen down. I was too tired to think clearly. Heading for bed, I just hoped I could eventually drift off if I counted sheep instead of suspects. Switching off the light, I lay back and pulled up the comforter.

Something was wrong.

My cats. All three of them had disappeared from their usual spots on the bed. "Boys?" I called.

No sign of them. I rolled out of bed and took a quick tour of the house to see whether they were eating my spilled cereal, playing in the toilet, or hiding in my laundry pile.

Nope.

I heard a noise. A low guttural growl. Coming from under the bed.

I got on my knees and peeked. Six eyeballs glowed in the darkness.

"Boys? What are you doing under there? Come here, kit—"

A thud. Outside the front door.

Cairo, aka Scaredy Cat, hissed. The blood in my veins turned cold.

In the darkness, I fumbled for my purse, finally locating Brad's business card at the bottom and my cell phone. Not daring to turn on the light, I touched the phone and called up the keyboard.

Before I could tap the number, the phone rang. Blocked number.

"Brad?" I answered, whispering urgently. "Brad, if that's you, there's someone here. Outside."

I listened for a response. Silence.

The line went dead.

"Shit!" I checked the business card and tapped out Brad's number.

"This is Brad Matthews at Crime Scene Cleaners. If you wish to leave a message . . ."

"Shit! Shit!"

Another thud. Just outside the front door.

My mouth went dry. In the darkness, I felt my way to the kitchenette and lifted a knife from a drawer. My hand was shaking so badly, I nearly dropped it. I crept back to the bedroom, bumping into a wall along the way, closed the door, and crawled under the bed with the cats. I lay there covered in dust bunnies, knife in hand, and listened for the intruder, hoping I had the nerve to slice his Achilles tendon, like the kid did in *Pet Sematary*.

Or at least cut off a toe.

I awoke, startled. Minutes had become hours. I must have been truly exhausted to have drifted off to sleep in spite of the scare, because the next thing I knew it was morning and I was lying in a pool of drool. At least it wasn't blood. I had a stiff neck, cramped fingers, and ached everywhere else. My cats were long gone. I slithered out from under the bed, sweeping the floor with my pajamas as I went. Slowly I sat up, unkinking my stiff joints with every movement.

At first glance, the room looked undisturbed. Using the bed for support, I drew myself up to stand, cursing my useless cats, who had abandoned me in my time of peril, and brushed off the cat hairs and accumulated dust. I found the boys curled up cozily on my warm, soft comforter, where I should have been. I thought about calling Brad again and took a look outside to see if his SUV happened to be there. No sign of it. He'd mentioned something about sleeping near the office building to keep an eye on things. Oh well. In the daylight, things looked less menacing.

After a long hot shower that loosened my muscles and washed away most of the tension, I dressed in my favorite black jeans, "Go Directly to Alcatraz" T-shirt, and red flip-flops. I whipped up a triple latte and sat down with the morning paper.

No mention of Rocco in the hospital—apparently not newsworthy enough. But there was a small story on the fire at my office building. The police were looking at it as part of the recent break-ins and vandalism on the island.

"These acts of violence are no doubt connected to the current power struggles over the future of Treasure Island," Mayor Green was quoted as saying, "and they won't be tolerated. I've increased security on the island and am looking into all possible sources of these malicious acts. In the meantime, I will hold my decision about the destiny of this historic piece of land until the perpetrators have been arrested and brought to the full measure of the law."

The mayor could use a good editor, but one thing was clear: He was pissed. Did his anger—or was it overreaction?—have anything to do with the fact that his future bride had been found floating nearby?

The plot had thickened. The mayor had indicated the recent trouble might have been connected to the groups demanding to see their visions of the island become a reality.

A knock on the door interrupted me from scanning the rest of the article. I went to the door and peered through the peephole.

Brad Matthews stood on the other side, holding two paper cups of what I guessed was coffee and a white bag filled with—please God—some kind of pastry. I checked to see that the fly on my black jeans was zipped, tugged down the hem of my "Alcatraz" shirt, and licked the coffee 'stache off my lips before opening the door.

"What are you doing here?" I said.

He held up the coffees and bag. "Brought you breakfast. Thought you might need something to start your day, like me." This didn't look like a man who'd slept in his car. His jeans were spotless, the black T-shirt fresh out of the laundry, and the black leather jacket was the icing on the cake. Even the soul patch on his chin had been neatly trimmed.

Did he think I needed *him* to start my day—or the coffee?

I widened the opening to let him in.

"Rough night?" he said, giving me a once-over.

Did I look that bad? I ran my fingers through my still-damp hair and brushed at the few cat hairs that decorated my shirt.

"How did you know?" I said, raising a suspicious eyebrow.

He nodded toward the knife on the table. "Awfully big knife for buttering toast."

"Oh, that. I thought I heard a noise last night, after you left. I guess it was nothing."

Brad's expression sobered. He looked me over.

"What's wrong with your face?"

I glanced in the toaster reflection and saw the sleep crease that ran across my cheek. That's what happens when you sleep on the floor. "Slept wrong," I said, rubbing the line on my face.

Pushing aside the newspaper and placing the coffees on the small table, Brad sat in one of my two wooden kitchen chairs and took the lids off the paper cups. "Saw you drinking a latte the other day, so I figured it was your drink of choice."

I glanced at my espresso machine and half-full commuter mug, then smiled at him. So he'd been profiling me, just as I'd been profiling him. I wondered why. Did he still think I had something to do with the murders? As attractive as he might be—and he was—my suspicions of him were never far from my thoughts.

"I can always use another jolt of caffeine," I said, taking the cup. I filled my mug with the still-warm latte, then stole a glance at his cup. No milk, no whipped cream, no nonsense. Just black. He opened the white bakery bag and pulled out two cinnamon raison bagels spread with cream cheese. They too were still warm. I took a huge bite before saying another word, then licked my fingers. Pastries from the Job Corps culinary school could not be beat.

I caught him watching me. "Thorry. Hungry. Thanks," I said with my mouth still full.

"This isn't strictly a social call," Brad said, setting down his cup after a sip of his coffee.

"What do you mean?" I said, joining him at the table.

"Melvin thinks he knows who set fire to your office building. Fire chief found the hot spots—the sources of the fire. One in the kitchen and one in the reception area."

I set my coffee down and licked my top lip. "That's great. Do they know who did it? Did they catch him?"

He took another sip of his coffee, as if it were liquid courage.

I leaned in. "So? Tell me."

He shrugged. "The fire marshal had some of the ash analyzed."

"And?"

He looked down at his coffee. "It was highly flammable material. Only took a match to get it going. In another few minutes, the whole building would have been an inferno."

And I would have been smokin'. . . .

He pulled a small, rolled-up sheet of paper from his pocket, uncurled it, and held it up for me to see. I recognized it immediately—one of the fake mug shots of the mayor I'd had made up for the party. "That's one of the decorations from the wedding. Where did you get that?"

"Melvin found it in your office. Apparently one just like it was the source of the fire. The chemicals used to make the photocopy made it catch quickly." Brad took another sip of his coffee. There was something he wasn't telling me.

I sat back, having suddenly lost my appetite for carbs, sugar, and caffeine. “So . . . someone went into my office, took a couple of leftover posters, and used them to light the fire? For God’s sake, who?”

Brad looked up at me. “The detective thinks it was you.”

# Chapter 26

*PARTY PLANNING TIP #26:*

***Don't let your party become a wild free-for-all, or you'll soon find uninvited guests at the door—such as the local police.***

I put down my coffee, forgetting all about Brad's untouched bagel, which had been on my mind seconds before. "Why would Melvin think I set fire to my own building? That's ridiculous."

He shrugged casually. "Get rid of evidence?"

"Shit. I gotta get out of here." I stood up and grabbed my SFSU hoodie and knockoff purse and headed for the door.

"Where are you going?" Brad stood up, coffee in hand, and followed me.

I spun around. "If Melvin thinks I set the fire, that's probably all he needs to arrest me! I've got to find out who did this before he locks me up. Once he does that, there's no way I'll be able to prove my innocence. He thinks I did it, and someone is helping him along with that ridiculous assumption."

I stepped out the door and waited for Brad to clear the entryway so I could lock up.

"How about I come with you?"

"Why?" I crossed my arms. "What do you really want, Brad?"

He shrugged. "Well, I don't have any pressing crime scenes to clean up right now. And . . ." He looked away.

"And what?" I snapped.

He met my eyes again. "And, frankly, I don't think you did any of this."

He looked sincere, and suddenly I had trouble finding words. Tears brimmed my eyes, but I quickly turned away and blinked them back.

"Then why did you pick up one of my business cards from the ground before you left last night? If you want to check my fingerprints, they're on file with the California Teachers Association."

Brad frowned. "If I wanted your fingerprints, I could find a much better set on that coffee cup I brought you."

"Then why? You got some kind of business card fetish?" I was only half kidding.

"You're right about trying to find prints. I think someone had your card, cased your place, then dropped the card accidentally. Your home address was handwritten on the back."

That stopped me momentarily. I thought about the noise I'd heard last night. Someone *had* been here. And his theory about the business card made sense. I bit my lip, then said, "Well, you'll have to move your car." I waved my hand toward his SUV, currently blocking my MINI Cooper.

He jumped in and backed the SUV out of the driveway. I did the same, then waited on the street while he reparked his car and returned to mine. I stepped on the gas before he even got his seat belt on.

"Where are we going?"

From my purse, I pulled out the latest version of my notes with the list of what were becoming my suspects and handed it to him. He read it over, then said, "Who's KTBNL?"

I felt my face color. I couldn't tell him it was my code

for Brad Matthews. "Uh, it's a free space, like in bingo," I said, and changed the subject. "Have you been to CeeGee Studio?"

He shook his head.

"I've heard from Raj it's pretty cool inside. They've filmed all kinds of movies in the old aircraft hangars—*Indiana Jones*, *Flubber*, *Rent*, and TV shows like *Battlebots* and *Nash Bridges*. Even *Monk*. It used to be a Pan Am hangar in the thirties." I glanced over at him. No reaction.

After a few turns, I pulled into the film studio lot and shut off the ignition.

"But why are we here?" Brad asked.

I released my seat belt. "Spaz Cruz is one of the people who has definite ideas about Treasure Island. I need to talk to him—see if he has anything to say about the mayor. He may know something Mayor Green doesn't want the general public to know. And he may be using it as leverage in his fight for the island. Besides, he might even be a suspect."

The hangar didn't look like much from the outside—just a ginormous windowless building—but I'd heard from Raj it was a whole other world inside. Tourists regularly tried to find the place, but if you didn't know where it was, it was easily overlooked. There were no signs on the doors or walls other than KEEP OUT. DANGER. Those signs were common all over the island, thanks to the toxic chemicals left behind.

We got out and headed for what looked like the front entrance—two huge double doors decorated with NO ADMITTANCE signs. By the look of the metal gizmo attached to the heavy doors, it appeared I'd need some kind of coded card to get in. With that kind of security, anything could be going on in there. Who would know?

I knocked. No answer. Duh. I cursed and headed back to the MINI, where Brad stood leaning against the front fender. "It's like a fortress," I said, reaching for my purse lying in the backseat.

"Boy, you give up easy," he said, his arms crossed over his chest.

"I'm not giving up!" I snapped, and pulled my cell out of my purse. "And I don't see you trying anything."

I scrolled down my contacts, touched a name, and held the phone to my ear, waiting for an answer.

"Yes, hello?" a voice whispered.

"Raj?"

"Yes, it is me. Ms. Presley?"

"Yeah, why are you whispering?"

"I am at CeeGee, on the soundstage where they are filming the new movie *Bad Ass*, with Jack Jason. I cannot make any noise or I will be removed."

"Perfect!" I said, glancing at Brad smugly. "Listen, I'm right outside the door. You've got to get me in there."

Hearing my side of the conversation, Brad grinned.

"Oh, Ms. Presley," Raj whispered. "I cannot do that, actually. It's what they call a closed set. No one is allowed inside."

"But you're inside!"

"Yes, but I am having a role in the film, remember?"

"Raj, this is life or death. I need to talk to Cruz. All you have to do is open the door for a second. I'll sneak in and—"

"You are asking me to break the law, Ms. Presley! That's going against the code."

"Entering a movie studio is not against the law, Raj. And I'll make sure no one knows you let me in."

"Ms. Presley—"

"Raj, the cops think I killed those two women! If I don't find some kind of evidence that clears me, they're going to lock me up. Do you understand?"

I glanced at Brad again. He was rolling his eyes and shaking his head.

"Okay. Okay. They are taking a break. Everyone will be

going to the catering table. Maybe they will not be noticing you. There is a door at the back—on H Street. Go there and be waiting for me."

"Thanks, Raj. You're saving my life."

I hung up, gestured for Brad to stay put, and headed to the back door. Moments later it opened a slit. A dark brown eye appeared in the crack. A brown hand grabbed my wrist and quickly pulled me inside, closing the door behind me.

I found myself behind a black curtain, which I assumed was there to keep any light from sifting in when the door was opened. Raj shushed me—for no reason—then gestured for me to follow him. The darkness abated as we came out from behind the curtain, and the bright lights nearly blinded me as I entered the humongous soundstage.

I don't know what I expected—maybe something like the magical lot on the Universal Studios tour—but what I found was akin to an enormous junkyard. Cement floors and ceilings were covered with wires that seemingly led everywhere and nowhere. While most of the crew were huddled around an expansive table covered in deli meats, cheese, breads, and spreads, a few in flannel shirts and baggy jeans appeared to be repainting cars in what looked like a chop shop. In another area, a couple of guys seemed to be playing with explosives. I heard the sound of little *pop*s. At the far end of the room I spotted what could have been a crack house, complete with skanky prostitutes and overdressed pimps in various stages of drug-induced apathy.

Hard to believe it was all fake.

Raj nudged me and nodded toward a thin man with a scraggly goatee and a scraggly ponytail sitting on the seat of a fake motorcycle, flipping through what I guessed was a script. Although he looked more like a longtime doper than a respected film producer, I recognized Lucas "Spaz" Cruz immediately from the wedding party. I turned around to nod my thanks at Raj, but he had disappeared.

Glancing around for something to make me look as if I belonged, I spotted a tray of cheeses on the buffet table and picked them up.

"How is everything?" I asked Spaz Cruz after sidling up to him. I held out the tray as an offering.

He glanced up from his reading and looked at me blankly.

"I'm the new caterer. Presley Parker." I held out a hand. "I did the event for the mayor the other day, and someone from your office hired me."

"Everything's fine," Spaz said. He shook my hand limply, then took a cube of cheese and returned to his reading.

"This is so embarrassing, but would you mind if I borrowed your cell phone for a minute? The battery is dead on mine, and I think one of my staff is lost. She's supposed to bring the dessert, and I see it isn't here yet."

Spaz Cruz frowned, then reluctantly pulled his cell from his pocket and handed it to me. An iPhone, naturally.

"Thank you so much. I'll be quick."

I turned slightly so he couldn't see the screen, then pretended to click on the push-button screen while actually pulling up his contacts list. Scrolling down I found Mayor Green's number. Not surprising. I scrolled further down until I hit another familiar name—Ikea Takeda. Why would he have her number on his contacts list?

"Whoops. Wrong number," I said, grinning at him. I pretended to redial while pulling up the recents list. Scrolling down, I found Ikea's name listed again. She had called him the day of the party. Odd.

I held the phone to my ear, pretended to talk to my fake assistant about the fake dessert, then hung up and handed back the phone. "Thank you so much! She's on her way. Just got a little lost."

Spaz nodded, forced a smile, and tucked the phone back into his pocket.

"Hope you enjoyed the mayor's party the other night," I

said, trying to figure out a way to ask him about Ikea. "You know, except for Ikea. It's so awful what happened to the mayor's fiancée, isn't it?" I said, shaking my head.

He stared at me as if I were some kind of alien.

"Of course, we're not using that chef anymore for our catering business," I rambled on.

Spaz glanced at the cheese tray, then looked at me.

"Oh, you have nothing to worry about. They have that guy in custody. He won't be poisoning anyone anymore."

Spaz Cruz put the script down on his lap and turned to me. Finally, I had his attention. "They do?"

I nodded, but before I could ramble further, he asked, "Who did you say you are again?"

"Presley Parker. The caterer for the mayor. And you." I offered the cheese tray again. He shook his head. "So did you know her? Ikea, I mean."

"No . . . ," he said, clearly puzzled as to why I was talking to him about the dead woman. I blathered on before he came to his senses and told me to get lost.

"They say the mayor might have had something to do with it," I said, "but he seems like such a nice man, don't you think?"

Spaz's mouth dropped open. He looked stunned by my boldness. And that was just what I was going for. The more outrageous I became, the more I hoped he'd talk. "Then again, you never know what goes on behind closed political doors, do you?" I gave him a knowing wink.

"Do you know something about Ikea's death?" he said, growing more interested by the second.

"Well, I'm not one to gossip," I said conspiratorially, "but I heard someone was trying to 'convince' "—I put the word in one-handed finger quotes—"the mayor to turn over the island to a special interest group."

Spaz Cruz got that thoughtful look in his eyes again. "Really?"

"Hey, weren't you one of those guys arguing with him at the party? Yeah—you're the one who wants to turn TI into a Hollywood of the North!"

Spaz abruptly closed the script he'd been reading and dismounted the motorcycle. "I'm not trying to pressure the mayor to do anything," he said, not meeting my eyes. "Where did you get such misinformation? The tabloids, no doubt."

I dropped the act and turned serious. "But you do have a stake in this, don't you, Mr. Cruz? And you did know Ikea Takeda, didn't you? Did you also know Andi Sax? She's dead too, you know."

Spaz's face reddened as he finally met my eyes. "I barely knew Ikea. I may have used Sax for a couple of parties, but I didn't really know her. My staff handles all that."

"Really? Then why was Ikea's number in your cell phone?"

The dawn of enlightenment filled Cruz's face. "I hope you're not suggesting . . ."

"No. I'm just trying to find out what happened to the mayor's fiancée and his former party planner. I think the mayor is somehow connected. If you know anything—"

He cut me off. "How did you get in here?"

"You're awfully defensive, Mr. Cruz. If you had nothing to do with any of this, then—"

"Jerry! Rob!" he called to a couple of guys carrying a long ladder nearby. "Would you escort Ms. . . . whatever . . . out of the building, please?"

Jerry the Giant and Rob the Robot set down the ladder and muscled their way over. When they started to take my arms, I jerked out of their reach, spilling the tray of cheese.

"Thank you for your time, Mr. Cruz," I called as I dashed toward the exit. "I hope you'll use Killer Parties for your next event."

"How did it go?" Brad asked. He was sitting in the passenger side of my car, listening to the radio. Country music.

I shrugged. "He's definitely hiding something—he was very defensive—but he won't talk to me."

"No shit," Brad said. He didn't look surprised. "You probably weren't terribly subtle."

"I thought I was brilliant," I said, as I started up the car. "I could be an actress if I wanted to. Piece of cake."

Brad laughed. On the way back to the office, I shared what little I'd learned. But the more I thought about it, the more I was certain that Spaz Cruz knew something.

When we arrived back at the building, I kept the car idling, waiting for Brad to get out. He didn't move.

"You're not coming in?" Brad asked, resting one arm on the windowsill and the other on the back of my seat.

"I'm going to see my mother."

"She lives nearby?"

I nodded. "In a care facility in the city. Alzheimer's. You know."

Brad nodded. "Sorry." He opened the car door, then turned back to me. "Do me a favor."

"What?"

"Don't go around interrogating people without me. You could get into some serious trouble, poking your nose into places that some people want to keep private."

I thought of Spaz Cruz. He knew my name and the name of my business. He knew where to find me. And he knew I was snooping around about the murders. If he had anything to do with it, I could be in real trouble. It was nice to know Brad was concerned about my well-being.

Then again, was he? Or was he just keeping tabs on what I learned?

As soon as he was out of the car, I shoved the gearshift into reverse and sped away without looking back.

"Mom?" I said into the phone at a stop sign, hoping a cop wouldn't catch me. This hands-free-while-talking-on-the-phone law was idiotic, and I tended to ignore it—when there were no cops around. One day I would get caught, but by then I'd feel it was worth the fine.

"Yes, dear?" she said. Good. She still recognized my voice. Although she might not remember what we did a few hours ago, she remembered me, and for that I was grateful. And while I'd learned that some Alzheimer's patients become surly as the illness progresses, so far my mother was her usual sweet, albeit ditzy, self.

"Are you free?" I pulled onto the Bay Bridge headed for the city, one eye on the road, one eye alert for the California Highway Patrol.

"Well, I think I have some kind of exercise class this afternoon. Tai Chi or yoga or something. But that's it."

"Want to take a little drive, maybe see an old friend?"

"That sounds lovely, dear! Male or female?"

"Male. I thought we'd pay a call on Admiral Stadelhofer. He's retired and lives on Yerba Buena Island."

"Wonderful! I haven't seen him in years! Oh, what shall I wear?"

"Keep it casual, Mom. You look beautiful in anything."

She giggled.

"I'll be there in fifteen, twenty minutes."

"That doesn't give me much time. But all right, I'll see you in the lobby."

Not giving her much time to primp was the point. I didn't want her changing into some kind of cocktail frock and full makeup for this visit.

Twenty minutes later I pulled up in front of her Victorian building. Double-parking the MINI, I rushed inside, signed her out, and led her to the car.

"When did you get this cute little thing?" my mother asked as she delicately snuggled into the cozy passenger seat.

"I've had it for a while, Mom. You've been in it before. Remember last week when we went to the de Young?"

"Oh, I love the de Young. We should go there."

I turned on my iPod, and selected one of her favorite songs from *Grease*.

"So, where are we going today?"

I smiled. "Yerba Buena Island. To see your old friend, Admiral Stadelhofer."

"Oh, I'm so glad I dressed for the occasion."

And she had. Her highlighted blondish hair was swept up in her usual French roll, her makeup expertly done but a little heavy for daytime. And she wore a frilly dress covered with red and yellow flowers, years too young for her age. It matched her scuffed red heels and red patent leather handbag.

I took the turnoff for Yerba Buena, passed the sign that read PRIVATE ROAD: RESIDENTS AND GUESTS ONLY, and waited for the usual travelogue my mother offered whenever we went somewhere. As a native San Franciscan, she knew more about the Bay Area than most history teachers, and her long-term memory was still very much intact. She didn't disappoint me.

"Did you know, Presley, that Yerba Buena means *good herb*?"

I nodded, wondering what the local pot smokers thought about that.

"The island used to be called Sea Bird Island and Goat Island, back when it was a Civil War military post. Then it became a naval training station, you know, with upscale housing for senior officers. . . ."

As she continued with her lecture, I focused on maneuvering the hairpin turns as we drove up the steep, narrow road. I caught glimpses of the natural topography of the island, dramatically different from the flat, man-made landscape of Treasure Island, its conjoined twin. Whereas TI is practically barren of vegetation aside from a few palm trees and in need of serious renovation, neighboring Yerba Buena Island is lush with sage scrub, wildflowers, eucalyptus, moss and ivy, live oaks, buckeye trees, and well-kept, albeit tiny, yards. A few retired officers—and civilians who could afford the high rent—currently lived in the stately two- and three-story homes. Though built closely together, the houses were mostly secluded from one another thanks to the trees. Since the coast guard keeps a minimal base there, a small portion of the area is restricted, but most of the island is open to the public, in spite of the less-than-welcoming sign. Still, there were never many cars on the road. There's not much to see or do unless you're visiting old military buddies, checking out the quaint, still-functioning lighthouse, or you're just plain curious.

I wondered what it must have been like living on the base during wartime. Much of the navy housing was simple—squat homes with flat, asphalt roofs built on stilts into the hills. Mother pointed out several playgrounds and mini-parks the officers and their families must have used in the postwar days, as well as other remnants of the past, such as the blue awnings, small windowpanes, and clotheslines.

We pulled up to the address on the private road listed in my notes, a four-story white brick and clapboard Victorian with three turrets at the top. The expansive front porch was covered with artificial green turf, and the top riser leading to the porch sported a brass plaque: ADM STADELHOFER.

"So Gene lives here?" my mother asked, finally ending her travelogue. I scanned what would have been the admiral's enviable panoramic view of San Francisco, the peninsula, and Oakland, but the fog had started to sweep in, obscuring the details. I felt my hair frizz as soon as I got out of the car. Helping my mother out of her seat, I noticed her hair seemed impenetrable, no doubt covered with layers of hair spray.

"Classic Revival," my mother said, staring up at the mini-mansion, noticeably larger than the three other homes located within a stone's throw of the place. "He's certainly done well for himself."

I followed her up the three steps but stopped short when she began peering into one of the two large-paned front windows that flanked either side of the palatial home.

"Mother!" I whispered as she cupped her hands around her eyes and leaned into the glass.

"Oh my!" she gasped. "Look at this!" She grabbed my arm and pulled me to the window. In spite of my sense of propriety, I peeked inside, curious about how a retired navy officer lived—especially this one.

Hardwood floors, a sparkling chandelier, fleur-de-lis wallpaper, and a brick fireplace created an impressive background for the blue velvet couch and chairs, antique tables, and Victorian lamps. A portrait of the admiral in full uniform and colorful medals hung over the fireplace. Before I could study the room further, Mother dragged me to the other side of the double front doors and leaned into the matching window. This room was almost a mirror image of the first room, with more hardwood floors, another chandelier, and a second fireplace. Only the furniture, while still antique, was maroon instead of blue. Incredible. The house had two living rooms.

Mother released my hand and rang the bell.

"Mother!" I whispered.

"What? We're here to see Gene, right? What's the problem?"

"I . . . I'm not ready," I stammered.

"What do you mean, you're not ready? He's my old boyfriend. I'll do the talking."

I had no choice but to nod as I heard muted heavy footfalls on the hardwood floors. One of the double doors opened and a red-faced older man stood in the doorway. He wore a silky, old-fashioned smoking jacket that was barely secured around his large stomach. This was not a man who stayed away from a mess hall. He wore leather slippers and argyle socks on his feet, but his legs were bare beneath the hem of the robe. He frowned at us with bushy white eyebrows that could have used my mother's expert styling and hair spray.

"Yes?" he said, pulling the belt tightly around his middle.

I started to say something but my mother interrupted me. "Gene! It's so good to see you!" She smiled, practically batting her eyelashes in time to her words. The old girl still had it.

"Ronnie?" the admiral sputtered.

"In the flesh, so to speak," she said, then blushed.

Instead of inviting us in, Admiral Stadelhofer glanced back into the house, then stepped onto the porch and closed the door softly.

"What are you doing here, Ronnie?" He turned to me, finally acknowledging me, and said, "I know you. You're . . ." He snapped his fingers, trying to come up with the answer.

Mother put an arm around me and gave me a proud squeeze. "This is my daughter, Presley. She's a college professor over at San Francisco State."

I started to explain: "I'm only an instructor, not a professor, and actually I was recently laid off—" I stopped when I saw the color drain from the admiral's red face. He looked at my mother.

"She's not . . . mine, is she?"

Mother laughed. I frowned. Of course I wasn't his daughter. God, I hoped not. Neither of us was pleased at the thought.

"Don't be silly, Gene. She came along way after you."

He looked visibly relieved, and the color returned to his Santa Claus cheeks and gin-blossom nose.

"So, may we come in?" Mother said.

The admiral shook his head. "It's not a good time, Ronnie. My wife is ill—"

"Your wife?" Mother frowned, then said loud enough for the neighbors to hear, "You're married?"

Uh-oh.

I had a feeling her Alzheimer's was kicking up a notch today. Had she really expected he'd been single all these years?

"You knew that, Ronnie. You planned our engagement party, remember?"

As my mother tried to focus her thoughts, I could see the admiral realize the situation. He looked at me—a look of regret flashed over his florid features. I gave a tight smile. Then suddenly, another look crossed his face—one of recognition. "Now I know who you are! You're that party gal from the mayor's wedding."

I started to nod humbly until he continued. "What a *snafu*! You really made a mess of things, didn't you? Not exactly a chip off the old block when it comes to parties, are you?" he said, glancing at my mother.

I knew my mother wouldn't take kindly to the "old block" reference. "Eugene! What are you talking about?"

I rolled my eyes. "Nothing, Mother. It was that party I planned for Mayor Green. There were a couple of glitches. . . ."

"Glitches?" The admiral laughed. "You call a murdered guest of honor a glitch? In the navy, we'd call that a major FUBAR. A clusterfu—"

"Stop it, Gene!" Mother stared at the admiral, horrified. "You watch your language in front of a lady." Then she turned to me. "What does he mean, 'murder'?"

"She didn't tell you?" the admiral said, his eyes on me. "At that so-called party she threw for the mayor, his bride-to-be turned up floating in the bay like an overturned boat. Apparently she was murdered. Poisoned. With chocolates your daughter served at the party."

"How did you know about the chocolates?" I asked, surprised he would have that kind of information.

He shrugged, as if realizing he might have said too much. "I got connections. Scuttlebutt is, you're their primary suspect."

Mother, eyes wide, mouth open, looked at me, then turned

back to the admiral and slapped him, hard, across his fat red cheek.

"What the fu—" he started to say, rubbing his face.

"How dare you! My daughter is no murderer. If anyone is guilty of a crime, it's you, Gene. I may have forgotten you're married, but I haven't forgotten the rumors about all that testing you did on those poor men."

The admiral took a step back, wild-eyed. Mother was onto something.

"That was never proved," he sputtered.

"Everyone knows how good you are at hiding things, Gene. You only got away with it because you paid off some self-serving committee. And now you're at it again, aren't you? You think your money and influence will buy you a place in history."

I stared at my mother, who seemed amazingly lucid at the moment. "You mean, you know about his interests in Treasure Island?"

Without taking her steely eyes off of the admiral, she nodded. "I have my sources too, Gene."

A female voice called from inside the house. The admiral whirled around and headed inside without another word. I jumped at the sound of the door slamming shut in our faces.

"Come along, dear," Mother said, taking my sweating palm in her dry, papery hand and leading me back to the MINI Cooper. "I'm hungry. How about we go to Tommy's Joynt for some buffalo stew and an Irish coffee? My treat."

I glanced back at Admiral Stadelhofer's stately home and caught a glimpse of a woman wearing a housecoat, staring out the window, her arms crossed over her chest. There was no sign of the former navy officer.

Tommy's Joynt at Van Ness and Geary is a popular tourist spot, but the locals love it too—the non-vegetarian ones, that is. My mother used to take me there every year for my birthday because she loved the Hofbrau and I loved the tacky retro signs and neon beer lights that covered the walls and ceiling. Now that she lived so close to the place, we'd become regulars.

I ordered the beer and bean soup, she had the stew, and we sat down at a small table under the stairs that led to the restrooms. She gave a brief history lesson about the place—built in 1947, Herb Caen's hangout, and so on—something she did every time we came. It was as if she'd completely forgotten about our recent encounter with the admiral.

"So, Mom," I said, after a spoonful of the spicy soup, "what did you mean about Admiral Stadelhofer doing tests on his men?"

She looked up from her stew and blinked. "Who?"

"Gene Stadelhofer. You said something about some testing he did while in the navy?"

She resumed eating her stew. Between bites, she filled me in. "There were rumors about a secret project called SHIP, or SHADE, or something like that. It was some kind of germ warfare tests or whatnot. When a bunch of sailors got sick from the tests, Gene tried to cover it up, denied everything. I don't think they ever proved any of the allegations, but a few of us know the truth—that he was into something secret—and dangerous." She looked at me pointedly. "That was *after* I dumped him, of course."

I ate and thought about what she'd said, hardly tasting my soup. Admiral Stadelhofer had been using his men as guinea pigs to test for some kind of germ warfare? Could that have something to do with the death of Ikea Takeda or Andi Sax? Could one—or both—have discovered proof of his involvement in something so unethical and diabolical it could have ruined him?

For the rest of the meal, my mother did the talking, mostly about her party heyday and plentiful paramours. Then, out of the blue, she said, "Dear, are you in some sort of trouble? You look a little pale."

I smiled and shook my head. "No, Mom, I'm fine. I'm just trying to find out how Ikea Takeda and Andi Sax were murdered so I don't end up—" I started to say in jail—or worse—but didn't want to alarm my mother.

"Murdered? Who was murdered?"

Apparently she'd forgotten what the admiral had said, another sign that her long-term memory was still good, but not so much her short-term.

I sighed internally, shook my head, and rose from the table. "We've got to get you back home. Your friends will be wondering where you are."

She stood and delicately brushed at the front of her dress, removing nonexistent crumbs with bright red nails. "Oh, I hope I haven't missed the party!"

"What party?" I asked, following her to the door.

"It's my birthday, silly! Did you forget? I'm having a huge gala to celebrate."

I didn't have the heart to tell her that her birthday had been six months ago. Why spoil an excuse to celebrate? "Happy birthday, Mom."

"I had a little chat with Admiral Eugene Stadelhofer," I said to Brad, who stood in my office doorway looking down at me. He pulled the folding chair up to my paper-littered desk and glanced down at the increasing notes I'd been making about the murders.

"Really?" He looked a little disappointed. Why? Because I hadn't taken him with me? Or because I'd learned something that he might not know? "So what did you chat about?"

I decided not to tell Brad about my mother's questionable relationship with Gene, as she called him. I didn't think it was necessary to involve her in this.

"How'd you get him to talk?" he asked.

"Rang the doorbell," I answered smugly.

"What, no breaking and entering? No criminal trespass?"

I glared at him. "Stop sounding like a cop. I thought you were interested in helping me. If not, go . . . clean something."

He sat back. "Whoa. We're a little crabby, aren't we? I just want to keep you from breaking any laws. How's it going to look if you're arrested for a 602?"

A 602? I assumed it was police code for trespassing, but how would he know that? Had he been arrested for a 602? I really knew nothing about this guy who had walked into my life so coincidentally. Brad Matthews might claim he was a crime scene cleaner, but I had a feeling he was something more. A snitch for the cops? Letting him get involved in this had been a bad idea.

I underlined Admiral Stadelhofer's name and added a fat question mark, along with the acronyms SHIP and SHADE my mother had mentioned.

Brad looked at my notes. "You're going about it the wrong way."

"Oh really? Got a better idea, Holmes?"

"Yeah, Drew. Think about it from the killer's perspective. That's what I do when I'm bored cleaning up a homicide. I try to imagine what happened and get inside the killer's head while I'm wiping up all that blood."

"Easy to say," I said, sighing. "I don't have any solid suspects, other than the mayor—and that's just because he looks guilty. I don't have any incriminating evidence, either—except my connection to the chocolates. Frankly, I'm running out of time. It's only a matter of hours before Detective Melvin reads me my rights—or I move to Argentina."

Brad patted my knee, then stood up and left me alone to my self-pitying thoughts. I turned on my iTunes, plugged in my earbuds, and listened to the Smiths sing "Girlfriend in a

Coma." Luckily for me, having ADHD is akin to multitasking, so while Morrissey crooned, I started to formulate a plan.

It was time to throw another party. The theme: "Catch a Killer."

# Chapter 27

*PARTY PLANNING TIP #27:*

***When you're desperate for a fresh party idea, search the Web and you'll find every theme from Redneck Trailer Park parties to Red Hat tea parties. But a Murder Mystery party is always a crowd-pleaser.***

Without a backward glance at Brad, I left the office and drove to my condo. My cats gave me a mixed welcome—Cairo hid under the coffee table, no doubt thinking I was an intruder. Thursby tried to attack my feet because he thought they were mice. And Fatman barely lifted his fat head from his place on the kitchen counter, probably because I wasn't food.

I plopped down on my couch and switched on my blue netbook. My laptop was still in the old smoke-damaged office—I hadn't had a chance to move it to the new barracks next door yet. My mini-computer would give me access to as much information as I could get before I took the next step.

I Googled "Bradley Matthews." Apparently it was a common name, since over a dozen hits appeared. I narrowed down the search by adding "San Francisco" and "crime scene cleaner" and came up with nothing. I took out the job, leaving only his name and the city.

Bingo. An article appeared, dated three years earlier, no picture. What I read sent a shiver through me.

Bradley Matthews had killed a man.

I reread the passage slowly, making sure I hadn't skipped anything important or misunderstood it.

> . . . The victim, Jerome "J.T." Thompson, was shot and killed coming out of the liquor store when he didn't respond to the police officer's command to halt.
>
> According to an inquest conducted by SFPD Internal Affairs, Officer Matthews claimed the suspect appeared to be hiding a weapon in the pocket of his hooded sweatshirt.
>
> After Matthews identified himself and repeated requests to "Halt and drop the weapon," he shot the suspect twice in the chest. Thompson died at the scene.
>
> The investigators later learned that Thompson was deaf, and the weapon he was brandishing was a BlackBerry, which he used to instant message other deaf people.
>
> Officer Matthews is on leave, pending further investigation.

Oh my God.

I knew it. Brad had been a cop. What I never would have guessed was that he'd killed an unarmed man. A disabled unarmed man.

That must have been devastating for him.

Was he kicked off the force? Or did he leave voluntarily? He had most likely suffered—was still suffering—from PTSD, posttraumatic stress disorder. Is that why he'd become a crime scene cleaner?

This bit of news took some of the wind out of my sails, but it still didn't explain everything about Brad Matthews. Or anything, for that matter. It was hard to read between the lines of the article, but had Brad been some kind of renegade cop who shot first and asked questions later? If so, I'd better not make any false moves.

I checked the time. I couldn't afford to waste another minute pondering Brad Matthews. I'd just have to watch my step and do what I had to do.

I Googled my interviewees one by one, but found nothing that offered a motive for murdering two women. In fact, the only thing they had in common was their interest in Treasure Island. It was no secret—at least on the Internet—that Spaz Cruz wanted to follow in the footsteps of George Lucas, whose film company basically owned San Francisco's Presidio. Cruz wanted his own private island to house his cutting-edge computer graphics studio.

Siouxie, aka Susan Steinhardt, got plenty of Internet hits. She frequently made the papers in the name of some save the animals/earth/universe cause. Her current campaign was "Save Treasure Island." I wasn't sure whether she meant the flora, fauna, or possibly future marijuana fields, but she'd certainly brought awareness to the need for cleaning up the toxic chemicals left over by the navy.

And speaking of the navy, the name "Eugene Stadelhofer" garnered over a hundred hits, most of them citing his military service records—all glowing. No wonder Stadelhofer wanted to turn TI into a monument to his arm of the armed services—not to mention his bust. At least the pigeons would have a new place to poop. But I couldn't find anything that linked him to germ warfare testing. My mother had probably confused him with someone else.

The only other person I still wanted to talk to was Dakota Hunter. His name Googled up as "chief" of the Gold Rush Casino in Calaveras County. In one article he talked about his desire to expand his Indian gambling empire into the mostly untapped and lucrative San Francisco Bay Area. Indian gambling clubs were hot and getting hotter. The only thing keeping more casinos out of the Bay Area was the lack of available land. Treasure Island would be the perfect place for his tribe to set up camp.

Aside from their interests in the island, I could find no other link to the mayor, still the most obvious suspect—at least to me. According to *Law & Order*, most spouses—and future spouses—are murdered by their not-so-better halves. Those TV shows were pretty accurate, weren't they? There was still a chance Ikea knew something Mayor Green didn't want exposed, and he killed her because of it. But why would he have murdered Andi? And why make me look guilty?

Under this cloud of suspicion, my time was running out. I had to get my party plan started. Much like gathering all the suspects in the parlor to unveil the killer, I'd gather a few key people at a GPS Treasure Hunt and maybe catch a murderer.

I pulled up E-vite.com, the online invitation service, and typed in the details, hoping the proposed guests would drop whatever they were doing and join me on such short notice, as in tonight.

On the Island, lies a Treasure,
Somewhere hidden, this I vow.
Book of gold, it dangled brightly
Then went missing—until now.

After I finished working out the rhyme, I filled in the rest of the pertinent information:

You're invited to a GPS Treasure Hunt!
Tonight, 8 p.m., the Officers' Club on Treasure Island.
Hosted by Mayor Green in memory of his beloved Ikea Takeda.

*Bad, bad party planner!* I admonished myself silently. Using the mayor's name like that could get me in big trouble. No doubt he'd come after me—exactly what I hoped.

Taking a deep breath, I clicked SEND and watched as the E-vite shot out to Siouxie, Dakota Hunter, Admiral Stadelhofer, Spaz Cruz, and, of course, Mayor Green, along with a few other names that had been on the wedding party list.

If my party plan worked, the killer would show up to retrieve the clue alluded to in the cryptic invitation—and then I'd know for sure.

Let the fun and games begin.

I fed the boys, then changed into khaki shorts, an old "Bay to Breakers" T-shirt, and my skates. The fog was filling in the landscape, so I pulled on my SFSU hoodie. A skate around the island would relax my knotted muscles while I placed the hidden clues.

It took me nearly an hour, but after everything was in place—a fake fur wrap, a copy of one of Ikea's books, and the "missing" gold earring—I skated back to the old barracks to move my smoky office supplies and party stuff to the building next door. When I arrived, Delicia was standing in front of what would be our new digs. She waved me over.

"What's up, Dee?" I called, skating over.

Delicia took me silently by the hand and led me up the steps to Barracks C, an identical building next door to our fire-damaged barracks.

"What's going on?" I repeated.

She said nothing, just led me through a matching reception area, down an identical hall to the first office on the right—what would have been my office in the old water-damaged building that still reeked of smoke.

Inside stood my other coworkers.

"Surprise!" they shouted, waving party flags, crepe paper streamers, and balloons.

I glanced from Raj to Delicia to Berk to Duncan. Behind Duncan stood Brad.

Grinning stupidly, I asked, "What's this all about? My birthday was months ago. You missed it."

"Voila!" Delicia stepped aside and waved an arm at the desk filled with my papers and the new shelves loaded with my party stuff. Hiding behind Raj was a big red ribbon on the open door.

I scanned the room. "Oh my God!"

Everything from my old office had been moved to the new site, right down to a fresh supply of chocolates in my drawer.

I turned to the gang, tears welling in my eyes. "You all did this? For me?"

"It was Brad's idea." Delicia beamed as if it were her own. "We just helped. He even hooked up the computers. We still need a few things—some of the furniture smells like smoke, and you lost a couple of those giant people cutouts, but we were able to save a lot."

"Actually," Raj said, "it was not too difficult. And you have done a lot for us, Ms. Presley. We were glad to return the favor."

Berkeley, who'd been filming the whole thing, added, "It's time for your close-up, Ms. DeMille."

I shook my head, overwhelmed by their friendship and support. I glanced again at my laptop, party props, and office supplies, all neatly arranged on my desk and shelves.

"Wow. Thanks, guys. This is too much." I turned and blinked away tears that brimmed my eyes. I didn't know if they were tears of gratitude at the generosity of my coworkers or sorrow that I might not have this office for long, thanks to recent events. When I turned back, I said, "I owe you all. Big-time."

Brad, I noticed, had mysteriously disappeared.

I glanced across the hall to see if he was in his new office opposite mine. The room was empty.

"Listen, guys," I said to them, lowering my voice. "I need one more favor." I checked again for Brad, but he was nowhere in sight. Just as well. "Believe it or not, I'm having a sort of party tonight—impromptu. And I could really use your help."

Berk lowered his camera. "You're kidding."

"Tonight?" Delicia blinked. "Isn't that kind of short notice?"

"What kind of party, actually?" Raj arched his eyebrows.

"A treasure hunt," I said mysteriously; then I glanced at Duncan, who was staring at Delicia as if he were a lovesick puppy. "Right, Duncan?" I asked, waking him from his coma.

"Uh, right," he said, his face filling with color.

Before I could say more, Brad reappeared from the back of the building, carrying a large box. He eyed me, then went into his new office to deposit the box.

"So what's this secret treasure going to be?" Delicia whispered conspiratorially. "Money? Jewelry? Some gourmet chocolates?" Realizing what she'd said, Delicia slapped a hand over her mouth. "Sorry about that." The others glared at her.

"I'm sure it will be something surprising," Raj said, trying to make me feel better. "Right, Ms. Presley?"

I smiled as mysteriously as I could, but I don't know if I pulled it off. I probably just looked constipated.

# Chapter 28

*PARTY PLANNING TIP #28:*

*As you get closer to party time, check, double-check, and triple-check the details. One small, overlooked point—a melting ice sculpture, an intoxicated parking valet, a misspelled birthday cake—can ruin an entire event.*

I gave each of my coworkers a specific assignment. Delicia would greet the guests at the starting point—the parking lot of the Officer's Club right inside the TI gate. Duncan would pass out the GPS units and show the treasure hunters how to locate the clues. Raj would keep an eye on suspicious players—his suggestion. And Berk would film everyone at the final destination where the "treasure" was hidden.

Ikea's gold earring.

Which reminded me, I *still* hadn't viewed copies of the tapes Berkeley had made of the mayor's wedding. The police, naturally, had the originals. No time now, with only a few hours before party time. Besides, I had a phone call to make.

I tapped the name in my recent calls list.

"Chloe? It's Presley Parker."

"Presley! What are you doing? I got the invite for the treasure hunt you sent to the mayor, and he's livid that you used his name to get people to come! What were you thinking?"

"I know, I know. That's what I want to explain. Can I come by the office?"

"Sure, but I gotta warn you. If he sees you—"

I cut her off. "I'll tell you everything as soon as I see you. I should be there within half an hour, traffic permitting."

I hung up, gathered my purse and notebook, and stepped out of the office, locking my door behind me with the keys we'd received from the rental office. Someone tapped me on the shoulder, startling me. I whirled around and came face-to-face with Brad, who always seemed to appear out of nowhere.

He stepped back, grinning. Apparently he liked startling me. "Another fire?"

"Uh . . . no," I stammered.

He leaned back against the doorjamb. "Where're you going in such a hurry?"

"Out . . . you know. Some errands before the . . . thing tonight."

"Yeah, I got your E-vite. Having a treasure hunt? At night, with the fog coming in? And hardly any notice?"

I nodded. "Yeah, uh, it's the mayor's idea. Another fundraiser, this time for one of Ikea's causes—in her memory, you know? Uh . . . Friends of the Painted Ladies. With his clout, most people will show up, even at the last minute. And the fog's never stopped a true San Franciscan."

He gave me one of those *Yeah, sure* nods and stuck his hands in his pockets. "Want company?"

"Don't you have any work to do? Blood to clean up? Maggots to kill?" I said, stepping toward the reception area.

Brad laughed. "Truthfully, cleaning out your old office was as bad as some crime scenes I've worked."

"Ha ha," I said sarcastically, then changed my tone. "Thanks, by the way, for doing all that. It was really nice of you—

and everyone." I checked the time on my cell phone. "I've really got to run. But see you tonight, right? You'll be there? For the treasure hunt?"

"Yeah, I'll be there." He reached over.

I reflexively pulled back. Slowly, he moved his hand forward and brushed my cheek, then held up his fingertips. "You had a little something. . . ."

I saw the brown stain on his fingers. Chocolate. Poisoned or not, I wasn't about to give up my addiction. I rubbed my cheek where he'd stroked it. "Thanks."

He smiled warmly. "You've got my number."

*Boy, do I*, I thought, and held up my cell phone to indicate I had it. Once inside the MINI, I checked the number and thought about deleting it. There was no way I was going to call him in an emergency now. Not until this was settled. Unfortunately, I wouldn't be able to delete it from my mind—I'd already memorized it.

After circling the city streets for fifteen minutes, I said, "Screw it," and parked my car in a yellow zone. What's another parking ticket compared to an arrest warrant for murder? I ran up the steps and had started to push my way through the door when it suddenly opened. I nearly fell into the arms of a man with long black hair, wearing jeans and a T-shirt that read "Homeland Security—Fighting Terrorism Since 1492." He caught me with two strong hands, frowning. He was so big and imposing, I thought at first he was some kind of undercover security guard. And then I recognized him.

Dakota Hunter.

What was the outspoken tribal leader doing at city hall? Had he just come from the mayor's office, pleading his case again for a casino on Treasure Island?

I brushed myself off but didn't move away, blocking his exit.

"You're Dakota Hunter," I said.

He blinked in surprise. "Yes, ma'am. Do I know you?" With his mocha skin, dark brown eyes, and long straight hair, he had an arresting presence. I froze for a second, suddenly intimidated by his air of confidence. Or was it aggression?

"Uh, I'm . . . Presley Parker," I stammered. "The event planner for the mayor's wedding?" Caught unprepared, I didn't know what to say now that I had him right in front of me.

He gave a single nod, waiting for me to continue—or get out of his way.

It was fight or flight. And since I still needed answers, I wasn't going anywhere at the moment. "You're the one trying to get an Indian gambling casino built on Treasure Island, right?"

This time, not even a single nod.

"How's that going?" I waited.

He gave a condescending smile, his eyes on the door. "I'm just one of many who would like to help improve the land, ma'am. It's really up to the mayor. Now if you'll—"

He started to edge past me, but in spite of being dwarfed by him—no easy task at my height—I stood my ground. "Have you and the mayor got some kind of special arrangement going?" I was blindly asking questions, but I couldn't let this opportunity slip through my fingers. Not until I came up with the right question.

"I don't know what you mean," he said, looking at me as if I were a nosy child. "I really have to—"

"If you get the contract, you stand to make a great deal of money, don't you?"

He frowned. "I thought you said you were a party planner. What does any of this have to do with you?"

"I think it has something to do with the murder of the mayor's fiancée," I said, blurting out my thoughts with abandon. Time to take a wild stab in the dark. "What was your relationship with Ikea Takeda?"

His face colored; then he raised a muscular arm. I flinched.

He reached over and pushed the door open with that big strong hand. "That was over a long time ago, ma'am," he said.

I ducked out from under his arm as he moved through the door.

*What* was over a long time ago?

Goodness. Had Dakota and Ikea been lovers at one time? Maybe this thing between Dakota and the mayor was more than just a negotiation over Treasure Island. Was Dakota holding some sort of grudge against the mayor? Or could it have been against Ikea?

I caught a glimpse of the back of his shirt as he headed down the steps. It read, "America Discovered Columbus." This was one angry American.

I was still unnerved by my encounter with Dakota Hunter—and puzzled by his reference to Ikea—when I entered Chloe's office. She was buried in paper. The element of chaos in her usually pristine office seemed out of place, but it helped distract me from the puzzling reaction I'd gotten from Dakota Hunter.

"Looks like you're busy," I said, stating the obvious. I took a seat opposite her. "Sorry to interrupt."

She waved my apology away, a silver bracelet jingling as she moved. She was dressed in an elegant maroon suit with matching spike heels, her signature triangle necklace dangling between her modest cleavage.

"I've been doing a lot of the mayor's work since . . . you know. Of course, you haven't made things easier with this so-called treasure hunt you're doing," she said, shaking her head. "What are you trying to do? Get me fired?"

"Listen, Chloe, the reason I wanted to talk to you is this: You probably know the mayor better than anyone, being his secre— I mean, administrative assistant."

The hint of a smile broke through her anger. Everyone loves a compliment.

"And I'm getting nowhere trying to find out who killed Ikea," I continued. "The cops won't let go of the ridiculous idea that I had something to do with it. I really need your help. Is there anyone—*anyone*—you can think of who might have wanted Ikea dead? Maybe to seek revenge on the mayor? Or someone who had a grudge against her—like an old lover?"

Chloe shook her head.

"Any chance the mayor had a reason to get rid of Ikea?"

"Absolutely not!" Chloe said, her face flushed with anger. "He loved her. He'd never do anything to harm her. Presley, you're way off base here."

Whoa. Quite a reaction. It was time to change the subject. I nodded, then said, "I just saw Dakota Hunter leave the building. Maybe he's pressuring the mayor to get that casino built?"

She shrugged. "Dakota Hunter is only one of several people trying to sway the mayor."

"Does he have anger management issues? Is he violent?"

"I have no idea," Chloe said.

"Or maybe he has another agenda . . . ?" I said, leaving the question open to possibilities.

Chloe frowned. "Like what?"

"I don't know. He mentioned something about a relationship with Ikea being over. . . ."

Chloe laughed. "In his dreams. Look, Presley, Ikea was an attractive woman. A lot of men . . . liked her. But as far as I know, she was faithful to Mayor Green. I really think you're on the wrong track." She began to play with the triangle charm on her necklace and glanced at her closed office door before taking a deep breath—or was it a sigh? "Listen, I can't talk to you about this anymore. You know that what goes on in the mayor's office is confidential." She squirmed and glanced again at the door. Lowering her voice, she said, "I will say this. . . ."

I nodded, encouraging her to continue.

"I don't believe Ikea was killed because of the mayor. I think someone had a grudge against her for some other reason. I told you—she was very ambitious."

"But both Ikea and Andi had a connection to Mayor Green. If he wasn't directly involved, then . . ."

"Like I said earlier, Ikea had a lot of influence over the mayor. Obviously he was smitten with her or he wouldn't have arranged that ridiculous wedding fiasco. I think that's why the surprise was such a disaster. Ikea was a control freak. She wanted control over everything—her career, her love life, her future, the mayor, and of course her eventual wedding. When he took that away from her, she really freaked."

"So why did she end up dead?"

Chloe shook her head wearily. "Good question. Maybe she did promise to influence the mayor in some way—and it didn't happen. Or maybe she made someone angry for some other reason—who knows? But the chaos of that wedding party was the perfect opportunity for anyone who knew her to . . ."

"Murder her," I said, finishing her sentence.

Chloe glanced at the door, then down at her desk. What was she worried about—that the mayor would come storming in and find her talking to me?

She abruptly rose. "Um . . . I have to use the restroom."

I started to get up, taking the hint, but she waved me down. "Would you excuse me a minute?" I stared at her, puzzled, as she pulled a manila envelope from a desk drawer. She set the envelope on top of a stack of papers, tapped it twice with a red acrylic nail, and said, "I'll be right back."

I watched her as she left the office and closed the door behind her.

I turned back to the desk. And the envelope.

Obviously she meant for me to open it. Was it some kind of a trap?

Holding the envelope up by a corner, as if it were a dead rat, I dumped out the contents.

A small notebook fell onto the paper-covered desk.

I flipped it open with a finger.

The page was filled with gibberish—random letters and numbers. I scanned through the first few sheets. Each page began with two different letters. First DH. Next XS. Then SC, ES, and so on. Down the left side of each page were what looked like dates—3/15, 4/14, and on. Next to each date was an indecipherable word with numbers next to it, plus the letter K—50K, 10K, 25K.

DH—

3/15—flsdnty—50K

4/14—drgdlr—10K

5/15—bnkrpt—10K

6/15—txccvrp—25K

If it was supposed to be some kind of code, it wasn't very intricate. It didn't take me long to guess that the double letters were initials—and familiar ones at that. DH was Dakota Hunter, XS Xtreme Siouxie; SC was Spaz Cruz, and ES Eugene Stadelhofer. There were several pages more with additional initials that I didn't recognize.

As for the K, that usually stood for thousand. So, were these amounts of money?

It was the gibberish that I had trouble translating. I figured this was hardly written by a CIA operative; it must have been a code simple enough for the writer to remember and read. Recalling a consonant code from a *Games* magazine where all the vowels were missing and the letters were strung together, I sounded out the letters phonetically, to see if they made any sense.

The first one: Flsdnty. I tried *flesed nuty. Felse denuty*? Then I got it.

False . . . identity.

Drgdlr. Drag dollar? Drug dealer.

Bnkrpt was easy. Bankrupt.

Txccvrp. Taxic—toxic. Cvrp—coverup. Toxic cover-up.

Oh my God.

DH—Dakota Hunter. False identity.

XS—Xtreme Siouxie. A drug dealer.

SC—Spaz Cruz was bankrupt.

And ES—Eugene Stadelhofer—was involved in a toxic cover-up.

God only knew what the others were up to.

Whoever owned this notebook wasn't the brightest balloon in the bouquet. Granted I couldn't decode all the pages, but the ones I could told me everything I needed to know. Except who wrote this.

Chloe? Not likely, or she wouldn't have shared it with me. To make sure, I pulled a sheet of paper out from a nearby pile and compared her signature with the handwriting. Not even close.

It must have been Ikea's. Chloe must have found it in Ikea's office—after her death. But why hadn't she turned it in to the police?

To protect the mayor, of course. If this got out, the scandal would kill his political career. And along with it, her job.

But why let me see it?

I didn't have time to explore her reasons. I just hoped it would help me find out who killed Ikea. With little time left before my GPS Treasure Hunt, I slipped the notebook into my purse and hurried to my car. Chloe had trusted me enough to show me the damning notebook; I had to keep that trust as long as I could by not turning it over to the police. At least, not until after tonight.

Breathless, I took a moment before turning the ignition. This thing was a whole lot bigger than I thought. Ikea had hidden information in that notebook—information about at least four people who had a major interest in TI.

At least four people who also had something major to hide.

And Ikea knew it all.

Did the mayor know? Highly unlikely. That way Ikea could collect money—hundreds of thousands of dollars—from these desperate people who thought she was going to sway the mayor in their favor. At the same time, she had all kinds of blackmail material on each of them.

She was killed because of it, I was certain. But by whom?

And what did Andi Sax have to do with all this?

# Chapter 29

*PARTY PLANNING TIP #29:*

*When life gives you lemons, have a lemonade party!*

*There's nothing like a festive gathering to give you and your friends a little boost when things look bleak.*

So. Ikea ran her own little business on the side, thanks to "referrals" from an unsuspecting mayor.

Or was he all that innocent?

Chloe had been a gold mine of information. She'd done the right thing by giving me that notebook—at least to my mind—in spite of the possibility she might lose her job. I hoped I could make it up to her one day.

I still had a few loose ends to tie up—including the part that Andi Sax played in all this. But I was sure everything would come together when the killer showed his or her hand tonight at the bogus treasure hunt. The invited guests wouldn't dare dis the mayor and not show up—would they? And when the killer discovered Ikea's gold earring hidden in the cache, I'd be right there to see the reaction. With Berk filming the whole thing.

Back at my office, I waved to Delicia, the only one inside the building besides me, then opened up my computer to do a little Googling. While I knew better than to rely completely on information I'd gathered from the Internet, it was better than nothing.

What I found was eye-popping.

To begin with, Dakota Hunter had apparently had a little trouble with his tribe. After fifteen minutes of searching dead ends, I found an Indian advocacy group called SmokeSignals.org. There were several posts questioning the authenticity of his Indian roots, including one member of the Miwok tribe who claimed he could find no connection to the tribe that Dakota claimed as his own.

Not a real Miwok? Whoa. Was he even an Indian?

Thirty minutes later I found a site called BoxOfficeBombs.com that had the scoop on Lucas "Spaz" Cruz. According to someone named Perez Hilton, Cruz had quietly gone bankrupt this year. The site mentioned half a dozen money-losing disasters, including *Vampire: The Musical*. Another writer, a film critic, said, "Cruz seems to be under the self-delusion that a bigger, fancier studio will turn things around. It'll take a lot more than an island to remake this man. And knowing Cruz, he's got a few special effects up his sleeve—not all completely legit."

So how did he think he'd manage the big turnaround? First by getting the mayor to hand over Treasure Island. And then what? By getting investors to buy TI real estate at a low cost? Possibly at a ballooning loan?

It didn't take long for Xtreme Siouxie, aka Susan Steinhardt, to pop up on a site called CaliforniaCrimeWatch. She'd been arrested numerous times for protesting to save the island as a nature habitat. But she'd also racked up some arrests for growing and dealing marijuana, claiming it was for "medicinal purposes." No real surprise there.

But did the lofty end justify the lawbreaking means? Or did it just justify her own personal—and financial—means?

And finally, Admiral Eugene Stadelhofer. By searching a few military fringe sites, I found the project my mother had been referring to—ProjectSHAD.com. It appeared the admiral was little more than a blustery egomaniac who used his power to try to cover up a scandal decades old. The site claimed Stadelhofer had supervised secret chemical and germ warfare tests conducted on TI in the fifties and sixties, called Project SHAD, an acronym for ship habitation and decontamination. There was little doubt that he'd been responsible for exposing his sailors to radiation, anthrax, plague, botulism, and deadly nerve agents. According to the site's chat room, the men, used as guinea pigs, had experienced headaches, memory loss, cancer, wounds that didn't heal, and so on. Thanks to Admiral Stadelhofer's insistence on military secrecy, none of the sailors could ever prove a connection to the testing, so they never received disability payments.

Outrageous. Had Stadelhofer really been covering up his part in contaminating—and killing—hundreds of innocent seamen all these years? How could he have gotten away with such atrocities in this day and age?

I sat back at my desk, overwhelmed with all the possible motives these "friends of the mayor" had. Except perhaps Siouxie. Although the most outspoken, she seemed to have the least to gain.

Unless there was a major drug connection . . .

A voice came from over my shoulder. "Whatcha doing?" I'd been so engrossed in my notes, I hadn't noticed Delicia come in.

I sat back and tapped my pen on my desk. "Just doing some research. You know."

She pulled up the folding chair and sat down. "Trying to solve this mystery by yourself, aren't you, Nancy Drew? Listen—you've got a great stunt planned for tonight. You're sure to find out something. Have you learned anything new?"

I shared my notes with her, ending with my suspicions about the mayor. She listened patiently while doodling on a scratch pad. When I was finished, and her pad was filled with little cartoon figures, she said, "The mayor does look good for this. Politicians do all kinds of bad things—including murder. They think they're above everyone else."

"I know, but I can't find anything concrete on Mayor Green. He's practically a saint."

Delicia spun my laptop around and started typing. "Let's try this. . . ." She punched in a couple of gossip sites, like Drudge.com and YouElectedThem.com. Nothing came up on the mayor, other than all his good deeds. She tried one more search, linking "Davin Green" and "Treasure Island." Bingo.

"Looks like he's been stalling on his decision regarding Treasure Island for over two years," she said, summing up the article, written by "A Disgruntled Supervisor." "This guy, whoever he is, says Green has his own secret agenda for the island—but it doesn't say what. Probably can't say, without getting sued for slander."

"Libel," I said, "but that's not exactly a motive to murder his bride-to-be. Or a party planner."

Delicia held up a finger. "Unless she—or they—found out something he didn't want anyone to know. Ikea was extremely close to him, so she could have learned something incriminating. And he'd worked with Andi a lot. Hey! Maybe they were having a secret affair . . . and Ikea found out . . . and he had to kill both of them. . . ."

I laughed. "Nice try, but I think you've been reading too many bad scripts. Actually, someone"—I decided to try to protect the innocent—"gave me a notebook that Ikea kept." I pulled the notebook from my purse and handed it to Delicia. If I couldn't trust her, who could I trust? "It sure looks like Ikea was either blackmailing a bunch of people, or taking their money and promising mayoral favors. Or both. But I still don't know who killed her."

"What do you mean?" Delicia asked, flipping through the notebook.

"Well, if there were all these people who were paying Ikea to insure their special interests with the mayor—each without the others' knowledge—she could have been pulling in hundreds of thousands of dollars with no intention of helping anyone. And they couldn't do anything about it because it would compromise them as well."

"That's what all these scribbles mean?" Delicia asked, looking up. "Hey, maybe Ikea was saving Treasure Island for herself. I mean, maybe she planned to take over the place, build a big mansion, keep the riffraff out. . . ."

I looked down at my list, remembering what I'd learned from watching *CSI*. Gil Grissom said it was all about the physical evidence.

So what was the physical evidence?

Close-up on the missing earring.

Chloe had said the mayor bought the earrings for Ikea as a surprise for that night and had had them engraved. He gave them to her so she'd be wearing them at the wedding.

Then one ended up in a geocache on Treasure Island.

How did it get there? Was that random—or deliberate?

"Well, I gotta get back to work," Delicia said, placing Ikea's notebook on my desk. "I've got a party to decorate, and my boss is a slave driver."

I smiled as she headed back to her office to finish creating the clues. I stood up, stretched, and glanced down the hall. Berkeley was in his office, fiddling with his video camera—which reminded me. I *still* had to look at that wedding tape—as soon as I had a free moment. Duncan was unboxing a bunch of GPS devices in the back office. I giggled when I spotted Raj. He was practicing his quick draw in one of the window reflections. What a team we all made.

I checked the time. Five o'clock. Three hours until showtime. Just enough time to make a quick trip to city hall.

According to Chloe, Ikea had her own office at city hall, thanks to Mayor Green. I passed through the metal detector and headed up the stairs, hoping her office would be near the mayor's, and easy to find. But a quick search of the doorplates proved me wrong. No IKEA TAKEDA.

I picked up a nearby wall phone and dialed the security number listed there for emergencies.

"Guard."

"Yes, hi. This is Presley Parker, the mayor's event planner. I left some of my things in Ikea Takeda's office, and I need them for another event I'm hosting for the mayor tonight. I wondered if you could let me in so I could collect them? The mayor will kill me if I don't bring the props for the treasure hunt tonight."

"Be right there," came the response.

Moments later a uniformed security guard met me on the second floor with a ring of keys. Fiftysomething, African American, he had a bowlegged walk and looked tired, with droopy eyes and a turned-down mouth.

"Hi!" I said too cheerily.

He nodded. "Got ID?"

I handed him my business card.

He took it between his bony fingers. "Killer Parties, huh? You did that wedding thing for the mayor. I read about it." He handed it back.

"Yep. That was me."

"Didn't go so well, eh?" He eyed me through the bottom half of his bifocals.

Not knowing what to say, I shrugged.

"Too bad," he said with little emotion. Perhaps Ikea wasn't a favorite around these parts? "I'll have to escort you in."

"Of course. Thanks a lot. I really appreciate it. I'll be in real trouble if I screw this one up."

I followed him down the hall to an unmarked room. That's why I couldn't find Ikea's office. No nameplate. He opened the lock, accompanied by a lot of jingling and jangling of keys. Holding the door open, he nodded for me to enter. I squeezed by him and headed inside.

The room had already been cleared out. Only an empty

desk and lone file cabinet remained. Had the mayor taken care of it? Or the police?

I shook my head, trying to look disappointed. "Wow. Looks like they took all my stuff." I turned to the guard. "Well, thanks anyway."

As I reached the doorway, I stumbled and dropped my purse. Knowing a gentleman when I saw one, I knew he'd pick it up. As he bent over, I wadded up my business card and stuffed it into the door notch. I hoped the trick would work as well with paper as it did with gum.

"Thanks!" I said again as he returned my purse. "I've got a big event for the mayor tonight and . . ." Blah, blah, blah . . . I rambled on as he pulled the door shut. As we started for the staircase, I asked, "Is there a restroom nearby?"

He pointed back to an alcove nearly hidden along the hallway.

"Thanks," I said, and gave a little wave. "I can find my way out."

"Have a nice day," he said robotically as he moved on.

I headed in the other direction for the restrooms, ducked inside, and wiped away the beads of sweat that had been tickling my forehead.

After waiting five minutes—a long time for a person with ADHD—I peeked out, saw the coast was clear, and returned to Ikea Takeda's office.

# Chapter 30

*PARTY PLANNING TIP #30:*

*If you plan to videotape your party, avoid playing the footage back during the event or you may find you've captured a couple of unsuspecting guests engaged in some compromising activities.*

The back of my neck tingled as I approached Ikea's unmarked office. I twisted the doorknob. It held fast.

Taking a deep breath, I pulled on the door, praying the business card trick would work like the gum had.

It gave easily.

With a last look down the hall, I slipped in and closed the door.

Light from a streetlamp lit up the room enough so that I didn't have to turn on the switch. I tiptoed to Ikea's empty desk, sat down, and began opening drawers, one by one. All barren.

I turned to the file cabinet behind the desk and yanked on the top drawer. Empty. All four drawers were the same. Cherchezing la femme was turning out to be a colossal waste of time.

I shoved the top drawer back in, then the second, third, and last one. The three top drawers glided in smoothly. The one on the bottom stuck out about an inch. Mad at myself for wasting my time, I gave it an ineffective kick with my flip-flip and stubbed my big toe on the corner. "Shit!" I said, shoving it again with the bottom of my shoe.

It stood fast.

Kneeling down, I pulled the drawer open, then slid it in and out a few times. There was something keeping it from fully closing. I pulled on the drawer until it came completely out. Setting it on the floor next to me, I retrieved my cell phone from my purse. I turned it on and used the light to see inside the dark cabinet.

I could just make out something white—a piece of paper?—at the back.

I reached in, straining against the cabinet to grasp the paper with my short fingernails. I managed to get hold of a corner, then inched it out slowly.

It was an envelope. Apparently it had fallen behind the drawer and gotten stuck.

Or had someone hidden it there?

I sat on the floor, my heart racing, and opened the sealed flap. Dumping the contents on the carpet, I held up my cell and scanned the materials: a map and a mini-videotape.

Unfolding the map, I immediately recognized Treasure Island. Someone had divided the island into sections and labeled each one. But instead of plans for a casino, movie studio, memorial, or habitat, these plans indicated areas for a multimillion-dollar commercial/residential development, complete with high-end shops, gated communities, and exclusive homes—including one marked "Mayor's Mansion."

It was all here. The mayor's—or Ikea's—real plans for Treasure Island.

I set the map down and held up the videotape. This I had to see. And with Berkeley's help I'd be able to view it as soon as I returned to the office.

A click.

Shit! Someone was at the door!

I stuffed the contents of the envelope into my purse and scooted under the desk, behind the chair.

The file drawer!

If the intruder entered the room, he'd quickly discover it lying on the floor. I reached out a hand, pushed the drawer out of the line of sight, and crossed my fingers I wasn't totally screwed.

I sucked in a breath. My heart beat like a trapped bird inside my chest.

The door opened.

Silence.

A flashlight beam swept the room.

The bird in my chest grew to the size of a turkey. I pulled back under the desk as far as I could, hoping the chair gave me extra coverage.

More silence.

I pressed my hand over my heart to keep it from pounding out of my chest. Could the intruder hear my heartbeat echoing like a drum?

An eternity later, the door closed. I scrambled out from under the desk and moved to the door, pressing my ear against it, listening for footfalls. Muffled steps faded away to nothing.

I exhaled, waited a few more minutes, then pulled the door open an inch and peered out.

Clear.

That was way too close.

When I thought about all the laws I'd broken and how narrowly I'd escaped being arrested—this time—my hands began to tremble. If anyone had caught me, there would have been no Camp Cupcake for me.

Holding the stair railing with a sweaty, shaky palm, I double-timed it down the steps and ducked out of the building in record time. When I reached my MINI Cooper, I cursed.

A ticket on the windshield.

Cursing again, I threw caution to the wind and drove over the speed limit back to Treasure Island. My thoughts were consumed with what I'd found in Ikea's abandoned office. Not only her plans for the island—or the mayor's?—but a mysterious videotape. I couldn't wait to see what played.

How much did the mayor know about Ikea's secret stash? And whatever was on that tape? Enough to have a reason to kill her? And how could he know for sure the party would end in such chaos?

I was going around in circles, my mind churning with possibilities like a whirlpool. I had to focus on the upcoming treasure hunt. That earring was the key to everything, I was sure. If the mayor showed up to retrieve it, that would almost prove he killed her. And he'd do it in front of witnesses.

Like a shower of snowflakes, everything seemed to be falling into place.

Or was it more like an avalanche—and was I about to be buried in my own scheme? After all, the killer knew I knew, thanks to that cryptic invitation.

"Berk! I need you!" I yelled as I entered the office building.

Berk looked up from the video screen he was watching. "'Yes, my precious?'" he hissed, quoting *Lord of the Rings*.

No time for games. "Can you play this?" I handed him the tiny videotape I'd taken—stolen—from Ikea's office.

He took the tape and turned it over in his hand. "Sure." Popping it into one of his smaller videocameras, he flipped open the viewer and turned the camera on.

Instantly the tiny screen filled with the image of two people having sex.

"Whoa. Is this you?" He turned and grinned at me.

"God, no!"

We both watched the action on the screen in stunned silence. Finally Berk said, "Oh my God. I see dead people! Isn't that Ikea?"

He was right. There she was, lying on her back on a mattress.

"Who's that with her?" I asked, referring to the muscular man on top of her. After a few mesmerizing moments—and a new camera angle—I recognized the long black hair.

"Ikea is having sex with Dakota Hunter!" I looked over at Berkeley, who was grinning like a horny schoolboy. But he wasn't lusting over the cheerleader; he was ogling the football quarterback.

"Dude, he's hot."

What was Ikea doing with Dakota Hunter, other than the obvious? In other words, why—if she was engaged to Davin Green?

"The photography needs work. Obviously the guy holding the camera is a rookie," Berk said.

"Oh my God! You're right—someone else is there. I didn't even think about that." So now the question was, who was holding the camera? Davin Green? Were they into that kind of thing? Who knew what went on behind closed doors?

"Can I borrow your camera for a little while? I want to watch the whole thing and see if I can figure out who's doing the shooting. I don't have time right now."

Berk clicked off the camera and handed it over, with brief instructions on how to play the tape.

"Thanks, Berk. And don't tell anyone about this, okay?"

He nodded. I left his office and went to check on the others. Delicia had the decorations and clues ready to go.

Duncan had packed up the GPS devices. Raj had ironed his uniform, and his badge shone like the top of the Chrysler Building.

Only Brad Matthews was missing from the roster.

I wondered where he was.

And whether he'd show up for the "party."

# Chapter 31

*PARTY PLANNING TIP #31:*

*If, in spite of all your plans, you commit a party foul, learn from your mistakes. If there's something more you could have done to give that party some pizzazz, try it next time. What have you got to lose?*

Back in my office, I tried to call Chloe but got her voice mail. Damn. I left a message for her to call me back as soon as possible, that it was urgent. Next, I turned to the pressing matter at hand.

"Okay, guys. Let's get this party started!"

I heard Berk chant a line from *Animal House* in the background. "Toga! Toga! Toga!"

If this treasure hunt didn't kill me, it just might save my life—and maybe a few others. I was sorry it was too late for Andi Sax and Ikea Takeda. I was still praying for Rocco's recovery. If my plan worked, the killer would get my clue about Ikea's missing earring and come after it during the treasure hunt. Of course, he—or she—might even come after me, figuring I knew something about how it ended up on Treasure Island. But that was a chance I'd have to take. The alternative was twenty-to-life.

"Duncan!" I yelled.

Duncan leaned out of his squatter's office, his red hair falling in his face. "Dude. *What*?"

"You ready?"

"Du-*uhh*." He flashed a freckled thumbs-up.

Duh. I wish I had that kind of relaxed confidence. "All right. Meet you at the Officers' Club."

After my coworkers had piled into their cars and started off, I checked one last time for Brad's SUV in the lot. Where the hell was our crime scene cleaner? Mentally shrugging, I followed the caravan to the starting point less than a mile away.

A few minutes later we'd pulled up to the club parking lot and had begun unloading for the game. I sidled up to Duncan, who was unboxing a couple dozen GPS units and absently setting them on a card table. His real attention seemed to be focused on Delicia. I caught him stealing glances at her as she covered another table with a tablecloth. She'd chosen camo fabric in an effort to coordinate with the theme. I wondered if she noticed Duncan's surreptitious looks.

Meanwhile, Berk began videotaping the area, with close-ups on the GPS units, the stack of clues, and my frantic-looking face. Raj just strolled around, hands clasped behind his back, watching for guests—invited and uninvited.

"Think the game is easy enough for beginners?" I asked Duncan, then chewed my nail nervously.

"Totally. With these new units, all they have to do is find the longitude and latitude for each coordinate." He picked up a unit as if it were a valuable relic. "These are state of the art. They have their own maps, built-in electronic compasses, even voice navigation."

"So the players don't need to know all that technical mumbo jumbo you're always spewing?"

He rolled his eyes. "No. You just enter the waypoint written on the clue. That's where the geocache—the *treasure*—is hidden. That's it."

"Hmmm. Can I track a player with one of these units?"

He looked at me like I was an idiot. "God, Presley! The units don't broadcast your *location*—unless you're an *alien* or something. I thought you knew all this stuff. The satellites use radio frequencies that broadcast *their* position. Your unit takes that information to figure out where *you* are. It's called *triangulation*."

"So they don't have to wear foil helmets to deflect all those gamma rays?" I asked, laughing.

He rolled his eyes again. If he wasn't careful, his eyes were going disappear into his head forever. That's what my mother had always told me.

"You know, someday they're going to be able to track Oldtimer's patients with these babies," Duncan said, practically petting the one in his hand.

I bristled at the euphemistic word. "It's Alzheimer's."

"Whatever."

I started to pick up a unit but fumbled it in my fingers. It landed on the table with a smack.

"Careful! Those are *expensive*." Duncan grabbed it up.

"Sorry. How much do they cost?"

"Some are only a hundred bucks, but those are crap. These cost five hundred a pop."

Whoa. I wondered who paid for them. Did Duncan make that kind of cash hosting his GPS hunts?

"What are you guys talking about?" Delicia appeared with a handful of leftover fabric she'd used as tablecloths. In addition to the camo, the tables now sported green, black, and brown balloons, along with signs that read CLUE #1. Ever the scene stealer, she was wearing camo overalls and Crocs that matched the tablecloths. Cute.

"I was just telling Dunk that I didn't realize these GPS units were so expensive."

She picked one up. Duncan eyed her. "That's a Cobra," he said, suddenly losing the attitude.

She turned it around in her hand. "So how do you play with it?"

Duncan smiled as he gently took the unit from her hands. "You use it to find a hidden cache. When you find it, you TSLS—take something and leave something. Then you write a note in the logbook."

Delicia scrunched up her nose. "You take something? Isn't that stealing?"

He laughed a little too loudly. "It's *trading*, not stealing."

"Cool. What kind of stuff is usually in the catch?"

"It's a *cache*, like C-A-S-H, not a *catch,*" he explained patiently. If I'd said it, he would have rolled his eyes at me again. What kind of a spell did Delicia have on him?

"Could be anything in there," he continued. I'd never seen him so animated as he was with Dee. "Stuff like Star Wars figures, baseball cards, army men, foreign coins, cool stuff like that."

I thought about the earring.

"No jewelry? Or chocolate?" Delicia joked.

Duncan laughed again. I hadn't even known Duncan had a sense of humor, and here he was giggling like a teenager—which he practically was.

That was all the time I could spare thinking about a possible Duncan/Delicia hookup. It was time for the hunt to begin, and none of the invited players had arrived yet. I paced the area, checking the time on my cell phone every thirty seconds, wondering where everybody was.

Moments later a white SUV pulled into the parking lot of the Officers' Club. Out stepped Brad, dressed in his crime scene jumpsuit. Had he been working?

"About time," I said, checking his uniform for signs of blood.

"Sorry I'm late. Had a job. How's it going?" he said, glancing around.

I looked at my coworkers, who were standing idly by, and shrugged.

Brad's eyes moved to the table filled with the GPS equipment. He stepped around me, picked up a unit, and examined it. "A Magellan? Nice model," he said to Duncan. "Parole officers are starting to use them to keep track of ex-cons. What channel do you use?"

Duncan lit up. "Channel two as the primary for both FRS and PMR, and twelve as the alternate FRS channel," he said in some foreign tongue. He may as well have been speaking Fo'Shizzle.

"Ah, so they're longer-distance walkie-talkies, like Nextels or Talkabouts."

Apparently Brad knew about global positioning satellite units. And ex-cons.

What didn't he know?

I glanced around for the umpteenth time. Where was everyone else?

What if you gave a party and nobody came?

Did they not get the invitations?

Or had the mayor circumvented the invitation and cancelled the party . . . ?

What had I been thinking? Hell, some event planner I was. Maybe I wasn't cut out for this entrepreneurial business after all. I shook my head at my office mates, who'd been waiting for my cue. The fog had come in and the darkness was swallowing up the creative decorations. Slowly we folded up the tables, popped the balloons, gathered up the clues, packed up the GPS units, and loaded everything into our various vehicles.

Delicia gave me a hug. "The mayor is a jerk," she said, trying to cheer me up. I sighed, which Berk caught on videotape. While Brad helped the others with their tasks, I caught him glancing at me several times.

An hour after the party was supposed to begin, I was already back at my new office, replacing party props on shelves. My tired coworkers had gone home, after trying to pump up my self-esteem. Even Brad had disappeared, apparently called to another crime scene. Only Raj remained to lock up the building after I left.

Before leaving my office, I checked my messages and listened to an "urgent" phone call from my mother. Turned out she wanted to know if she'd left her panty hose at Tommy's Joynt. I didn't even want to know how that might have been possible, and I deleted the message. Tomorrow I'd stop by to see her again. Every day I didn't visit her, I lost another small part of her.

The other "urgent" call could wait until morning—the one from Detective Melvin. I pretty much knew what he wanted.

Me.

In an orange, county jail jumpsuit.

Not my color.

Remembering the videotape in my purse, I gathered my notes and headed for the door. "Have a good night, Ms. Presley," Raj said, peering out of his office.

"Thanks, Raj. And thanks for your help tonight."

"It was my pleasure, actually. Drive yourself safely."

As I backed out of the parking lot, I also remembered the earring I had buried at the last cache, hoping to catch a killer. Damn. In my haste to clean up and clear out, I'd forgotten to retrieve it. I made a sudden left turn onto Avenue B, followed it to Perimeter Road, then pulled over at the rocky edge, not far from where Ikea's body had been found.

The fog seemed thicker in the darkness, making it even harder to see. A few lights glowed through the mist from the Bay Bridge, but the island had few streetlights. We'd had to set up our own lights for the hunt, but of course, now they were gone.

I used my cell phone to light the way, creeping along the rocky shore while half feeling my way to the cache spot. Running my fingers into a crack in the rocks, I felt the treasure box and pulled it out. As I opened it, I half expected the earring to be gone, thinking maybe the killer had somehow figured out my plan and beat me to the punch.

There it was, mocking me and my stupid idea.

I tucked it in my pocket and returned to my car. Locking the doors, I switched on the headlights and checked the mirror before pulling out.

I thought I heard the sound of an engine just before I turned the ignition, but I couldn't make out where it was coming from. Checking my mirrors again, I scanned the road, but saw nothing. I was about to pull out when the crash came.

I thought I'd been jolted by an earthquake.

Then I realized I'd been hit!

The crash sent my MINI sailing into the deep ditch on the side of the road, dangerously close to the precipice that led to the bay. I bumped my head on the wheel—I hadn't bothered with my seat belt for the short drive—and hit my knee on the dash. That was going to bruise.

With my head throbbing, I sat there gripping the wheel, my body wet with perspiration, my heart racing wildly, my leg aching.

Once I'd calmed myself down and took stock, I looked out the windshield, hoping to catch a glimpse of the monster that had deliberately sent my car careening off the road. But all I could make out in the foggy, semidarkness before it disappeared was the receding back of something big and white.

An SUV?

# Chapter 32

*PARTY PLANNING TIP #32:*

*Every party has its surprises. When something unexpected occurs at your event, just pretend you planned it. Guests will think you're the most creative party planner on the planet.*

My hands shook as I pulled my cell phone from my purse, causing me to bobble the phone to the floor. Damn! I needed to put a string on that thing. Searching for it in the dark, I found it underneath the brake pedal and grabbed it up. I held it as steadily as I could and tapped what I hoped was Raj's number. The ache in my leg went into overdrive as I waited for him to answer.

Finally, a male voice said, "Hello?"

"Raj, this is Presley! I need your—"

"I'm sorry, this is Richard's Craft Store. I think you have the wrong num—"

Shit. I clicked off before the man finished talking and punched the number above it, my fingers trembling even more. The phone rang forever before being picked up.

"Yes, Raj Reddy here—"

"Raj! Thank God! I'm—"

Raj's voice interrupted me. "I'm out of the office at this

time, but if you leave me a message, I will be calling you back. Thank you very much and have a very nice day."

Double shit!

I dialed 911.

"Nine-one-one. Hold please."

Hold?

I hung up.

What the hell was I going to say anyway? *I think someone's trying to kill me?* I couldn't prove it, even with my car in a ditch. I had no ID on the driver, other than the car was big and white. Maybe.

I tried Delicia, then Berk, then Brad. Where the hell were all these people? At some party I wasn't invited to?

As my pulse slowed and my shaking eased, I realized Raj would call back. Eventually. In the meantime, the menacing SUV seemed to have disappeared. I had to get my MINI Cooper moving in case it returned for a second swipe.

I spun my wheels in the dirt for several minutes, then gave up in frustration. The car was going nowhere. I got out, putting my weight on my sore leg, and immediately tore my shin on a sharp outcropping of rock. The gash burned with pain, the ache in my leg kicked up another notch, and the throbbing in my head returned with a vengeance.

I locked the car and set out for home on foot, using my cell phone to light my way between frantic redials. The walk would take less than fifteen minutes, and I knew some shortcuts that would keep me off the main road where I was more likely to be a target. But my leg injuries wouldn't make it easy. Still, it was better than sitting in the car. Alone. In the dark.

*"There won't be anyone around if you need help . . . in the night . . . in the dark. . . ."*

Damn that Berkeley and his movie game! Pushing scenes from *The Haunting* away, I limped as fast as I could through deserted backstreets, black alleyways, and makeshift paths, past vacant lots, a long-abandoned gas station, and a decrepit bowling alley. Finally I cut through a dilapidated elementary school until I reached my housing development.

Cursing myself for watching too many horror movies, I sensed I was being followed, but saw nothing big or white in the foggy darkness. Still, I was certain someone had forced me into that ditch. Had Ikea's killer figured out my plan—and decided I needed to join Ikea and Andi?

"Thank God!" I whispered, spotting my condo. In my excitement to reach the safety of my home, I tripped over a chunk of concrete left over from a recently razed building. I sank to the ground in pain, gripping my wounded leg, and wincing at my own touch, tears brimming my eyes. I could feel the warm blood ooze down my shin, between my fingers. I tried to push myself up, clinging to the thought of reaching the safety of my nearby home. Once there I could lock the door, arm myself with my big knife, and hide under the bed with the cats until morning.

With as much energy as I could muster, I pushed myself up and tested my leg. It hurt like hell every time I put weight on it. "Ow!" I said, every time I took a step. Only a few more feet and I'd be home.

I hauled myself over the low fence and headed for my end unit. Out of the corner of my eye, I caught a glimpse of something big and white. An SUV sat across the street from my condo.

Windows dark. Engine idling.

No CRIME SCENE CLEANER sign.

Keeping my eyes on the SUV for any sign of movement, I pulled out my keys, my hands trembling. I dropped the keys, bent over stiffly, and picked them up, nearly overcome by the pain in my leg. Hobbling on, one eye on the SUV, I jammed the house key into the lock. I yanked the door open, dragged myself inside, and gave a last glance toward the white menace.

Gone.

I shivered and slammed the door behind me, sending my scared cats flying in three directions. After bolting the lock, I shoved a chair under the knob like I'd seen a frightened Eleanor do in *The Haunting*.

Not that it did her any good.

What had happened to the SUV?

I flicked on every light in my condo, including the one over the oven. Next I checked to make sure the windows and backyard sliding glass door were secured. Finally, I set down my purse and called my boys, who had fled in terror.

At the sound of my soothing *Here, kitty-kitty* voice, they crept in, one by one. I sat down in my kitchen chair, my wounded leg outstretched, and gave them all fur massages, while I tried to slow my racing heart and catch my breath. My cats are just about as good as Ritalin for calming me down in a crisis.

Once I'd gathered my wits, I cleaned up my bloody, swollen leg with damp paper towels, dabbed it with Mercurochrome, and carefully covered the three-inch-long scrape and two-inch gash with half a box of Mickey Mouse cartoon Band-Aids. Limping over to the cats' bowls, I filled them with food shaped like little mice, then helped myself to three Tylenol and a beer with still-trembling hands.

Pulling the video camera from my purse, I sank into the clothes-strewn couch, propped my throbbing leg on the coffee table, and switched on the recorder. I rewound the minitape while chugging half the beer, then restarted it, bracing myself for the footage. Holding the viewer up close, I watched for clues to the identity of the person holding the camera. Nothing. Just poorly framed shots of the couple doing their thing. Funny how sex can be so wonderful in person, and so silly-looking when you're a third-party voyeur.

I was about to turn off the tape when the camera zoomed in close on Ikea. Naked, she sported only a delicate necklace I hadn't noticed before. The camera jiggled, and I lost sight of the necklace. A few minutes later, it came into view again. In fact, it seemed as if the person holding the camera was trying to feature it: a tiny silver triangle.

Where had I seen that before?

I remembered Berk's copy of the party tape I had yet to see, and leaned over to retrieve it from my purse, trying to avoid moving my leg. I removed Ikea's tape and popped in Berk's tape, also micro. After another long sip of beer, I switched on the PLAY button.

Berk had apparently videotaped "the whole parade," as he called it. He'd started with footage at the barracks, where we were preparing for the wedding party—Delicia working on decorations, Raj surveying a map of Alcatraz, Rocco arranging his chocolate birds, and me running my fingers through my hair and shaking my head, mumbling something unintelligible. There were also several more shots of me chugging champagne.

I rewound to Rocco and slowed down the video to watch him work. As Berk panned the kitchen, I saw no sign of poison vials or toxic containers anywhere. I fast-forwarded through the rest of the preparations, then slowed it again as the guests arrived—Dakota, the admiral, Cruz—and briefly Miss Marple, aka Andi's party sidekick. I slowed the tape again as Mayor Green and Ikea, aka Bonnie and Clyde, stepped from the ferry onto the Alcatraz dock.

From their body language, it appeared that Ikea and Mayor Green were having an argument. Odd. I hadn't noticed that before. They'd certainly tried to keep it private. I couldn't hear their hushed words, thanks to the background noise of the water, the ferry, and the foghorn, but their knitted brows and unsmiling lips told the story.

So Ikea was already upset by the time she'd arrived at the party. Was she still bothered about her costume? Or was it something else?

The videotape missed the tram ride, but picked up again as the couple entered the cellblock building. I could hardly believe this was the same couple. By the time they arrived, the mayor had a full-on grin, obviously expecting a joyful reaction from his future bride. And Ikea had pasted on her public smile.

But as soon as Ikea took in the scene and realized what was happening, her mouth dropped open. Her confusion quickly turned to anger, evident in Berk's close-up of her face. When he pulled back, I caught a glimpse of Chloe, glancing around. Probably looking for a way off the island.

Then Berk swung his camera toward the door, catching Ikea as she stormed out. He focused on a close-up of the mayor's grimacing face just before he bolted out after the runaway bride-to-be. A pan of the crowd showed half a dozen others following him out the door, their backs to the camera.

I watched the video a while longer, hoping to see something in the faces of the other guests that might indicate an intent to feed Ikea poisoned chocolate. Although he had done his best, Berk never focused on any one person for long. It was just a blur of guests enjoying the loud music, gourmet snacks, and plentiful bubbly.

When the mayor finally returned, Berk was there to capture the unfolding drama. As he panned the room full of partyers, I tried to make out some familiar faces, but there was no sign of my new list of suspects—Stadelhofer, Cruz, or Dakota Hunter. And Siouxie was long gone.

Or was she?

Berk shot a close-up of the grieving mayor. Someone was patting his back in an effort to comfort him. I recognized Chloe's fingernails, painted black to match her outfit. She turned around and waved off the camera. Something caught my eye.

I backed up the video and reran the close-up of the mayor in slow motion, with Chloe at his side. As she turned around to face the camera, I saw it clearly this time. Around her neck she wore a small silver triangle.

I rewound the tape back to the point where Ikea entered

the cellblock. Berk had not only filmed a close-up of her horrified look when she realized this was to be her wedding, he'd also captured the details of her oddly mismatched jewelry.

The gold earrings.

And a silver necklace.

I stopped the tape and stared at the necklace. The sharp tip of what looked like a triangle peeked above her neckline, the rest of the charm hidden beneath black fabric.

The video camera suddenly clicked off by itself.

Then the lights went out throughout my condo.

My home was plunged into darkness.

A floorboard creaked.

Someone was in my home.

Whoever it was must have been waiting for me. After trying to run me off the road.

The white SUV.

The sound had come from my bedroom. I held my breath, not moving.

I had to get out of there.

I slid from the couch to the floor, dragging my aching leg, half crawling toward the front door. Another creak of a floorboard at the threshold of my bedroom stopped me cold.

The intruder was only a few feet away. But where exactly, in the dark, I couldn't be certain.

I scrambled forward to the door on my hands and one knee. Just as I was about to reach it, I bumped into something hard. The damn chair I'd propped in front of the door. It came crashing down on my sore leg.

I cried out in pain

Shit. That was a dead giveaway of my location.

I tried to pull myself up but the chair now blocked the door. Using the chair as a crutch, I tried again to stand up, but couldn't get my balance.

Another noise only inches behind me.

A second later something slammed into me, hitting my leg again, knocking me back to the floor.

I felt—and heard—my ankle snap from the impact. I cried out again from the searing pain.

My ankle throbbing, I dragged myself back toward the living room as silently as possible, trying not to groan with every movement. When I reached the small hall closet, I had an idea. Straining to find the knob, I finally managed to open the door, hoping to use it as a temporary shield. My leg and ankle throbbed with each heartbeat, but the adrenaline of fear kept me focused on survival.

The big question was, where was the killer?

Blindly groping in the darkness, I pulled boxes of stored party goods down from the closet shelves and heard them crash to the floor. So much for stealth. I patted the floor around me in search of anything I could use as a weapon. Feeling around in the dark, my hands touched something familiar.

Party poppers!

"I've got a gun!" I screamed into the black hole that was my condo.

Grasping the party popper, I found the string and pulled it.

A loud *pop* rang out.

I set off another and another until I ran out. Hearing shuffling nearby, I threw the exploded favors in the direction of the sound. Panicked, I felt around for something else to use as a defense.

My fingers touched a spray can, but as I grasped it, a cold, bony hand grabbed my uninjured foot. Frantically, I ripped off the cap of the spray can, aimed the nozzle toward the person yanking on my foot, and pressed the button. I heard the hiss of streaming tendrils of Silly String being released.

Pressing the spray button down until my finger ached, I emptied the can, then threw it at the killer. But before I could find any more props to use as weapons, a beam of light hit my face, blinding me.

The intruder had a flashlight.

I put up my hand to block the light and see my attacker, but I could make out only a shadowy outline.

"I think you're out of party favors," the voice said calmly.

I recognized it instantly.

Chloe Webster.

# Chapter 33

*PARTY PLANNING TIP #33:*

*If you find a boorish guest is monopolizing other partygoers, step in and distract her with a task, such as carving butter tabs into seashells or making radish flowers. That way she won't ruin the event for everyone else.*

Ice flowed through my veins. I stammered, "Chloe! What—?"

"Shhh, shhh."

In the glow of a flashlight, I saw Chloe lift a finger to her lips. She was shushing me as if I were a crying baby.

"Don't talk," she continued. "It's not necessary."

*"But . . . why?"*

"I said *shhh*!" This time she said it like an overworked librarian. But instead of lifting her finger, she lifted a gun.

My heart dropped into my bladder. I may have wet my pants.

Holding the gun on me, she pulled up a kitchen chair and sat down. Resting the flashlight by her side, she raised her other hand. In it she held what looked like a Baggie, but in the dim light, I couldn't make out the contents.

"I know you're scared, Presley, but you need to calm down. Here." In the shadow of the flashlight, she looked completely different from the friendly, caring administrative assistant I thought I knew. Instead of her professional suit, she wore black slacks, a black turtleneck, and black athletic shoes. Only the silver triangular necklace caught the light now and then. While her mouth and eyes were smiling, there was no warmth behind them. She held out the bag to me. "These should make you feel better."

I didn't move, just sat frozen to the spot, holding my swollen, throbbing ankle. She tossed the bag at me, and I jumped. The pain in my leg increased exponentially.

Chloe picked up the flashlight and shifted the beam to the bag that now rested in my lap.

I looked down and grimaced.

Chocolates.

"Go on. Eat one. They're good for you. Full of antioxidants. Helps prevent cancer. And chocolate gives you a natural high, you know. Makes you feel good. I think it has the same stuff that's in Prozac. Serotonin or Valium or something."

I stared at her. She spoke so sweetly; I think that's what scared me the most. This was not your average sociopath.

"Chloe, why?"

"I'll tell you what," she said, sounding condescending. "While you eat, I'll explain everything, okay?" She waved the flashlight, gesturing for me to get started. "That's what you want, right? That's what you've been trying so hard to find out, isn't it?"

I nodded. I figured I'd pretend to eat the chocolates while listening to her brag about her accomplishments and her superior intelligence—classic behavior for a sociopath. Meanwhile I'd stall as long as I could.

She waved the gun at me, this time more menacingly.

I pulled a chocolate from the bag.

"Good girl." Chloe sat back in the chair, the flashlight in one hand, the gun in the other, both resting on her thighs, but pointed in my direction. In spite of the outfit, she still gave the appearance of the perfect administrative assistant. Expensive outfit, right down to the shoes, and not a hair out of place. Maybe once she started her story, she'd forget about the chocolates. Obviously they were tainted.

I held the first chocolate aloft, as if about to pop into my mouth, and said, "You're a lot smarter than I thought, Chloe. I didn't suspect you at all. I still don't understand though. Why did you murder Ikea—and Andi? And try to kill Rocco? And me?"

Chloe laughed. "Oh, you had it all wrong, right from the start. Everyone thinks the administrative assistant is just a drone, with no brain of her own. Meanwhile our party planner here thinks she's Nancy Drew."

"I never thought you were a drone," I said. "That's why I'm surprised you committed the murders. Were you in on Ikea's scheme to blackmail people who had an interest in Treasure Island? Or did you just find out about it and want a piece of the action?"

Instead of responding, Chloe nudged the air with her gun. It clearly meant *Eat up*. I put the chocolate in my mouth and held it between my teeth, trying not to touch it with my tongue. Fear had dried up most of my saliva, which would slow down the melting process. If only she'd look away, I could spit it out—

"Good girl. Yummy, isn't it?" Her voice was filled with sarcasm. She began fiddling with her necklace as she talked. "So anyway, you're half right. Ikea and I did have a good thing going—manipulating people who wanted something from the mayor. Ikea and I always talked about how we were going to be rich when we got out of college. We were sorority sisters at Berkeley. Tri Delts. So when the job at the mayor's office opened up, I knew it would be a door to something big and lucrative."

"So you were in on it together," I managed to say around the lump of chocolate in my teeth.

"Yeah, but I was the brains behind it all. I introduced Ikea to Davin. He was just coming off a bad relationship, and I knew he'd fall for her. Who wouldn't? It wasn't long before she had him wrapped around her ring finger, if you know what I mean. I started giving her inside information about the special interest groups who wanted to influence the mayor, and she used it to our advantage. The money just poured in." She paused, seemingly lost in a memory.

"Then what went wrong?" I said, trying to keep her talking as long as possible. The words came out more like, "Den wa wen wong?"

In the dim light, I could see her face darken, the lines around her mouth and eyes deepen. I stuck my tongue into my cheek and pretended to chew, then nodded for her to continue. At this point I couldn't talk or she'd know I wasn't eating the chocolate.

"He proposed," she said simply.

I nodded as if I sympathized with her.

She played with her necklace as tears glistened in her eyes. She sniffed, then said, "Oh, she was so thrilled. Neither of us expected the relationship to last. But I didn't expect her to accept his proposal either. She certainly wasn't in love with him. In fact, she had a few other men on the side."

I thought of Dakota as she paused, tears brimming her eyes again. Instantly I knew why—it was right out of my psych textbooks.

"You were in love with Davin Green, weren't you, Chloe?" I could barely get the words out without dribbling chocolate down my shirt.

The gun in her hand snapped to attention. I was onto something.

"And if she married him, that would change things, right?" I prompted her, then wiped the chocolate saliva off my bottom lip. *Just keep her talking*, I said to myself, hoping she didn't notice the chocolate pouring from my mouth with each word.

Chloe gave a bitter laugh. "Oh, Ikea decided she liked the idea of being the First Lady of San Francisco. She had her own personal plans for Treasure Island and knew she could talk Davin into doing what she wanted. Forget about those other groups. After scamming them out of all that money, there was nothing they could do. They certainly couldn't tell the mayor they'd been bribing her to influence him." As Chloe spoke, her voice grew raspy, her words biting.

Wow. As a psych teacher, how could I have missed this other side of her?

I squirmed, trying to get my leg comfortable on the floor, but moving my ankle sent a jolt of pain to my brain. The chocolate was really beginning to melt now. I had an overpowering urge to swallow the liquid that had gathered in my mouth. Another drizzle made its way down the side of my mouth and dripped onto my shirt. I hoped Chloe didn't notice.

"Aak!"

Chloe suddenly jumped up from the chair. She swung the flashlight down at the floor in front of her, and with her gun hand, pulled up one of her pant legs.

Three bloody lines ran down her ankle.

Thursby, my attack cat, had apparently found a new scratching post.

"Stupid cat!" she hissed, rubbing at the scratches. She tried to shoo him off with the gun but he just sat there, wondering, I'm sure, what all the fuss was about. "I really hate cats," she said.

While she was temporarily distracted, I took the moment to spit the remaining mouthful of chocolate into my hand and slipped the melted glob into my pants pocket.

When she looked back up, I chewed on my tongue, wondering how long I could stall until the next dose.

As if reading my mind, she shined the flashlight in my face. "I think it's time for another chocolate." She pointed the gun at my head.

My heart skipped a few beats.

"Swallow it, Presley. You're taking too long. You wouldn't want anything to happen to your kitty, would you? Maybe he'd like a chocolate." She looked down at Thursby. "Kitty wanna chocolate?"

Thursby didn't move, but Fatman appeared and started for the sweet in her hand. Fatman never refused a meal. At his size, one bite of that chocolate and he'd be dead in seconds.

I pretended to swallow. "Okay, okay, don't hurt my cats."

"Good girl," Chloe said, smiling. "Have another."

I fumbled with the bag, eventually pulling out another chocolate. Before I popped it in my mouth, I asked, "How would their marriage really change anything? The two of you could still go on taking bribes and making money."

Chloe sighed. "Isn't it obvious? She wouldn't need me anymore. What's his would be hers—and he had plenty, believe me. I'd be out of the picture, with no more money coming in, other than that lousy paycheck. I can't live on that."

I had to keep her talking, keep her distracted, buy time until I had a chance to figure out how I was going to get out of this.

"So why did you have to kill her? Couldn't you just blackmail her?" I glanced around my familiar little living room, searching for something, anything, to clobber her with. A lamp. A cat bowl. The video camera.

There was nothing within reach.

"She had . . . stuff . . . on me," she said slowly.

I knew my time was short. "But you helped with the

wedding plans. Why would you do that if you didn't want her to marry Davin?"

"Because," she said, "we used to talk about our dream weddings, back in the sorority house. She'd always wanted a big society wedding at a huge mansion with all the important people there. A surprise wedding would have pulled the red carpet right out from under her. And that's exactly why I suggested it to the mayor."

She waved the gun at me again, indicating it was chocolate time. Using my clean hand, I palmed the next chocolate while pretending to pop it into my mouth.

Chloe leveled the gun at my forehead. "Oh, come on, girl. You're not much of a magician. Put the chocolate in your mouth and then open up and show me."

I should have practiced my prestidigitation skills a little more when I was a kid, but I could never make a rabbit come out of a hat, let alone do a card trick. Reluctantly, I obeyed.

After verifying the chocolate was in my mouth, she lowered the gun and nodded. "Good girl."

Trying not to swallow the saliva that was puddling in my mouth, I asked again, working my tongue around the mouthful, "Did you really have to kill her? She was your friend."

Chloe frowned. "I know it sounds harsh, but after all I'd done for her—introducing her to the mayor and helping her get all that money—she was turning her back on me. I was about to lose my best friend *and* my bonus income. These shoes don't come cheap, you know." She aimed the flashlight at her black suede Eccos. Perfect for working out at the gym or murdering a victim in her condo.

"Besides, she threatened to have me fired! Like I said, she'd been collecting evidence against me all along—insurance, she called it—while destroying anything incriminating about herself. Couldn't have that now, could I?" Sarcasm rolled off her tongue like liquid chocolate.

I thought about the sex videotape she'd made of Ikea and Duncan. That piece of evidence had slipped through the cracks, so to speak.

"So you poisoned Ikea at the wedding," I managed to say around the viscous mass oozing in my mouth. In spite of my efforts, it was melting fast. I wondered just how much poison I was actually absorbing.

And how much it would take.

"Yeah," she said, a smile curving her lips. "It was so easy, thanks to a little help from this young punk I hired."

"You hired someone?" It sounded more like "Ooo ired um un?" with the chocolate goo in my mouth.

She nodded, grinning at her own cleverness. "Kid named Geoff Pike. Calls himself the G'Man. Ironic, since he's a criminal, not a crime solver. When one of the island cops arrested him for breaking and entering and car theft, I checked him out. Paid him a visit at the city jail and made him an offer he couldn't refuse. I told him I'd get him released in exchange for some 'assistance.' It was a simple matter of forging the paperwork."

*I guess it pays, in more ways than one, to work at the mayor's office*, I thought, fighting down the urge to swallow.

"Once he got out, he had no choice but to do what I asked. He knew I could send him right back again. I set him up in one of the apartments on the island for convenience, got him an SUV and a cell phone, and just called him whenever I needed something. He was very accommodating."

"So he did all your dirty work," I managed to say, dribbling a little chocolate spit down the front of my shirt.

She shrugged, like it was no big thing.

I figured the more I talked, the more I'd dribble, so I kept going, starting with the break-in we'd had at the office building. "He's the one who stole the chocolate birds from Rocco's supply the night before the party."

Chloe blinked, confirming my guess.

"And injected the poison?"

"Oh no," she said, shaking her head. "He was too stupid to do that. The guy was a real rookie. After he got the chocolates, I injected the poison. Learned how from the Internet. Then all I had to do was smuggle them onto Alcatraz for the wedding—piece of cake, so to speak. Then I just waited for the opportunity to use them. When I saw Ikea on the dock, heading for the ferry, I knew I had my chance. I joined her, gave her a little hug, a few sympathetic words, and some chocolates to make her feel better."

"And after she ate them and started to get sick, you shoved her into the water," I said. I choked on the collection of slime in my mouth.

My cell phone suddenly rang. Chloe spotted my purse on the couch, grabbed it, and dumped out the contents, including my phone. As she glanced at the caller ID, I spit out the mass that had been the second chocolate and hid more of the sticky glob in my pants pocket, praying it wouldn't show. At some point the moist chocolate would leak through, but for now I could keep it covered with my chocolate-covered T-shirt. When Chloe looked up, I had my tongue firmly stuck in my cheek again.

"Nobody important," she said, tossing the phone aside. "Time for you to swallow that."

Nobody important? Except maybe Raj. Or even Brad. Now no one would ever know the trouble I was in. I pretended to do as she asked, praying I wasn't ingesting much of the poison while wondering if I'd be dead in a few minutes. Feeling dizzy, I rolled my eyes and swayed. Chloe watched me intently. I forced myself to focus—I had to keep her talking. She gestured with the gun again.

I brought the third chocolate to my mouth, then stopped, hoping to stall with another question. "What about Ikea's earring? How did it end up in the cache? Did you do that—or did you get your thug do that for you too?"

Chloe pointed the gun at my mouth. I popped in the chocolate.

"When Ikea started to fade, I took the earring off, figuring I could use it as a plant later. Pike was supposed to place it in your office for the cops to find, but the stupid kid apparently dropped it on the way over there."

I thought about the sequence of events that had followed: Duncan had found it, put it in the cache, and I'd discovered it soon afterward.

I met her eyes. "So you planned to make it look like me all along?" I mumbled the words around the slimy wad as best I could.

"Who better? You had the best motive. First you killed your party planner rival, Andi Sax. And then you killed the woman who ruined your big breakout party, Ikea Takeda. Made sense to me."

"But why kill Andi? You murdered her even before you killed Ikea."

"Andi, Andi, Andi." Chloe sighed. "She just sort of got in the way. We had this fight about the party details—she hated the ball-and-chain theme—so I told the mayor he should fire her and hire someone who wasn't such a diva. Andi was so mad about being let go that she told me she'd ruin the surprise for Ikea. And that, of course, would ruin my plan. So, before she left my office, I gave her some chocolates as a peace offering—chocolates I'd been practicing with—and promised I'd talk the mayor into hiring her for the next big function."

Chloe was on a roll. She'd temporarily forgotten about the poisoned chocolates she'd been forcing me to eat. That was the trouble with sociopathic egomaniacs with delusions of grandeur—they felt like they were the only ones in the room. All I had to do was keep the questions coming. "What was Andi doing on Treasure Island that day?"

She laughed again. "I told her you were taking over the

job and had stolen all the plans and ideas she'd already prepared. She said she was going straight over there to confront you about it. I guess she ate the chocolates on the way."

I needed another question to keep her distracted. Fast. "But, uh, why Rocco?"

"Why not? I thought it would make you look extra guilty. The cops were already on your ass and I figured that would cinch it." She waved the gun again. "Now, how about another chocolate? It's time for your suicide. Obviously you've made a mess of things, the police are about to arrest you, and you can no longer live with your guilt. You used to be a psychologist. Isn't that about right?"

I suddenly groaned, clutched my stomach, and bent over.

Chloe leaned forward in her chair.

Feeling her breath, I raised my head and spat the chocolate into her face.

"Ack!" she screamed, caught off guard. The gun went flying. I pulled my chocolate-covered hand out from under my leg and thrust the saliva-soaked poison-laden goo in her face, pushing her back as I smeared it. Rising up on one knee, my injured leg outstretched, I grabbed the helium tank that had tumbled out of the closet and brought it down on her head. She lost her balance and fell off the chair.

Using the closet doorknob for support, I pushed myself up and hobbled toward the front door of the condo. I shoved the overturned chair aside, yanked the door open, and limped out. I heard Chloe cough as I staggered into the carport.

I must have dazed her.

That wouldn't last.

Outside, I saw a white SUV parked on the street.

Brad!

I dragged myself over and pounded on the door screaming his name. "Brad! Brad!" No response.

"He's not in there," a voice behind me called.

I turned to see Chloe in the doorway, her gun pointed directly at me. Her face looked like it was covered in shit. Ooey gooey chocolate.

I yanked open the side door of Chloe's SUV and scrambled in, the pain in my leg throbbing with every move I made. I pulled the door closed and locked it, then strained to lock the rest of the doors.

Seconds later Chloe appeared at the driver's side window waving the gun. I hunkered down out of sight, but I could still hear her voice.

"It's okay, Presley. Lie down. Relax. It won't be long now. You've had more chocolates than I've given anyone else."

Was she right? Was it only a matter of minutes? Panicked, I stuck my fingers down my throat and tried to gag. How did bulimics do it?

Getting nowhere, I looked around, searching for—I didn't know what. On the passenger seat I recognized Chloe's Coach bag. Purse meant cell phone. Obviously she wouldn't bring her own phone into my condo and risk having it go off while she lay in wait.

I grabbed the purse, emptied the contents out on the seat, and found the phone. As I flipped it open, I glanced back out the front window.

Chloe was gone.

I turned around.

Her face appeared in the passenger's window. She began pounding on the glass like a madwoman. When she saw me with the phone, she froze, her lips pulled back into an ugly grimace. She knew what I was about to do.

Trying to stay focused, I punched in 911. When I looked up, Chloe had disappeared again. As I waited for an answer, she reappeared again at the driver's side—this time lifting her gun to the window. Her arms shook as she held the gun in both hands. It was aimed directly at me.

A gunshot rang out.

The driver's-side window shattered, filling the front seat with glass confetti. My ears rang as I gripped the phone tighter. I couldn't hear whether anyone had answered the call. I couldn't hear much of anything, except the ringing in my ears.

I crawled to the back and screamed into the phone. "Help! I need help! She's got a gun. She's trying to—"

Another shot rang out. A bullet whizzed by my head and ricocheted inside the SUV.

An arm reached in through the front window. The door opened.

Chloe was coming in.

I scrambled over the backseat and scrunched down, not breathing, not moving. I was clearly at a disadvantage. I was injured, I couldn't hear anything, and I didn't have a gun. I could only pray someone had heard my 911 call—and then I remembered. I hadn't given my address. The police couldn't trace a cell phone call.

A shadow moved across the ceiling of the SUV. Chloe was in the backseat. Moving my hand down and around the side of the seat, I felt for the lever that folds the seat. With all the strength I had left, I jerked it, throwing my weight against the seat. It fell forward and on top of Chloe.

I felt her thrashing through the seat. Digging in my pocket, I grabbed a handful of still-gooey chocolate and shoved it in her open mouth. If it didn't poison her, hopefully it would choke her—at least long enough for me to get the hell out of there.

I hurled myself over the seat, my leg screaming in pain. Ignoring it as best I could, I scooted headfirst out the driver's side door and onto the pavement. As I hit the road, skinning both my hands as I caught myself, I turned over and gave the door a shove with my good leg.

A screech of tires filled the air.

I could hear again!

I pushed myself up into a sitting position and spotted another white SUV zooming up behind Chloe's SUV.

Pike—Chloe's thug?

I started to crawl away as the door to the second SUV flew open. The driver shot out and quickly ducked out of sight behind the opened door. A gun appeared over the top of the door.

Oh shit. There was no way I was going to get away now.

"Police!" a familiar voice called out. "Drop the weapon! Now!"

Brad!

"She's back there," I squealed, pointing toward the backseat of Chloe's SUV. Brad approached, holding the gun at arm's length with both hands. With his head, he gestured for me to lie low.

He pulled the driver's door open.

I could hear Chloe coughing and gagging inside.

Brad aimed his gun toward the sound. A moment later, I heard Chloe's gun hit the windshield after her attempt to either drop it or throw it at Brad. She slowly rose, chocolate smeared over her face. She raised her chocolate-covered hands.

Together, I'm sure we made quite a sight.

"Get out of the car," Brad commanded, gesturing with the gun as he moved around the front windshield. The side door opened. He waited for her to step out, never lowering his gun. Pulling out cuffs hidden beneath his shirt, he slammed her against the car and cuffed her.

Raj pulled up in his beat-up old Chevy and hopped out. He ran over to me and helped me to the curb. I couldn't stand on my bruised leg and possibly broken ankle, so he eased me down.

"I just got your call, Ms. Presley. Are you all right?"

"Call an ambulance, Raj," Brad ordered. With one hand

against Chloe's back, he pulled out his cell with the other. He punched three numbers—the police.

I knew it. Brad was much more than a crime scene cleaner.

And thank God for that.

# Chapter 34

*PARTY PLANNING TIP #34:*

*After hosting a big event, give yourself a full day to recover.*

*Sip the last of the champagne in a bubble bath as you relive every delicious detail all over again. Then start planning your next party!*

"You lied to me!" I yelled at Brad from my hospital bed as he entered my room.

"You lied to me," he replied calmly, and sat down on a nearby chair. He'd obviously cleaned up from arresting criminals. His wavy brown hair was neatly combed, his jeans were fresh, and he wore a blue T-shirt with the Crime Scene Cleaners logo emblazoned on the front. But it was his smile that made me self-conscious. I pulled down the hospital gown, tried to fluff my hospital bed hair, and licked my lips wishing I had some lip gloss.

He picked up the remote and switched the TV to mute. Dr. Phil rambled on, using his pop psychology on some neurotic couple, but I could no longer hear his down-home soliloquies.

"So they pumped your stomach, huh?" he said, smiling with empathy.

"Yeah, not fun. My throat still aches from the tube." In

fact, it hurt even more now, making me wish I hadn't yelled at him a moment ago.

"Heard you have a broken ankle"—he glanced at the foot-to-knee cast—"along with multiple contusions and abrasions on your leg, and a sore mouth."

Yeah, from tripping and falling on my way home, getting in a fight with Chloe, and holding quantities of poisoned chocolates in my mouth. Plus a huge headache—from the poison? Or the car accident? Luckily, the doctor had promised I could go home—with crutches—after a few more hours of observation.

In the meantime, I was lying in a hospital bed watching Dr. Phil talk about people who had stressful lives. Ha.

"Are you even a crime scene cleaner at all?" I asked hoarsely, then coughed. It hurt to talk. My voice changed to a rasping whisper. "Or are you really some kind of undercover cop?"

Brad gave his lopsided grin and shrugged. He looked great in his blue shirt, while I felt like a hag in my tent-shaped hospital gown.

I eyed him as he pulled up a chair next to me, seeing him in a completely different light. Someday I'd have to ask him about the accidental shooting of the disabled man that must have had a huge impact on him. No one walked away from something like that without a degree of posttraumatic stress disorder. But now was not the time.

"How did you know I was in trouble?" I asked. "Were you spying on me? Did you hope to catch me in the act of murdering my next victim?"

He laughed. "No. I told you, I knew you didn't do it. It was the mayor who sent me to TI to keep an eye on you. He's not as stupid as Ikea sometimes made him appear. When he started receiving death threats about his upcoming decision for the island, he suspected the vandalism there was somehow connected. I was hired to check it out. Turns out he was right about that. Chloe managed to find a punk named Geoff Pike to do some of her dirty work. All except the murders. She saved those for herself."

"So you're not really a cop?"

He shook his head. "I do a little private investigating. For SFPD, the mayor. This time I was hired to find out what was up."

"And did you?"

"With a little help from you," he acknowledged.

"You bet your ass. Did they catch that Pike guy?"

"Oh yeah. We found all kinds of information about him locked in a file in Chloe's office. Tracked him down to the apartment she'd rented him on the island. When he found out about the murders, he gave her up."

"Wow. I never realized how much power an administrative assistant had." I paused. "But that doesn't answer how you found me—and so quickly."

"I was in the office when your call to Raj came in. I just beat him to the scene."

I smiled.

"Doc says you can go home soon," Brad added. "Thought I'd give you a lift."

"Thanks. Not sure I want to get back into another SUV anytime soon though." I took a sip of water. Even that hurt. "Have you seen Rocco?"

Brad nodded. "Good news. He's awake, alert, and out of danger. Can't remember much about what happened to him—something about chocolates—but other than that, he seems fine. He'll be released in another day or so."

"Thank God." I sighed, a combination of exhaustion and relief. Raising an eyebrow, I said, "So, you got a license?"

Brad leaned to one side and pulled his wallet from his back jeans pocket. He flipped it open and showed me the official form. I took it and checked out his ID picture. Taken a couple of years ago, it didn't look much like him, now that his hair was longer and he had that soul patch on his chin. But the dark eyes were definitely his.

I handed it back. "So you're friends with the mayor, huh?"

Before he could answer, Detective Melvin appeared in the doorway. I tensed up reflexively. What now?

"Got a warrant?" I asked weakly, only half teasing.

Melvin stepped in, dressed to kill in a designer suit, silk tie, and shiny Italian loafers. I wondered for a moment if he was on somebody else's payroll. When he shook hands with Brad, I decided I had to stop being so suspicious of everyone.

"Six o'clock? Firing range?" he said to Brad.

Brad nodded. "Wouldn't miss it. You'll be buying the beer afterward."

"In your dreams, buddy. Remember last week?"

I stared at them, watching their back-and-forth banter openmouthed until I'd had enough. "You guys are *friends*?"

Melvin finally turned his attention to me. "Went to Cal together," he said. "Sorry about giving you a hard time, Ms. Parker. When it became clear that someone was trying to make you look guilty, we did our best to find out who it was, and protect you at the same time. Obviously we couldn't let you know."

"Well, you sure made it look good, Detective."

"Sorry about that. But you were under surveillance twenty-four/seven. At least, for the most part."

Yeah, except when I wasn't.

After it sank in, I realized I still had a few threads to tie up. "All right. I have a couple of questions for you guys," I said, looking back and forth between the two men. "And I want answers."

Brad glanced at Detective Melvin, who clasped his hands protectively in front of his groin. They both nodded.

"Who tried to run me off the road?"

"Which time?" Brad said.

I shook my head. "Both times!"

"That first time, when you were coming down Macalla to the island, that was me. I wasn't trying to kill you. I was in a hurry—I'd had a call from one of the officers on the island about another break-in. I've already apologized for that."

"Apologized? You should have your license revoked." I took a breath. "So what about the second time. Was that you too?"

"No, that was Pike, driving the SUV Chloe rented for him. He was just supposed to scare you."

"What about that phone call, with my voice threatening to kill Ikea?"

"Chloe must have caught you on tape at the party," the detective said. "We found a mini-recorder in her desk. She was probably waiting for you to say something like that at the party so she could use it."

"And the fires at the office building?"

"Pike."

I suddenly had an epiphany and looked at them. "Was I your—decoy?"

Melvin shook his head. "Absolutely not. I assure you, you were well protected."

"Except when I wasn't! Like when my car was sideswiped, my office building was torched, and my home was broken into, and—"

Detective Melvin flushed. "Like I said, I'm sorry about not being able to let you know, but we had you covered, most of the time."

I pointed to my leg cast, indicating one of the times I wasn't protected.

"You want me to sign it?" he said, pulling out a pen.

I looked at him in disbelief. Before I could kick him with the cast, I heard a Southern-accented voice outside the door. "Mama always said, 'Life is like a box of chocolates.'"

A hand appeared from the side of the door, holding—wait for it—a box of chocolates. Berkeley stepped into the room, followed by Delicia, clenching a handful of "Get Well" mylar balloons featuring Mickey Mouse. Duncan entered with a bouquet of California golden poppies, no doubt freshly—and illegally—picked from Treasure Island. Finally Raj peeked in holding a small gold-wrapped present with a red bow.

A rush of emotion overwhelmed me and I felt my eyes sting. These people weren't just my coworkers; they were my friends.

Detective Melvin and Brad stepped back to make way for the new visitors. After a few minutes of answering their questions and listening to their condolences, I realized Brad and Detective Melvin had left the room.

"You must open your gifts," Raj said.

Berk handed me a heart-shaped package. Inside were a dozen fancy chocolates.

I looked at him, horrified.

"Chocolates?" Delicia said. "Berk, what were you thinking?"

He grinned. "They're porcelain. Just for decoration. At your next party."

I laughed and thanked him.

Delicia tied the balloons to my cast while Duncan put the flowers in an emesis basin, unable to find anything else. He plucked off a bud and stuck it between my bare toes, which tickled.

"Thank you, guys," I said, blinking back the tears. "This is all too sweet. I owe you all so much."

"Don't worry," Delicia said. "You'll pay us back. By the way, the governor called again! He's hot for you, Pres." She clapped.

"Great," I said, although I didn't feel as enthusiastic as I once had about doing an event for the governor. In fact, I'd planned to read the want ads and see if there was some other job I might be more suited for, such as mattress tester or governess.

I unwrapped the gold paper and opened the small bejeweled box. Inside was a pink enamel pin shaped like a balloon. Printed on the balloon were the words "Killer

Parties!" I guess I'd be keeping the name, no matter what I did.

I thanked them all again and gave them bedside hugs. Then the doctor appeared and shooed everyone out so she could check me one last time.

"You're looking good, Ms. Parker," Dr. Vassar said. "Do you feel up to going home or would you prefer to stay an extra day?"

"Go home," I said, through my sore throat. I sounded like E.T.

"I'll write a prescription for pain medication." She pulled out a pad, scribbled something, ripped it off, and gave it to me. "Come by the office tomorrow so I can check you. Do you have a ride? Or shall I call you a cab?"

"I got her, Doc," Brad said from the doorway.

The doctor nodded, shook my hand, and left after signing my release. A nurse appeared with a wheelchair. "I'll be back in a few minutes to take you to your car," she said.

When she left, Brad said, "You ready?"

I glanced down at my gown.

He grabbed the bag with my clothes. After untying the balloons from my cast, he lent me a shoulder and helped me into the small bathroom.

"I'll go fill your scrip while you change," he said, then closed the bathroom door.

With my leg in a cast, I felt like a contortionist inside the little room. It took me ten minutes to dress. The doctor had cut my pant leg above the knee, saving me the trouble of having to make the alteration myself, but it still wasn't easy getting my jeans on. After combing my hair and wiping the mascara shadows from under my eyes, I opened the bathroom door.

Brad was waiting for me, holding the balloons. I didn't know who looked more ridiculous—me wearing half shorts and half long pants, or him holding Mickey Mouse balloons.

"You want these?" he asked, lifting the balloons.

I shook my head. "Leave them for the next patient. I've got plenty more."

Brad helped me into the waiting wheelchair. He piled the chocolates and gifts on my lap; then we started out of the room. A nurse appeared and blocked his path.

"I've got it," he said.

She tried to argue hospital policy, but when Brad flashed his PI badge, she must have mistaken it for a police badge and gave up, handing him a pair of crutches.

As Brad wheeled me to his SUV, I had a growing sense of dread.

"I hate SUVs," I said, grimacing. "Especially white ones."

"You're stereotyping. Not all SUVs are evil. Not all party planners are murderers."

"*Event* planner!" I snapped, and then realized I was more upset about being called a party planner than a murderer.

Brad helped me in and buckled me up. As he started the car, I asked, "Can we stop by the office—"

Brad held up a hand. "No. I'm taking you home."

I nodded, too tired to argue.

I dozed off on the drive from San Francisco General to Treasure Island, and woke up when he turned off the engine at my carport. He carried me into my condo and helped me into bed, then made a second trip to the car for the crutches and hospital goodies.

Heavily medicated, I fell asleep before he returned.

The next morning, aching everywhere but my hair, I rolled up, grabbed the crutches that lay on the floor nearby, and hobbled to the kitchenette for my pain meds. I was surprised to see Brad sitting at the table, drinking coffee and reading the newspaper. He was wearing the black Alcatraz T-shirt from the party. It looked great on him.

He must have seen my startled look. "Just got here. Made you a latte."

I blinked. "Where did you sleep?"

"In my SUV."

"Really? Where?"

"In the driveway."

I dropped into a kitchen chair. The front page of the *Chronicle* was spread out on the table. Chloe, Mayor Green, and I had made headlines, but I didn't feel like reading further. I folded the paper over to the want ads and scanned them.

"Good story. Sure you don't want to read it?" Brad said.

"Maybe later. Right now I need drugs. Got any heroin?"

He laughed and brought over my pain pills, along with the latte he'd made using my espresso machine. Multitalented.

"What, no medicinal marijuana?" I swallowed the medication.

He sat down. "How're you feeling?"

"Like I partied all night."

"Yeah, I know that feeling." He looked down at his foot. Thursby was brushing against him.

"Hey. You're not sneezing!" I said.

"You're not the only one on drugs. Took some Claritin."

After I'd had a couple of swallows of my latte and felt my head begin to clear, I asked, "So what's going to happen to Chloe?"

Brad shrugged. "Trial. Sentence. She'll probably get life for first-degree murder."

Too bad Alcatraz wasn't available, I thought.

"So your assignment for the mayor is over?" I said.

He nodded. "Piece of cake, as they say in your business."

"Will you be moving out of the barracks?" I squeaked. I sounded like helium escaping from a balloon and hoped the disappointment on my face wasn't that obvious.

A wicked smile crossed his face. "Well, it looks like the crime scene cleaning business is about to pick up. Davin's got another job for me."

"Really? What?" I couldn't contain my excitement.

"If I tell you—"

"You'll have to kill me, I know."

"Seems there's some kind of monkey business going on at the de Young Museum."

"Really?" I looked up at Brad. I don't know if the tickle in my stomach came from hearing his startling news or looking into his sparkling eyes. "That's interesting. One of the calls I got after the mayor's so-called wedding was from the curator at the de Young. She wants a murder mystery fundraiser for a new wing or exhibit or whatever."

Brad smiled. "Sounds like a killer party to me."

Jeez, I certainly hoped not.

Still, I was no party pooper. I knew that now. And working with Brad Matthews again might just be my party favor.

# *How to Host a Geocaching Treasure Hunt*

## Introduction

Adventure parties like Geocaching Treasure Hunts are raging these days, thanks to new technology and new twists on a popular theme. In the past, miners and explorers would hide a cache (pronounced "cash") with food and emergency items. Today they're filled with trinkets, pens and logbooks, and other fun discoveries. Teams use GPSs—electronic global positioning satellite units—to find hidden caches set up locally. The game is deceptively easy. Just key in the waypoint—longitude and latitude—to find the coordinates and off you go. But you still have to find the hidden cache, somewhere within six to twenty feet, a fun and challenging task. For added fun, consider giving your hunt a theme, such as "The Secret of Nancy Drew's Clues," "*CSI*—Your Town," or "Halloween Haunted Hunt," then create invitations, decorations, and caches to match the theme.

### *Invitations*

Photocopy a local map, mark the party location, including coordinates, then write party details on the back.

Include a toy compass and a clue to the first cache inside the envelope, then mail to guests.

### Costumes

Divide up the teams ahead of time and ask each guest to come dressed in the selected team colors.

Have everyone wear camouflage.

Tell the guests to wear sport clothes and athletic shoes.

### Decorations

Decorate the starting point with maps, arrows, street signs, and compasses.

Set out some of the tiny trinkets teams will be searching for, such as:

Troll dolls
Foam letters of the alphabet
Stickers
Pins
Candy
Magnets
Keychains

### Games & Activities

#### To Prepare:

You'll need at least two GPS units for two teams, more if you divide up into more teams. Ask the guests if they have a device—many people are buying them because the prices are reasonable, as low as $100—and they're fun to use. You can also rent a couple from electronics, camping, or boat stores, if you prefer.

To prepare the hunt, choose a starting point—your home or off-site, at a café, park, or local landmark.

Choose five to ten sites for the hunt, depending on how long you want the party to last, and write down the coordinates of each.

Fill a small container, such as a plastic lidded bowl, small box, or lidded can, with enough of the same trinkets for each team. For example, if there are two teams, place two trolls in the bowl. Then insert the coordinates for the next cache.

Hide the container at the first site.

Repeat for each site, leaving different trinkets behind, along with new coordinates for the next sites.

### At Game Time:

Gather the guests and divide into teams. Have them give their teams a name, such as "Trezure Seekers," "Gold Diggers," or "GeePers Creepers."

Give each team a "cheat sheet" that lists the coordinates, along with a "give-up" sheet that indicates where the hunt ends—at your home, a restaurant, etc.

Tell the teams they must find each site using the GPS unit, retrieve a trinket from the cache, replace the cache where they found it, and continue to the next waypoint. Include a puzzling clue for added fun, such as "Look up high, perhaps a tree holds the cache for all to see."

Each trinket is worth a point.

If they can't find a cache, they can use the "spoiler" sheet to move on to the next site, but they will lose a point since they won't be retrieving a trinket.

The team who arrives back to the end site with the most trinkets wins the game.

## *Refreshments*

Geocaching teams are likely to get thirsty on the hunt, so provide them each with a bottle of water or a sports bottle with a sports drink.

For fun, hide some candy in a couple of the caches to discover—this will help keep the players' energy up.

When the teams arrive back to the end point to count up trinkets and decide on winners, they're apt to be ravenous, so provide a buffet deli lunch or bake DIY pizzas.

If they've been out in hot weather, welcome them with refreshing drinks and cold-cut platters, or make a hearty soup with hot French bread for the cold weather hunts.

Serve food to match the terrain—gourmet entrees for city treks, veggies and salads for hunts in the park.

Offer beer, wine, and/or soda, along with sports drinks if the weather's warm, and hot chocolate or lattes if it's cold outside.

If you're celebrating a special occasion, make or order a cake shaped like the cache—a box or bowl—and top it with all the trinkets from the hunt.

Serve cupcakes decorated like compasses.

## Favors

If money is no object, give them all their own GPS units.

Have extra trinkets and give them a cacheful to take home.

Hand out maps of local historic areas, along with recommendations for attractions.

Give them inflatable globes, compasses, or a subscription to Google Earth.

## Tips & Options

Send them on a tour of your town, or a historic section of another town, and offer interesting information about each place. Then quiz them when they return to the end site.

Have them take pictures of each cache, using a digital camera or Polaroid camera, instead of taking a trinket.

Watch out for GeoMuggles—people who might spot you finding the cache. Be subtle—remember, this is supposed to be a treasure hunt with hidden loot. You don't want GeoMuggles to crash the cache!

For more information about GPS hunts, go to Groundspeak at http://www.geocaching.com. It's a great site listing all kinds of hunts in your area, where to get equipment, and how to play the game.

Try a Letterboxing party! It's much like a Geocaching party, played outdoors, that combines orienteering, puzzle solving, and personalized stamping. You'll find clues hidden in boxes in public places, along with a logbook and rubber stamp. Collect the stamps in your own logbook, and leave your stamp in the letterbox logbook. For more information, go to http://letterboxing.org.

# Acknowledgments

Thanks to everyone who helped me with the development and realization of Presley Parker: Gay Carter, Corinne Davis, Staci McLaughlin, Ann Parker, Connie Pike, and Carole Price. To event planners extraordinaire Andrea Campbell and Patty Sachs. And those who prefer to remain nameless: the police officers, security guards, and shopkeepers on Treasure Island, the park rangers at Alcatraz Island National Park, the police officers at the San Francisco Police Department (850 Bryant). Oh, and Nancy Drew.

A very special thanks to Andrea Hurst, Amberly Finarelli, Kristen Weber, Claire Zion, Rebecca Vinter, and Sandra Harding for all their help, support, and enthusiasm.

Turn the page for a sneak peek of
Penny Warner's next Party-Planning Mystery,

# How to Crash a *Killer Bash*

*PARTY PLANNING TIP #1:*

*When planning a murder mystery party, make sure you don't use real weapons as props. They may be too tempting for some of the guests.*

The murder weapon lay on a black velvet cloth, traces of blood so deeply embedded in the carved hilt that centuries of wear hadn't eroded the terror it could still induce in the viewer.

At least it looked like blood.

In the dimly lit room, the ivory and jade dagger glowed an eerie greenish hue. I was dying to touch this exquisite artifact, which had been used countless times on helpless, horrified victims.

I reached for it. My fingers collided with the cold, protective Plexiglas case.

*Too bad it's locked up*, I thought. The real dagger would make the perfect weapon for the murder mystery play I'd be hosting the next evening at San Francisco's world-renowned de Young Museum. Instead we would have to make due with a Styrofoam prop from the museum's art restoration department.

I set my venti latte on top of the case and pulled out my iPhone to take a picture. Glancing at the security camera high on the wall, I noticed the motion-sensing light was yellow. Alone in the room after hours, I was being watched—and probably filmed.

A footfall creaked behind me.

My heart skipped a beat.

I snatched the latte from the top of the case.

A hand clamped down hard on my shoulder and I nearly dropped my coffee.

I whirled around, raising the only weapon I had besides lukewarm coffee—a Killer Parties promotional pen. At a moment's notice I was ready to stab—or at least heavily mark up—the shadowy figure. He stepped into the glow of the spotlight that illuminated the case.

"There's no food or drink allowed in here, ma'am," the uniformed security guard said.

I lowered my killer pen and caught my breath.

"You scared the crap out of me!"

The guard raised an eyebrow. Apparently he meant to scare the crap out of me.

"Ma'am, you're also not supposed to be in here after hours."

I raised my latte in apology. "Sorry. I just wanted to take another look at the dagger."

"I'm afraid the museum is closed to the public tonight."

"Oh, I'm not the public. I'm Presley Parker, the event planner for the mystery play tomorrow night. I have permission from Mary Lee Miller to be here." That was stretching the truth a bit. I had permission to be in the museum for the rehearsal, not necessarily to have free run of the place.

The security guard held up his flashlight and shined it on my face.

"Oh, yes, I recognize you. You've been here several times lately, haven't you?"

"Yep. Trying to get ready for the big fund-raiser." I tried to sound casual.

"Sorry about sneaking up on you. Didn't mean to scare you. I know this place can get kind of creepy when there's no one around." He looked me up and down. I must have appeared suspicious wearing an old-fashioned button-down jacket and loose-fitting khaki pants, not to mention the leather boots. He eyed the badge pinned to my lapel.

I looked down at my outfit. "This is my costume," I explained. "Tonight's our dress rehearsal and I'm going as Kate Warne, the first female Pinkerton detective."

The guard surveyed the room—probably making sure I hadn't stolen anything—then looked back at me. "So what are you doing up here? Isn't that event taking place on the main floor?"

"Uh, I just wanted to see the dagger once more, to make sure the art department copied it accurately. After all, I can't have six of the world's most famous fictional detectives trying to murder the museum curator with a rubber knife, can I?" I gave a nervous laugh.

He didn't crack a smile.

"And you are . . . ?" I reached out my hand.

Stone-faced, the guard shook it. "Sam Wo. Head of security."

I took a moment to study—and diagnose—him, a habit I'd formed while teaching abnormal psychology at San Francisco State University. He was Asian, in his sixties, and shorter than me by several inches. His hand was small, dry, and ringless; I noticed a tan line around his ring finger. He wore standard black loafers, the discount variety from Target or Wal-Mart popular with underpaid service employees. From his impeccable uniform and well-worn but polished shoes, I guessed he had a touch of OCD—obsessive-compulsive disorder—a trait well matched for this particular detail-oriented job.

"I wish Ms. Miller would tell me when people are going to be running around the museum after closing." Eyeing me again, he added, "So you're the one who's putting on this mystery thing?"

"That would be me. And I'd better get back to the rehearsal. Make sure no real murders are being committed. Although I suppose if that happened, you guys could figure out whodunit pretty quickly." I nodded at the nearest camera, watching us.

"True. This wouldn't be the best place to kill someone. The cameras are motion triggered—that's how I knew you were here. Just be careful about touching the cases. You could set off an alarm."

My eyes widened. "Really? Are the alarms that sensitive?"

"Sure. Especially the ones with priceless pieces inside, like that Dogon statue over there." He gestured toward a nearby case.

I glanced at the piece he was referring to and grimaced. The grotesque three-foot-tall statue looked to be carved out of wood. Shaped like a human body, the figure had long pendulous breasts that hung nearly to its waistline. But that wasn't the disturbing part. Dangling from just under the waist and nearly reaching the feet was an equally pendulous penis.

The guard broke into a grin, showing a mouthful of crooked teeth. "Naw, I'm just messing with you. We don't have alarmed exhibits here. That's an East Coast thing. But I love to tease the schoolkids when they come. They couldn't care less about the art. All they want to know is whether anything's ever been stolen and whether we have alarms."

"You're quite the kidder, Sam Wo," I said, forcing a friendly laugh. A little surprised at the low-level security, I glanced back at the case holding the ceremonial dagger. "Seriously, has there ever been a theft?"

"No, ma'am. Surprising, perhaps, since we have more than twenty-five thousand works of art from around the world. Top names, too—Homer, Cassatt, Frank Lloyd Wright . . . But we still manage to keep an eye on things."

I scanned the room, which was filled with incredible artifacts from Oceanic, Mayan, African, and Andean cultures. "So you've never had a problem?"

"Not on my watch. At least not with thefts. This is a friendly museum, a museum for the people, not like some of those hoity-toity ones back East. The biggest problem we have are the transients who come to the Friday night open house for the wine parties and end up drunk and lying on the marble floor." Sam Wo chuckled. His stiff, official manner had softened, replaced by an easy smile and contagious laugh. Being in charge of these irreplaceable objects insured for more than $90 million would have made me nervous, but Sam Wo appeared relaxed.

"What about fakes?" I said, lowering my voice to sound conspiratorial. "I mean, does the museum have any art scandals I could include in the script?"

"You mean like questions of provenance?"

I made a face. Museum-speak was a whole new language for me.

His face lit up. I had a feeling he got pretty bored on the job and loved the opportunity to share his authority and expertise with the public.

"Provenance means where the objects come from and whether they're authentic."

"That's a concern in this day and age?" I asked.

"Yes, ma'am. Some museums take a 'don't ask, don't tell' attitude. But not the de Young. Our curator works only with reputable dealers."

I sensed his feeling of pride about the objects that surrounded him.

"There are museums that don't?" I took a sip of my now-cold latte. It was my third of the day, but I needed regular doses to help control my ADHD—attention deficit/hyperactivity disorder. It was either triple the caffeine or go back to Ritalin, which pretty much turned me into a zombie. Old psychology secret: While caffeine is a stimulant for most people, for those of us with ADHD, it does the opposite—it calms us down.

Sam Wo shined his flashlight around the room while he

talked as if it was habit. "I guess you didn't hear about the Getty or the Met scandals? They made the news a few years ago. There were questions about how they acquired some pieces."

"You mean they had fakes?" I stole another glance at the encased dagger, wondering how one could tell a replica from an authentic piece. I'd been impressed with how much the Styrofoam stage dagger looked like the real thing, right down to the dried-blood effect.

"More like they were 'taken without permission,'" he said, making finger quotes. He stepped over to another display and shined his flashlight inside the case. "See these ceramic bowls and whatnot? They're authentic. We have the documentation to prove their provenance. But similar ones were recently acquired illegally at another museum."

Surprised, I asked, "How does that happen?"

"Some museums aren't as careful as the de Young. They'll deal with the black market."

"Where does the black market get them?"

Sam tucked his thumbs into his black leather belt. "Professional thieves usually steal them from the country of origin and sell them to questionable curators who think art should be 'shared with the world for the greater good.' But if you think about it, it's like taking pieces of the Statue of Liberty and displaying them at, say, a museum in Egypt."

I saw his point. Not only was I unaware that this kind of looting occurred, but I was impressed that a security guard knew so much about art. More than I did, anyway. My walls tended to display posters from classic movies such as *The Maltese Falcon*, and my "display cases,"—aka table- and desktops—showcased party props and event catalogs. I guessed Sam Wo had absorbed a lot just by osmosis.

"There's a lot of competition between museums to build world-class collections," he added. "And the de Young—"

His words were suddenly cut off by the echoing razor-sharp click of heels and the yapping of a small dog coming from down a shadowed hall. As if he recognized the sounds, Sam Wo jerked to attention, pulled down the front of his jacket, and adjusted his hat.

Mary Lee Miller stepped into the dim light. The woman who'd hired me to produce a murder mystery at the museum was the de Young's major fund-raiser and philanthropist. She was a petite blond woman who was clearly older than fifty but tried to look younger than forty. Tonight she wore a pink Chanel suit and matching stiletto heels that would have made killer weapons. Peeking out of her pink Coach bag was a teeth-baring, pink-ribboned purse pooch. A pit bull wrapped in a poodle's clothing? The metaphor fit both the dog and the woman.

"Oh, God, Sam. Do hush!" Mary Lee said to the security guard. She waved him away with a whisk of a manicured hand. Sam nodded, tipped his hat to both of us, and shuffled off into the darkness, waving his flashlight from side to side as if a blind man with a cane.

"Sam's a character. The older he gets, the more he talks. We keep him around only because his father was my father's gardener." Mary Lee patted her poodle with a diamond-riddled hand. "No doubt he was telling you one of his exaggerated stories, right? I do believe he's a frustrated Indiana Jones."

I smiled. "Well, a museum can always use a little mystery."

Mary Lee raised a perfectly plucked eyebrow. "Yes, but it can't afford a real scandal. See that Dogon figure over there?"

Oh, God, not that piece again.

"Superb, isn't it? We paid over one million dollars for this truly incredible piece. The de Young would rather have one great object than a hundred ordinary ones. We strive to make sure our museum is *not* your dowager grandmother's provincial museum. It's contemporary, user friendly, and, with my name on it, it has to be the best. Believe me—I have the scars to prove it."

She was referring to the controversy that had dogged the museum since she first took on the job of major money raiser a decade ago. Everyone in the San Francisco Bay Area knew about the frequent arguments over everything from the architecture and location to the financing and environmental impact. But somehow Mary Lee Miller had managed to overcome these obstacles and raise more than two hundred million dollars worth of funding in the process.

"Blockbuster art brings in millions of visitors—that's a fact. And we now rival the Met, the Louvre, and the British Museum with our collection. Plus, the art-related trinkets we sell in the gift shop make great refrigerator magnets for tourists to purchase. When the Tut exhibit was here, we made more money selling Tut shirts and bags than we did on admission."

Remembering what Sam Wo had said, I asked. "Is it difficult to make sure all the objects are legitimate?"

"Absolutely not," she snapped, petting her purse pooch vigorously. He . . . She . . . *It* panted in response. "We trust our dealers implicitly. When we acquire something like the Dogon statue, we make sure it has a reliable provenance."

I nodded my understanding, but she continued as if I were a schoolchild on a field trip.

"Provenance, Presley, is the ability to document an object's origin and history of ownership."

I tried to ignore her condescending tone but it irritated me. "Sam said there's still a black market for things like the Dogon statue?"

Her eyes narrowed. I knew I'd offended her as soon as the words "black market" tumbled out of my mouth. It was like saying "plastic surgery" to a trophy wife.

"Certainly there are still looters, smugglers, unethical dealers, and desperate collectors who will turn blind eyes to the origins of some art," Mary Lee said, "not to mention the occasional forgery. But our staff is top-notch, impeccable. I personally recommended Christine Lampe, who was hired as our curator. And that's why this fund-raiser is so important. If it's got my name on it, it's sure to bring in hundreds of thousands of dollars we need for the new wing and collection. And it has to be perfect."

Her minispeech reminded me how pompous Mary Lee really was. When she'd hired me for this gig, she'd insisted she be given full credit for the fund-raiser. I'd agreed, as long as a percentage of the money raised went to the Autism Foundation. My friend and part-time assistant, Delicia, had a sister with the disorder, and I wanted to do something to help stem the puzzling rise in cases.

"Now, shall we return to the Grand Gallery, Chou-Chou?" Mary Lee said to her dog in a nauseating baby voice. The dog licked her fingers as if they were covered with gravy.

Mary Lee spoke to me in a normal voice, "Do I have to remind you, Presley, that I hired you to do an event, not wander around the museum unescorted? The rehearsal is not going well, and you won't see a dime for your company or your charity if this event isn't perfect." Her face tightened.

I stole a last glance at the bloodstained ceremonial dagger, safe in its plastic case. *Good thing it is inaccessible*, I thought, or I might have borrowed it to use on Mary Lee. Instead I followed her down the stairs, her stilettos tapping out a strident beat as she led the way. Her threats had been repeated so many times over the past couple of weeks that they no longer struck terror in my heart as they had initially. Still, I wasn't above the occasional dagger-in-the-back fantasy.

But before I could picture shoving the blade between her pink-clad shoulders, I heard a scream echoing up from the stairwell ahead.

A scream so loud that it could have shattered Plexiglas.

The **Crime of Fashion** Mysteries

by Ellen Byerrum

# *Killer Hair*

An up-and-coming stylist, Angie Woods had a reputation for rescuing down-and-out looks—and careers—all with a pair of scissors. But when Angie is found with a drastic haircut and a razor in her hand, the police assume she committed suicide. Lacey knew the stylist and suspects something more sinister—that the story may lie with Angie's star client, a White House staffer with a salacious website. With the help of a hunky ex-cop, Lacey must root out the truth...

# *Hostile Makeover*

As makeover madness sweeps the nation's capital, reporter Lacey Smithsonian interviews TV show makeover success story Amanda Manville. But with Amanda's beauty comes a beast in the form of a stalker with vicious intentions—and Lacey may be the only one who can stop him.

Also in the **Crime of Fashion** series:

*Designer Knockoff*
*Raiders of the Lost Corset*
*Grave Apparel*
*Armed and Glamorous*